Wild Grow the Lilies

Christy Brown

WILD GROW THE LILIES

Scarborough House/*Publishers*

Scarborough House/*Publishers*
Chelsea, MI 48118

FIRST SCARBOROUGH HOUSE PAPERBACK
EDITION 1990

Wild Grow the Lilies was originally published
in hardcover by Stein and Day/*Publishers*.

Library of Congress Cataloging in Publication Data

Brown, Christy, 1932—
Wild grow the lilies.
I. Title.
PZ4.B874917Wi3   [PR6052.R5894]   823'.9'12   75-37905
ISBN 0-8128-2470-9

For Mab, Edie, Tulsa & Peach:
at the last count, the girls in my life,
without whom not a single lily would have grown.

Following up the acclaim of his autobiography *My Left Foot* and the international bestsellerdom of his novel *Down All the Days, Wild Grow the Lilies* revisits that same raucous Dublin. Irish journalist Luke Sheridan, newly jilted, sets out to cover the story of a poisoning gone awry and ends up in a boisterous party that moves at the pace of the Keystone Kops set loose in a fun house. From Madame Lala's house of pleasure, with her most alluring "girl" Babysoft, and Count Fustenhalter, the designated murder victim, through gallons of drink and hours of orgy, we are exposed to a multi-bedroom farce of the good, old-fashioned, earthy, laugh-out-loud kind.

In the end, we no longer feel like visitors in Christy Brown's Dublin. We *know* it, we're part of the family, and we love it.

From his moving appearances on the "Today Show" and "The David Frost Show," Christy Brown is still remembered as a man of incredible courage and good humor, an almost total spastic, typing with his left foot, the only limb over which he had full control. Although he died in 1981, audiences all over the country can now meet Christy Brown again through actor Daniel Day-Lewis's dazzling portrayal of him in the equally acclaimed film of Brown's life, also entitled "My Left Foot."

Part One

I

'My weary head to rest upon a pillow
next my favourite girl in Lala's bordello.'

Half singing, half muttering the words under his breath Luke,
stood at the base of the slender obelisk, squinting querulous and
famished up at the emblazoned head of Charles Stewart Parnell,
which glinted wanly under the watery January sunlight; the
eternal flame of revolution above the head that never wore a
crown, and the graven words proclaiming the folly of putting
boundaries to the forward march of a nation, a little tarnished with
the droppings of generations of heedless unpatriotic pigeons.

'Tonight I shall sleep in Paradise, good fellow
just round the next corner in Lala's bordello.'

Luke on his hunkers now peering still at the fallen leader, lost
in the lugubrious din of traffic, thinking of his last unconsum-
mated supper, a regal repast of spare-ribs and bread and butter,
a mug of stout gone dead and somewhere an evening bell telling
him the time he did not want to know.

A shadow fell across him.

'Wasn't he a lovely man, all the same, sir? A terrible pity about
himself and that Kitty O'Shea wan.'

A friendly open-air voice and the woman who spoke stood near
gazing up at the monument, clasping to her a bundle of rags which
stirred and gave a weak hungry whisper as she shushed it sooth-
ingly, standing there with the proud impassive mien of Indian or
Eskimo in an ageless near perfect near sexless symmetry of shape

3

and line, thick plaid shawl wrapped several folds round her. Tiny spumes of breath issued from her mouth and nostrils in the bright brittle air as she lifted a mannish wrist to wipe away a single gleam of moisture gathered on the blunt tip of her nose.

Resignedly he straightened up and put a hand into the narrow side pocket of his anorak, fumbling for loose coins, and the woman with disappointed eyes turned away, unstressed dignity in the set of her shoulders and firm buoyant sway of her hips.

'O thou crass ignoble creature,' he said fiercely to himself as he began walking. 'Shame and shit on you.'

Walking past the upended cakestand of a cinema on the corner that once in better slower days had echoed with the pipes and flutes and oboes of chamber music, he passed the pugnosed tarnished little Grecian folly of an amphitheatre with tattered windswept posters telling of the latest premiere, the newest spawn of Sheridan and Goldsmith arrived in the tawdry tinsel township.

'Rash and impertinent parasite,' muttered Luke again to himself, head down and hands clenched in pockets. 'That lady was worth more than your miserable ashes.'

Swiftly now past the bestial monstrosity of a discotheque squatting next door like a predatory hybrid about to pounce raucous with mechanical mayhem to drown the limpid tide of rhetoric that would rise later that evening and mutilate the pluperfect language of native genius under a witches' chorus of banalities—

'O Oscar, thou shouldst be living at this hour.'

Crossing the frantic street, unheeding of the horns that screeched at his meandering progress and once safe and fairly sound on the opposite side, he stepped up to the canopied portals of his modest Eden.

'I am come, I am come, my heart's delight.'

Into the vestibule grey and sonorous with echoes, potted plants and climbing shrubbery dimly seen against faintly glimmering walls and ostentatious chandeliers hanging from the vaulted ceilings like grotesque genitalia, the slightly nauseous aftersmell of cigar smoke lingering on the air, a place of damask curtains and stern ivory pillars.

'Has anybody here seen Kelly,
Kelly from the Isle of Man?'

He sat down at a table in the huge front parlour, candles already
lit even at that early hour stuck in empty wine bottles, yellow
coagulated layers of grease coiling round the sides, and heads
turning towards him from neighbouring tables.

'Bejasus, you're early today, Sheridan—who is guarding our
free press while you're here on the hunt for your bag of coal?'

A long lewd guffaw and the sudden flare of a cigarette flowering
in the murky gloom.

'He hasn't lost the horn he had last night.'

'Bit early in the day for carnalities, isn't it, Sheridan?'

'Ever the time and the place, gentlemen.'

A bloated face floated up to his table. 'How's the crack, Luke?
Buy you a gargle?'

'That is warmhearted of you, Conor abu. A large brandy.'

'Piss off.'

'That's what I thought.'

'Have a glass of stout and shame the divil.'

The leery beery moonface drifted away.

Another porter voice boomed out across the flickering candlelit
infinities of the room. 'Lost that nice chirpy Ballsbridge bird of
yours, have you?'

Luke turned his head and smiled into the shadows. 'Ours but
for a little while, O'Brien, the sweet bird of youth.'

The slight absurd vacuum Tessa had left in her wake worried
him now and fretted the fine placidity of his life, grown used to
her with custom, her dark hellenic face over the bacon and eggs
making a minor feast of it all, more sister than mistress, spinning
a luscious web out of her own sensual vacuity.

'Don't think dark sanguine thoughts of slitting your wrists,
Luke oul' son. It's a poor mouse that depends on one hole.'

He smiled again looking into the candleflame. 'Your wisdom
is shattering at this hour of the day, O Lalor of the faulty pipes
and ragged drums.'

Moonface swam back with a glass of creamy stout and put it
before him. 'Get that down you before you do your stud duties.
It is injurious to ride on an empty stomach, as my brother Father
Malachy is forever belting into me.'

'Conor abu, for this relief much thanks.'

'She's scarpered, has she, your mot—done a moonlight?'

Luke touched the froth with his lips. 'I cannot deny it.'

'Well, you know what they say about the fishes in the sea,' consoled Moonface. 'You've come to the right place anyway, and that itself is a sign of sanity.' Moonface sipped his beer sloppily and grinned.

> 'You're in the right direction
> if you're suffering from erection
> walk past Parnell and come to Madame Lala's
> You'll find warmth and consolation
> and all the copulation
> you could ever want in life
> at Madame Lala's—'

'I made that up on the spur of the moment, Luke.'

'I'll see to it that you are included in the next anthology of New Irish Verse, Conor.'

Moonface got up. 'Well, I hope you'll get over your mot leaving you, seeing that you can't get on top of her anymore.'

'You are too good by far for this world, Conor abu.'

The raddle of that morning rankled somewhere in him, Tessa moving quiet not to wake him and him wide-eyed watching her gather up her few belongings, placing each item neatly in the black suitcase as though leaving for a peaceful weekend in the country, turning at the door, a look of vague concern on her face as if about to remind him not to forget his dinner, the next instant gone, her wedge-soled shoes echoing down the corridor, muffled a moment on the carpeted staircase, the halldoor opening and shutting behind her—

Leaning out the window watching her go clutching the suitcase in both hands as a nun might her breviary, climbing into the waiting taxi with never a backward glance, he at the window looking on dimly amused unreal, detached with cool eyes, watching the taxi slide down the leafy avenue out of sight.

And that was finally that.

A heavy hand landed on his shoulder and he looked up.

'Luke son, you come so early. Something wrong?'

The face smiling down at him was remotely feminine, lips a

vivid orange streak, flat toadlike nose pitted with blackheads, hairs sprouting out of nostrils, several layers of jowl falling in terraced slabs into goitre-thick throat and neck.

'Madame Lala, I come to you a broken man.'

The soft sultry voice strangely alluring and disembodied emanating from a solid chunk of mascaraed muscle and flesh, the topheavy head wobbling slightly with thin reddish-tinged hair plastered to the skull, vacuous blue eyes sunk deep staring down at him, slobbery babyish mouth trembling on the verge of mirth.

'Have you put your poor Mother in her grave at last?'

'My Mother is ageless and enjoys excellent health. It is I who am at death's holy door and halfway over the threshold.'

'Wait, wait.'

Waddling away to the cubbyhole in the wall, skirt hammocked over rolling expanse of hip and buttock, small white hands fluttering up and down in front of her gypsy-red blouse, and returning with bottle, lowering her gigantic girth into the chair, pushing two glasses towards him. 'You say you are distraught, Luke, son?'

'Did I say that? What a beautiful word, "distraught". Your very good and everlasting health, Lala.'

Madame Lala across the table in uncertain candlelight, puckered lips breaking in a smile over glass rim, her face puzzled sad unbelonging, lapping down brandy with lascivious relish, stirring in him a begrudging affection for things incomplete and maimed.

'Tessa left me this morning, Lala. Not again, but for good.'

'Who is Tessa, Luke son?'

'Who but my lady of exceeding grace and tribulation?'

'I never knew you were married, Luke.'

'Married? Not I, dear lady. I have yet to enter into that blissful state.'

Lala joined her suet fingers together. 'So you lived in sin, did you, with your Tessa?'

'Sin most hale and hearty, while it lasted, in my little grey hole in Ballsbridge. Now my bird of paradise has flown, and I come to you for creature comfort.'

'I can only pray for you, Luke.'

'Your prayers are welcome, I assure you, but at this moment I confess I am much more embroiled in mortal conflict.'

Lala wistfully stroked a thick clotted vein in her throat. 'You want one of my daughters?'

'Solely for solace, Madame Lala, a little spiritual solace.'

Lala sighed. 'You will be wanting Rosie.'

'Rosie?'

'I'm Rosie,' a voice said. 'Anything I can do for you?'

A girl with dark insomniac eyes, bright as blighted berries, intense and thin-lipped, hair coiled like sleeping serpents on her shoulders taking a seat at the table.

'Have we met before?' he asked.

'Does it matter?'

'It doesn't matter in the least.'

Madame Lala rose ponderously. 'She is a good girl, is Rosie. She is a listener. I will leave you two alone. And Luke'—she patted his arm as she passed—'I am sorry about your lady.'

'You are a dispenser of much comfort to us all, Madame Lala.'

Lala paused a moment, her canine ugliness softened by sudden maternal affection, and then once more waddled away, a dwarf duchess going forth to greet her first callers of the evening.

'Will you have a drink?'

'I'm not here for the good of me health.'

He filled her glass and she held it at a coy theatrical angle. 'I didn't quite catch your name.'

'How could you forget a name like Rosie, for Christ's sake?'

'Ah, Rosie. Your health, Rosie.'

She drank from her glass in slow disdainful sallies, elbows on table measuring him up as if for a shroud, putting in the final stitches with the black needlesharp points of her eyes, her sandalled foot barely touching his under the table.

'I've seen you in here before.'

'I'm sure you have, Rosie. Your glass is empty.'

'One of them newspaper blokes, aren't you?' she said pushing forward her glass.

'A member of the press gang, Rosie, to my everlasting ignominy and shame.' He studied her for some moments. 'Your face comes back to me now.'

'Great. I was beginning to think I was losing my appeal.'

He gazed at her steadily. 'Appeal. Yes, you do have considerable appeal, Rosie. It's a quality I admire above all else.' He reached over and touched her hand.

'Jasus, are you sick or something?' she cried snatching her hand

8

away as if from fire. 'Holding me hand like that—do you think I've nothing better to do with me time?'

'I do beg your pardon, Rosie. No offence. It is such a nice elegant hand, it was suddenly irresistible.'

'There's other parts of me, you know.'

'I'm sure there are, Rosie, and all equally irresistible.'

She looked closeted and impregnable though her arms were bare to the shoulder and the dress dipped to reveal the crevice between her breasts.

'I don t know what you're like, but if it's kinky stuff you're after—'

'Might I be allowed to ask what makes you think I want anything more demanding of you than a sympathetic ear?'

Her eyes narrowed. 'Now listen, mate, don't get funny—'

'I remember now your queenly gait honourable among the drab press and confraternity of bodies—'

'What?'

'That droll and unique turn of head and hip as you weaved your sinuous way between tables—'

'What are you bleeding talking about?'

He leaned forward. 'I would talk with you, Rosie. Believe me, that is the only solace I ask of you.'

'Then for the love of Jasus will you talk sense?'

'Sense, Rosie—do you really want me to talk sense?'

'You'd put years on anybody with that kind of bullshit out of you, anyway.'

He sat back relieved. 'We could get a taxi and go out to Ballsbridge after a few more drinks.'

'Ballsbridge? What the hell would I be doing out in Ballsbridge, in the name of God?'

'I have a nice little pied-à-terre out there.'

'You have a what out there?'

'A room, lady, just a room, humble but my very own. I would deem it an honour to have you grace its modest threshold.'

'Nothing doing, mate.'

'I assure you, my intentions are dishonourable only, not homicidal, Rosie.'

'Nothing doing. It's strictly business on the premises.'

'But what possible difference would it make?'

Her manicured fingernails beat out a taut tattoo upon the coarse wooden tabletop. 'Never stray from home-base. You could call it union rules. I come from a good union family. Me Da was a personal friend of James Connolly until he collapsed and died from drink six months ago—'

'Your Father?'

'Well, it wasn't bleeding James Connolly, was it? They strapped him in a chair and shot him in the GPO.'

'James Connolly?'

'It wasn't me effing Da'—she stopped and gave him a sharp angry look—'Are you trying to make me nervous or something? I always get nervous when I lose me temper. Why do you want to make me lose me temper?' She glared at him and it excited him to notice that she was getting a little intoxicated, anger pushing her out of her immobility and remoteness.

'Lose your temper, Rosie, if it pleases you.'

'It doesn't please me. I hate losing me temper.'

'Then keep it by all means.'

'Have you got such a thing as a cigarette on you?'

'Certainly.' He lit her one, and she drew on it throwing back her head, smoke issuing from her nostrils.

'Broke it off, have you?'

'Broke it off?'

'With your girl?'

'Oh, Tessa. Why do you call her my girl?'

'Well, she was, wasn't she?'

'Yes, I suppose she was. I never thought of it like that before. At the threadbare heel of the hunt it's odd to think of her as just my girl. She might just have been any girl, put like that, a bit on the skinny side, wearing jeans and a sweater several sizes too big for her.'

'Did a bunk on you, did she?'

'She left this morning on the ten o'clock train to Limerick Junction. She always did have exotic tastes.'

'More bleeding power to her,' said Rosie with sudden fervour.

'You mean you like Limerick yourself?'

'I've never been outside Dublin.'

'Oh then you mean you applaud her decision to leave me?'

'Couldn't care less, mate.'

'Don't you approve of me, or is it men in general?'

'I've no feelings one way or another. Me glass is empty.'

The room was filling up, the rising hum of conversation lending a companionable intimacy to the bleak walls. Couples at tables were holding hands and presently the desultory tinkling of a piano in the background fell faintly on the ear.

Rosie placed a hand decorously in front of her mouth to suppress a hiccup. 'If you want to come upstairs now we'd better go before all the rooms are booked.'

Her voice was ordinary flat unemphatic, a telephonist answering a call giving the requisite information, her face blank and impassive save for her eyes dark and restless fastening defiantly on a neutral middle distance, sipping her drink with the air of one drinking afternoon tea in a sedate drawingroom above a quiet tree-lined square.

'That is the last thing I want now, Rosie.'

Her eyes darted at him. 'Look, I don't know what you're after—'

'I am loth to touch your hand again, but can't we just sit here and enjoy the bread and wine of brothers?'

'If you think or imagine—'

'What, Rosie?'

Her shoulders visibly relaxed, the rigid lines of her mouth softened, the shards of glamour falling from her, a mask being slowly discarded.

'That's better, Rosie. You're smiling.'

'Am I?'

'For the first time.'

'You're a funny bloke. What's this your name is?'

'Luke.'

'Luke. Short and sweet. Luke. I think I'm getting a little drunk, Luke.'

'Is that unusual, Rosie?'

'I don't often get drunk. It makes me sick.'

'But you feel all right now, Rosie, drinking with me?'

'I feel fine. I'm ready for another one, Luke.' Her voice slurred somewhat in a soft seductive way.

'Your health, Rosie.'

'Cheers. What was she like?'

'Who?'

'Tessa. Your ladyfriend. Did you make a scene when she left?'

'No last-stand quarrel, no recriminations, no hate or fury, nothing like that. She just packed and left.'

'Better that way.'

'Oh much better.'

'Did you love her a terrible lot?'

'Do we ever really know whether we love or not? Can we ever really tell from one moment to the next whether we are in love or out of it?'

She almost drank her glass empty, dashing a hand across her smarting eyes. 'Jasus, no wonder she blew town! Anyone with a heart would know whether they were in love or not without all that bleeding shilly-shallying and hemming-and-hawing! No wonder Tessa or whatever her name is beat it hotfoot down to Limerick—you're as cold as an effing fish!'

Heads were beginning to turn towards their table as her voice grew, the boldness of brandy making her reckless and excited.

'You're losing your temper, Rosie—'

'Bullshit! I'd lose more than me temper if I had to stay with you for long—I'd lose me bleeding mind! That's why your Nessa ran off—'

'Tessa.'

'Bleeding Tessa then—that's why she scarpered—she couldn't stand all that oul' guff out of you any longer! I wouldn't stand it either—not if you were William Butler Yeats himself!'

A hesitant form sidled up and stood on the edge of their talk. 'Good on you, Rosie—that's the spirit.'

She looked up. 'And who asked for *your* opinion, Marmaduke?'

'I couldn't help overhearing—'

'Earwigging, you mean.'

'Ah now, Rosie, you know me—'

'To me grief. What do you want?'

The thin stoop-shouldered young man, all twitching irresolution, stood at their table shifting stance from one foot to the other, his weak ineffectual mouth trapped between a brave smile and a look of abject pleading, a thin sheaf of papers folded under his arm. 'How's it going, you two?'

Luke sighed and picked up his glass. 'You have a rare genius, Brian, for suddenly appearing where you are least wanted.'

Rosie scrutinised the young man shrewdly. 'Put your hand in

your pocket and do something mad for once in your life—like buying us a drink.'

The halfhearted smile momentarily grew bolder. 'Do you think I'm shitting pound notes or what?'

Rosie smiled. 'That would be a change from shitting yellow, which you're still doing.'

The unsuccessful smile faltered. 'What is it you're drinking anyway?'

'It isn't Robinson's barley water, for one thing.' Rosie lifted her glass up to him. 'Smell.'

The slightly effeminate nostrils twitched. 'Expensive privilege, talking to you. Honest to God, Sheridan,' he reproached petulantly, 'you'll spoil the whole orchard with your cavalier ways, paying all that attention to one little cherry—'

'Who are you calling a cherry, you under-nourished little ferret? You do nothing but whine and moan out of you. You look as if you've just come straight from a meeting of the Legion of Mary or the Dispossessed Sons of Unmarried Mothers.'

The weak mouth almost stiffened. 'Now look, just because I happen to have a social conscience—'

'Ah, social conscience me arse. G'wan and play with yourself.'

The mouth tried valiantly to maintain a martial steadfastness. 'I deem it beneath my dignity to pay heed to such gross unladylike language, or indeed to bother to reply to such—'

Luke picked up the bottle. 'This is almost empty, and I agree with the lady. Methinks you protest your impecuniosity too much, and besides surely you haven't forgotten the benign beatitudes of the slate, have you?'

'No I haven't, but the point is—'

'The point is I have always admired the pilgrim soul in you, O Brian of the dirty fingernails and greasy locks. Bend thou thy parched young lips to the pulchritudinous ear of Lala the bountiful and all will be forgiven.'

'The night is young and I'm so beautiful,' added Rosie.

Brian appeared at once mollified and greatly flattered with their seeming appreciation of his influence. 'I was just having you on. Hold on to this a minute, Luke,' he said placing on the table a thin coarse-papered periodical. 'I won't be long.'

Rosie relaxed again when the intruder had gone. 'I don't know what to make of that bloke. He goes around as if he had just pissed in his trousers, that shy little wriggly walk of his. I declare to Jesus I think he's bent.'

'Maybe, though personally I think his particular bent is purely of the literary kind.'

'I heard tell he was a bit of a poet right enough, God bless the mark.'

Luke leafed idly through the periodical. 'He edits this noble tome. *Poet and Peasant* they call it, an inspired streak of originality. Ah, here are some of his latest emissions right here. Listen to this and be duly chastened.'

Luke smoothed out the pages and cleared his throat, drawing nearer to the candlelight.

> 'In the eyeless vortex of the night
> You willow down the void
> To where dreamless I lie
> Your breath anointing my glued lids—'

'Jasus,' said Rosie into the pause. 'No wonder he's off his rocker, the poor bastard, if that's all he has to be doing with his time. Writing bits of things like that, bejasus, and him not a day under twenty-five.'

'Charity, Rosie, charity. It covereth a multitude. Ah, I see they have included some of my own little gems as well in this issue, which modesty forbids me to quote—'

'Don't tell me you write bleeding poetry too?'

Her voice was low and conspiratorial as if the whole room waited with stopped breath upon their next words.

'I share Washington's affliction of not being able to tell a lie, or at least to tell one convincingly. I plead guilty to aspiring to the mantle of Mangan—'

'The mantle of who?'

'James Clarence Mangan, our noble countryman who perished in the mists of Parnassus.'

'Ah well, sure all them countrymen are the same. As mad as the heifers they milk.'

Brian returned flushed with pride and bonhomie, sitting himself down at the unwelcoming table, an intruder at a private banquet.

Rosie viewed the half-bottle with disdain. 'You broke your bleeding heart.'

Brian rushed in with mongrel apologies. 'She said it put her to the pin of her collar to let me have the half-bottle. I have a slate here as long as Dollymount Strand—' tentative as a sparrow on a wintry branch he raised the glass to his lips—'Still, let us not pour scorn on well-meant offers, be they ever so humble.'

Rosie was looking steadily at Luke, taking in each pleasing detail of his features. 'You're not bad-looking, all the same.'

'And you, my dear Rosie, *are* beautiful.'

As if on cue from an unseen stage prompter they reached over towards each other, wrists touching, sipping from behind the other's eyes, their foreheads together eyes half closed in mock dumbshow of imminent yielding.

Brian the dainty dilettante once again ignored and cast out from the cosy ring of their growing intimacy, trying to conjure up a manly frown between his pale gingerish brows, biting his nether lip with yellowish teeth, draining his glass halfway in search of bravado and sustenance in the midst of this elaborate exclusion of his presence.

Brian coughed and spluttered a little. 'Did you see we put some of your stuff in this month's broadsheet? I like the one where you're looking out to sea on a windy day—' he picked up the periodical—'Was it out in Howth or Bray?—and you're thinking of some girl from the past, and on the sands below you there's a couple making love. The imagery's terrific, Luke, terrific.'

The high voice humming tensely, rushing ahead of the words, faltered, the thin mauvish lips worked and broke into a snarl. 'For fuck's sake, is it to myself I'm talking?'

The two stopped and disengaged, turning slowly towards their fellow-reveller.

'I'm sorry, Brian. What did you say?'

Rosie giggled. 'He wanted to know if he was talking to himself.'

'And what better man to talk to than yourself, Brian? I do it all the time, and derive considerable amusement, if not edification, from the exercise.'

'Did you see these, I asked you,' quavered Brian, holding out the periodical, 'your poems we printed in this issue.'

'No, but one or two of yours caught my eye. Let's see now—' Luke took the magazine and hand on breast started to declaim:

'In the eyeless vortex of the night
You willow down the void
To where dreamless I lie—'

He stopped. 'Or should that be "up the void", Brian? Never
mind—

Your breath anointing my glued lids—

Did I get the intonation right, Brian?'
   Brian's caged animal's face was pale under its rage. 'Cut it out,
Sheridan, you bastard. Give me back that—'
   Luke easily evaded the grasping fingers and held the loose pages
aloft.
   'No, no, my dear chap, you are far too modest. Listen to this—

Faltering I follow my lifeline of hope
Down wine-dark canyons of night
To swoon at last in the duck of peace
Under your heaven-pointing breasts—

I don't think I got the metre exactly right, do you, Brian? I think
I should have put more feeling into

Your heaven-pointing breasts

But you're the poet, Brian—what do you think?'
   'Give it back to me, you poxy bastard!' hissed Brian and then
feebly grinned in placation. 'Come on, Sheridan, give it back to
me and stop messing, for God's sake.'
   Luke affected a look of puzzled reproach. 'I honestly don't
understand you, Brian. You are the new voice of the time-
honoured literary hostelries of Dublin's fair city, the voice of lucid
language, of unclouded vision, of erotic verisimilitude, and you
want to gag that voice, to muffle it with a swab dipped in the
chloroform of false and excessive modesty! Nay, friend, nay, I'll
have none of it—'
   Luke thumbed quickly through the roughened pages, drilling
for more dross as Brian's small womanish hands knotted into mute
rage and entreaty on the table.
   'Hah! A line plucked from the rich vein of your poetry to amply
illustrate my contention:

O give to my famished mouth
Your nutbrown nipples
dipped in the honey of love—'

Luke paused with closed eyes as if quivering on the last falling note and savouring it deeply, reiterating slowly with a fastidious gourmet's relish:

'Your nutbrown nipples
dipped in the honey of love—'

Luke opened his eyes and regarded Brian with serene esteem. 'Does that not make your pulse race and pound with pride?'

Rosie yawned and drained her glass. 'Jasus, wouldn't that make you sick, all the same? A grown man writing shit like that.' She reached for the bottle as with a feline snarl Brian grabbed it up, clamping the cork back into it and clutching it fiercely under his arm.

Rosie laughed. 'Are you bringing that home with you or what, Thomas Moore?'

Brian sprang up wildly, almost upending the table as his chair crashed backwards to the floor, short spiky beard and hair erect as he confronted the two and the room in general, bile-eyed and viperish with flailing arms slicing the air.

'You bastard, Sheridan! You're nothing but a pimp and a ponce, selling your balls to every man-mad prick-happy lady columnist in Dublin for a bit of buckshee freelancing while you write *the* great definitive Irish novel out there in some seedy genteel dosshouse in Ballsbridge! You're a classless parasite, Sheridan, not fitting in anywhere because you turned your back on your own people—!'

'Good God, Brian, you make me sound almost biblical, like Saul when he had that bad turn on the road to Damascus. Now there's a marvellous description of that to be found in *Quo Vadis*—'

Brian brought his rabbity inflamed face down close to Luke, white flecks of foam gathering on his lips, breath redolent of rancid grease. 'It's the last time any of your half-baked pseudo-intellectual crap will be published in *my* magazine, so help me God!'

'Whom we must thank for small mercies,' murmured Luke with bowed head and folded hands.

'Yevtushenko!' screamed the other, jack-knifing upright again and pointing an accusing rigid finger at Luke. 'That's who he thinks he is, ladies and gentlemen—fucking Yevtushenko!'

Brian wildeyed, spittle flying out of his mouth, hopping frantically from one foot to the other as if walking on burning stones.

'I've been accused of writing with my penis, ladies and gentlemen, and maybe it's true—' He stopped and pulled the cork out of the bottle, gurgling down brandy, his thin windpipe jerking, wiping his mouth on his sleeve. 'But your man there—Gregorio or Yuri or whatever grand name he gives himself—that half-shit Cossack from Cabra—he writes with sweet fuck all, with not even the ghost of an erection to lend a bit of human warmth to all that cold dead cardboard stuff he churns out by the hundredweight!' Once more he wheeled on Luke, an inner fury welling out of his angular frame in almost tangible waves, the little fanatical eyes ablaze and tormented.

'You're a shit artist, Sheridan! You're found out now, have no fear! You can't hide behind those smart cynical smug remarks of yours any more!' He flung his arms wide in a gesture of crucified sorrow and wailing, 'Jesus, when I think of all I've done for that bastard, all the times I've pulled him up out of the gutter!'

Lala rumbling forward, drawn out of her lair by the commotion in the room, masculine shoulders set and fists doubled up took Brian roughly by the arm.

'What is going on here, hah? Do you think you are up in Leinster House, hah, with all that shouting and bawling? What do you think I run here, hah, a pitch-and-toss school or something?'

All the fight went out of Brian, his arms dropping at his sides and head on chest ashen and defeated, shuffling off Lala took him out of the room, patting him none too gently on the back, wagging her toadstool head in reproach.

People settled back in their seats, the buzz of talk rising again and Rosie with unbelieving eyes looking at Luke her mouth slightly ajar.

'Does he often take fits like that?'

Luke not answering her immediately looked away, a cold raw feeling in his belly.

'I didn't enjoy that one bit.'

'He's bleeding mad, that's all there is to it. There's saner people locked up.'

'No, he's not mad, Rosie. No madder than the rest of us anyway. I think for the first time since I've known him I admire him.'

Rosie shook out her massed hair. 'Well, I suppose it takes one to know one. You're both mad.'

'He blew up. Perhaps for the first time in his whole little bleak existence he blew up. It gave him a sort of nobility, a sort of dignity which must have been there all this time, submerged under all that fawning, all that whining—'

Lala returned, still glowering brows drawn. 'What the hell happened just now, Luke? You had that poor man reduced to tears, crying like a whipped mongrel dog. Who or what brought it about?'

'A mismarriage of true minds, you might say, Lala—'

She leaned forward heavily, cutting him short, a squat staunch defender of the faith she expected all her clients to uphold. '*You* might say so, Luke, not me. Here I will be master of my own ship, you understand?'

'I understand, Madame Lala. I did not anticipate the consequences of our little prankstering. I am sorry.'

'It is not a nice thing to see a man cry. It is not a nice thing to see a woman cry either. But it is especially not a nice thing to see a man cry. It offends against something in my nature, to see a man cry, a grown man cry like that. You understand, Luke, I know. So please don't let it happen again, hah?'

'You have my word, unworthy as it is.'

'Am I not like a second mother to you all?'

'You are indeed, and in grace abounding.'

'So no more tricks behind my back, hah? No more naughty games between my girls and boys, no more sly digging and pinching in the ribs when I am not looking, hah?'

'No more, Lala, no more.'

He beckoned the pimply young floorboy wandering dreamily about with an empty tray and ordered another bottle.

'Will you perhaps partake of a glass with us as a sign of my atonement and your own stout-hearted forgiveness?'

Lala snorted like a befuddled heifer. 'You're crazy, Luke, you know that? Crazy. No wonder you put your own Mother into that early grave.'

'My poor Mother, I am glad to say, is seventy next birthday and very much alive. It was my poor Father I put into an early grave, I'm afraid.'

Rosie hiccuped. 'What did you do to the poor man?'

'He died of cardiac arrest brought on by the fact that I was going into the newspaper business. He thought at first that I was only going to sell papers on O'Connell Bridge, which would have been perfectly acceptable, but when I told him I was going to write papers it killed him straight off. What really brought on the final attack was when he saw my first poem published in the *Cork Examiner*. Now the *Times* or the *Press* or even the *Independent* would have been bad enough, but the *Cork Examiner* was beyond redemption. He knew that I was irretrievably lost to reason and all decent intercourse with my fellow man.'

Rosie picked up her glass and poured from the new bottle. 'If there's one thing I hate it's smutty talk. I am what I am, but I have me scruples.'

Luke held up a protesting hand. 'No, no, Rosie, not that sort of intercourse. Do not, I pray you, add incest to injury. I was speaking in terms of social communication, of empathy, the spread and exchange of ideas, that "sweet conjunction of the mind" of which the poet sings—'

'And anyway,' spoke Lala swooping forward, finding a new outlet for her frustrated pique, 'what are *you* doing still sitting here?'

'Me, Madame Lala?' faltered Rosie.

'Yes, you. A real lady of leisure we are tonight, are we not? Do I pay you such good wages to sit on your throne like the Queen of Sheba?'

Rosie, momentarily stumped, glanced at her companion and gallantly he rose to her defence.

'I believe I have the signal honour of enjoying the young lady's company for the rest of the night, Madame Lala. An arrangement which I hope will be agreeable to you?'

'I don't know. I have my other gentlemen devotees to consider. It is not my policy to show favouritism. It is so greedy of you, Luke,' said Lala irritably, 'wanting the one girl to yourself the whole night.'

Luke bowed. 'I acknowledge the enormity of my cupidity, Madame Lala, and ordinarily I would not impose, but so sore is my heart and craves such solace and surcease from anguish that

nothing short of this young lady's full and undivided attention
will suffice to give it ease, for which pleasure and privilege I would
gladly pay a king's ransom, but alas, being only a struggling
journalist I must throw myself upon your charity and under-
standing and those fine maternal instincts which have given me
such succour in the past and will I pray not fail me now in this
the hour of my greatest—'

Lala threw her arms up in front of her as if warding off a hail
of blows. 'Take her, take her! You'd talk Jesus Himself down off
the cross if He listened to you long enough. O Sons of Eireann
arise,' muttered Lala as she moved off shaking her head from side
to side. 'O Sons of poor Eireann arise.'

Rosie laughed. 'Jasus, she's right. You would talk your way
into Hell and out of it. I heard the one about the pen being
mightier than the sword, but your tongue is better than both of
them put together.'

'I must admit the verbosity of my own exuberance overwhelms
me at times.'

'Sure why wouldn't it?' Rosie lifted her glass, unsteadily peering at him over its rim. 'Jasus help me innocence, but it's two of
you I see over there.'

'That, I assure you, is a privilege granted only to a rare few.
A mystic manifestation such as had the ancient anchorites fasting
themselves to glory and immortality in the burning deserts of the
East—'

'And why wouldn't they, bejasus? "O Roll me over in the
clover, roll me over, put me down and do it again." Do you love
your Mother?' she asked with sudden solemnity, squinting over
at him defiantly. 'Honest. Straight up. Do you love your Mother?'

'Ah, the Irish Mother, Sublime embodiment of the immemorial
Earth-force. Ageless epitome of Eve, of Isis, of Lilith—'

'Me own poor Ma is dead and gone a year ago now.'

'I am sorry to hear it, Rosie. Ah yes, the Irish Mother is truly
a karmic phenomenon, a continuing emanation and epiphany of
that dark primordial life-force which stirs inexorable and unalterable in our deepest consciousness and which at any time—'

'She dropped dead last year in the Daisy Market.'

Luke blinked. 'Who did?'

'Me poor Ma did. Fell over dead on top of her fish stall.'

'Her fish stall?'

Rosie sniffed. 'Yeah. She had a fish stall for over twenty years, me Ma had. A heart attack in the middle of the Friday morning rush, best day of the week for fish. There's luck for you. Never a day sick in her life. Just keeled over into the cod and mackerel without as much as a whimper out of her. Me younger sister Carmel just had time to whisper an Act of Contrition in her ear before she was gone like that—' she snapped her fingers—'There was always the smell of fish about me Ma, God be good to her, and even to this very day I can't look at a piece of cod or mackerel without the tears coming to me eyes.'

Rosie morose, looking into the malodorous past, eyes fetchingly moist with tears, pulled herself upright and swivelled round in her chair. 'I wish somebody would give us a song. Sure you'd think you were at a hooring wake in here!'

A rotund barrel-organ of a man was aloft on the cramped improvised stage at the far end of the room, bald-pated and profusely perspiring, open-neck shirt loose to the navel displaying a pink continent of chest covered with dense charcoal outcrops of hair, his eyes screwed up tight as he warbled in the throes of some unheard melody.

'Hey there, Mongoose!' yelled Rosie getting to her feet. 'Give us your masterpiece, give us "Thora" for the love of God and lift me out of this deep trough of depression I'm after falling into!'

At once there were cries and cheers and handclapping and table-slapping all round.

'Come on, Mongoose—"Thora", "Thora"!'

'We want Mongoose, we want Mongoose!'

'A noble call for Mongoose and "Thora"!'

'Me life on you, Mongoose, never let it be said!'

On stage Mongoose beamed with cheerful modesty and held up his clasped hands with the gesture of a prizefighter entering the ring to the plaudits of his fans, waiting for the ribald applause to die down, and then standing still, a look of intense abstraction on his round childish countenance, staring hard at the floor until with an abrupt rearing-up of head he flung himself recklessly into song:

> 'I stand in a land of roses
> but I dream of a land of snow
> where you and I were happy
> in the days of long ago.

The nightingale sang in the branches
the stars in the midnight sky
I only heard you singing
I only heard you sigh
I only heard you singing
O I only heard you sigh.
Speak, speak, speak to me, Thora
Speak from your heaven to me—'

Voices murmured admiringly as the falsetto middle-aged boy-soprano vocal chords of Mongoose climbed quavering but heroic towards the rafters and after an agonising quiver of uncertainty reached crescendo, to be immediately drowned in a wild outburst of approbation and acclaim.

'Me life on you, Mongoose!' enthused Rosie on her feet. 'That would bring tears to a stone!'

Luke after a desultory flap of applause poured for them both. 'A pleasing lilt of a melody.'

Rosie stopped clapping and sat down. 'That oul' cumawla, is it? Sure for Jasus' sake that was being sung and slaughtered when me Granny was alive. It's just that we haven't the heart to hurt poor oul' Mongoose—he's one of the regulars here, you know. A sloppy oul' fool, God love him, but as good as gold behind it all.'

Mongoose was still standing up on the stage in a rapt pose of oily gratification as the applause and encouragement continued, albeit with a little more restraint as it became clear that the star was not about to wane as speedily as they had hoped.

'Encore, encore!'

'A bit of order now for the singer!'

'Give us "Smilin' Thru", Mongoose oul' son!'

Rosie picked up her drink. 'Oh Jasus, I wish they'd let him sit down before he starts off again. I feel sorry for the poor oul' bugger, but enough is enough.'

'You mean there are limits to even your charity, Rosie?'

She spilled a few drops of the liquor down her chin and wiped it with the back of her hand. 'I'm not hardhearted or anything, but bejasus some people are gluttons for punishment.'

Mongoose invincibly immune to sly hints of abatement was again wafting mellifluous, lost in his own intense appreciation of himself:

'There's a little brown road winding over the hill
to a little white cot by the sea
There's a little green gate
at whose trellis I wait
while two eyes of blue come Smilin' Thru'
at me—'

Rosie hiccuped. 'I wouldn't mind so much if he sang something that you could join in with, but every bleeding song he sings has hairs on it.'

'You know what they say, my dear Rosie. Once you are famous you can get away with murder.'

At long seemingly unending last the song and the singer concluded and with a final wave of fidelity to those who still had the impetus to clap wanly Mongoose vacated the stage and went laboriously back to his seat mopping his gleaming egg-smooth pate and lifting a foaming tankard wearily to his mouth.

The pianist, left with the stage, drifted moodily into a waltz.

'Do you want to get up, Rosie?'

'Jasus no, not yet. I'd be falling all over meself.'

A woman stood on the fringe of the crowd as the floor filled up with dancers, her back to their table, shoulders bare, the V of her dark green gown running almost to the dusky hollow of her spine, her shoulderblades sharp and as they moved making delicate little statements beneath the light gauze of skin, the fine tracery of her vertebrae perfectly delineated and the abrupt perpendicular line of her short-cropped intensely black hair strangely stark and martial, appearing to sever the soft nape making her look guillotined and brutally abbreviated.

Seeing the look of surprise on Luke's face Rosie laughed and tapped his shin with her foot. 'It's all right, for God's sake. Sure it's only Babysoft.'

At that moment the girl turned round with a laconic smile. 'Is there room for another at your table? I won't have any effing feet left if I don't get off the floor.'

'Sit down, Babysoft—you must have eyes in the back of your head.'

'Ah, thanks, Rosie. You're a treasure. Who's your friend?'

'A famous millionaire from Cabra. He deals in scrap, so you should be all right.'

Babysoft regarded him more closely. 'Now I'm not going to ask whether you come here often, but haven't I seen you before somewhere?'

Luke filled a glass and handed it to her. 'I am known to have several twin brothers, but I have been here before, in happier times.'

Babysoft raised an eyebrow. 'Happier times?'

'His girlfriend did a moonlight on him today,' supplied Rosie.

'I'm sure you're heartbroken, you poor man.'

'Utterly devastated.'

'Jasus, doesn't he look it?'

Babysoft drank and held out her glass for a topping-up.

'Hey you,' snapped Rosie. 'Go easy on that stuff—it's not Lourdes water. And anyway you know it always brings you out in spots.'

'I was always partial to Napoleon,' said Babysoft picking up the bottle and peering at the label. 'Fair play to yourself, Rosie. You know how to pick them. Me, I'm stuck with the likes of Mongoose, bejasus.'

'He isn't your type anyway,' said Rosie. 'He writes poetry.'

'Mongoose write poetry? I didn't know that—'

'I was talking about Luke here—'

'Ah, so that's your name, is it? I always fancied the name of Luke.'

'Leave off the torchlight procession, Babysoft,' warned Rosie with a moist pout of lips. 'Go back to Mongoose.'

Babysoft drew back her head and looked thoughtful. ' "Oh to have a little house of mud and wattles made . . ." I often wondered what the hell wattles were. Would *you* know, Luke, being a poet?'

'Yes, they are a variety of brick laid out to dry in the sun.'

'The very thing. Why don't you ask me up to dance?'

Luke rose at once. 'My very great pleasure.'

'Now look here, you thieving cow—'

Babysoft smiled down at her. 'Relax. I won't ate him for Jasus' sake! I thought we trusted each other—sure aren't we like sisters, me oul' mate?'

'I don't trust me sisters neither.'

'We can't do anything on the bleeding floor, can we, and all them people milling around us?'

'You don't need the Phoenix Park for *your* manoeuvres.'

'Lookit, can I have a loan of him or not?'

'Shag off, then,' said Rosie sullenly. 'Just keep your hands to yourself, that's all.'

On the dance-floor Babysoft fitted snugly into his arms, easily accommodating his clumsy movements to her own, and after a brief struggle to assert himself he succumbed and let her guide him around while he gave himself up solely to enjoying the warm sensuous feel of her body brushing and pressing against his own.

'Am I dancing too close to you, Lukey love?'

'Nearer my God to thee. Why do they call you Babysoft?'

'I suppose it's because I'm only a baby at heart, and I'm soft all over. As you can feel, I'm sure.'

'You dance well, Babysoft.'

'I do everything well.'

'That I can well believe.'

'You might believe it, but wouldn't you like to find out for yourself sometime? Just to satisfy your own curiosity, like?'

'Is that an invitation?'

She moved irritably against him. 'Of course it's an invitation! What do you expect—gilt lettering on embossed paper requesting the pleasure of your company in the upstairs lounge of The Maiden Head?'

'I think you mean The Brazen Head.'

'I know what I mean.'

'You wouldn't try to entice me away from Rosie, would you?'

'I'm effing sure I would. Don't be afraid to hold me, Lukey love —I'm not made of candyfloss.'

Her hands were under his jacket by now stroking his back.

'I think you have the right philosophy in life, Babysoft.'

'Sure haven't I the right everything?'

'You are utterly amoral, like myself.'

''Deed I am, but as long as it doesn't break out in pimples and yellow spots I don't mind.'

People bumped and swayed against them jarring them roughly, but Luke felt peaceful as though marooned on an island with the soft sighing and purring of surf in his ears and slender grass-shoots licking his face with teasing indolence.

'You're not bad-looking,' she told him feeling his cheeks with her fingers. 'A bit scrawny, but nice.'

'I am excruciatingly sensitive, too.'

'Ah, so you would be.'

'I shrink and cower away whenever I enter a strange room full of people I don't know.'

'You should see a doctor about that. Hydrophobia they call it.'

'Claustrophobia.'

'What's that you said?'

'It's called claustrophobia. Fear of enclosed places.'

'Isn't that what I said? And anyway, isn't one bleeding phobia just as bad as another? Jasus, all the same, you're terrible thin. I can nearly feel your ribs. Haven't you got anyone to look after you at all?'

'I left the family fold as soon as I could. That was claustrophobia with a vengeance. Now I have a little pad in Ballsbridge.'

'You're coming up in the world, Lukey.'

'I rather think I'm coming down. Ballsbridge is just a dandified wasteland of stupendous dullness. One big vacant plot.'

'I live in meself. Like the nurses, you know.'

'I suppose one could say you are a kind of nurse, Babysoft, ministering to the slings and arrows and the thousand and one ills that flesh is heir to.'

'Yeah. I suppose you could say that, right enough. I'm sensitive too, you know.'

'I can quite believe you are, Babysoft. There is this aura of sensitivity about you, of exquisite receptivity to people and things—'

'I wouldn't mind showing you me sensitive spots sometimes, when you're not carrying the cares of the world around with you. Ah, Jasus, there's the dance over, just when I was beginning to get the feel of things, you might say.'

Back at the table Rosie watched them approach, baleful and surly, her eyes clouded with brandy. 'Well—did you manage to ravish him while you were at it?' She appraised him as he sat down. 'He looks drained.'

'We talked about life and Ballsbridge,' said Babysoft resuming her drink.

'What's bleeding Ballsbridge got to do with life and death?' demanded Rosie pulling herself stubbornly forward in the chair.

'According to your Romeo there—' Babysoft nodded towards him—'Ballsbridge hasn't got nothing to do with anything.'

'Not even balls, I suppose,' said Rosie arms folded on table and eyes rapidly closing.

'I fear even that half of its name conveys a false impression.'

'Sure the whole world's just a matter of balls.'

A sudden pounding on the piano and in unison everyone stood up.

'A little order for our National Anthem, please!'

Everyone erect in military fashion, an awkward cough here and there, and after the final flourish of keys Madame Lala smiling and shaking innumerable hands in farewell, Godspeeding the unchosen ones on their way with a prayer of good fortune and fond expectations of their continued patronage, waving them out into the raw January night to catch bus or cab or stagger homewards and then bolting the heavy oak front door and switching off lights, leaving the room in candleglow again.

Lala sat down at their table, poured herself a drink. 'That's another night over and done with, thank God.' She raised her voice a little as she looked round. 'Those who are staying will please be quiet and retire as soon as you can. Thank you.' She turned to Luke. 'Well, Luke poor boy, is that heart of yours still broken in two?'

'Still somewhat fractured, Lala, but not as irreparably sliced as I had feared.'

'Maybe it was just a hairline fracture,' yawned Babysoft. 'Or a case of the windy colic.'

Lala wet her finger and brushed her thin charcoal eyebrows slowly. 'You gave her no babies I hope, this Tessa of yours?'

'I gave her only heart's love and mind's torment, Lala. Man's supreme gift to woman.'

Lala nodded. 'That's all right then. Babies out of wedlock bring trouble, more so than in it. How will the ball bounce now, Luke son?'

'Favourably, I hope.'

'How will you live? Who will look after you all alone in that cold empty flat?'

'Perhaps, Lala, a handmaid of the Lord will appear when I least expect her, floating along on a white cloud up Eglington Road, two perfect red roses at her feet and a string of lilies flowing round her perfect waist.'

'Mind there's no thorns in the roses,' cautioned Babysoft.

Lala looked sternly at the drowsing Rosie slumped forward across the table. '*She* is no handmaid of the Lord. Can't cook, can't sew, can't do anything except tell you lies in bed—can you, my baby duckling, hah?' Lala said as she reached out and pinched Rosie's chin, clucking like a brooding mother-hen. 'Can't do anything, can you?'

'Ah, but I can tell lies beautiful,' murmured Rosie hearing the last part of the statement and struggling up. 'And anyway I'll be the handmaid to no bleeding man.'

'Never fret, my friends,' said Luke stretching himself. 'I will make highly improper and erotic advances to my landlady Mrs Tombs, sixty-six and buxom and a genius with cabbage and pigs cheek. Fear not, my worthy comrades. With gritted teeth and chin thrust out, I *shall* survive, in the hallowed heritage of my calling, dug deep in the trenches of adversity. Per ardua ad astra—'

Babysoft dipped a finger into her brandy and licked it. 'Or as the man said—Onward Christian Soldiers, before you miss the last bus.'

Lala looked past Babysoft towards the great blazing fireplace at which Mongoose lay curled up on the floor like an enormous seal. 'Your friend appears to be quite exhausted. You had better get him up to his room.'

Babysoft threw her eyes to heaven and grimaced. 'He'll be snoring and grunting all night, like a pig in mortal agony. I'll get Freddie to give me a hand with him if I can drag him away from that effing piano.' She drained her glass and got up. 'Nice meeting you, Lukey love. Will you be staying for breakfast?'

'Don't be cheeky, you!' Lala snorted. 'Go and tend to your poor fallen friend.'

'Ah, sure aren't we all fallen, for Jasus' sake? I'll see you in me dreams, Lukey, and exchange the time of day.'

Babysoft swaggered off towards the supine Mongoose, a long streak of white leg showing through the slit in her gown.

Lala gave a deep sigh. 'A crazy girl, full of vanity and impudence, but at least she can cook.'

'Yeah,' retorted Rosie. 'Bleeding stirabout.'

Lala took Luke's hand fondling it warmly. 'I will pray tonight that you will find peace of mind and warmth of belly, and don't forget to lock your door, Rosie. Goodnight, children.'

Fresh logs were thrown onto the smouldering wreckage in the

hearth, sending green and orange flames spiralling up the chimney and Rosie tottered into the chair and turned to Luke. 'For the love and honour of Jasus, would you ever be a gentleman and take me up to bed before I drop out of me standing?'

Luke smiled and got to his feet, bending over and placing his fingers gently on her elbow. 'If you will step this way, madam.'

II

Staggering up unending centuries of padded stairs, the soft scented cargo of love burdening his shoulders and Rosie losing her sandals, muttering Hail Marys liberally strewn with curses, wailing for her dead mother, her hair in her mouth. 'Shut up, for God's sake,' Luke implored, feeling for her in the musky black of the final twist of a passageway as rising bayings of protest came from behind draped sealed doors, not a candle in sight to light the way of the unwary celebrant on this treacherous stretch of via dolorosa olive-dark to the point of extinction. 'Just a few more paces and paradise will be gained,' Luke puffed prodigiously, grappling for her again as she slithered downwards in a soft swish of fallen linen.

'O Jesus put me to bed.'

The very last door was reached, the dead wall ahead of them saying the merciful end had arrived, he fumbling for the handle, putting bruised shoulder to door and pushing as he turned the lock, both shooting into the room headfirst as the unlocked door easily succumbed, a tangle of arms and legs thrashing about on the carpets, crawling over each other, heads bumping until Luke gained the approximate vicinity of the window on all fours and pulled aside the curtains, praying for a moon and there it was big as a melon flooding the room with sharp spun silver washing over everything.

'Switch off that bloody light, can't you,' cried Rosie struggling upwards by the side of the bed, 'it's blinding me.'

'It's the moon, lady,' Luke gasped gulping in air as he opened the lower window, 'the good and gracious moon—'

'Switch it off, moon or no moon,' Rosie belched, digging her fingers into the sheets, dragging herself off the floor onto the bed where she sprawled face downwards, head turned sideways into the blankets, low moaning noises coming from her. 'Jesus I'm dying.' She twisted round towards him as he squatted on the floor at the window hungrily sucking in night air. 'God forgive you anyway—'

'Forgive me?' he echoed breathing less raggedly now.

'For dragging me all the way upstairs like that,' she said striving to lean forward on an elbow. 'Like a bloody animal.'

'My dear girl, you were in no condition to skip the light fantastic, I assure you,' he replied, gingerly examining his sides. He winced. 'I think I've cracked a rib or two somewhere.'

The window overlooked a small courtyard ringed by an enclosed mews with windows still burning here and there, moonlight on garbage bins and refuse sacks and bicycles leaning like skeletal derelicts against walls, cats stalking their own shadows, arching stiff-spined over bins in search of sustenance and beyond the serrated rooftops and ubiquitous spires of the city gleaming, falling away into the inky depths of encircling hills, and not a phantom wind anywhere abroad.

'Jesus I feel sick.'

Seismic rumblings from the bed, and Rosie kneeling and beating her breasts, frantic to contain the rising pitch of bile inside her, as Luke scrambled hastily to his feet diving under the bed, banging his forehead against the hard steel handle of a bucket which he pulled out just in time as the pallid face of Rosie swam over the side of the bed, hand flying from mouth to let loose a cataract of vomit into the black metallic depths of the utensil, hair raining down and shoulders heaving as convulsions racked her while the amber trove of that evening's pleasures fell into the bucket held fast in Luke's knightly hands until the storm receded in little ebbing forays, leaving her limp, drooping over the side of the bed, arms like two white strips of willow, naked and innocent as the grave in the moonlight.

From the yard below the scalded fearful screech of a cat as Luke emptied the contents of the bucket out of the window, returning and replacing it under the bed, pulling the gurgling befuddled Rosie up onto the pillows, wiping her soiled mouth and drawing her hair back into place from the cold expanse of her forehead.

'I'm cold, cold,' she said her teeth knocking together. Her eyes fluttered open. 'Is this the right room we're in?'

'I fervently hope so,' he declared, bending irresolute over her. 'Er—don't you think you ought to take off your clothes?'

She moaned and turned her face aside. 'Jesus—is that all you can think of and me dying by the second? The more I know about bloody men—'

He backed hastily away, holding up a hand in disavowal. 'Not at all, not in the least, I do most earnestly assure you—' His heel struck against something on the floor, and he realised it was the brandy bottle still half full that had somehow stayed magically intact during the ascent from the bowels of the building. 'I seem to remember my Mother saying you should never go to bed in your clothes as you're liable to catch a chill on getting up—'

'Go away,' she mumbled tossing onto her side, burrowing deep into the blankets until she was submerged completely, 'go away and let me die in peace.'

At the window he sat on the oak ledge resuming his nocturnal eye-wandering, all lights extinguished now and the cats gone skulking home thin-ribbed and unsatisfied from the black hole of the yard. The snorings and fretful nasal mumblings of Rosie behind on the bed were a comic accompaniment to his fancies.

Eyes hurting with moonlight he rose stiff-jointed and stood by the bedside looking down at the blanketed bundle of Rosie, softly touching and caressing where he imagined her shoulder to be much as he would rub a sleeping puppy, sighing because she was lost, so manhandled by life and prone to the wiles and vagaries of blunt-witted schemers. He blew her a vague kiss and tiptoed out of the room unbearably wakeful and seeking nothing save to pad about in stockinged feet sure and safe as a ghost.

Darkness dense and deceptive swarmed over him, and he grew into it as into a second skin. As tentative as an Indian scout he inched forward smoothly rounding corners, moving with fox-footed sureness through a labyrinth of corridors with hardly a let or stumble up and down unexpected steps pausing to pilot the bottle mouthwards, lounging against wall or banister.

'Jesus Christ almighty—who's that?'

A sucked-in feminine shriek and a hand flung out in protection as he slid round a corner and collided with a fellow night-traveller, the cool touch of flesh at his inquisitive fingertips.

'Fear not, fair damsel.'

A quick drawn-in breath of relief ending in a smothered giggle. 'Oh, it's yourself,' came the hoarse gushing tremolo he knew at once, her hands holding his own keeping them where they had strayed. 'I was on the way back from the lavatory—'

'Ah,' he said unremarking, moving away.

Her fingers tightened. 'What's your hurry sure?' her small breathless whisper soft-winging into his ear. 'Where's Rosie?'

'Sick unto death, poor lady.'

Babysoft gave a sagacious sigh, and he saw her shake her head in the greyness of the wall behind. 'Brandy. She always throws her guts up after brandy. I'm forever telling her to stick to vodka.' Her fingers roved up his forearms drawing him closer. 'I forgot your name—'

'An entirely understandable lapse,' he whispered back unresisting as she drew him nearer.'

'Well, what is it, for Christ' sake?' she asked spanning his waist with her arms.

'It's Luke.'

'Luke,' she murmured as she drew the folds of her nightgown around him, 'Luke . . . hmmm . . . of course it is, a nice strong name, no messing about a name like that.' Babysoft lifted her face to him. 'Kiss me, Lukey darling.'

'Madam, mine not to reason why—' He stooped and featherly touched her forehead with his lips. 'It would be rude and craven to refuse so innocent an importuning.'

'Stop mouthing out of you,' she rasped fastening her mouth upon his as her hands fought for his, writhing and wriggling against him. 'Hold me, you fool—crush me,' she panted against his mouth, grabbing his hand and pushing it downwards, imprisoning it between her thighs. 'Do things to me, Lukey, oh yes do things—anything—just *do*—' There was a plopping sound as the bottle slipped and a stifled screech escaped her. 'Oh Jesus Christ—what's after falling on me foot?' She staggered away from him hobbling on one foot and holding up the injured one in her hands. 'You fucking eejit—you're after breaking me instep! The curse of Jesus on you anyway! Oh mammy!' She stumbled against the wall clutching her foot, whimpering. 'Don't just stand there gawking and you after afflicting me like this,' she wailed. 'Pick me up and help me to me room—down there first on the right—Oh Jesus the pain is running right up me leg!'

Once more sleep-thick voices were rumbling out in protest and door handles beginning to rattle, and hastier than post-haste Luke rushed forward and swept the wincing near-naked Babysoft up into his arms, instantly staggering to his knees under her large-boned deceptive weight, which occasioned a further stream of wailing and invective out of her as he manfully strove to regain the perpendicular, reaching the door of her room on his knees still gallantly clasping her, she almost garroting him as she clung to his neck and then inside at last where she miraculously regained both her composure and use of her foot, sitting demurely down on the bed.

'Are you kilt?' she asked softly in lisping solicitude, rubbing her foot and wriggling her toes. 'Poor Lukey,' she cooed, the nightrobe slipping from her shoulders. 'It's all right now, darling.'

'Well, if you're sure?' he said his breathing yet again in a state of turmoil, backing towards the door.

'Don't be silly, Lukey love,' spoke Babysoft rising and closing the door. 'You're not going yet—I want you to kiss me foot and make it better.' There came a loud funnelling snore from the bed behind her. 'Don't be minding him sure—'

'Who?'

'Poor Mongoose,' she replied languidly, 'sure he's harmless and out to the world as usual.' She sat down on the bed and held out her foot towards him. 'Kiss it.'

'What about—er—*him*?' he whispered.

'I want you to kiss it, not him,' Babysoft hissed back, disrobed now and shoulders all a white winsome blur silhouetted against the paleness of the window, wriggling her foot at him. 'I only want you to kiss me poor injured foot, Lukey love—honest to God, nothing mortal or anything.'

Resigned and bowing to his fate, parfit gentil knight kneeling to receive the sword-touch of honour upon his unlined brow the sooner to return to poor hapless Rosie, he kneeled with closed eyes, moulding his lips in reverent chaste shape of every brotherly kiss given in need and platonic fidelity, touching the girlish foot as he would in greener days the holy water of communion, lingering and musing on each separate toe as on a string of rosary beads held up for his homage and swinely adoration.

'Oh Jesus come to me *here*!'

Her sudden thrust forward, her legs closing in a clamp round his neck, her warm cushiony thighs manacling him trussed like a village idiot in the stocks, her hands holding his ears for reins tight-held, her feet dug in the middle of his spine like spurs digging into him, yanking him face-forward into the full unimpeded path of her pelvic charge. 'Lukey love, Oh Lukey love, you wild sweet demon—'

He struggled to say something as she straddled his shoulders cowboy fashion bearing him implacably to the floor as his knees gave way sliding and slewing out from under him and his overloaded spinal arch in imminent danger of cracking—

'Carmelita!'

A loud fearful wail from the bed followed by a convulsion of heart-wrung sobbing.

'Carmelita—a candle, Carmelita—say you'll light a candle for me when God finally takes me.' A dull thudding sound like knuckles beating on someone's chest. The cry again merciful to Luke's ear. The unwieldy pyramid of their bodies tottered and collapsed amid a tangle of groping limbs, he uncoiling himself from beneath her and tentatively exploring his musculature to happily encounter only a few unspectacular contusions.

'Who is Carmelita?' he asked. She sat panting on the floor facing him, her head drooping to one side like a rag doll.

'His effing wife,' she replied. 'He lets on she's Mexican but she's one of the Donoghues from Sherriff Street.' Babysoft in no mood to be softtalked out of her indignation, thumped fists on her knees in a drumbeat of teeth-clenched rage, then forthwith leaping to her feet and proceeding to transfer her tattoo onto the openshirted mountainous chest of the fondly sleepdreaming Mongoose. 'I'll Carmelita you!' she screeched, out-screaming every fishwife that ever swam unannounced into any man's cosy little harbour of domestic placidity, her hands flailing that slumbrous expanse of flaccid flesh. 'Get up out of that you horny oul' truckster and let a girl go about her God-given work in peace!' Babysoft had worked herself up into a fine fury, her eyes ablaze and her delicate features suffused with El Greco luminosity. 'Bejasus I know the candle I'll be lighting for you and where to effing well put it too—'

Mongoose the belaboured and berated dreamer rose up on the pillows like a bemused whale unexpectedly harpooned, foolishly shaking his great gleaming head and opening his mouth to gulp in lungfuls of air and on beholding Babysoft and her rough tender ministrations, he smiled, a half-awake middleaged cherub, taking her hands between his own, commencing to let forth as though he had never left the tawdry little stage below in the dark:

> 'Speak, speak, speak to me, Thora
> speak from your heaven to me—'

Babysoft went mute as she strove to wrench her wrists free from the clammy grip of Mongoose waxing lyrical, but he reading in her agitation a mere feminine pique changed song effortlessly in mid-stream:

> 'O Maiden, my maiden, dear love divine,
> O Maiden, my maiden, dear love be mine—'

Mongoose on a wave of histrionic passion injudiciously placed his hand upon his breast to give earnest of his fervour, thus releasing one of the captive maidenly hands of Babysoft and straightway she grabbed ferocious hold of his jowls, instantly reducing his soaring boy-soprano crescendo to the guttural squeaks of an impaled pig.

'I'll guzzle you so help me Jasus!' she swore, her flashing fangs snapping inches away from the thick jugular swelling in his neck.

Luke in no little wonder and mystification backed mesmerised to the door seeing Babysoft of a sudden go limp and subside in a fit of weeping on the broad acres of Mongoose, that bewildered soul cradling her head and patting her shoulder as if lulling a child to sleep.

Outside in the good dark again, the cold creeping about his ankles, Luke followed a thin greyish vapour of light down coils of corridor, his faithful senses telling him this was the same via dolorosa he had taken an hour or two back with Rosie as he now picked up and followed a trail of faint music below in the profound night.

Pausing on the last staircase, the piano tones stronger now and light coming from the door of the front parlour, his feet making no sound he stepped into the eerily ringing room, a large glow still alive in the hearth and in the shadows a dim form at the piano playing Chopin. Advancing into the welcoming glow Luke discerned a squat immobile shape seated at the foot of the stage, head buried in folded arms, listening, intent, carved into the texture of the night. Firelight playing on her near naked skull, charcoal streaks of hair plastered to it, Lala sat in silence, deaf and mute to all save those love-led fingers straying over the keys, herself the sole and only audience the pianist craved.

On an abrupt unfinalised passage the music stopped like something falling over a precipice. 'I can't, I can't,' the man stammered between harsh dry sobs, rising from his stool and moving about like someone blind.

Without a word and hardly stirring Lala held out her hand, and he came haltingly like a truant schoolboy and sat down beside her, letting her hold his head against her breasts, rocking back and forth until gradually he ceased to quiver and lay passive and harboured in her oceanic embrace seeming to fold up like a concertina, and there Luke felt with a strange conviction they would remain until morning, a fixed sculpted tableau finding home in each other.

Luke retraced his steps out to the hallway again, his feet frosty and Rosie uppermost in his thoughts, the image of her blended in strange alchemy with the scene he had just witnessed in the last light of the fire.

Crossing to the bar, hand guided by unerring instinct, Luke gently eased a bottle of brandy off the bottom shelf, making a mental note to reimburse his hostess for this and sundry pleasures before departing the establishment next morning, and once more ascended, crafted now in the night ways of the house, on up lush storeys of stairs, singing his silent way to Rosie.

Arrived unmolested he pushed open the door gently and went inside, the moon throwing a bright shaft across the bed showing the foetal shape of Rosie under the blankets. He sat down on the bed and uncorked the bottle, putting it to his mouth.

A strange noise insinuated itself into his hearing like the flapping of a loose window shutter; it was Rosie and it was indeed her teeth chattering.

'Jesus Christ, I'm freezing. I can't stop meself from shivering— might as well be up in the Park.'

'Sit up,' he said putting an arm under her shoulders.

'Are you mad—do you want me to catch me death of cold?'

'Sit up,' he told her more brusquely, pulling her into a semi-sitting position against the headboard, bringing the bottle forward. 'Take a good mouthful of this.'

'Oh Jasus I couldn't—take it away,' she moaned, the smell wafting strong and pungent into her nostrils. 'It's turning me stomach—take it away before I throw up.'

'Alas, sweet maid,' he sighed, holding her head steady in the crook of his arm and bending her back, forcing the neck of the bottle between her teeth, 'in thy orisons be all my sins remembered.'

She choked as the brandy trickled down her throat, and he took the bottle away briefly to enable her to catch her breath but put it back at once, and more composed this time she drank carefully, her shoulders heaving and the rigidity melting away from her as she lay back against the pillows, drops of brandy glistening on her chin.

'Jesus, that nearly killed me,' she told him. 'Where did you get yourself to?' she queried him, pulling the bottle to her and taking a steadier draught. 'I might've been found dead in me bed for all you bothered your arse.' She sniffed fastidiously. 'Don't tell me,' she said with lip-curling disdain. 'You're reeking with Babysoft's bleeding perfume. Her sister works in a scent shop in Grafton Street and gets everything buckshee by giving the manager a bit on the sly.'

Luke in turn sniffed himself, curious to discover if indeed he was carrying Babysoft's spoor around with him. 'I did happen to encounter the lady during a cursory tour of the establishment,' he admitted. 'It was, shall we say, a brief encounter but one not entirely devoid of incident—'

'Did she drag you into bed with her or did you go peaceful?' Rosie asked with a brave attempt at a sneer which to her obvious mortification turned instead into a painful grimace. 'Some women have no respect,' she announced haughtily pulling the blankets chin-high, making a tent-like hump with her knees, 'and most men have no effing taste.'

He contemplated her sleepstarved sunken eyes and ruined make-up. 'I fear I must agree with you,' he said, untwining her hands from around the bottle and hoisting it to his lips, 'sorely though it irks my masculine conceit, though in my own defence

I must point out that I valiantly resisted the lady's none too reticent advances.'

'The brazen bitch!' exclaimed Rosie, much impressed and more than a little envious of what seemed to her proof of her friend's superior arsenal of allure. 'You have to hand it to her all the same —she never went to school, you know, not even to the Sisters of Charity, and there she is today, able to walk down the best streets in Dublin and pick and choose to her heart's content—none of them halfeejits out of Trinity for her, all balls and no bread—' Rosie giggled and pressed her hand to her mouth. 'God, I get awful common sometimes when I've a sup taken. Don't be minding me, Liam.'

'Luke,' he gravely corrected.

'Beg your pardon? Oh, you mean you're not—'

'Liam.'

This time Rosie quite definitely lowered her eyes. 'Of course you're Luke—I knew it all the time. I was just kidding you. Anyway Liam is my twin brother.'

'Of course he is. Have another drink.'

'Do you want to get me drunk all over again?' she asked, accepting the invitation, and even in the unreal shrine of the moon he imagined he discerned colour returning to her cheeks.

'I don't feel a bit sick now.'

'I'm delighted to hear it.'

'Funny you should know Liam.'

'Sorry to disappoint you, but I must make it quite clear that I am totally unacquainted with Liam.'

'Then how did you know he was my brother?'

'I had no knowledge that he was until you told me so.'

She looked at him. 'And you believed me?'

He smiled, knowing it was the smile that showed off his rather good teeth to the best advantage. 'But of course,' he said not letting up on the charm now that the uncertain tide was turning in his direction. 'I always believe the word of a lady.'

Again she drew her brows together as if irritated, but unconvincingly. 'Don't be funny,' she said lifting her shoulders defiantly. 'Ladies are born, not made.'

'Then you were born a lady,' he persisted, gently touching her chin with thumb and forefinger.

She twisted away her head rather fiercely. 'Bullshit,' she said with somewhat uncertain force. 'I was born in North Brunswick Street in a tenement with two rooms and rats as big as kittens playing tick-tack all over the place, the smell of stale piss everywhere—'

'Which does not make or unmake a lady,' he intervened. 'I am unimpressed with your social antecedents, the present alone interests me, and nothing you say or do will dissuade me in my unerring and unalterable conviction in your ladiness.'

Rosie half glared up at him from the pillows. 'Jesus, do you always talk like that? Would you not be afraid of doing your jaw some terrible injury?' Her voice and look softened. 'All the same, you say nice things, if I could only understand them. I like it when you're masterful.'

'And when have you allowed me to be masterful?'

'You know—just now when you made me take that drink—I thought you were going to stuff it down me throat—that kind of thing—you know what I mean—I like it.' She looked at him critically. 'You don't look the masterful type, sort of delicate and downy, a bit under-nourished I suppose, but I bet you could be a real bastard if it came to the push. I bet,' she went on rather breathlessly, 'I bet you could give a girl a good clatter in the puss if she got out of line.'

Rosie was leaning forward looking up at him, eyes bright with masochistic fervour, and he was hearing the swish of leather thongs slapping happy-go-luckily on bare palpitating buttock and belly, stinging like wet nettles the willing flesh to ecstasies of pain.

'I've a terrible thirst on me.' She took another meaningful mouthful, rolling her eyes comically, then rested the bottle lightly on her chest, fingernails tapping. 'You'll owe Lala a bomb by the morning,' she said. 'Rothschild isn't in it. I didn't think newspaper fellas got such good money. I knew a fella once,' she mused, 'had a paper stand at the corner of Parnell Square, ran a fleet of taxis and a house in Rathmines, a Mercedes and a Humber in the garage and a string of girls on the game for him, his brother was secretary to the Archbishop of Dublin, oh money no object to Eugene.'

'I'm afraid I'm in the poorer end of the trade,' Luke sighed. 'I just subscribe supremely irrelevant articles and an equally menial bit of occasional reporting on the side.'

'But what do you do for a living?' she asked in some considerable perplexity.

He smiled into the comradely darkness. 'That, dear lady, is a question that shall continue to harass and occupy me for the rest of my natural and unnatural life, the great question-mark of my existence, what do I do for a living. I haven't got the guile to be a parasite, or the stamina to fend for myself, hence I fall down miserably between two stools.' He retrieved the bottle and nourished himself once more. 'Shall I tell you something?' he said, bending and assiduously wooing her ear. 'I am writing a book.'

She gave him a look compounded of pity and alarm. 'Never mind, sure you'll get over it.'

'Hah!' he proclaimed, lifting a prophetic finger, 'you fail to comprehend. I am writing no mere tome of spurious content to flatter the infantile aspirations of the pseudo-intelligentsia or fan the peacock feathers of the petty rabble rousers—Mein Gott, nein!' he declared striking his chest with clenched fist. 'What I am creating is a chronicle of Dublin writ large and writ loud for generations to come that will reawaken the splendid spirit of satire and the high art of asperity once more throughout the land and summon all the poetic and literary sons of Eireann to unite under one flag, one bright and indivisible star to reach out once more and reclaim our ancient and inalienable heritage of blinding genius—'

'And why wouldn't you?' said Rosie; her fingers tightened on his arm. 'It must be all hours—are you coming to bed at all or what are you doing?'

He looked at her sadly. 'Ah! You too have inherited the incurable curse of the Irish,' rising to strut around the room giving a woefully inept impression of an imprisoned soul in wrath and anguish, beating his forehead carefully with the soft underpart of his hand. 'The moment you come upon anything that threatens your own snug little shell of blithe ignorance and cosy unquestioning acceptance of the prevailing status quo, you immediately run and take refuge in mockery and derision and become absorbed in tremendous trivialities—what time is it? did you set the clock? did you put the cat out? did you post that letter to my Aunty Kathleen I gave you today?'

'What letter?' asked Rosie thoroughly addled. 'What are you bleeding on about?'

Luke stopped at the foot of the bed spreading his hands out

wide. 'An analogy, dear girl, I am merely drawing an analogy in order to underline and put into perspective the kind of mental malaise that has plagued Ireland since the dawn of our cultural history, the ostrich mentality that refuses to look openly into mirrors when they are held up to us—what about Mangan, Swift, Synge, O'Casey—what about Joyce and Beckett, what about—'

'Well, what about them, for Jesus' sake?' Rosie broke in exasperated. 'They're all bloody well dead, aren't they, so let the poor buggers rest.' She flounced over onto her side pulling the bedclothes high. 'Jesus, you'd think all belonging to you had just died.'

He stood at the end of the bed putting on an expression of ineffable melancholy, remembering a painting he had once seen of the head of John the Baptist reclining on a plate after it had been smoothly severed from the rest of that beatific personage at the behest of some dancing lady and hoping his face held the same look of unmentionable woe, martyring for all he was worth. 'Ah, Rose, matchless Rose,' he said drawing up a sigh from the belly-depths of him, 'you cut me to the quick. Let me not go gentle into that good night of the soul ere my salad days have in truth begun—'

'I'm getting out of here,' she growled, about to toss the blankets aside.

He sprang forward, words wise and comforting on his tongue, soothing the flare of revolt out of her, the wealth of ageless benisons in his fingertips as she allowed herself to be cajoled back into peace again, relishing the undemanding warmth of his fingers stroking her hair as he might a forest creature staying its flight awhile and Rosie her face lying in the softness of his armpit smiled at the great foolishness so easily risen in a man, he meanwhile lying in an easy state thinking of no worrisome particular and she grew gradually restive under so leafy an aegis of concern.

'Are you asleep?'

'Oh, I am far from the arms of Lethe,' he replied, dangling the bottle over the side of bed, no longer feeling the night chill.

She twisted her head higher on the pillow. 'You're not a queer, are you?' she asked as if much puzzled. 'You wouldn't fool me like that, would you?'

'No, Rosie, God's wrath on me if I fooled you like that.'

'Then don't you like me?'

'Hmm, very much I like you.' He raised the bottle, sipping. 'Want some?'

'No, thank you,' came her brusque answer, then after a pause: 'Do you think I'm nice—do you fancy me?'

'Fancy you? That's quaint.'

'Quaint or not, do you?'

'Why else would I be sharing your bed and a church bell in the distance telling me it is gone two in the morning?'

She stirred uneasily, for once tongue-tied and inwardly railing against it. 'God, do I have to spell it out for you, will I draw you a bleeding map? Do you want me to take me clothes off?'

'If that would make you more comfortable—'

'Look, I'm not here for comfort.'

'Oh, I was forgetting your trade union principles.'

'Do you want us to say the Rosary together?'

'I thought you were tired?'

'See what thought done.' She stretched her full length in the bed. 'The sooner it's over the sooner I can get some shuteye.'

The silky shifting and crumpling as with precise time-drilled manoeuvring she slid out of her clothes under the blankets, kicking them to the bottom of the bed in a rumpled heap, suppressing an involuntary shiver and feeling for his hand, finding and placing it peremptorily upon her breast as though slapping a piece of cold dead fish down upon a plate, clearing her throat and flexing herself like a sprinter poised and waiting on the go-line.

'Goodnight, Rosie,' he said, withdrawing his hand and turning over on his side away from her, placing the bottle carefully down on the rug and pulling some blankets over his shoulder.

'What?'

'Sweet dreams,' he said mumbling setting his head into the pillow, drawing his knees up comfortably.

'Look, what ails you?' she demanded digging her elbows into the mattress and sitting up. 'I don't want you to start bothering me towards morning.'

'Word of honour.'

'I must have me night's rest like anyone else.'

'Of course you must,' he concurred crossing his arms and hugging himself tightly. 'Are you warm enough?'

She momentarily choked on her words. 'Am I warm enough! Now see here you, don't you start insulting me!'

44

'Insulting you? I assure you, nothing could be further from my thoughts. Are you sure you'll be warm enough?'

'Don't you start treating me like I had leprosy.'

'*Do* you have leprosy?'

'No, nor nothing else neither! Do I have to show you me clean bill of health? I get one every month, you know, but I don't go around wearing it on me chest or hanging it up on the wall.'

'I'm sure you're a very healthy girl, Rosie—I did say goodnight, didn't I?'

'Look,' she said torn between supplication and rage, 'I never gave anyone a dose in me life, and I'm not about to start now.'

'That is a very salutary and most salubrious consideration on your part, Rosie. Would that others were equally meticulous and dedicated in their chosen professions, myself not the least. Be good, sweet maid, and let who will be clever.' He gently pummelled the pillow into a more comfortable position against his cheek.

Rosie's voice faltered. 'Look, tell me straight—I don't smell, do I? I'm no bloody fanatic about taking baths twice or three times a day, mind you, but I do keep meself clean.'

'Fresh as morning dew, Rosie. A Rose by any other name could not smell sweeter than you.'

'Then what's bugging you?' she asked, fretful and confused. 'Why are you lying there like a bloody altarboy or a priest wore out from listening to too many confessions?'

'You have a very original line in similes.'

'Jesus Christ,' she said totally exasperated, 'do you want to or not? You'd think it was me who was doing the paying.'

'Goodnight again, Rosie.'

'I've never been treated like this before in all the time I've been working here,' said Rosie fuming. 'If you don't like me say so and no hard feelings, only don't insult me or treat me like dirty. Just because I don't go around like that Babysoft tearing the clothes off a fella with her eyes doesn't mean I have no feelings —I've me feelings same as anyone else, and me pride too—' she nudged him sharply in the back with her elbow. 'Do you hear me —don't be letting on you're asleep.'

Luke yawned, flattening down the covers with his chin. 'I hear you very well, Rosie, but alas, I think I am just about to yield to the blandishments of Lethe after all.'

'Oh, to hell with you anyway,' she snapped drawing away to the other side of the bed. 'Go and play with yourself for all I bloody well care. Your father must have been a Jesuit, though if he was itself you'd have more gumption in you.'

'Rosie, Rosie,' he chided, 'the spoiled priest syndrome is no longer in vogue. You really should keep in touch with events and changes in the modern world. The priesthood is no longer synonymous with fearful bogeymen and goblins of starved carnality, no longer the happy hunting ground of Freudian free-for-alls—'

'Stuff you.'

'And goodnight to you too, good daughter.'

Limbs pleasantly warm pervaded by a fine lassitude, the accumulated aches of the day ebbing slowly out of bone and sinew, Luke felt easy and totally belonging, as if lying in his own bed under the low ceiling beside the window looking out over the tree-lined avenue beyond in dead-of-night Ballsbridge, the neat shelves of books lining the corner wall, the desk green-leather-covered at which he wrote down shop-soiled oddments of thought in the slim abstemious days of industry before Tessa had nudged him into disarray, and happily he waited now for sleep to settle heavy and sensuous upon him and in that luxurious pause before dovetailing into oblivion there came the sound of Rosie sniffling tearful and tense beside him. 'Are you crying?' he asked, turning over on his back.

'Who—me? Oh no,' she answered swallowing noisily, 'sure I'm breaking me sides laughing.'

'I'd like to comfort you, if I knew how.'

'Say ten Hail Marys for the repose of me soul. I can't wait to see the back of you anyway.'

'It would help if I knew the precise nature and enormity of my sin,' he told her.

'Sin!' she exclaimed, 'God between us and all harm, I don't think you know the meaning of the word. Have you even heard of it?'

'Oh, that word. Yes, I have come across it during my terrestrial procrastinations, though I am not sure what relevancy it bears to the situation in which we now find ourselves. For instance,' he said putting hands behind head, 'if we were to make love now would you consider that to be sinful?'

"Course not!' said Rosie spiritedly, then she hesitated. 'I wish you wouldn't ask me such questions—why do you always have to ask questions? A girl would be driven demented by talking the effing night away.'

'What are you trying to fight, Rosie? I know it isn't just me—what is it?'

'Talk, talk, talk—'

'Why are you afraid?'

'Me, afraid? Sure what would I be afraid of and a big strong fella like yourself beside me?'

'I won't go all mystical and metaphysical on you,' he said, 'but it strikes me that you're afraid of yourself much more than you could ever possibly be of anyone else.'

'Jesus, you're a right effing Confucius.'

'I may not have put it very well, but it seems to me you're longing desperately for a kind of—of, well a kind of mental and spiritual ejaculation.'

'Wha—?' Rosie faltered. 'I'm longing for what?'

'An ejaculation of the spiritual kind,' he expanded with conviction, 'as much as any other kind. You crave for it as other people look for that other, more orthodox ejaculation in the throes of coitus—a kind of soulful dénouement, a mental climax as powerful, as shattering as the final upheaval of passion when all petty constraints and taboos are swept away. What you need is a climax in reverse—a sexual purgation of the psyche, if you like—'

'I don't like the sound of that at all.'

Heedless of her rising unease, 'You've been suffering,' he went on, 'from a pernicious flagellation of the soul, lashed by merciless whips of indifference, stung into rebellion by the perversities and abnormalities of others tossing you into a kind of psycho-sexual frenzy—'

'I've heard of fellas like you,' she said drawing further away from him, 'effing sex maniacs up to all kinds of kinky goings-on, leather boots, studded belts—the lot—well, you've come to the wrong shop, Sonny Boy.'

He laughed. 'You misconceive my meaning, Rosie—my metaphors got rather tangled.'

'What, between whips and strangulations and frenzies and what have you, I don't know whether I'm coming or going with you—don't you ever give your jaws a rest?'

47

'I put too great a strain on your pristine innocence,' he conceded, feeling for her hand under the bedclothes. 'I think perhaps it is time I began to woo you.'

'Woo away till you're blue in the face, but you won't get Rosie bending over to get her arse whipped and be beat black and blue just to please some effing maniac—oh bejasus no. I'm not just up from the bog, you know. I'm not shit-ignorant.'

'At least let me kiss you goodnight—sure that would not be an act of criminal irresponsible debauchery?'

'Well, if it would tire you out,' Rosie relented turning her face to him.

A grave cool kiss, a gentle penitential coming together of lips, his hands cupping her face, she static and obedient giving up her mouth to his safe-keeping in a determined docility grown hardy through familiar usage, faltering slowly now as his tenderness persisted, his fingers storytelling her to peace, her own hands now feeling him as with tongue and fingertip he unhurriedly explored her downy secrets, igniting little runaway fires, jerking her into dismay at such alien magic things dancing in her limbs as he softly persuaded her knees apart and she grew taut expecting the old gruesome invasion, but he had already entered her as he would a temple, avoiding advances that might knock or jar her, and it was new day to her, a slow procession of measured delights, striking rapid response in her, spreadeagled with wonder beneath him, her body shook with the long shuddering, choked little birdcries twitching in her throat swelling at last to one prolonged gasp of bewilderment primal as the pulse and pain of earth.

She lay afterwards as if stunned, eyes flickering open and shut, hand clutching her left breast as though to still the erratic thumpings of her heart, other hand lying upon her thighs feeling the dew there, a quiver still passing through her body, a gleam of sweat upon her as her breathing subsided to a low ragged rise and fall.

'Rosie,' he said presently, leaning over her a trifle concerned, 'Rosie, are you all right?'

She opened her eyes. 'Jesus, what happened to me?' Her voice was hushed, staring up at him. 'What was it?'

'Don't you know?'

She shook her head, hand still clasping her breast. 'How would I? I—I never felt like this, never before—Christ, it was—it was like some kind of heart attack.'

48

He looked down at her a smile on his face. 'I do believe it was the very first time for you, Rosie.'

She continued to stare at him blankly. 'What do you mean—the first time?'

'I could do with a drink,' he said, picking up the bottle from the floor. 'You too?'

'Please. A good one.'

He passed the bottle to her and she drank gratefully, then he put it to his own mouth as she looked on at him as at some enigma.

'Ah, that's better,' he said smacking his lips, wiping the neck of the bottle with his palm, leaning back against the pillows. 'Lord, I feel good.'

'Tell me what you meant—about this being the first time,' Rosie became conscious of her nakedness and drew the blankets up around her shoulders. 'Don't tease me.'

'I won't tease you, Rosie,' he told her gently. 'Tell me how you feel.'

'Feel?' she echoed, eyebrows rising. 'I—I don't know—I feel funny—not meself, kind of—' She stopped, angry and puzzled. 'How do you expect me to feel? Stop grinning at me.'

'I beg your pardon. I didn't intend to be facetious or cast ungallant aspersions on your sincerity. You simply stun me with wonder and breed in me a most unfamiliar sense of humility.'

'I wasn't born yesterday, if that's what you're trying to say.'

'Pardon my seeming indelicacy,' he continued, clearing his throat, 'but in the course of—er—circumstances you have no doubt found yourself in a similar situation as now—with a man, that is—' he hesitated. 'It would hardly be with a baboon, would it?'

She replied, 'But if you're asking me if you're the first bloke I've ended up here with—come again—'

'Yes—precisely,' he muttered vaguely. 'Exactly. What I meant was—before, you know—did anything happen?'

'Happen? Sure what would you expect to happen? Look, stop acting the eejit,' reprimanded Rosie sharply. 'The same as what happened just now with you and me—'

'Ah!' he darted in quickly, '*exactly* the same?'

'Certainly,' she answered decisively, 'a few drinks and a chat first downstairs, then up here after closing time, and after that—'

49

She stopped, suspicious again, eyeing him up and down. 'What are you up to? If it's kinky stuff you're still after.'

He held up his hand. 'On the collective tombstone of Eireann's patriot dead, I repudiate such base leanings.'

'I'm not as green as I may look.'

'I'm trying merely to ascertain a certain pertinent fact,' he said sighing. 'When it happened before, as you say, on those other occasions, with those other gentlemen—well, did anything happen to *you*?' He stopped and waited but she went on looking up at him as if she in turn expected some relevant revelation from him. 'I mean,' he continued rather desperately, 'did you have a heart attack?'

Rosie looked at him for some moments, then her mouth opened out into a perfect O and her eyes widened. 'You mean,' she gasped, 'you mean . . . Jesus,' she ended, sinking back onto the pillows. 'Imagine . . . oh imagine . . .'

It was the wrong setting for wonder, the wrong end of the world for such tremulous glad amazement, but the moon was there to see and quiet magic moved in the shadows attending Rosie and played about her face, making a marvel of it softened with a new fullness. Rosie murmuring, 'Imagine, oh imagine,' over and over softly under her breath, oblivious even of him who had brought her beyond the door of her gnarled ignorance. Her mind careered dazedly down ways of fancy, and with a cry she flung her hand before her eyes. 'Imagine, oh imagine . . .'

He dared not touch her nor speak, knowing himself at that time to be outside of her small intense world, not moving to jar such perfect possession till she opened her eyes and reached for him.

'For God's sake, come to me.'

Part Two

III

Three months had passed. Luke stepping it out boldly through dawn-grey back-alleys and sidestreets, shortcutting it to the press offices in time for the first black coffee of the day, ink, rubber and resin in his nostrils already, hearing the tell-tale rattle-tittle-tattle of typewriters tolling out the daily litany of murder, rape and mass starvation, the back page neat with births deaths marriages, the endless presses rolling in that bird-stained citadel of desiccated doom-mongering on the quays, spilling out its sewerage of fact and fiction into the unbeautiful river, polluting the veins of its naïve natives, that citizenry of light-hearted genuine genuflectors lifting the glass, raising the shifts of their women.

'Lovely fresh daffodils, sir, the dew still on them, plucked with me own hands, a shilling for two.'

Buying a bunch of the luscious glories from the puckered-eyed woman on the corner, the shawl slipping from her grizzled head, toothless gums spread in a smile as she gathered the garland together, her fingers gnarled and loving handing him the flowers, pavement princess, and thanking him the woman stepped back, the coins jingling and singing in her voluminous apron pocket. Bending to the flowers, burying his face in them, feeling their cool morning flesh startling him into joy, wondering why they should call to his mind that night's culmination with Rosie three months ago, he moved out at last into the broader thoroughfares, torn pink slips of clouds in the sky wisping over the rooftops and a broken-rimmed sixpence of a sun nudging its way between black chimneystacks nerveless and without warmth. Gaining the spattered ribbon of the quays he paused, elbows resting on parapet, the scavenging gulls already beginning to wheel and wail low over the green-scummed water, breathing deep and filling his lungs with air as though bracing himself to meet the leering scowl of Mulligan the night editor firing him for the umpteenth time.

A flap of wings shadowed his face and looking up he saw a gull settling on the parapet to his right regarding him with dark-green scrutiny, questioning his bona-fides to be there at that hour of the gull-swarming morning, scruffy lag-eyed alien on its territory with only flowers to offer it, every feather a livid quill of indignation—

'Stay awhile, friend,' intoned Luke edging a tentative forefinger towards the forked beak, 'and sway the burdensome weight of my thoughts a little to the side of indolence.'

Viper-tongued the bird shot its head at him, villainous eyes flashing, missing the proffered digit narrowly and hopping on its rapier toes angrily disgusted with its own failure, lifting its muddied wings in agitation but grimly footholding its position on the parapet, thirsting for another chance at bloodying the hand that fed it not.

'Art thou Poe's horrendous raven come back in meaner feathers?' asked Luke the loose-brained ornithologist leaning elbows on the river wall, regarding the beady-eyed baleful bird as would a consultant a difficult morbid patient while it in turn studied him unblinkingly intent on vampire rites. 'What quote you now, O ramshackle raven, hungering after a neat nibble of my poetic flesh so you might enjoy me as the Roman worms feasted on the holy bones of Keats?'

The dull-yellow streak of beak in the air snapped viciously shut like a nutcracker a hairsbreadth distance off target.

'Who knows who you are?' mused Luke, the astonishing yellowness of the daffodils through which he peered contrasting with the soiled grey breast of the vigilant gull, bringing him a certain obscure sadness. 'You are perchance one of Lir's unfortunate progeny doomed forever to feed on the rank befouled bosom of Anna Liffey with plurabella no longer attached to her name.'

Swayed unwisely by his fanciful surmising, Luke for a second forgot the perilous proximity of the ready beak, and in less than a wink it had snapped fast on his unmoving finger, biting quick and sharp into the flesh, sweetly drawing blood. For a moment the fanatical eyes held his in triumph, and then with a contemptuous rise of wings the gull rose up over the river with a loud contented cackle.

'Touché! Bravo! Viva rara avis!' Luke called after it, painfully sucking his afflicted finger, rueful and humbled, waving the bright laurel of flowers after his victorious duellist, murmuring low as he nursed his wound, 'May the decapitated head of a Dublin Bay herring stick in your gullet this day, you skyborne bugger.'

A few drops of his blood smudged the flower petals and with surprise he studied for some moments the scarlet stain against the fragile yellow, marvelling at the mingled colours, the throb of pain stinging the bitten tip of his finger. Then off again down the river walk he went gladful of that rude prick of victorious nature chastising him for stepping out of his station, quickening his sluggish senses, rushing forward into the day, and passing a bus-stop he stopped and thrust his bloodstained circlet of flowers into the hand of a young woman absorbed in a newspaper.

'Poor jewels for so beautiful a madonna,' he murmured briefly pressing her gloved hand. 'Adieu.'

'Hey you, do you mind?' the girl spluttered letting her newspaper fall. 'This town's full of fucking lunatics,' she added.

Dancing backwards on his heels he threw her a wide flamboyant kiss, careering into a plump bag-laden matron who muttered a curse as he turned, profuse apology on his lips, doffing his non-existent hat as he continued on his way, skipping over imaginary squares of hopscotch from foot to foot, hot-griddling along, the sullen morning clouds massing in the river below, factory smoke pluming into the sky, the city beginning to belch forth its heavy farts, rumbling and grumbling as it begrudging awoke. Fat green buses swollen with disgruntled worker-ants lumbered past like lugubrious Trojan horses, blind impervious faces staring out of windows or hidden behind newspapers held in front of them like shields, warding off the tentative blows of camaraderie. Carts trudged topheavy with useless litter, horses backbeaten between shafts, plodding clodding over bridges down innumerable bone-rattling streets, saliva dripping from their shaggy mouths. The little bells on huckster shopdoors tinkled as they opened for the day's garrulous haggling; and loose torn hoardings swung and flapped in the spiteful squalls of wind while the huge neon letters were dead and foolish now in the broadening hangover daylight and Luke with his delighted eyes embraced everything in sight, tossing unspoken felicitations into the air, prodigal as confetti, dancing to the charnel house of the press offices across the last bridge but one spanning the gull-loud ravaged river.

Water splashed in the pails of the cleaning women mopping the dull brown parquet floor of the gloomy entrance hall, sleeves rolled up businesslike over dimpled elbows, stout town women, red-cheeked, turbanned, broad bosoms rolling in rhythmic collusion with their sturdy arms splashing and wiping and wringing dry, absorbed by toil in the vineyard of the Lord, telling bedroom jokes about their men, looking fondly up at him as he waltzed past stopping to cluck a few of his motherly favourites familiarly under their jolly chins, 'Ah, my damsels of scrubbing brush and pail, you make the morning loud with music.'

'Oh, you're light on your pins this morning, Mr Sheridan.'

'Ah, Mr S, you're like a fresh breeze blowing from Ringsend.'

'You make me feel seventeen again, Mr S.'

And when he had waltzed and charmed his way out of earshot: 'Mulligan will soon put that grin the other side of his kisser.'

'A terrible waste of young manhood on all them little hoors he does hang around with—I'm at the age when a young buck would do me a world of good.'

'Ah it's past that kind of thing you are now, Bessie, and yourself with eight of the little effers.'

'Still and all, what I wouldn't give.'

Maternal musings quite empty of lewd succulence, they wistfully eyed Luke's twinkling goblin form, his hands in trouser pockets ringing the few loose remaining shillings inside, exchanging ribald pleasantries with weary-eyed colleagues yawning past him, pens and notebooks stuck in stiffened fingers from the night-long vigil of no news, and at length stopping outside the office with M. MULLIGAN emblazoned on the frosted glass panel in arrogant black capitals, fingers straying to brush back his lank unruly hair, humming The Marseillaise as he turned the handle and sprang inside the dusty sanctum, the poetry of centuries on his lips—

'Mr Mulligan would like to see you.' The first words of chilling civility dropping from the thin dry lips of Miss M. Springett from behind the impregnable ramparts of her desk, not lifting her bespectacled thorny blue eyes from the barking little typewriter in front of her.

'Ah, dear Miss Springett, your musical notes drop into my heart like—'

'Immediately.' Miss Springett, forefinger pointed and cruel digging into the typing keys, hair drawn back in a well-polished coil of titian tinfoil gathered in a ball at her stringy nape, spindly-heeled majorette-domo to Matthew Mulligan night editor, defender of his faith, vicarious maternal aunt and mistress and mother of Matthew's nocturnal scribbling hours, implacable foe to all who would demean him, especially the lesser minnows jacked up by their own bloated importance whose every footfall across that hallowed threshold she resented with all a fanatic's bile.

'When are you going to relent and tell me, Miss Springett?'

'Tell you precisely what, Mr Sheridan?' volleyed Miss Springett, fingers flying on the keyboard like a cloud of insatiable wasps, the downward tip of her thin fastidious nose on a par with the tip of her chin which curled upwards in severe comradeship.

'Why, the great enigma that has scourged me since I first entered this venerable precinct so many countless decades ago,' Luke said leaning forward with both hands on the desk. 'What the M in your name stands for. I cannot bear the suspense a day longer —is it Margaret? Surely not, I tell myself, it must be more exotic than Margaret. Marigold, then? Ah-ha, I tell myself, that is a distinct possibility, containing as it does so many beautiful connotations. Or could it be, I wonder, could it possibly be Melissa, a name that rolls off the tongue like cool smooth syrup?'

'I repeat,' announced Miss Springett amid a mounting crescendo clatter of keys, 'Mr Mulligan would like to see you.' A determined thump hard on the capitals. 'Immediately.' The face at a downward slope abbreviated, showing all smooth unwrinkled forehead with the faint sheen of a duckegg shell.

'Miss Springett,' said Luke gravely sliding a tentative buttock onto the desk, 'I must confess. My levity merely disguises an inner conflict of truly agonising dimensions. I am confronted with an area of dark and terrifying confusion in my life out of which I see no escape unless it be through the superior sagacity of one wiser and slightly, only marginally, older in years. Miss M. Springett,' said Luke throwing out his arms in a gesture of crucifixion, 'I therefore fling myself upon you—metaphorically speaking, alas-Oh,' he asided rolling his eyes ceilingwards, 'What joy unutterable to fling myself upon you *literally*—Ah, what mad foolish dreams we weave in our dark insufferable night—Where was I? Yes, I have it. This dark terrifying inner conflict—would that I could rest this tired world-weary head—' pointing to his forehead—'upon *that* soft haven of succour'—pointing with his other finger in the direction of Miss Springett's decorous tweed-clad frontage.

At last Miss Springett raised her eyes and instantly robbed him of rhetoric, all the cold sunken distances and impervious dominions of the sea swamping him mercilessly behind inscrutable magnifying glasses making her eyes two small concentrated points of beady implacable disdain.

'I'm going, Miss Springett,' he said, hastily, backing away appalled by her marvellous malevolence, 'I—*am*—going.' Stumbling backwards like a flunkey in the presence of royalty, a sickly hangdog smile on his face he felt behind him for the handle of Mulligan's private office, almost floundering inside with the speed of a bandit seeking sanctuary from the deadly cobra of the law.

It might still have been deadfall of night there in the office, a thick palpable nicotine-laden penumbra draping everything and windows still shuttered against the siege of daylight. On the oval desk a beacon lamp burned, lulling the unwary into false peace, for behind the disgruntled presence of the night editor, large leonine head and gargantuan torso shrouded in smoke and shadow lamplight falling on bulging waistcoated belly, two small pudgy hands eternally knotted into tight, twitching fists of frustration renowned for the snapping of pencils and the recalcitrant wills of subordinates, bunched now rigidly as Luke steered a wellworn path towards the unwelcoming shrine.

'Matthew, Oh Matthew, when are you going to replace that dreaded Medusa outside your door? I swear to God the woman is composed entirely of ice upheld throughout by solid steel girders—'

'Sheridan, you're fired.'

'Certainly, Matthew,' Luke nodded agreeably as though impatient to press home his point, 'certainly, whatever you say. But as I was saying—what about that female Yeti outside your door? There I was quite gone in the middle of a rhapsodic eulogy in praise of her entirely mythical charms when quite without provocation she lifted her evil-eyed head and hissed at me—yes, *hissed* at me, right in my face—'

'I said, Sheridan,' came the booming snarl from behind the

desk and the smokescreen of cigar smoke, 'I said you're fired.'

Luke again nodded rather absently. 'As you say, Matthew, as you say. But you know,' he went on joining his hands behind his back and rocking back and forth on his feet, 'I have a pet theory about our Miss M. Springett. She is the kind of unbelievable freak female who arouses in the most sluggish imagination unending fantasies of speculation—that is about all she does arouse, need I say—but my own particular theory—nay, daily it is becoming a conviction—is that she was spawned one unfortunate day by an oversized superannuated toad in a moment of unforgivable distraction by the Creator and ever since she has been dangling in a sort of terrible suspension between the underworld of toads and creatures of similar ilk and the bright clear upperworld of honest normal clear-as-day creatures like you and me. Therefore it follows—'

A clenched fist rose and crashed down on the desk, thunder-clapping pencils jotters inkstands ashtrays and everything else within a radius of the volcanic belly-roar, behind the perimeter of the desk—'YOU'RE FIRED!' the unseen mouth bellowed, accompanied by another shattering slamming of fist upon desk. 'Understand me? F.I.R.E.D. Fired!'

'Finally?' Luke ventured.

'Irrevocably!'

'Oh well—'

'If you think or imagine,' bellowed Mulligan, heaving himself laboriously to his feet, 'that you can breeze in here like Fergus the fucking leprechaun after screwing half the brassers of Dublin all night when you were supposed to be in here at two this morning —if you think you can do *that* and expect me to have hot coffee and buns waiting for you with maybe a curer thrown in—'

'Stop,' pleaded Luke licking his lips, 'you'll have me drooling in a minute—'

'Shut fucking well up when I'm speaking to you!' Mulligan yelled, knocking over the chair behind him as he swung around and yanked the blinds with a vicious tug then staggered back as the light hit him. 'God curse it,' he cried puffing heavily, resting a moment on the desk rubbing his afflicted eyes. Blinking rapidly he turned to Luke in full flood once more, shaking a fat quivering forefinger to underline his invective. 'If you think or imagine I'm going to mollycoddle and pamper you like some middleaged philanthropist who's just been made a father—by God, you're mistaken, me randy bucko, you're badly mistaken! Out all night hoormastering on the taxpayers' money and me with one of the best stories of the year lined up for you.' Mulligan's overhung brows shot up, his eyes shooting out like bulbous blowlamps. 'What do you expect me to do—wipe your arse with a lilypad?'

'A story, eh?' said Luke ruminatively studying the corded distended veins in Mulligan's neck. 'A good one, you say?'

'Yeah,' replied Mulligan, his mood abruptly changing to one of muted excitement, picking up a cigar from an ornate box in front of him and chewing it distractedly. 'Remember your woman —some foreign countess or something—has that big filthy cathedral of a place out in Howth?'

'Madame Karina Fustenhalter,' Luke volunteered, sitting down in a chair for the first time feeling suddenly tired. 'Her maiden name is Kathleen Furlong, originally from Booterstown and latterly of Baden-Baden. Society wedding of the year when I was still a green lad. What has Kathy done now?'

'Poisoned her old man and written a best seller.'

'In that order?'

Mulligan took the unlit cigar out of his mouth and waved it extravagantly. 'Does it matter a fuck what order it was in?' He stood still a moment thinking. 'She wrote the best seller first— last year. All panting tits and a fuck on every page. Being made into a film of course—don't you read the newspapers?' he demanded angrily quirking a spiky eyebrow.

'As little as possible,' answered Luke lifting a hand and stifling a yawn. 'I feel guilty enough writing them.'

'Hottest story of the year—'

'Seeing it's only January, that is understandable—'

'And you have to go absent without leave knocking sparks off some hoor's arse—'

'Is the good count dead?'

'What good cunt?'

'Count, Matthew, Count Otto von Fustenhalter, Kathy's husband.'

'Oh, him—no, of course he isn't dead,' said Mulligan impatiently, puffing furiously on his cigar then realising it was unlit fumbling on the desk for his lighter. 'The old bastard's strong as a horse and built like a tank, in spite of the fact that he's some kind of cripple or other.'

'I thought you said Kathy poisoned him?'

'That's right,' Mulligan agreed, his face soon wreathed in smoke. 'She tried to, but she got their drinks mixed up and she fucking near died herself.'

'How did all this world-shattering information reach your ears —something more substantial than a little bird, I hope?'

Mulligan's eyes twinkled. 'A very substantial bird indeed—the count's sister. She phoned me after midnight—a gem of a story she told me—'

'And you believed her?' asked Luke trying to pierce the stratosphere of smoke surrounding the domed planet of Mulligan's head and reassure himself that the eyes were as canny and perceptive as ever.

'Of course I didn't believe her,' retorted Mulligan. 'What do you take me for? She told me a beautiful pack of lies and that's good enough for me.'

'What about the verisimilitude of the press, Matthew?'

'Fuck you and the verisimilitude of the press,' said Mulligan equably, the glowing tip of his cigar faintly obscene as he waved it expansively up and down. 'I want you to get out there to Howth and get it all down on paper and ready for tonight's edition— better bring a bottle of Irish along—she sounds the thirsty type.'

'You honestly mean you want me to shag all the way out to Howth at this hour of the morning just to interview an elderly alcoholic German noblewoman who has accidentally strayed from the pages of Agatha Christie?'

Mulligan loomed over him. 'You're not fucking Tolstoy yet— move your arse.'

Luke rose wearily from the chair. 'I was hoping something might have been happening down in Fenian Street—more evictions from derelict tenements by brute bailiffs from Dublin Corporation, women with crying infants clasped to their bosoms and fierce young men in caps and Wellingtons standing guard over them with pickaxes—' Luke put a hand on his breast—' "Shades of Colonial Despotism" the banners would scream, "Lackeys of Cromwell's Tyranny Abroad in the Streets of Dublin"—'

'You get hotfoot out to Howth and leave the socialising to

Marx,' Mulligan said. 'And don't have any misconceptions either about your elderly alcoholic German noblewoman.'

'You mean she isn't alcoholic or noble?'

'I mean she isn't elderly—but you've had more than enough of that for one night.'

'For the love of Allah or Jehovah or Cormac MacArt or whatever godless deity you worship, Matthew,' said Luke with a very exaggerated totter, 'wet my parched lips with a drop of whiskey before I set off for the unknown trackless wastes of Howth, to say nothing about confronting once more your guardian angel beyond in the outer sanctum.'

Mulligan stooped, rummaged in a lower drawer of the desk, finally bringing out half a bottle of whiskey. 'You make me flounder on the rock of my good nature,' he said, surlily pouring. 'And I would thank you to refrain from making these disparaging remarks concerning Miss Springett—the whole of my deplorable staff could take a lesson from her efficiency and dedication, not to mention her loyalty.'

Luke surfaced briefly from his drink. 'Ah, but mention must be made of her loyalty, must it not, Matthew?'

Mulligan frowned. 'I want none of your sly insinuations, Sheridan—remember you're only here by the skin of your teeth yourself.'

'I assure you, Matthew, I intended no disrespect towards the lady, quite the contrary, in fact—I was merely extolling one of Miss Springett's—shall we say?—more discernible attributes?' Luke continued in a determinedly conciliatory tone, the whiskey sending ripples of good tidings throughout him.

The willingness to be flattered vied visibly in Mulligan's florid countenance with the urge to maintain professional decorum. 'I hold Miss Springett in the highest esteem,' he declared, airily picking up his glass and ruminatively gazing at it before drinking. 'She has given me loyal uninterrupted service these past—ahem—few years, and I am full of admiration and fatherly solicitude towards her—'

'Fatherly?' echoed Luke, sure now of the receptivity of his audience. 'Surely not "fatherly", Matthew. Surely that is a total misnomer in the circumstances?'

'What circumstances?' Mulligan barked, thrusting out his lower bull-mastiff lip.

Luke's eyes widened ingenuously. 'Why, your age, Matthew, your age—you're much too young to harbour "fatherly" feelings towards anyone.'

'Oh aye, yes, I see, umm,' Mulligan mumbled, pacing up and down on the solitary quasi-Indian rug in front of his desk, seven precise strides to the length, cigar-chewing happily glass in hand. 'Well, yes, I suppose I do push my age a bit far—been in this fucking job so long I'm beginning to grow antlers—' He stopped and craned his head towards Luke with a fatuous schoolboy leer. 'Nota bene, I was almost about to say?'

'Horns,' supplied Luke dutifully when Mulligan paused on cue.

'Exactly. Horns. Yes. And speaking of which,' Mulligan gulped down his whiskey and reached for the bottle. 'In my job you must have a keen sense of observation and, despite my entirely platonic feelings towards the lady, it has not escaped my notice that Miss Springett possesses remarkably attractive legs—well, I mean,' said Mulligan with florid condescension, 'for a woman of her age.'

'Of course,' Luke instantly concurred, measuring the contents of the bottle in Mulligan's hand and estimating how much his parrot-like collusion was worth. 'The lady is indeed well endowed —for, as you so generously point out, a woman of her age.' He coughed, holding his glass a little nearer. 'No doubt those sterling qualities of hers help to provide you with a welcome measure of distraction from the ardours of high office?'

'You said it,' Mulligan nodded taking another large swallow, eyes misting up somewhat, ignoring the empty chalice in Luke's hand. 'Only the other day as she was leaning over my desk—it was hot in here—that bloody central heating—a dead loss, never did take to it—unnatural you know—opens your pores—Oh, you're empty.'

'You were saying she was leaning over your desk,' Luke prompted when his glass had been refilled.

'Who?'

'Miss Springett,' said Luke knowing the game well, knowing it was a matter of brief time for the snail to come wriggling out of its shell.

'Oh her. Yes. Platonic, you understand—my feelings—fucking hell, I'm not a spring chicken—but I'm observant—in my job you have to be—and it was hot and Miss Springett had opened a few buttons on her blouse—and as she was leaning over I couldn't help but see—well, you know—' Mulligan made a vague enveloping gesture in front of his chest. 'Jesus, they were big, you know —big—'

'You mean I suppose the lady's—'

'Tits,' Mulligan said softly, the while slowly licking moist lips. 'Miss Springett's—tits,' he repeated half closing his eyes as he padded up and down voice husky behind the glass. 'Quite by accident—but very plainly—through a chink in her blouse I saw she was wearing a black bra—lacey stuff—and they were bursting out of them—bursting, bejasus, as God is my judge—shaking with milk.' Mulligan made a loud gurgling noise as he drank his whiskey. 'And later the same day—looking up from reading a report by young Barney O'Halloran about that stabbing case out in Ringsend—what should be staring me straight in the face but Miss Springett as she bent over looking for something in the wastepaper-basket.'

'A delightful vista, no doubt?'

'Her arse,' Mulligan said softly lisping on the word, swilling it round on his tongue like choicest brandy, 'Miss Springett's—*arse* was practically in my mouth—tight as a drum—neat and rounded to a tee—a pearl waiting to be prised open—and she couldn't find whatever she was looking for and had to stoop lower—the skirt riding up behind her higher and higher—Oh Jesus, and there I was reading about a stabbing match in Ringsend and me with a horn as big as bejasus.'

The door opened and Miss Springett was in the room, pencil and notebook in hand, prim and brisk as starched linen, the sanctified odour of ink and mothballs billowing about her.

'Do you wish me to remain on for anything else, Mr Mulligan?' she enquired, her voice like the crisp staccato beat of her typewriter, standing to attention, pale and severe as a suffragette.

'For fuck's sake, Miss Springett—'

'*Mr* Mulligan!' gasped Miss Springett, two perfect little roses flooding her cheeks.

'Forgive me, forgive me,' Mulligan gulped, trying ineffectually to wipe the whiskey off his rumpled check shirt and breathing hard like a swimmer struggling against the tide. 'Pardon my language, but you should've knocked.'

'I never do.'

'No, but I was having a serious business discussion with Mr Sheridan here—a matter of newspaper politics—'

'Oh, I *am* sorry, sir,' said Miss Springett inclining her stiff neck a few inches forward in recognition of her impropriety and stepping up as Mulligan continued to brush himself, fishing out a hankie from the sleeve of her jumper. 'Let me do that—'

'No!' Mulligan almost screamed, backing away and barging into the desk behind him.

'But Mr Mulligan, I merely wished to—'

'I know, I know,' Mulligan acknowledged recovering hastily, swallowing hard. 'Most kind of you, most kind, but it's nothing —a little accident—'

'Then there isn't anything further you want me to do?' Miss Springett asked, slipping back into martial gear.

'As a matter of fact, Miss Springett—' Luke said easily moving from the window.

'No, no!' Mulligan interposed quickly, his voice still not quite steady, a furtive sickly found-out smile on his face. 'Nothing at all, Miss Springett. You may go now—see you tomorrow.'

'As you wish, Mr Mulligan,' Miss Springett said tucking notebook under elbow and moving towards door, then turning as if remembering something. 'By the way, Mr Mulligan, that report is waiting for you.'

'Report?' asked Mulligan picking up the bottle and pouring with shaking hand. 'What report, Miss Springett?'

Miss Springett's thin eyebrows arched up in surprise. 'Why, the report on the pregnancy test, Mr Mulligan.'

As Mulligan was about to lift the glass, a considerable seismic convulsion seemed to grip him and once more his shirtfront was liberally anointed with spilled whiskey. 'Jesus Christ, woman, what are you talking about—what pregnancy test—are you gone mad or something?'

'On your bitch, Mr Mulligan.'

'My what?'

'I think the lady said—' began Luke from the side, immensely enjoying himself, marvellously free and lightheaded from such early morning libations.

Mulligan swung around with a goaded bull's bellow. 'You shut your fucking gob, Sheridan—I beg your pardon again, Miss Springett,' he switched to her almost in the same breath, panting, 'but what bitch do you mean? I mean, what do you mean by bitch?'

Miss Springett brought to bear upon the hapless befuddled Mulligan the full arctic force of those piercing iceberg eyes. 'Verona, Mr Mulligan,' she said her voice wire-clipping. 'Your Irish setter—ahem—bitch. You asked me to write the vet since we could not contact him over the telephone.'

Mulligan's wobbling jowls sagged and relaxed visibly as he weakly picked up the bottle again. 'Oh that—thank you, Miss Springett.' Mulligan's voice rose to a high-pitched giggle of relief. 'I should've known you meant Verona all the time.'

'I might point out,' said Miss Springett as rigid as Victoria unamused, 'that the tests proved positive.'

'Just my fu—just my luck,' sighed Mulligan looking at Miss Springett with lowered eyes. 'Miss Springett, is there anything else you want to tell me? You see, I don't want to spill my drink again.'

'Good morning, Mr Mulligan,' she said, hands clasped sedately together, mouth shut clamtight, a thin unyielding line of disapproval shooting a last parting glance at Luke, pointedly saying nothing and marching out, her sensible shoes clicking on the hard polished floor.

'Stupid woman,' said Mulligan when his paragon had safely left. 'Stupid oul' hoor, going on like that about my fucking dog. Wishing it was herself that was up the pole, no doubt, and myself to have put her there.' Mulligan held the bottle up and squinted at its depleted contents, pouring what remained into his glass. 'See the way she came clutching at me? It was all she could do to keep her hands off me.'

'Precisely,' said Luke putting down his drained glass.

'Could see it a mile off,' continued Mulligan blithely beyond irony. 'The sly way her eyes kept dropping to my balls—didn't think I copped her on behind her specs. The poor woman must be famished for a bit. If this keeps up,' ruminated Mulligan leisurely sipping, 'I'm greatly afraid Miss Springett will have to go bag and baggage—no other way for it. A woman of her age, you'd think she'd know better, ogling me like that.' Mulligan paused, holding the glass delicately between his hands, an improbable beef-red bloated mandarin. 'But you know, when they get to that age and with life slipping past them—well, they get desperate—getting themselves up on all sorts of things—door-handles and things like that—so I'm told,' Mulligan added quickly obviously straining to reveal the source of his information at the slightest insistence. 'Of course you can't believe all you hear, but in Miss Springett's case—well, you can see it in her eyes, can't you? That mad fixed stare, the twitching hands, the slight frothing at the corners of the mouth—poor woman,' Mulligan sighed, 'she's more to be pitied than envied.'

'Amen and aren't we all?'

Mulligan glared. 'You should be in Howth by now instead of standing there like Moses drawing the Labour—'

'I'm gone.'

'Where were you last night, anyway?' asked Mulligan drawing him instantly back unable to subjugate the vile twitchings of his curiosity to the higher demands of commerce. 'You look like a biro sucked dry.'

'If I'm ever to get out to interview this Transylvanian countess I'd best be on my way,' Luke said, no longer prepared to pander now that the well of inspiration had dried up. He stopped on his way to the door. 'My wallet received rather a nasty accident last night—'

Mulligan smirked and belched at once. 'Expenses, expenses. Put it all on expenses. Except screwing. That is strictly a private indulgence paid for with strictly private funds—but maybe Madame Fustenhalter will pay you. She likes them young and foolhardy, so I'm told.'

'My commiserations, Matthew.'

'Fuck off, you bastard.'

With that morning salutation ringing in his ear Luke sauntered out past the bent intent sleek-brushed head of Miss Springett putting the hood over her silent typewriter, gathering her few toiletries into her very utilitarian handbag, not looking up as he paused—

'Can I see you to the bus-stop or something, Miss Springett?'

Her pinched face somewhat flushed was averted as she rummaged with her things. 'Thank you, Mr Sheridan, that won't be necessary.'

'No doubt, but I asked not because I thought it was necessary, but simply because the pleasure of accompanying you even a few steps homeward exhilarates me beyond words.'

'You are most kind, Mr Sheridan—thank you—but no.'

Luke sighed. 'Then adieu, fair maid, parting is such sweet sorrow—'

'Good day to you, Mr Sheridan.' Clasping the handbag decisively shut Miss Springett retreated into the cloakroom adjoining, his last meditative glimpse of her the peculiarly youthful vulnerable turn of her ankles in the deadly sensible blockheeled shoes as she walked away, a frigid bloom encased in airless plasticity ravaged ten times daily by the ghoulish eyes of Mulligan splitting her apart, grunting and groaning his way into her as she sat prim and remote on the far side of the desk across the great all-merciful divide, taking dictation with mute precision unheedful of the hand lying far from quiescent in Mulligan's stout lap beneath the concealing shelf of the desk, a frosted Lucrece he had already heartily devoured between bland successive paragraphs, bearing in his lurid mind's ear her lamblike bleatings above the dry scrape of her nib.

Out again on the hard resounding pavements, the morning now quite ordinary, blurred and raucous with traffic, yesterday's news swept along swollen gutters blowing round his shins in tattered ribbons, dust gritting his redrimmed unwilling eyes. Luke felt a dull gnaw of hunger in his guts, stung at every second step by luscious wafts of food from the inviting doors of cafés and kerbside delicatessens torturing his brain with images of impossible largessè heaped high on steaming plates, gastronomic fantasies rioting in his mind, his belly fast held in by the band of his skimpy jeans grumbling in revolt, but onward he went, head bent against a mean scurrilous little midmorning wind nipping his nose and the lobes of his ears, hands thrust in jacket pockets knotted in spartan valour, struggling onwards to the oasis of the taxicab rank strung down the spine of O'Connell Street praying to high or low heaven that number IOU 1066 would be there, singing as he crossed the hazardous strip:

> 'I know where I'm going
> and I know who's going with me
> I know who I love
> but the —— knows who I'll marry.'

Receiving a surly bilious glare from Paddy Mulcahy blue and

bitten in his serge uniform freeing and stopping traffic with a contemptuous wave of his whitegloved hand.

'What are you so fucking cheerful about so early in the day?' snarled that bold gendarme out of the crooked corner of his broad stirabout mouth as Luke slid past him.

'You wouldn't have an odd pound on you, Paddy, would you, by some divine act of the holy ghost?' Luke fired back in faint-hearted hope, briefly pausing at the side of the law.

Mulcahy's lips curled slightly over irregular nicotined molars, arms windmilling rigidly. 'You literary fuckers are all the same,' spoke Mulcahy eyes sternly on duty staring into traffic-loud distances. 'A right shower of bums, always on the love-and-honour, cadging at every fiddle's fart—why don't you fucking well work for a living?' Mulcahy held up an imperious hand arresting a snakelike stream of cars ahead. 'Will you be beyond in Mooneys at lunchtime?'

'I will with all my heart,' agreed Luke hunching his scrawny shoulders together against the wind whiplashing down the broad acres of the populous thoroughfare, 'if you provide the lunch.'

'I got a tip for the Curragh today,' Mulcahy side-mouthed, waving on an opposite flow of vehicles. 'Take it or leave it.'

'I take it with a heart and a half, only—'

'Jesus divine saviour,' Mulcahy snapped, 'is it asking me you are for something to put on the bleeding nag? Talking about looking a gift horse in the mouth—' Horns were honking querulously as Mulcahy was momentarily distracted by indignation. 'Get to the other side of the street with you before I pull you in, you cow's melt, and the feet falling off me with the weather—'

'And a happy new year to you too, Patrick, you great Tipperary shit,' Luke pleasantly rejoined, yanking fiercely at his forelock as he skipped across the street between bonnets and bumpers, winking in friendliness at the blank faces wizened up behind steering wheels and resenting his brash pedestrian freedom.

Eagle-eye open for business he spied out IOU 1066 snuggling pug-nosed behind the mobile X-ray van in the taxi isle as if the car like its driver was trying to remain anonymous and unmolested by the slings and arrows of outrageous friendships, and glimpsed at once reclining against the leather top of the driving seat the cloth-capped skull of his quarry snoozing, hands folded beneath the sports pages of the *Times* spread out on the thin topcoated belly and at last the side of the check cap moved a reluctant few inches to reveal a small blue inflamed eye as Luke opened the door and slid in beside him on the seat.

'The dead arose,' muttered the driver immediately closing his eye again and pulling the peak of the cap further down, touching his squat pudgy nose. 'Kindly fuck off.'

'The frosty top of the morning to you, Ranter,' greeted Luke, pulling the door shut and burrowing into the back seat. 'How are you fixed for a fiver till Friday?'

'I repeat—'

'Don't. It offends against all the singular virtues of my genteel superior upbringing. Are you fixed badly?'

'Would I be sitting here freezing to death if I wasn't?' Ranter replied twisting his shoulder away in annoyance, the sports pages slipping to the floor. 'I thought you were on expenses?'

'I am, I am,' said Luke picking up the paper and scrutinising the racing page, 'but I got a living certainty today for the Curragh and a fiver is the lowest I could in all conscience put on it, otherwise the animal would refuse to start being a most noble high-spirited specimen with an aristocratic sense of pride.'

'Did Paddy Mulcahy give you this tip?'

'He did, like the good public servant he is.'

'Forget it,' advised Ranter turning away and curling his feet up underneath him. 'Don't you know that bastard takes sadistic delight in seeing you throw away your bread on the fucking hobbyhorses he gives out as tips? How much was it we lost last time—a whole bleeding monkey!'

'Admitted, his advice is not always infallible, but his brother-in-law is a trainer in Meath—'

'He must train fucking rabbits, if that's the case,' Ranter retorted, drawing the end of his long heavy topcoat tighter round his legs. 'Never trust a rozzer. They'd nick their own mother for taking a penny extra in her change and not reporting it to the proper authorities. Steer clear of your man Mulcahy and his like —renegades from justice that's what they are.'

'I refuse to believe that our resources are so meagre that we are incapable of raising a fiver between us if we pooled said resources together,' said Luke, damming the rising flood of bleak prospects welling up within him. 'Have you no money at all on you?'

'Of course I have money on me,' Ranter answered indignant, vainly trying to pull the cap down over his ears. 'I work for a living, don't I? I have exactly three pounds fifty p lining me pocket at this exact perpendicular point in time. I also have a wife and five kids and a mortgage on me house and besides which I also happen to be up to me balls in bills of one variety or another, but of course them little incidentals mean nothing to a genius like yourself walking around Dublin with your head swimming in the clouds of Mount Parnassus the whole bleeding time—shag off and let me rest!' Ranter finished, the little pig-like blue eyes more inflamed than ever.

'You also possess that most invaluable of all modern conveniences,' said Luke easily, 'a cheque-book. Now don't tell me,' he went on holding his hand up as Ranter opened his mouth ominously, 'I know it's slightly in the red—'

'Slightly! It's fucking scarlet.'

'But that will be put right by the end of the week upon my Father's revered bones.' Luke ferreted out a ballpoint. 'Here you are, good neighbour, make it out for twenty.'

Ranter shook himself up into a sitting position, cap going askew on the side of his rapidly balding head. 'Are you off your fucking rocker? You owe me fifteen already from last week.'

Luke struck his forehead with his clenched fist. 'So I do. An unforgivable lapse of memory on my part. Make that out for forty so and we'll be all square.' Luke held out the biro politely.

'Are you getting up on me back, bejasus?' Ranter demanded, looking at the proffered pen as if it were a missile. 'Do you want me to end up flat on me back in the gutter with not a penny to me name? When I give you the shirt off my back to wipe your arse with, will you be satisfied then?'

'Look,' said Luke as to a chronically retarded pupil, 'it is all perfectly logical. I owe you fifteen quid already—right? I now wish to borrow a further twenty off you, making in all thirty-five —correct? Therefore by giving me a cheque for forty you make sure I repay you your thirty-five plus a fiver to spare for us to drink the health of brothers together beyond in Mooneys—get it?'

Ranter shook his head, slightly appalled by such dense logic, taking the pen as if mesmerised. 'Gertie will have me certified,' he said, his hand moving to the glove compartment and extracting a cheque book, hardly taking away his fixed incredulous stare from Luke as he made the cheque out with the ease born of jaded familiarity. 'I swear to Jasus she'll have me certified before the day is out.' He tore the slip from its perforated dotted line and handed it over.

'First satisfactory business transaction of the morning,' said Luke pocketing the captured prize. 'What time do you make it? I must remind someone to buy me a watch on my birthday.'

Ranter pulled up the sleeve of his coat and looked at the large moonfaced watch on his wrist, each numeral decorated with a strategic part of the female anatomy over which the hands passed caressingly. 'Just eleven.' He put his hand to his mouth yawning. 'Jasus, I'm knackered. Been out half the night—so have you be the state of you,' he added taking in Luke's appearance and insomniac eyes. 'It wasn't in the line of duty either?'

'In a manner of speaking,' Luke answered feeling the renewal of hunger pains in his belly. 'Let's saunter over to the warmth and welcome of Mooneys—I must get a bowl of soup inside me before my entire system seizes up—and after that and a few medicinal libations we'll head for Howth.'

'Howth?' Ranter repeated. 'Are you going fishing be any chance?' He shook himself a few times, straightening the peak of his cap, and switched on the engine.

'Again in a manner of speaking, yes,' said Luke, feeling his eyes burning as he closed them and opened them again blinking. 'I hope to land a certain peculiar kettle of fish. We must be out there by half past one or two at the latest, otherwise my last duchess might have lost herself beyond recall in the land of Nod, pickled beyond redemption.'

'You wouldn't be hinting that you want me to drive you out there, I suppose?' enquired Ranter as he pulled out from the rank into the traffic lane. 'If so, start walking—I've a living to make while you're expending your energies chasing after married women in the middle of the day—'

'The marital status of the lady in question bears no relation to the context in which I wish to see her, and anyway let me put you at rest and say that I am engaging you to convey my weary bones out there.'

'It'll cost you a fiver easily,' warned Ranter swinging past the Parnell monument, 'to say nothing of me waiting time.'

'This is strictly duty and therefore on expenses.'

'But you use all your expenses on yourself,' said Ranter parking expertly outside Mooneys between a bread van and a coal cart with a venerable horse steaming between the shafts. 'On gargling and hooring.'

'Let's not be petty, my friend. We stand in a hallowed spot,' Luke informed him as they stood awhile on the pavement. 'Over yonder,' he went on, raising a prophetic finger and pointing across to the domed and cupolaed building facing, 'is where I first assumed this mortal coil, where I first breathed life outside my Mother's womb—'

'The Roto you mean?' asked Ranter stepping aside to let a heavily pregnant young girl pass with a pram overburdened already with two identical children.

'Ah, the Roto, as you fondly remark, the natal Parthenon of Dublin,' continued Luke gazing with moist windswept eyes, see-ing the fleet of ambulances lined up in the quadrangle outside, those unique delivery vans forever traversing the veins of the city in a shuttle service of new mortality. ''Twas there I was born on a bright harvest morn and 'tis there they will erect a plaque to my immortal memory when the Glasnevin worms grow rich and opulent on my bones, mark my words—'

'I was born in Castletown House meself,' Ranter replied resenting the bite of the wind as it came sweeping at them with the tang of fresh fruit and vegetables on it. 'I'm bursting for a piss—will you c'mon in out of that and stop standing there like a transfixed eejit—people are looking at you waving your hands and jabbering out of you.'

'Ah, but it holds you, you know, it draws you,' said Luke, turning and following Ranter through the diamonded portals of Mooneys. 'Like a giant umbilical cord attaching you to its cavernous womb. The most popular holiday resort in town.'

'Gertie seems to like it anyway,' Ranter said almost visibly lapping up the cushiony warmth and snugness of the lounge. 'She had her last four in there. I'll have a large one,' he said as he headed for the gents, shoulders hunched forward in his customary slouch-like shuffle, head pressed down upon his neck.

All was gloom and vague outlines in the lounge, reverential as a chapel nave with a faint confluence of light from the curved circular portholes in the ceiling, the thin solitary tinkle of the till from the public bar behind the partition, desultory voices raised in hesitant pre-noon conversation, the dull leaden sheen of the brass footrail of the bar worn smooth, necks of bottles glinting on the tiered shelves, the traffic outside a lethargic drone, the good comradely smell of old leather and pipesmoke hanging soft in the air, a white smock coming towards him from the far end of the counter—

'What will it be, Luke?' asked Gerry the foreman, his fingers drumming a tattoo, towel thrown lightly over his shoulder, regarding Luke with sleepy heavy-lidded eyes.

'Two large Powers, Gerry. No water.'

'Oh, divil a bit of water.'

'And two bowls of hot mouth-watering soup.'

'With lashings of pepper and mustard.'

'As you say, Jeremiah. And while you're at it—'

'You want me to cash a cheque.'

'Clairvoyant.'

'For how much?' asked Gerry placing the glasses of whiskey on the counter.

'An absurdly insignificant amount.'

'How much?' Gerry asked again, face and voice impassive.

'Forty.'

'You getting married or something?'

'I'm attending the coronation of my Uncle Gerontius in Rome as the new Papal Legate in the township of Dunquin. How long will you be with the soup?'

'This won't bounce, will it?' Gerry said taking the cheque from Luke and scrutinising it methodically back and front.

'Who are you calling a forger, you dirty great big heap of Cork manure?' Ranter said returning and zipping up his fly. 'Is it a belt in the kisser you're looking for? When has a cheque of mine ever bounced anywhere in this metropolis?'

'Peace, O'Rourke, peace,' rejoined Gerry, accepting the cheque resignedly and moving to the till. 'No need to have a coronary on the carpet. Merely making customary formal enquiries, all in the line of business, you understand.'

'Ah go and get a Mass said for yourself,' Ranter said picking up his glass. 'All Corkmen are plagued with suspicious natures—'

'Especially when it comes to Dublinmen. There's a tenner,' said Gerry coming back and placing the note between them. 'All that's in the till at the moment. You'll have to wait for the rest.'

'We're not going anywhere foreign for an hour or two,' Luke said putting the money into his top pocket. 'And post haste with that soup, will you. I'm famished.'

'Will do.'

'Who's this quare one you're seeing out in Howth anyway?' Ranter wanted to know when they were comfortably seated in an alcove next to one of the radiators. 'Another one of your little mysteries in silk and lace? I swear to Jesus,' cautioned Ranter lifting the glass to his lips, 'one of these days if you're not careful—'

'A lady of noble birth and degree,' said Luke forestalling any rush of brotherly sagacity, 'whom I have never clapped eyes on.'

'That won't stop you.'

'Her Irish sister-in-law tried to murder her brother, the count, and ended up on the danger-list herself. Not exactly a very credible impersonation of Mata Hari, from all reports.'

Ranter stared. 'For a bloke who fancies himself as a bit of a writer you have a terrible tortuous way of explaining things. Among all them counts and countesses and in-laws who tried to do in who?'

'Have you heard of Kathy Furlong?'

Ranter's eyes widened. 'Oh her. Booterstown Belinda we used to call her. More blokes passed through her than what would go through Westland Row station on All-Ireland day. Still,' Ranter mused, cosily sipping his drink, 'she did all right for herself, marrying that foreign duke or something—Oh, I see,' Ranter echoed slapping his knee, 'now I'm on to you. You're saying Kathy tried to practise culpable homicide on the poor bastard?' He nodded in fond reminiscence. 'She always was a high-spirited little bitch, right enough. And what happened?'

'Events are rather clouded at present,' said Luke, 'but the upshot of the captivating little operetta is that poor Kathy is in hospital hopefully recovering from severe poisoning self-administered purely by accident and the count's sister spent half the night over the telephone regaling Matt Mulligan with the story, hence the expedition to Howth—Ah, Gerry, you cometh at the eleventh hour.'

Luke's stomach exulted exceedingly as the soup was at last before them strong and aromatic and chunky with chicken laced throughout with black pepper and gut-warming mustard, soaked sweetly into his tongue. He called for another deep bowl when he had cleaned the first, slowly assuaging his hunger, dipping crisp slices of fresh breadroll into the steaming soup hot and savoury assailing his palate unheedful of his friend across the table.

'Bejasus,' said Ranter as Luke finally pushed away the empty bowl, 'you gobbled that up like you were going to drop dead the next minute and not wanting to go to hell on an empty belly. You know,' Ranter added, 'why don't you get a woman to look after you proper—a good woman I mean, not one of your one-nighters, settle down you know before you die of malnutrition.'

'Wedlock?'

'Why not?' Ranter said defensively. 'It's no bed of roses but it's better than a kick in the balls. Where's that tenner?' he asked as Gerry came up with the drinks. 'It'll get green mouldy lying there in your skyrocket. When all's said and done,' Ranter continued, sitting down again after Luke had paid and Gerry had retired behind the bar, 'there's worse things in heaven and earth than man and wife. I mean, it's unnatural for a fella to live completely on his tod—isn't it now?' Ranter stated half defiantly and half for want of reassurance. 'Be honest now and tell me I'm right.'

'Some of the greatest minds and purest intellects in mankind's history were honed and developed in solitude,' said Luke sententiously philosophising on a bellyful of chicken soup. 'Plato, Homer, Michelangelo, all the great mystics too—Buddha, Mohammed, Jesus Christ—'

'And oul' Jemmy Carney from the Coombe,' Ranter intervened, impatiently waving his hand. 'I know all that, do you think I'm ignorant or something? But for Jasus' sake I'm not talking about great effing minds or intellects or things like that, I'm talking about ordinary everyday chiners like me and you—' Ranter held a hand up to forestall any counter-argument. 'Now I know what you're going to say, sure we all say the same from time to time, but where would we be without the women—hah? Tell me that!' Ranter nodded his head vigorously several times, the cap slanting again to one side at an incongruously rakish angle. 'We might give out about them—oh, give out the pay about them, moan and groan and curse the day we ever let them softsoap us into marrying them, the scheming bloody bitches—oh aye, that's all very well,

76

McGuggin, all very effing well, but where would we be without them—hah? That's a point to ponder well on, I'm telling you—'

'Ranter, your inspired advocacy of the wedded state leaves me breathless,' said Luke as his friend sat back in his seat contemplating him with a defiant stare. 'It would encourage a man of nobler instincts than myself to rush out this minute and ask the first unpregnant girl to marry him.'

'Oh, you can laugh all you like,' said Ranter immovably, 'you can laugh and joke about it to your heart's content, oul' son, but it all comes back to the one thing—where are we without women? Look at yourself, for Jasus' sake,' Ranter said by way of emphasis. 'The wind is whistling between your shoulders for the want of a good tightener, you wouldn't see your shadow if you turned sideways—and why? I'll tell you why,' Ranter bent forward across the table, little eyes bright and intent. 'You need a woman —Oh hold on now,' he said without pause, again silencing the wordless Luke, 'I don't mean what you're thinking—that's the trouble with yous hotblooded young rams—all you think about is the horn, the horn, parting the whiskers at every hand's turn, thinking it's going to be like that all your life through, up and down, in and out,' said Ranter in some agitation unconsciously adopting a rocking seesaw motion on the seat. 'But it's not, you know—oh bejasus no. It's not *that* you'll be thinking of with the belly falling out of you with the hunger and your teeth chattering with the cold with no one beside you in bed in the depths of winter—it's not the opening between a woman's legs that will occupy your mind, but how well she can make a pot of stew or a coddle and wash and iron the sheets and make the bed—that's when you start asking *real* questions, chiner, questions that have to do with *real* things like stew and coddle and making beds and to hell with the passing horn!' Ranter finished on a high note of conviction, his cap almost slipping off in his excitement, leaning back against the seat upright and stern, regarding Luke with the eye of a strict but fair-minded executioner.

'You never spoke a truer word, Mr O'Rourke.' A woman's voice from the other side of the leather shoulder-high partition. 'If only the men of today had your far-reaching outlook!'

Cool slight feminine hands groping for him in the narrow darkness, hair like shadow in his mouth came back and a bleached mountain of a man prostrate on the bed singing in a cracked falsetto voice of roses and snow and captured nightingales and the same madonna hands beating upon that broad gentle chest in little-girl fury.

'There's yourself,' said Babysoft emerging from obscurity, holding the hand of her companion, a thin sepulchral elongated totem-pole, spikey tufts of hair standing erect, eyes dead and gutted in his waxed face. 'May we join you or is it too early in the day?'

'Be our guests,' invited Luke half rising. 'Both of you.' He raised a finger towards their glasses. 'Something similar?'

'Brandy and soda,' answered Babysoft coming round and sliding in beside Luke, letting go the limp hand of her companion who sat woodenly down on a stool a little distance away. 'Haven't seen you in months. Did you get home last time all right after?' she asked Luke, turning a smiling face to him nudging him slyly in the ribs.

'After?' parried Luke politely catching the foreman's ever-ready eye. 'Oh—after. A hazardous trek, but I made it in one piece, thank you very much.'

'Are we going to be on our best behaviour today, Miss Brogan?' Gerry said with heavyhanded sarcasm as he came up to the table.

'What do you mean to insinuate, you bleeding turfcutter?' Babysoft retorted, giving him the full frontal assault of her vixen-eyed wrath, deliberately crossing her legs and letting her abbreviated skirt ride even higher. 'It's not one of your country heifers you're addressing now.'

'Just a joke, sure,' Gerry hastily amended, eyes trapped by the silky sheen of allure as he took in the soft dimpled knee and plump upper leg so casually revealed. 'Sure isn't yourself and Miss Hand among our best customers—I—I mean—customers in the proper sense—'

'Now lookit, Hector, don't get smart,' Babysoft warned. 'Fill that glass and keep your tongue on a leash. Them bleeding culshies would walk on you if you let them,' she said when the foreman had gone away with their order. 'He'll find himself back building stone walls in Connemara if he's not careful.'

'He's from Cork,' Ranter informed her. 'I'm very meticulous about the geography of things.'

'Cork or Donegal,' Babysoft said lifting her shoulders, 'a

culshie is a culshie just as a Jew is a Jew whatever side of the Jordan he comes from.'

'I enjoyed your playing that night,' Luke said, addressing himself to the thin man sitting solitary on the edge of their little group. 'I thought Chopin was a surprising choice under the circumstances, and your rendition was excellent.'

The man stared ahead as if he had not heard, long-fingered hands clasping each knee, a study in absolute immobility save for a muscle twitching in his jaw, his nondescript suit hanging limp on his long emaciated frame, a faint indescribable odour as of damp embers seeming to emanate from him.

'Freddie is it?' remarked Babysoft looking at the man with fond daughterly eyes reaching over and giving his hand a friendly tap. 'Ah, don't mind Freddie, for God's sake. He never hears a word you say to him. Not that he's deaf—he just doesn't bother to listen. Just give him an oul' piano and he's happy tinkling out little tunes on it. I take him out every day at this time for a little bit of fresh air. Cheers everyone,' she said when their drinks had duly arrived. She picked up Freddie's glass and put it between his fingers patient as with a child. 'Drink your drink, Freddie, it will do you good. That's the ticket,' she said satisfied as the man obediently sipped. 'Sure he's as good as gold, poor Freddie, no bother at all.'

'You—er—know your friend well?' Luke ventured.

Babysoft looked nonplussed for a moment. 'Know him? Course I know him—sure everyone knows Freddie.'

'The Rachmaninoff of Rathmines,' Ranter put in easily, hardly giving the strange newcomer a second glance. 'The life and soul of every occasion in the social calendar. I wonder did he ever finish that symphony bit of his?'

'You mean he writes music—a composer?' Luke asked, feeling distinctly odd speaking about someone who was actually present and within earshot in such a disembodied manner.

'Certainly he composes,' Babysoft affirmed, 'sure it's common knowledge. He once played in the Gaiety in a symphony concert before the President of Ireland. He played something he wrote himself—'

' "Lament for the White Swans of Coole" for piano and flute,' said Freddie suddenly looking fixedly at the oak panelling directly in front of him, his voice issuing clear and strangely warm.

'Exactly,' Babysoft nodded, 'just what I was about to say meself. He's quite intelligent really—aren't you, Freddie?' she said patting his jutting angular knee. 'We'd be lost without poor Freddie sure. Lala dotes on him something terrible.'

'I gather he—er—resides permanently in the hotel?' Luke said in what amounted to a whispered aside to Babysoft.

She again looked at Luke as though he were badly in need of some redeeming wits. 'Where else would you expect him to stay,' she challenged, 'and him her husband?'

'Her—husband?' Luke echoed, taking a quick swallow of his drink. 'I had no idea they were even related and I prided myself on being perspicacious.'

'You pride yourself on being what?' This from Babysoft.

'A bleeding know-all,' supplied Ranter.

'Sure you don't think Lala would have him there otherwise, do you?' Babysoft said, a little scandalised.

'Certainly not,' Luke replied at once.

'He was begging her for years to marry him, but it was only when he had the accident that she gave in.'

'Ah,' said Luke looking more closely at the man's curiously disjointed hands, 'you mean—'

'His hands were crushed when a barrel of wine toppled over on him as he was helping Lala below in the cellar one day. Lala has always said it was poetic justice or something like that.' She sighed. 'Terrible romantic. You could see they were made for each other.'

'As I see it,' Ranter opined cap keeling back on his head, 'there was neither a man lost nor a woman thrown away.'

'Ah now, that's a matter of opinion, Mr O'Rourke, surely?' Babysoft said stoutly. 'Granted, he's no Cary Grant and poor Lala, God love her, would never be mistaken for Sophia Loren, not even if she wore dark glasses. But sure beauty is only skin-deep—'

'Then it's a wonder some people don't get skinned,' Ranter said, 'it might make a considerable difference to their appearance.'

'Charity, Mr Rourke,' Babysoft reproved gently, 'a little charity never did anyone any harm. But listen here,' she said spinning off on a tangent, turning to Luke reproach and envy fighting for supremacy in her eyes, 'talking about appearance—what did you do to poor Rosie that night?'

Off-guard against such quixotic challenge Luke blinked. 'Rosie —is she all right?'

Babysoft pealed a thin brittle grudging laugh. 'All right! She got up that morning looking like Cinderella after coming back from the ball. She gave me an effing headache with her humming and whistling and talking nineteen to the dozen. Like a little girl in her first communion dress, she was, skipping about like a bird —most mornings she hasn't a word to throw to a dog and a face as long as a late breakfast—but that morning she even made the tea.'

'He waved his magic wand,' Ranter said flatly, eyeing the now empty glass in Babysoft's hand with a comical mixture of admiration and disapproval. 'He's a great man with wands.'

'Ah now, keep the party clean, Ranter,' she giggled, the slightly refrigerated pasty look slowly melting from her face as the brandy took effect. 'I only call him by his first name after the third glass,' she explained to Luke linking her arm through his, smiling up at him confidently, her teeth a faint white gleam in the heavy leathery gloom of the lounge.

'An expensive bloody privilege,' Ranter grumbled puffing to his feet. 'Same all round, I suppose?'

'No more for Freddie,' Babysoft put in, 'he's had his quota for today. He goes mad on the piano when he gets a few over the mark.'

Freddie stirred and lifted his hands slowly, looking at them with eyes that were wide baleful accusing. 'He cried, they told me,' Freddie muttered thin lips working strangely. 'The President of Ireland cried when I played the "Swans of Coole" that night.'

'Ah, so he would,' Babysoft said placatingly, 'he didn't mean any harm, pet.'

'He cried,' Freddie went on, eyes black and fanatical staring at his gnarled distorted hands. 'There were tears in his eyes when he came around backstage to see me afterwards. "My dear sir," the President said to me not letting go of my hand, "my dear, dear sir, I am proud to shake the hand of Ireland's Paderewski".' Freddie's voice deepened and trembled slightly. 'And there were tears in his eyes.'

'Sure Mr O'Kelly was always the gentleman,' Babysoft commented with the air of one who rubbed shoulders and knocked shins with the high and the chosen on a lifelong footing. 'There may not have been much of him in it, but a gentleman to the last inch, though I didn't know he had a musical ear—'

'And he wasn't being kind,' Freddie continued his clear and intensely personal monologue, 'he wasn't. He knew. I wasn't quite Paderewski then, I wasn't quite Rachmaninoff, but I was on my way, oh yes I was about to arrive.' Freddie glared at his stiff hands with unimaginable hatred. 'Then a ton of crushed grapes put paid to all the applause and the accolades—doing a labour of love—seeing the barrel slipping—rolling—Get out of the way, Lala!' Freddie suddenly shouted, flinging out both hands wildly, fingers stark and forked in the air, his elbow striking his glass, knocking it flying.

'What's going on over here at this hour of day?' Gerry growled arriving with a fresh round of drinks, looking uneasily at Freddie and moving obliquely around him. 'Is he having a fit or what?'

Babysoft fired a killing look at the foreman as she leaned forward taking both of Freddie's hands in her own. 'Would you blame anyone taking a turn for the worse looking at your face? There now, pet,' she cooed, kissing and fondling Freddie's hands gently as though stroking a maimed captive bird. 'It's all okey-doke, sure you're the bravest of the brave, God love you, com-pared to the likes that go around masquerading as men today—' she shot another venomous glance at the unfortunate Gerry—'go-by-the-wall-and-tickle-the-bricks, holy communion every morn-ing, eating the statues and stripping the young girls naked with their eyes, the dirty oul' vomits—'

'Arrah, now, Miss Brogan,' said Gerry with a slack-jawed smile, eyes unable to steer clear of her black-sheathed knees, ''tis a fierce tongue you have in your head, oh fierce altogether, and a poor man like meself only doing his duty.'

'Whereas you'd give your eye tooth to be doing something else, wouldn't you, Boris?' snapped Babysoft. 'You'll go gunner-eyed if you keep looking at me legs like that.'

'God, you're a caution, to be sure,' Gerry said brushing the table top ineffectually with his towel, 'a real caution.'

'Ah caution me arse, you oul' ravisher of holy pictures, upset-ting poor Freddie like that, a poor inoffensive soul.'

Gerry stepped back astounded, palms spread out. 'Me, is it? Sure I never opened me mouth to the creature.'

'Beethoven never heard a single note he composed,' announced Freddie with inexpressible sadness, calm again, sublimely remote and outside of the little ripple of disharmony.

'Or maybe it was he never composed a single note he heard,' Ranter said returning. 'Anyway he wasn't missing much. I'm a Tom Moore man meself.' Ranter settled back on the seat and started in a good clear tenor voice:

> 'O believe me if all those endearing young charms
> which I gaze on so fondly today
> were to fly by tomorrow and fleet in my arms
> like fairysong fading away.'

'Infidel!' rasped Freddie smiting the table with his knuckles, his eyes no longer vacant. 'Barbarian! Philistine! You dare couple the Holy Ghost with the cloven spawn of Judas, the sacred sweat of angels with dog's sperm!'

'Oh Jasus, you have him going again,' Babysoft complained, tugging at Freddie's sleeve as he half rose from his stool, 'and me enjoying meself with a full glass before me. Freddie!' she called out sharply, 'if you're not easy I'll take you back at once and tell Lala you were obstreptious.'

Freddie subsided meekly. 'I merely wish to engage this gentleman in a discussion on basic musical principles of relative aesthetic values strictly within the context of tonal singularities.'

Ranter blinked. 'Bejasus, that sounds bad. No need to get narky, oul' son,' he said, winking amicably across at Freddie and lifting his glass. 'Sure I wasn't trying to belittle poor oul' Beethoven by any manner of means, a decent enough oul' skin for all I hear even for a Prussian—I get a lump in me throat every time I hear Claire de Lune on the wireless.'

'Debussy,' Luke whispered loudly.

'Eh? Oh aye—your man Alfred Debussy to be sure,' agreed Ranter. 'Sure I always get Clair de Lune mixed up with the Moonlight Sonater—very similar tonal qualities you might say, though I'm not too well up on the oul' keys—'

'Well now,' Babysoft broke in, nudging her knee against Luke's under the table, beginning to count on her fingers. 'There's Ussher's Quay for one, where me married sister has a room—a filthy effing place—and of course Burgh Quay where all them dirty-minded newspaper blokes hang out fiddling with more than their pencils—and not forgetting Sir John Rogerson's Quay where the girls do meet the foreign fellas coming off the big ships. Oh, there's more quays in Dublin I'm telling you than what you'd find on any piano.'

'Jasus preserve me from female Charlie Chaplins,' Ranter remarked sourly. 'You will cut yourself if you're not careful, you're that effing sharp.'

Babysoft laughed, throwing her head back. 'There's that gleam in your eye, Ranter, and us not a stone's throw away from the Roto!' She turned to Luke fumbling for his hand, her pert hoydenish face with shining brown eyes slanting coyly. 'You're a real Silent Night all of a sudden—you're not pining for Rosie, are you. Ah don't. Sure amn't I here to divert you?'

Her voice teasing, dark helmet of hair clinging to her skull, an improbable Maid of Orleans rattling her silken armoury of allure in a city lounge, her fingers finding his own, guiding them up the path to her thigh under the tight skirt spreading her knees, her other hand adventuring fingertips hard probing and prodding, her smile angled up at him triumphant, finding him primed under the rough cloth, the table all concealing arching over them like a covenant shrouding these furtive gropings, the faint metallic rasp of nylon as her thighs contracted his hand captive between and it was last time again.

'Are you forgetting about Eva Braun?'

Ranter rancorous, nursing the last golden drops in his glass, eyeing the two of them scornfully.

'Who—what?' asked Luke as if waking from a swoon.

'Your bit of German mustard—this Brunhilde beyant in Howth.' Ranter raised his wrist. 'According to my pornographic watch here, it's almost one.'

'As always, Iago, you pull me back from the edge of doom,' said Luke abruptly withdrawing his hand and finishing off his drink. 'Leave the lady a parting glass on the way out.'

'Howth, did you say?' Babysoft enquired, quite ordinary and composed again. 'Sure I might as well go that far with you.'

'We're not going on a bleeding excursion,' Ranter told her as they all stood up except Freddie who sat carved in stillness on the stool. 'It's business.'

'I haven't been out there in years,' Babysoft sighed, 'not since

I was in me teens. I used to cycle every step of the way out there on me Norman Invader—'

'Your what?' asked Luke having visions of her being borne aloft through the city on some exotic craft fashioned from the hands of Nordic deities ringed in dark bloodred nebulae.

'Me bike that me Ma got me for me sixteenth birthday with a loan off the Jewman,' Babysoft explained. 'They used to say I'd get muscles on me legs like a fella from all that cycling, but I loved going to Howth—all them gorgeous rhododendrons—or whatever you call them.'

'Now lookit here, Snow White—' Ranter tried to intervene.

'I wouldn't take up any room at all in the back seat of your Rolls-Royce, and we can drop Freddie home on the way.'

Ranter straightened his cap determinedly. 'I told you, it's strictly business.'

'That's right, love,' Babysoft agreed sliding her hands down over her hips smoothing out her skirt. 'I wouldn't have it any other way.'

'I have a reputation to keep and a living to make.'

'Haven't we all?' Babysoft turned to Luke placing her hand on his sleeve. 'You wouldn't begrudge a girl a ride, would you, Lukey love?'

Luke enjoying himself grinned widely. 'Welcome to my chariot, Mam'selle. You shall drown in rhododendrons.'

Ranter sighed defeated. 'Remember, chiner, you're paying, and certain passengers cost more.'

'Ranter, I love you,' cooed Babysoft.

'Get stuffed,' growled Ranter recoiling from her proffered cupid's mouth and going out in stoop-shouldered dudgeon, muttering imprecations under his breath.

Babysoft flung her arms round Luke's neck. 'You're massive, Lukey,' she said clinging onto him and kicking her heels in the air. 'Take me now, in case I'm not in the mood later.' She looked thoughtful. 'I don't think I've ever been took in the backseat of a motor car before.'

'What about your Norman Invader?' Luke grinned into her face.

'Oh, dozens of times,' Babysoft said solemnly. 'The handlebars got buckled more times.'

'I can let you have another tenner now, Luke,' said Gerry

coming out from behind the counter shuffling some notes in his hands. 'The remainder will be here waiting for you.' He leered at Babysoft. 'Off for a jaunt are you, Miss Brogan? Arrah now, 'tis well for ye. What I wouldn't give to be coming.'

'I'm sure you'd give your all,' Babysoft said doing up the zip of her skirt, 'such as it is.'

'It was George Sand,' Freddie suddenly spoke up, 'it was her who enslaved and destroyed Chopin as surely as—as surely as—' Freddie stopped befuddled and uncertain, blinking vaguely into space.

'Indeed it was, Freddie love,' Babysoft instantly concurred, going up to him and taking hold of his hands, guiding him to his feet like a blind man. 'Come with us now, Lala is waiting for you.'

Out once more in the bleak January noon, the wind's claws less vicious now slapping petulantly at ears and noses and Ranter huddled disapprovingly behind the steering wheel, cap pulled down, hidden behind the racing page of the newspaper.

'After you, Mam'selle, and you, good friend, said Luke opening the back door with a flourish. 'Off we go on the golden road to Samarkand.'

'Jasus,' Babysoft giggled, 'I could have sworn it was Howth you said.'

IV

'O Wild grow the lilies
in the wilds of Kimmage West
but of all the darling lilies there
'tis Maisie Mooney I love best
for though she only has one eye
and a hoppy leg to boot,
her garden's full of turnips
and wild forbidden fruit.
Thou shalt not covet another man's wife
so the Lord unto Moses said,
but all that I covet in wild Kimmage West
is my Maisie's maidenhead.
For God and all harm be forever between us
she is my own one-eyed hoppy-legged Venus.
O long may the lilies grow luscious and wild,
wild grow the lilies forever.'

Along the windy ribbon road to Howth, past the greenery and
sudden vermilion chaos of Fairview Park they went, passing
Ringsend, in the plumed distance glimpsed across the estuary,
pylons and power stations and factory stacks and the masts and
funnels and iron spidery limbs of berthed ships rising against the
skyline under a grey pall of industrial smoke, then the svelte
sombre-slated habitats of Sutton, clean-limbed trim-lawned twin
balconied, homes of captains and petty officers and well-kept
galley slaves of commerce, half hidden from common view behind
leafy apple-blossom walls, lords of the needle's eye pin-striped
credit-card yacht-club denizens, two cars in the garage, beach-

playing sons already earmarked hallmarked and pockmarked for the playing fields of Blackrock and Belvedere far from the rough rudiments of secondary citadels of learning. Luke was singing a song of perishable goods in a lost quavering choirboy voice, the salty lash of the Bay fumigating his lungs, a valiant virtuoso doing his weedy best to keep the ragged little party from becoming a windblown wake, and a solitary light aeroplane doing lonely inaudible cartwheels in the middle of the jagged-stepped sky.

'Jesus, I'm only freezing,' chattered Babysoft huddled in the backseat hugging her knees.

'It's a grand fresh day, sure,' Ranter reassured her, well muffled up with a thick blue-and-white woollen scarf and cap pulled down over his ears.

Babysoft shivered. 'I'm puce all over with the cold.'

'You didn't cry crack till you came with us,' Ranter growled. 'A bit of sea air you said you wanted.'

'I didn't ask to be refrigerated, did I? You'd catch treble pneumonia by just sticking your nose out the window.' She looked reprovingly at Luke's skinny long-maned nape. 'And all that John McCormack there can do is sing dirty songs.'

'I cry bitter tears over your abysmal ignorance, Sister Dandelion,' Luke sighed. 'I weep for your lost unmusical soul. What you are hearing are nuggets of pure untrammelled imagery forged in the primordial heat of instantaneous creativity designed to re-create the lost conscience of my race—'

'Dirty songs,' Babysoft repeated. 'A writer how-are-yeh. It's nice pleasant things you should be writing about, and leave the poor girl's maidenhead to fend for itself.'

'Maidenheads, bejasus,' Ranter remarked, lowering his window down briefly to spit out. 'Miracles will never cease.'

'Ah now don't be too sure, Ranter,' Babysoft said stoutly. 'There's still a few knocking around Dublin.'

'Miracles or maidenheads?' Luke queried.

'One and the same thing is what I say,' replied Babysoft.

'There is in my ballocks,' Ranter affirmed heatedly. 'Where would you expect to find a maidenhead nowadays, I ask you, and nothing but swinging tits and bare arses all over the place?'

'Taximan or no taximan,' said Babysoft, 'you keep your oul' weather-eye open just the same, Ranter.'

'A man would want to be a Trappist monk not to notice.'

'Ah you're right, Ranter,' Babysoft said primly. 'Sure the scarcity of maidenheads is something shocking.'

'I mean to say,' Ranter went on, the opening clear bright vistas of coastline quite lost on him, 'looking for a virgin in Dublin nowadays is like expecting to find a half sovereign in your change.'

'You took the words out of me mouth, Ranter. Virgins is desperate hard to come by.' Babysoft kept blinking as if trying to concentrate on any subject that would take away her mind from the cold. 'Sure isn't the Mother of God the only virgin left today?'

'I blame the government,' Ranter said decisively.

'Sure who else would you blame?' Babysoft instantly concurred. 'That shower up in Leinster House is capable of any and every evil under the sun.'

'Allowing all them fucking foreigners in,' Ranter continued indignantly. 'Germans and Swedes and Frenchmen, buying up half the country and sipping their martinis in the lounge bars of the Shelbourne and Gresham, corrupting the youth of the land, boys as well as girls—' Ranter swerved violently to avoid a large yellow limousine appearing unexpectedly out of the tree-shrouded gateway of a big oppressively luxuriant house. 'There you are!' Ranter snorted honking his horn furiously. 'Going around in their flashy jamjars like they owned the bleeding place.'

'Sure it's enough to make Wolfe Tone or Robert Emmet or whatever his name is turn in his grave,' Babysoft said through intensely chattering teeth as she turned to Luke appealingly. 'Lukey love, would you ever be an angel and shut that effing window before I catch me end?'

Luke grinned in reply and lowered the window further still, thrusting his head out and raising his voice, his words again whipped away by the wind:

> 'When I think of the lilies of the field
> I'm considering how I might make them yield,
> for there's no harm in hoping
> that some judicious groping
> might bring the wild lilies to yield.'

'Fucking foreigners,' Ranter reiterated still shaking off some of his disdain. 'The country is desperate with foreigners fornicating all over the kip.'

'Sure a girl isn't safe walking the streets,' Babysoft assented, adding devoutly, 'thanks be to God.'

'All foreigners is horny bastards anyway,' Ranter monologued to himself, eyes blue slits of fire. 'I wouldn't trust me Granny with one, or me Granny's cat for that matter. They'd get up on the crack of dawn, bejasus, whether Dawn was awake or asleep.'

'It's something to do with the food they eat,' Babysoft opined, trying to pull her short inadequate leather jacket further across her knees. 'All foreign food is funny, unnatural like.'

'It's a few pigs' feet they'd want to get into them,' said Ranter, 'and a couple of sheets of ribs to knock the foreign divilment out of them.'

'Oh now, I don't know,' Babysoft rejoined, 'pig meat only makes a man worse. Me own Da never ate anything else in his life but pigs' cheek and ribs and the likes, and he never let me poor Mammy alone till there were twelve of us crammed into two rooms on the quays. It killed him in the end—'

'What killed him in the end—the pig meat or the other?' asked Ranter in a tone of genuine interest and curiosity.

'Oh, a bit of both, I'm sure,' replied Babysoft most seriously after some consideration. 'Sure most of the men that I do meet in the course of business you might say are notorious eaters of pigs.'

'Bejasus,' said Ranter begrudgingly, 'it's a wonder there isn't a pig famine if that's the case.'

'Ah thanks, Ranter,' said Babysoft bravely smiling. 'Sure I always said you were a gentleman, paying a girl compliments like that.'

The craggy serrated summit of Howth thrust itself forward through an aureole of mist and cloud like the head of some peevish giant emerging from a dip in the sea, white roofs of houses and faint milky veins of meandering hillside roads, far away squares of glass glinting, sails strong and taut in the wind rising and dipping blue and red and faint yellow and white and Luke thinking of the charming indolence of people out there in the bay playing Ahab on their little toy crafts chasing the white whales of fancy and dreaming deeds of nautical daring on a cold hangover Monday as the meeker purblind creatures of the city scuttled along shuttered devious bylanes and sidestreets nursing sadder dissipations, in and out of dark pawnshops and cloistered snugs, standing sentinel in cold bleak betting shops pursuing modest dreams of avarice of greed and glory up and down the lists of runners and starting prices to assuage pint cravings and more rarely catch the gleam of redemption in a ball of malt in the public bar next door. All on a raw-boned hangover Monday the coloured little boats sailed and the tills and the bells rang and dogs and children howled and whimpered and out over the rock-ringletted Hill of Howth an uncertain unwilling sun was trying to shine. Luke looked for relief at the gay shivering girl behind him in the backseat, catching a warm rewarding vista of smooth plump haunch as she sat huddled, her knees touching her chin, a bedraggled anemone wilting under the lash of the weather but strong-stemmed and stout-veined refusing to bow to the earth. He smiled at her in salutation and remorse and closed the window, then vaulted lightly over the seat and sat beside her, taking off his lightweight jacket and draping it around her shoulders as she burrowed into the wiry warmth of him. 'You're a real gentleman, Lukey,' murmured Babysoft, the lanky length of her coiled against him as she continued her assiduous licking of his hand. 'Jasus, I feel like a reheated corpse this minute.'

Ranter screwed up his pale blue piglet eyes at them through the rearview mirror. 'No grunting and groaning in *my* jamjar,' he warned. 'I only got the seats reupholstered last week in pure leopardskin.'

'I know—the smell of cat off them would turn your stomach,' rejoined Babysoft still shivering. 'And anyway a girl has to keep warm somehow, so don't be minding our panting.'

'Here, for Jasus' sake,' Ranter said hastily fumbling in the glove compartment and bringing out a naggin bottle. 'I was putting this by for Gertie, but if it will stop you from fornicating all over me new covers.'

'You'll have it all before you in heaven, Ranter,' Babysoft assured him, grabbing the bottle and twisting the screwcap. 'Not as nice as brandy, mind,' she said spluttering, 'but grand and warming just the same. Here, darling.'

'Gracias,' said Luke accepting, taking a respectable swig. 'Your wry and wistful good health.'

Babysoft inclined her head delicately back with a certain absurd lascivious abandon, allowing Luke to pour a careful trickle of the whiskey down her throat. She swallowed with relish, her eyes closing in bliss, then opened them and laughed. 'Isn't the scenery only massive!' she exclaimed, hugging Luke's arm and giggling. 'A few jars in the morning-time always makes me randy.' She hiccupped. 'Or I should say a few jars anytime.'

'Holy hand of Jasus,' swore Ranter exasperated as the car slid and slithered round the wet twists and curves of the road. 'Will you control yourself and don't bring the malediction of God down on me for letting me car be used for immoral purposes—and don't be guzzling all me Gold Label either.'

'Your fears are groundless, friend o' mine,' Luke said putting the bottle to his lips again. 'I have never yet attempted to deflower a lady in the backseat of a vehicle, at least not while it was in motion.'

'That's a beautiful word, that is,' Babysoft said, 'deflower. Sure only a gentleman would think of that—deflower. Gorgeous.'

'It is an exercise fraught with more than the usual amatory perils, with the most dire and possibly injurious consequences, besides being an extremely intricate and difficult lesson in callisthenics, which I as a mere initiate would not dare within an inch of my foreskin—'

'Now there's another word to tickle your fancy,' Babysoft said considerably revived now. 'A funny word, that. I mean, why not afterskin if all comes to all?'

The sun had escaped from the clouds after a struggle and was powering its way clear up a long thin blue blade of sky slicing upwards to the centre. The pirouetting aeroplane had vanished behind a thick cumulus bank leaving the wailing gulls supreme to rend the air, and Luke told himself excitedly that the day was spreading itself out before him, dull enough to look at but revealing layer after layer of tantalising coloured layer of hidden surprises as it opened and shed its protective wrapping. He felt good just to be there, the sun out at last unchaperoned, anaemic as an invalid perhaps with not much strength in it, but bright and ready to be adventuresome. It seemed to him, ensconced in the cosy leather depths of the speeding car, singular and touching for the sun to be there at all on a day of such cemetery weather, the little frail yet indefatigable terrier sun snapping at the dull-skirted clouds that sought to smother it and its blithe nerveless rays dancing in his eyes and lighting the gloomy interior of the taxi with the friendliness of matches struck in dank cloistered places, and in a dumbshow of delight he hugged the girl beside him in a comradeship of absurd disparate complexity that linked them each indissolubly to that moment of Howth sunlight and waves and gleaming cliff faces and sleek swooping gulls, making that moment seem indelible in his mind though he would step out of it round the next bend in the road.

Mistaking the sudden tightening of his arms around her, Baby-soft instantly responded by twisting round with a little glad cry of pleasure and putting her hand without preamble on the inside of his groin, resuming their little amorous cameo in the lounge back in Mooneys, her fingers glorying in their knowingness, finding again the coiled sleeping growth of his maleness stroking and rousing it as she would a cat drowsing in the sunshine. Immensely against his will, the surprise dimming out the sun, the contours of the day became hard and brittle once more, everything large and small ordinary and in its place, his five uncouth senses roped in again back behind, their neat level fences pulled back into the set predictable lines of stimulation and response. Babysoft bright-faced and scrubbed to a brisk healthy sheen occasionally closing her eyes and licking her lower lip with pink tip of tongue chattered mindlessly on as she went about her work like any factory girl at a bench exchanging small gossip with her neighbour, the glow of satisfaction rising in her cheeks as the certain design and shape of her handicraft became alive in her fingers, turgid testimony of her skill, and he staring fixedly ahead out the window as the houses and the lawns and the trim wooded estates gradually receded before the encroaching turbulent miles of sea, his bearded apostolic face rubbed of emotion, detached as the face of a patient on the operation table given himself up to the smooth manipulations of another, nothing in his sombre spaniel eyes, as though the thing that was happening was entirely exclusive to that rigid region of his anatomy now firmly clamped between the cold no-nonsensical hands of Babysoft, as though the hot nerves connecting it to his brain had been severed leaving the rest of him aside to look on with the cynical perception of a spectator watching a particularly intricate display of solitary amusement as the green and blue and smudged shades of the early afternoon whirled past outside and he could just about will himself to hear the lost savage cry of the insatiable seagulls above the clamour of the car engine.

'Howth coming up at last,' Ranter announced as they rounded a bend and the topsy-turvy array of masts and rigging and hulls swaying in the little harbour came gaily into sight. 'And not a minute too soon, for I'm bursting for a piss meself.'

'I never felt the drive,' Babysoft chimed in calmly, taking her hands away and patting her hair, licking a finger to smooth back her eyebrows. 'It was a lovely drive, though—' she gave Luke a heavy arch look—'Wasn't it, Lukey?'

'Most enjoyable,' Luke replied, draining the last of the naggin bottle with relief, glad of the chance to talk the usual safe inanities again and grateful too for the welcome feel of whiskey once more in his gut. 'You have a heart as big as the Rock of Cashel, Ranter, though not nearly as hard.'

'Ah,' whispered Babysoft leaning over to him, 'but I know something else that's big and hard, don't I, and much nearer than the Rock of Cashel.'

'What's that you said?' Ranter asked as they entered the village.

'No names, no packdrill,' squealed Babysoft, clapping her hands together like a teasing child.

'Randy bloody bitches, women,' Ranter growled as a flurry of agitated pigeons flew squawking past his windscreen.

'I'll take a walk and commune with the druidical spirits of the place while you relieve yourself,' Luke said as they slid to a halt outside a tavern on the seafront. 'Treat the lady to some ambrosia in my brief absence,' he added passing over a five-pound note.

'Jasus, it's a quare time and place you picked for a walk,' Babysoft said, getting out, shivering once more as the strong sea wind tugged at her. 'I love nature meself, but in moderation.'

'The essence of true enjoyment,' Luke agreed, putting on his jacket again. 'And in any case you wouldn't like the sea today— it has a lean and hungry look à la friend Cassius and might blow the comfortable cobwebs away. Far better that you retreat to your natural environment underneath the rafters of yon convivial hostelry. Adieu for a little while, dear friends of my bosom.'

'Good luck on your travels, nature-boy,' Babysoft trilled happily, following Ranter through the swingdoors of the public bar.

'That effer is mad,' affirmed Ranter, 'stone bollocking mad.'

The wind cut across the near-deserted promenade in vicious little scurries, slashing at the taut overhead cables that curved and twisted sinuously and emitted a thin humming sound; there was a wan forlorn look about the empty amusement arcade, its scarred billposters flapping in surrender to the dead season, the doors and windows padlocked and shuttered. Putting an ear to one corrugated wall he fancied he heard from within footsteps and coughing and hollow fairground jingles as though the stone floors echoed with last summer's revellers and the swirling and whirling and rusty creaking of the ghost trains had never stopped. There were few cars in the carpark on the front, one man asleep behind the wheel, hat pulled down over eyes snoozing his lunchtime away, an elderly aristocratic lady, face hidden behind hat-veil, straight and stiff as justice walking along the grassy verge of the long sea road exercising an abbreviated vile-snouted lampoon of a dog held rigidly on a leash, impudently barking above its station at imaginary adversaries; the serrated pyramid of houses rising like a Dutch dresser against the harsh rocky backdrop of the Summit, their façades severe and chaste in January, petite decorous bed-and-breakfast dwellings out of tune in winter like deserted icecream stands but during the festive months of high summer and apple-rosy autumn alive with business and choosy in their taking-in of clients; the many hotels with names that promised quixotic exotic mad Mediterranean frivolities now empty, the wide seafront street devoid of the heedless throng of city holiday-makers and gaseous city buses disgorging hordes of little bucket-and-spade demons frightening the fish back into the sea. Finding now a space between the iron pailings embedded at the end of the pier Luke went through onto the beach, trudging head-bent against the wind, his shoes already beginning to fill up with sand, hurting his feet, leaving great smudgy footprints behind him as he went, the dull gleam of a half buried upturned shell sticking out, the muted deep-bellied sealion roar of the waves thudding in his ears, and stood at last on the soft spongy fringe of the sea braced against the wham of the wind, looking across at the squat darkbrown thumb of Lambeg and beyond to Ireland's invisible Eye dim-lidded and shrouded in mist, the long sibilant sigh of the fathoms throbbing under his feet and dull wet seaweed flung out of the gleaming sand spelling things only the gulls and the shells could decipher with their old dark intelligence, and standing there as if on the lip of the uncreated universe Luke felt the ancient pull of the sea bidding him enter, and he felt the thrill of succumbing to it in one quick rush of yielding more imperious than the swoon of love and passion, a siren-mother beckoning him. He stumbled back with a dry harsh shout of defiance, his senses racing rudderless and reckless as the waves and sank to his knees in the sand, panting and laughing like a frightened child hearing tales he finally did not dare to hear.

Scrambling to his feet, drenched with spray, his wits carefree and scattered he turned back and regained the road and started off on the rocky trail to the summit, at times hardly more than a goat's trail climbing higher the shaley face of the cliff dropping sheer beneath his feet, the waves crashing and foaming on the rocks below as up he climbed, meeting an occasional cow forlornly chewing the sparse famished grass regarding him with great limpid suffering eyes, or a tight nervous cluster of sheep bleating loudly as they backed away at his approach, jumping over each other in their panic, and a hawk hanging motionless high up against a cloud poised like doom ready to swoop on its mesmerised prey. His thin nylon jacket flapped in and out like a parachute as the wind tore at it as he clawed his way upward with fingers and feet, every nerve and sinew aching and exulting till he heaved himself at last over the ultimate outcrop of rock and straightened up on level ground looking out over the sea, the wide scimitar of bay looping round the horizon, the beaches spread out like damp smudged foolscap pages ravelled at the edges, boats in the harbour barely stirring remote and undefined in the mist like shapes in a dream suspended and floating invisibly in a middle distance. To his madcap pleasure lumbering out of the fog like a bulbous blunt-snouted whale bellowing its impending arrival came the Mailboat, black smoke pluming from her red-striped funnels sailing in from the dark exotic climes of Liverpool laden with fabulous merchandise stuffed in coarse sackcloth bags, her decks dotted with a few returning emigrants home on sentimental sick-leave and full-pay, compassionate furlough from across the galling main to go awkwardly to mass again on Sunday morning and sup black pints of stout in shabby well-remembered bars and drown in heartfelt nostalgia for the old wayward ways and the old fond comradely things they had fled from in despair and disgust and would not embrace again for all the lost treasures of Tara, however they might weep on the shoulders of loved ones on the pier when their little green pilgrimage was over and it was time to depart once more to the well-paying overlords in Cricklewood and Kilburn with a tear and a smile and a long-suppressed sigh of relief, and he watched now as that dream-laden whiskey-befogged ship of bellicose church-mouse souls slurped and snorted and morosely snoozed its oily green-scummed way over the last dreary stretch of beloved water to belch querulously into port, and Luke looked coldly down upon the crabbed piteous comings and goings of frantic blinkered creatures below on the impervious earth.

Starting out of his noontime reverie he began wading knee-deep through bracken and gorse happily free of directions, until he finally came upon a narrow twisty lane rutted and furrowed by tractor marks, content to follow its zig-zag random course to somewhere in all that drenched green early afternoon, lost in the rowdy midst of sedge warblers flashing from branch and hedge in a perennial mêlée of joy, outraged by the spectacle presently of Luke having perforce to relieve his overburdened bladder shame-facedly up against the venerable bark of an arthritic elm, feeling as though he were doing so into the mothballed skirts of an austere dowager while the entire populace of branch and hedge and sky looked on in twittering sharp-beaked indignation. As hastily as nature allowed he finished, zipped up again and resumed his way.

He came to a wide enough road that spun downwards from the summit, and espied well back from the verge a squat sleeping toad of a tavern, windows half-lidded and heavily thatched roof slipping down over the edges like a woolly nightcap; making his way across he walked up the short paved path and looked up at the weather-worn sign creaking in the wind, bearing in over-elaborate lettering the legend, The Arms of May, and below in smaller but no less emphatic capitals language to the effect that the proprietor, Octavius McSweeney, was duly licensed and hopefully prepared to sell wines, beers and spirits, and consider-ably heartened and lightening his step Luke gently pushed open the heavy oak front door and went in.

A business-like little bell tinkled behind him as he stepped into the gloom of the stone-floored parlour, the bar lit by the dim spectral glimmer of the signs of draught beer on offer, half-seen hunting prints on rough white-distempered walls, light coming uncertainly from a small window high up almost level with the low beamed ceiling. A step and a cough from behind the counter, a youthful voice asking if he would be wanting anything, and on turning Luke looked into a boy's large country fresh wind-chafed face, eyes berry-black and impassive regarding him, thick hair falling in a fetching calf's lick across a wide ingenuous forehead, the youth waiting imperturbably for the order, leaning big spade-shaped hands on the counter.

'A Gold Label, if I may,' Luke announced coming up to the bar, sorting out the loose change in his pocket.

'Certainly, sir,' the youth replied, going about his job with sure unrushed movements, filling the glass from an upended bottle hanging on the shelf behind, ringing the cash register with the pleased authority of an adept. 'Anything else you would be wanting, sir?' he asked with natural courtesy, handing back the change.

'A fine day to be going mad on,' remarked Luke, picking up his drink.

'A fine day it is, sir,' the boy rejoined equably. 'You wouldn't be wanting water with that, would you, sir?'

'I would not. Will you join me in a drink, or is your youth against you?' asked Luke as he took a sip, feeling fraternal towards the good-natured open-air friendliness of the boy and wanting to spoil him in a big-brother way while they had the shop to themselves.

'I'll have a glass of cider, sir, and thank you,' came the reply as the boy filled a glass and dipped it in salute towards Luke as he took a mouthful. 'Is it fishing or sailing you are, sir?' he enquired, heartened, leaning his arms on the counter in a confidential grownup manner.

'Fishing in a manner of speaking, and sailing in unknown waters you might say,' Luke feinted. 'Whereabouts in the country do you come from, may I ask?'

'Kerry, sir,' the boy answered.

Luke smiled. 'You said that as if there could be no other possible place for a fine upstanding respectable young man like yourself to come from.'

'Nor is there, sir.'

Luke gave an exaggerated sigh. 'I envy you your unquestioning acceptance and acknowledgment of your antecedents. Do you not feel a bit like an exile from Eden transplanted up here amid the dross of Dublin?'

'It's a living, sir. Down there I'd only be making Denny sausages.'

Luke pondered this a while and nodded. 'And you perceive there is rather more to man's mortal estate than the making of sausages, no matter how delectable?'

The boy nodded gravely in turn. 'It's the truth, sir.'

'And so you'd sooner pull pints and dish out glasses of whiskey to uncouth pretentious jumped-up jackasses of Jackeens like myself than spend the rest of your days turning and churning out sausages in Paradise?'

'It's a living, sir.'

Luke sipped meditatively. 'And the knack of discovering relative sanity on this tired old planet is to choose a less crucifying way of making a living—in other words, not by sausage meat alone shall the true worth of mankind be known?' Luke put down his glass and regarded the boy solemnly, arms folded. 'You appear to have found at least a temporary compromise with life, my friend, and I suppose we need a respite even from Paradise.'

The boy carefully drained his glass and wiped his mouth with the corner of a very white towel he carried over his arm. 'Is it on a walking tour you are around these parts, sir?'

'Every foot of the way from the vast metropolis,' said Luke, 'in the backseat of a Wolseley saloon, drinking whiskey and disporting with a charming sample of prime Irish womanhood. The best of all ways to walk.'

A woman's voice came slicing from the obscure regions of the stores behind, cutting through their easy talk like a slap of Atlantic wind.

'Ultan McSweeney! What is it you're doing idling beyant and these barrels wanting to be tapped?'

'Serving a customer, Mam,' Ultan called back, stooping to the low-headed door in the middle of the wall behind. 'Won't be much longer, Mam.'

'Jesus Christ, amn't I scourged altogether?' the banshee wail continued as children began to cry loudly.

Ultan wiped a row of pint glasses methodically. 'My Mam,' he informed in a flat unemotional monotone. 'She's tending to the young ones.'

'How many?'

'Three at home,' Ultan explained. 'The other five will be arriving from school shortly.'

'And your father, Ultan?'

'Upstairs,' said Ultan, finishing with one tumbler and picking up another. 'Sleeping it off.'

'So, in a manner of speaking, you are really Mine Host?' queried Luke, respectful as in the presence of an equal in age.

'In a manner of speaking, as you say, sir,' said Ultan, 'though it's little enough I'm able to do—'

'Ultan McSweeney!' again came the strident cry from the stores.

'In a minute, Mam,' the boy called back, polite but firm, almost tangibly assuming the adult role that Luke had just conferred upon him. He looked at Luke, concerned, marginally ill at ease. 'I hope it doesn't worry you, sir, my Mam calling like that?'

'I am well used to the Elysian trillings of the female vocal chords, Ultan. I am wondering if perhaps you can be of assistance to me in a certain matter?'

'If I can, sir,' said Ultan, eager, yet courteous.

'How does one find the Fustenhalter place from here?'

Ultan stared back with cool unblinking eyes. 'What name would that be again, sir?'

'Fustenhalter,' repeated Luke, starting to spell it out: 'F.U.S.T.E.N.—'

'What manner of name I was meaning, sir,' the boy interrupted patiently as if dealing with a particularly dense tourist. 'The nationality of it, in other words.'

'Oh—I see. Er—German, most assuredly,' answered Luke, puzzled. 'Why? I mean, is there a foreign colony in existence out here?'

'I wouldn't rightly know about that, sir,' said Ultan going on with his tumbler cleaning, 'but there are some foreign people living in and around here, to be sure. We have the Bonniers, French, the Happenzells, Dutch, the Olaffsons, Swedish—'

'Stick to the Germans please, Ultan.'

Ultan stopped the summary of foreign domiciliaries and regarded Luke shrewdly. 'Ah,' he said, 'you would be meaning Count Otto, wouldn't you, sir?'

'The man himself,' Luke nodded. 'Then I take it he is still alive and in one reasonably recognisable piece, if not exactly doing a hornpipe on the top of Howth Head?'

'Alive, sir—the count alive? As you and me are, and himself only in with us this morning for his usual.'

'His—usual?' echoed Luke interestedly. 'And his usual usually consists of what, precisely?'

'The usual,' explained the boy. 'Three large Paddies and three pints of stout, and the same for the lady, except for the stout—hers is three half pints.'

'My admiration for Count Otto grows apace,' said Luke. 'Poisoned only yesterday, and downing whiskey and stout by the cartload today. To say nothing of this dark lady who accompanies him on these little therapeutic hillclimbs. You happen to know her well, too?'

'Oh no indeed, sir,' said Ultan instantly disclaiming such a privilege. 'Not well, sir, not at all, no more than I know the count except for their dropping in mornings and sometimes in the evenings. She is a great lady,' Ultan emphasised not in awe as much as merely stating a self-evident fact.

'She sounds a most remarkable one, at any rate,' said Luke urged by an ungracious inclination to scoff.

'Oh indeed she is, sir,' Ultan asserted earnestly. 'She walks for miles, never takes a taxi, and spends all her time looking after old people and trying to clean up the canals in Dublin and keep the old Georgian houses from falling down. They say she's a walking angel—'

'With a commendable capacity for whiskey and stout coupled with the sweet qualities of mercy. And the name of this angel?'

'Her name, sir—the count's sister?'

'His sister is she?'

'Sure everyone knows Countess Sonny—'

'Countess Sonny? Is that her real name, Ultan?'

'I wouldn't rightly know, sir,' said Ultan as if surprised at the question. 'Sure she isn't known by anything else except Countess Sonny—'

'Ultan McSweeney, you witches' spawn!'

Again as from a great subterranean depth the weird banshee wail dirgeful and bitter falling between them like a malediction lying upon each of them like cold salt spray.

'Coming, Mam—'

'Now, now, *now*!' came the venomous order, the voice growing louder as the noise came of chairs and tables being moved and pushed aside. 'In the name of God, boy, where are you?'

'Here, Mam, here in the bar,' said Ultan going hurriedly to the dividing door behind him. 'Serving this gentleman—'

'Amn't I blessed with the fine men living under my roof!' the voice cried coming nearer. 'Is it out there you are ogling the women like your prostrate Da beyant and having dirty thoughts in your head?'

'Serving a customer, Mam, a gentleman customer—'

'A fine pair of heroes I'm burdened with, to be sure,' the wail went on, growing in screeching volume as a long angular form appeared in the doorway. 'One too young to know for sure, and the other old enough to know better!'

The figure stooped and bent forward, a narrow vulpine head extended on a scrawny coarse antenna of neck, and let forth a vengeful hysterical scream.

'Ultan McSweeney! What is it you are drinking under my very nose, you son of Satan incarnate?'

'Only a glass of cider, Mam,' explained Ultan, picking up the tumbler from the counter for his Mother to examine. 'This gentleman was kind enough—'

'Amn't I scourged on this earth!' cried the woman, knocking the glass from her son's fingers and sending it crashing to bits on the hard stone floor. 'I'll not stand idly by and see the sins of your Da being visited upon you, boy, without raising my fist and smoothing the devil out of you!' she cried breathing hard and clawing at the boy's abundant mop of hair. 'You hear me, boy—hah? You hear me?' She paused briefly as though in the middle of a household chore and turned to Luke, looking on dumb-founded on the safer side of the counter. 'Be going on with your drinking, sir,' she said in an ordinary pleasant tone, 'and don't be minding us while I teach this young villain son of mine some manners. You hear me, boy—hah?' she roared again resuming her assault on the youth. 'You hear me? So help me God, I'll save your soul yet from the temptations of drink and loose females!'

A demonic force had entered the room as the woman set determinedly about berating her son, her talon-like fingers en-twined in thick tufts of his hair as though trying to pull them from the roots while the youth stood passive and dumb before her awesome vengeance, a slim lithe craft being buffeted and battered by barbarous unremitting waves, the woman doing a sort of mad dervish dance around him as she held on to his hair, he rotating docilely with her gyrations like a spinning-top being whipped around on its axis, knocking over bottles and glasses, sending them toppling and rolling about on the floor, she meanwhile keeping up a barrage of high-pitched abuse intermingled with scalded cries and yelps of bitter self-commiseration at the atrocious inordinate wrongs and black-starred ill-doings the world had visited upon her in the villainous shape of her husband and son. Then slowly the heads of the three youngest children appeared peering over the tops of beer barrels, watching with grave unalarmed eyes their Mother doing her dance of wrath and ritual retribution around the upright manly form of their brother as though they had watched the performance many times before and had season all-year-round tickets for it.

A door that apparently led to the upstairs rooms opened and a heavy hobnailed step sounded behind him. With difficulty Luke took his fascinated gaze away from the spectacle and turned, to see shambling forward a large befuddled beached whale of a man in shirtsleeves and braces hanging loose, rubbing his eyes with his knuckles and suppressing a yawn as he came reluctantly into the centre of the bar, thick grey outcrop of hair sleep-tossed, scratching the protruding bulge of his abdomen and peering short-sightedly into the gloom.

'Ah now, Ethel-May, what is it at all in the name of the Almighty?' the man asked in a reasonable placating voice, shrewdly keeping his distance. 'Is it at the boy you are again? God, woman, don't you ever leave the poor unfortunate lad alone for an hour itself?'

Ethel-May abruptly ceased flagellating her son and rounded flame-eyed on her spouse who instinctively stumbled back a few steps. 'Lad is it?' she screeched. 'He's as much of a man now as ever he'll be, and every day he grows more and more into the godless soul-damned spitting image of yourself, Ocky McSweeney! Drinking already and smoking fags behind my back and casting his hot lustful young eye on women, looking at them as if they had not a stitch on their bodies.'

'Sure what women are you talking about, in the name of God?'

her husband asked, mildly exasperated, rubbing his stiff grey-stubbled chin. 'There's not a decent-looking lass within a potato field of this place—'

'Hah—so you've been looking, have you?' Ethel-May pounced, squaring up to him, hands on hips. 'Lustful oul' demon that you are, you've been dragging yourself after young girls again, have you?' Ethel-May pounded her thin flaccid bosom in an attitude of martyrdom. 'Nine children you begot between the lawful sheets of matrimony, and it's nine more you'd be wanting to sire out on the hills like a billygoat.'

'Christ forbid,' murmured Octavius fervently, skirting warily round her and stepping over the three small buttercup-headed children on the floor to go behind the bar. 'One halter is enough for any man to hang himself with.'

'You're not starting off again, surely to God?' cried Ethel-May as her husband reached up for a bottle from the shelf. 'And you beyant in bed snoring in a drunken fit all morning!'

'I've a killing thirst on me, woman,' Octavius told her, unsteadily pouring himself out a tumblerful of whiskey.

'There's lashings of good clean God-given water in the taps.'

'You know I'm allergic to the fluoride or chlorine or whatever the bastarding hell it is that does be in the drinking water nowadays,' said Octavius lifting the glass. 'It brings me all out in a rash that's most unbecoming to look at and itches like bejasus.'

Octavius stood for a moment or two looking intently at the glass in his hand, then in a single convulsive movement he dashed the whiskey down his throat, his body seeming to be seized with a seismic shudder as he shook his head from side to side and gripped the edge of the counter, holding on tightly.

'Look well, boy,' Ethel-May cautioned her son who was now standing quietly in the shadows. 'Look well and see what you are turning into!' she said, pointing a thin withering finger at Octavius. 'See the work of Satan staring you in the face, the devil that never sleeps drawing you down into the nether depths with every accursed glass you raise to your lips—'

'For the love and honour of Jasus, woman, would you ever shut up and let a man sink down to hell with a little peace and quiet itself?' said Octavius, emboldened as the fresh liquor brought alive the stale contents of the bottle drunk earlier, filling his glass again. 'You'd make any mortal man fall in love with the devil himself with that mouth of yours.'

Ethel-May's pinched face grew mottled at this unexpected effrontery. 'That's a fine gentlemanly way to address your own wife in front of your own children!' she panted, hands working as though the greatest ecstasy she could imagine was to claw her husband's round bonhomie-bright face to shreds. 'You weren't saying things like that when you came courting me and took me away from hearth and family and comfort with your smarmy talk and silver lies—and to think I could have had the pick and pride of County Kerry at my feet!'

Octavius belched. 'No horse-thief would look at you twice— you'd give a bloody aspro a headache, and to think that once upon a time I thought you were the Lily of Killarney herself. Bejasus I must've been stone effing blind.'

Ethel-May looked apoplectic, the ferret eyes leaping out of her head. 'To think I let myself be tricked and fooled by a Dublin slob and my own darling Papa giving you the biggest dowry that was ever handed out in all the Kingdom to set you up in business with a pub—and here I am now straddled with nine brats and tied hand and foot to a whiskey bottle!'

'Oh aye, I see,' said Octavius addressing the glass in his hand. 'It was all sweet suffering for you, wasn't it—you never got any effing pleasure out of it, did you, and many's the night when I lay on the broad of my back dog-tired after working my fingers to the bone and all I wanted was to sleep, you'd creep up to me with that begging little voice of yours and whisper things in my ear— it was Ocky this and Ocky that and show me you love me, Ocky, show me you're a man, Ocky, do anything you want with me, Ocky—just *show* me!' Octavius took a long careful swig. 'Every bloody kid that came along you squeezed out of me, and bejasus I'm going to enjoy every last day that's left to me, for I'd have to be permanently pissed to go on sharing the same roof with you, never mind the same bed.'

Strange strangled animal sounds were coming from Ethel-May as she stood confronting her husband large and easy and dignified behind the counter.

'You—you Liffey scum—' she started.

Ultan, every manly inch a diplomat, stepped forward.

'Would you be wanting another drink, sir?'

'Well, as a matter of fact—' began Luke.

'Who the hell are you talking to—who's that over there?' Octavius asked quickly, straightening his shoulders and peering suspiciously over. 'Jesus God,' he said, drinking rapidly and pouring another. 'Don't tell me we're under surveillance—don't tell me we're after behaving like that and a customer present?'

'Don't be minding us, sir,' Ethel-May chimed sweetly as she gathered up the three infants off the floor who clung listlessly to her skirts. 'Sure we're married, and you know what married people are like.'

'Er—yes, of course—'

'A drink for the gentleman, Octavius McSweeney!' she said sharply. 'Where's your manners?'

'Bejasus, yes, darling, you're right,' responded Octavius, coming forward and placing a large glass in front of Luke, suddenly grinning like a shipwrecked sailor waving to a rescuer appearing on the horizon. 'Your very best health, oul' son.'

'Why, that's extremely generous of you,' Luke said, full of a new respect for all manacled mankind.

'My pleasure,' beamed Octavius, pulling up his braces. 'My great pleasure.' He turned to his wife, swelling with new-found authority. 'Is there something you have to be doing, woman?'

'Something, Octavius dear?'

'Like getting my dinner ready,' prompted Octavius heavily.

'Oh, certainly so, dear, certainly so,' responded Ethel-May, shushing her offspring away into the back stores. 'Do you fancy anything special today, Octavius?'

Octavius looked at her stonily. 'I don't think there's anything special you can set before me.'

Ethel-May's eyes flared briefly and her hand half reached for a bottle on the counter, then she looked at Luke and smiled nervously and very nearly curtsied as she hurriedly left and vanished into the stores.

'Women,' said Octavius with a sigh, turning to Luke. 'Women are a mixed blessing at the best of times and a bloody crucifixion most of the time. Are you married yourself, by any misfortune? No,' he went on not waiting for an answer, shaking his head sagely. 'I can see you're not, lucky sod. You haven't got that look of mortal agony on your kisser.'

'The gentleman was enquiring after Count Otto and his sister,

Da,' said Ultan who had been cleaning the floor of broken glass.

'Oh aye,' said Octavius, nodding. 'There's another poor bastard that's suffered the iniquities of matrimony.'

'From all reports he suffered a rather more positive fate,' Luke put in. 'Or almost.'

'You mean about the rat poison his darling missus put into his gargle when he wasn't looking?'

'I don't think that the exact nature of the poison has been ascertained yet,' volunteered Luke carefully.

'Rat poison, weedkiller, arsenic—what the hell does it matter?' Octavius opined. 'It would've killed him just the same. Are you a newspaper fella or what?'

'I have that dubious distinction.'

'Out to do a story on the goings-on up at that place last night, eh? Will there be pictures and things like that?'

'There might be, but—'

Octavius brightened and began buttoning his shirt. 'I can give you all the information you're likely to want,' he announced with a broad confident wink. 'I'm your man, your usually reliable source, so to speak. All the inside information. You get to hear things in a business like this. Things that they wouldn't print even in the *News of the World*, bejasus.'

'That's very kind of you, Octavius,' said Luke, 'but I'd like to talk to the count and countess themselves.'

'Countess Sonny is it?' Octavius said, lowering his voice and leaning closer. 'Now there's a quare one for you. They all say she's a living saint, and far be it from me to say otherwise, but bejasus if she's a saint then I'm well on the way to canonisation.'

'You mean the lady has a certain—er—reputation?' said Luke, looking around and glad that Ultan was not within earshot.

Octavius nodded approval of this approach. 'I see you're a man of discretion. Mum is always the word with me, oul' son, but there are certain things you cannot ignore even if you were blind and deaf itself—' He paused.

'Things?' queried Luke as obviously required.

'Things. Things that no lady would be up to, never mind a countess. Sure do you know what I'm going to tell you?' Octavius said, his voice even lower. 'I don't think your woman is even a German, never mind a countess!'

'What makes you think that, Octavius?'

'For Jasus' sake, man, sure she hasn't even got an accent, as any self-respecting German would have!' said Octavius on a high note of disapproval. 'She has more of a Rathgar accent than anything else, if you ask me, real posh and refined like as if she was talking with a hot potato in her mouth. And the characters she does be hanging around with!' Octavius rolled his rather inflamed eyes. 'All bejasus hippies and junkies and—what's this you call them?—oh aye, dropouts. And as for her title—sure can't you buy yourself any kind of effing title if you have the money? Isn't that a fact now?' Octavius asked earnestly.

'I really wouldn't know.'

'And let me tell you another thing about her ladyship—it is my own honest and unswerving belief that she and that Otto character are not related to each other at all, certainly not in a brother and sister way. What do you make of that now?' Octavius challenged triumphantly, crossing his arms.

'You leave me speechless, Octavius,' said Luke admiringly. 'Then in what other way would you say they are related?'

'Ah now come on,' said Octavius reprovingly. 'Use your head. Sure what made his wife try to poison him?'

'Ah-hah,' said Luke, again on cue. 'The ould triangle.'

'Exactly!' Octavius rejoined, nodding. 'She's no more his sister than I am the Earl of Desmond's twin brother. There's quare goings-on up in that house, I'm telling you. Hear no evil, see no evil, speak no evil by all means, but . . .' Octavius picked up his glass. 'And that bloody funny name she calls herself—the Countess Sonny—now I'm asking you as one reasonable man to another— what woman would go around with a handle like that? Countess Sonny!'

Just then the doorbell jingled and a woman's bright voice called out. 'Did someone mention my name?'

Octavius started out immediately from behind the counter, his face positively aglow, arms outstretched in greeting. 'It's yourself, countess! Come in, come in, my good woman, and rest your bones awhile in the Arms of May!'

V

Luke leaned on the counter sizing up the improbable sample of Teutonic nobility who had seated herself at a table on the other side of the room, Octavius fussing and fawning over her with much clasping and unclasping of his large uncomfortable hands, regaling her with anecdotes careful in their ribaldry, regarding her reaction shrewdly to ascertain how outrageously he might proceed further along the well-worn path of his imaginary quixotic adventures, a performance received with a mixture of grace and amusement and a nodding of blonde head that indicated familiarity with many of the diversions being related to her, an affinity which Luke found intriguing in such a slight bit of feminine gossamer. With an imperious sweep of hand Octavius beckoned to his son to bring drinks and trying visibly hard to maintain his natural dignity and sense of propriety Ultan laid the glasses on the table before the personage who obviously embodied for him the highest attributes of womanliness to be found anywhere in the four lush corners of his own green little cosmos, looking at her with un-abashed wonder and reverence as he backed mesmerised away to stand in the safer less rarefied atmosphere behind the bar watching his Father play the traditional host and virtuoso raconteur with respect rather than envy.

Luke on the perimeter of the little show felt a strong surge of sympathy for the boy, himself a child again gazing fascinated and forlorn into a shop window stacked with dazzling trinkets and fabulous tinselled things; he caught now the same lost look of wonder and longing undiluted by greed in the large unclouded eyes of Ultan as he beheld his princess across the room drinking her whiskey and stout with petite relish, inclining her small shining marigold head at a charming attentive angle and her slight perfect hands making eloquent little movements of their own in gracious response, her light laughter rising from time to time to join in Octavius' own coarse guffaws.

Presently Octavius returned to the bar. 'Yon woman wants to have a dickybird with you,' he told Luke out of the corner of his mouth as he stood beside him at the counter, his chest heaving and forehead full of sweat. 'I'm bandjaxed bejasus trying to keep her entertained.'

'Do you have to?' asked Luke.

Octavius looked at him as if he had asked a question of amazing innocence bordering on the idiotic. 'Of course I have to!' he replied, drawing his hairy forearm across his brow. 'Isn't she my best bloody customer, man? She comes in here expecting me to act the eejit, and act it I do bejasus as long as she drinks like that.' He looked admiringly over his shoulder. 'You'd ask yourself where the hell she manages to put it all in that little dawny whippit of a frame of hers. The dustmen fellas do drop in here for a jar, and they say the trail of empty whiskey and vodka and gin bottles up at your woman's place would stretch across the Gobi effing desert, and to look at her she hasn't a pick on her, like an advert for Oxfam bejasus. Still and all,' mused Octavius, 'I wouldn't turn me back on it—a fine enough little arse on her when she moves.'

'You say she wants a word with me?'

'What? Oh aye. But listen—a word in your ear before it's too far gone,' added Octavius guarding the side of his mouth with his hand, bending close. 'Watch yourself with that one, don't be taken in by that sweet little Red Riding Hood carry-on, because like all effing women she keeps her fangs and her talons well hidden and out of sight before she pounces and then a man is a goner, an effing goner, mark my word.'

'Thanks for the warning, brother Octavius,' said Luke putting down his empty glass.

'Keep your distance and your guard up, and you should come out of it all right,' said Octavius, going behind the bar. 'Good luck, oul' son.' He grinned, making a thumbs-up sign.

Luke sauntered over to where the lioness sat tapping the rim of her glass with cool faintly varnished fingertips, an absent look on her pretty birthday-fresh face, as he halted at her table and coughed; seeing this had no discernible effect, he started to hum a tune, and for a while this too produced no response, and her dewy eyelids flickered and she lifted her doll's face, enveloped in a hazy insubstantial halo of blonde hair, focusing on him eyes very blue, a face about which he could write every cliché under the sun.

'I know you didn't ask,' he said, 'but my name is Sheridan.'

She regarded him steadily, a half-open smile on her face. 'How do you do.'

'May I get you a drink?' asked Luke confidently, observing the full glasses.

The smile opened a little more. 'Thank you.'

Flummoxed, Luke coughed again. 'Er—whiskey, isn't it?'

She barely nodded. 'Umm.'

Back at the bar Octavius rolled his eyes again as he poured. 'I told you, didn't I?' he hissed loudly, regarding Luke sorrowfully. 'Your woman will ate and throw you up again in a flash if you're not careful. What're you having yourself?'

'A good cool pint for the love of God.'

Octavius waved away the proffered note. 'This one's on me, out of the pity and charity of my heart. Sure you'd throw a crust to a stray dog, and you're going astray like billyo, bejasus.'

'For this relief, much thanks,' acknowledged Luke gathering up the drinks.

'How kind of you, Mr Sheridan,' she said as he came back and put the glasses down between them. 'Do sit down.'

'Do I bow or pull my forelock?'

'You may pull whatever you desire, Mr Sheridan. Cheers.'

Luke sat down grinning. 'You said you wanted to see me.'

'I should have thought it was exactly the other way around, Mr Sheridan.'

'Do you have to call me Mr Sheridan?'

'I don't have to call you anything, Mr Sheridan, but what would you suggest I call you?'

'I can offer no other alternative than Luke—will that suffice?' he asked, lifting his pint.

'Luke will suffice perfectly.'

'And what do you suggest I call you?'

'The first thing that comes into your mind, as long as it is original,' she said, licking the creamy film of stout from her lips.

'I can't call you that funny name—it sounds like something out of a failed Gilbert and Sullivan operetta.'

'Then you certainly couldn't call me by my real name, which happens to be Countess Fustenhalter. Do you happen to have a cigarette, Luke?'

'I'll stick to Sonny,' he said, lighting a cigarette and handing it over to her. 'You sound determinedly non-German, almost English in fact, with the impeccable diction of someone who has studied the BBC's foreign language broadcasts.'

She sighed. 'I think it's a great pity not having an accent, a dialect, an idiom. Not having one makes you so nondescript, anonymous, a nonentity.' She played the full Hansel-and-Gretel impact of those bluer-than-blue eyes on him. '*You* have such a strong, rich, beautiful, unmistakable—' she paused, blowing a perfect smoke-ring, 'Mid-Transylvanian agricultural accent.'

'I was weaned on vampire milk. If you watch closely you will observe the telltale bulge of my fangs in the region of my upper jaw. Already I contemplate your juicy jugular with ill-concealed lust—'

'You were making certain enquiries about me via our host— may I ask why?'

'Things that go bump in the night—or rather,' he corrected, dipping his forefinger into the foam of his pint, 'that go plop in the early evening. Please tell me it was Socratic hemlock—'

'Arsenic, rather severely diluted.'

It was his turn to sigh. 'Nothing's perfect in this world. Will you give me the full, definitive, unexpurgated story of the abortive attempt?'

'Ask again—properly,' she said calmly.

He suddenly pulled down his bewhiskered jowls and licking the beer-wet table with his lolling tongue, slobbering, emitting high whining animal sounds, looked over at her with cowering hangdog eyes. 'Please, meine Frau.'

'Bravo!' she cried, clapping her hands in delight, jumping up and down on the wooden bench excited as a schoolgirl at a magicians' party. 'You shall have your story, and any number of others you want me to invent.'

He straightened up distinctly uneasy. 'You mean it's all a mere invention?'

'No invention is ever mere,' she remonstrated primly, exchanging her stout for whiskey. 'But I can assure you that the arsenic, meant for poor Otto and which by angelic misadventure ended up in my sister-in-law's stomach, was real enough.'

'He managed to swap glasses, you mean?'

Her small nose wrinkled in fastidious distaste. 'You, too, are afflicted with the newspaperman's malady of vulgarising even the most miraculous occurrences of life. Dear Otto owes his life to the direct intervention of Fate.'

'Don't we all?' he shrugged. 'And how fares the wicked witch of the piece, your sister-in-law, if that's not altogether too irrelevant a question?'

She smoked thoughtfully. 'She survived with a mere feeling of nausea in her guts,' she sighed. 'Nobody dies any more, really, not in the romantic sense. We either drop dead, which is thought-less, or we go out so bunged up with drugs that we leave absolutely without a squeak, which is cheating. People should be more discerning about how they're going to die.'

'Now that smacks too readily of the bould Oscar to be com-pletely original,' said Luke.

'Oh, I am too, too clever to be completely original,' she replied, tossing back her hair. 'Nobody is ever original in the first place—you wear the old skin under layers of new clothes bought and borrowed.' She looked at him directly, challengingly. 'You think I'm a phoney, don't you?'

Luke pondered. 'I don't know,' he answered, drawing circles in the beer droppings on the table. 'It really doesn't matter, though on the other hand maybe you want people to think you are a phoney, which is an art in itself. I should know.'

She leaned forward, chin in hand. 'I want to know about you. I may forget all about it in the next hour or so, but I want to know about you now, which is all that matters. What do you do?'

'You know what I do. I work for a newspaper—'

She shook her head impatiently. 'No, no, not that,' she said, her voice Sunday-school bland. 'I mean, when you are not caught up in this newspaper nonsense, what do you do?'

'Oh,' he said, 'you mean my mind and what I do with it?'

'Your mind, for want of a better word, yes.'

'I labour manfully along under the illusion that I am writing a novel of truly Promethean proportions, which will probably end up as a forlorn little fart brought forth with much toil and trouble from the bowels of hardbound ambition.'

'If you write the way you talk,' she said, 'your Prometheus will turn out to be no more substantial than an under-nourished verbose hobgoblin. Do you always talk like that, or is it some inexplicable malady you hope to recover from quickly?'

He smiled. 'Don't look now, but I am hiding behind this enormous Freudian front from the ogre of my true self which daily threatens to devour me.'

'And what is your novel about? Magic casements and faery lands forlorn?' Her eyes were studying him, smiling.

He nodded. 'Hmm. And cabbages and kings, and despots and slaves, and people carrying cardboard Calvarys through alleys perennially smelling of cabbage, that sort of thing, all very simple and mundane.'

'You are piqued,' she told him happily. 'You are not amused.'

He looked at her steadily for a moment. 'You know, it galls me, but I think you're dead right. Now isn't that extraordinary? Why should I be annoyed by what you think or say? I don't know who the hell you are, but to me you're a celluloid figure, a sugarplum fairy, a doll in an absurd pantomime full of inept would-be assassins and dubious Franz Lehar counts from Bavaria who seem to spend all their time quaffing inordinate quantities of Irish whiskey and stout—'

She clapped her hands joyously. 'More, more!'

'So why the hell should I give a damn what you say?' he shook his head. 'It's beyond my poor wafer-thin comprehension.'

'One day I am sure you will be quite famous.'

'Famous my discourteous arse, my lady,' he said decisively. 'Just give me the gen on what happened up at the ancestral manor last night and I'll be on my way.'

'Don't you like my company?'

'Immensely, but to paraphrase Micawber my present pecuniary state forces me to deny myself that pleasure. So give a poor newsboy a break and tell me exactly what went on up there in the Palace of Varieties last night. You see, I have this dateline to keep.'

She finished off her drink and stood up, shaking out her hair and edging her way from behind the table. 'You must make your story authentic and visit the scene of the would-be crime in order to soak in the atmosphere—is that not correct?'

'That is very correct.'

'Then come—I will take you there.' She came around and, placing her hand on his sleeve, looked up at him with such entrancing trust that he almost expected her to flutter her eyelashes. 'But first, I must go to the loo.'

She made her way towards the back stores as though familiar with the journey, and Luke went to the bar for a quick one.

'Bejasus, you need some fortifying, I'm telling you, man,' said Octavius as he served him. 'You weren't the swish of a cow's tail getting off with your woman, fair play to you.'

'Strictly in the line of duty, Octavius, I assure you,' said Luke, swallowing the whiskey down cleanly.

'Oh aye,' winked Octavius, picking up a towel. 'The ship's name is Murphy, but good luck on your travels, oul' son. Just one thing—'

'What's that, Octavius?'

'Your man the count—he's a bit deformed, you know, a bit of a cripple, if you get my meaning?'

'The significance of which is?' asked Luke as the older man paused.

'Well, you know how it is with such people—they have more bloody strength than normal people like me and you, to sort of compensate for their deformity or disability or whatever the effing hell it is, so if I was you I wouldn't turn my back on him while making sheeps' eyes at your woman—not worth it, oul' son, not worth it. He's built like an effing ox, sure, cripple or no cripple, so watch your Ps and Qs up beyant.'

'If I'm not back by six send a posse after me,' said Luke draining his glass.

'Oh now you can make a joke out of it if you like, but a gorilla with bad eyesight and a gammy leg is a gorilla just the same— Ah there you are, countess!' said Octavius all smiles as she came back through into the room. 'Sure you're not off already, are you?'

'The gentleman and I have some business to attend to, Octavius,' she said, linking Luke's arm with ease. 'Haven't we, Luke?'

'That we have, Sonny. Lead the way.'

'Good hunting!' Octavius called after them as they went out into the raw day. He flung away the towel and shambled over to where he had hidden his tumbler under the coun er. 'Aye, a quare hawk, to be sure, and all that oul' guff out of him thinking he was fooling me—' he took a long mouthful and straightened up, drawing his wrist across his mouth. 'Me, Octavius McSweeney, that made a lifetime's career out of fooling thousands, bejasus!'

Outside they turned past the shaky creaking sign in the wind and started to climb, walking vigorously side by side, her stride matching his own, heads bent forward, hardly speaking; she was slight, even diminutive, borne along on the wind, yet she strode on with purpose, a certain tough grittiness about her as if those small fish-thin bones of hers had stood up to many a stern tempest and could weather inclemencies of living that might crack and splinter sturdier frames. She walked briskly along, throwing up her head from time to time, stopping to draw the sea-washed air into her lungs, hugging herself happily, peering down at the rocks and the bay from the edge of the twisting road, somehow a different person away from the dank low-raftered gloom of the tavern, lithe, resilient, birdlike.

He could imagine her scampering down the sides of the cliffs with spidery agility, skipping from ledge to ledge hanging almost motionless in the air, the image flowing through his mind like a swan-flight caught in slow motion, a small golden blue against the mossy darkgreen cliff-face, the seabirds hardly stirring a wing as she alighted amidst them. He watched her on the verge silhouetted against the oatmeal-lighted sky, small and shapeless in her long loose peasant garment, red squares on dark green, watery sun catching her blown hair. He fancied if he closed his eyes and opened them again she would have vanished leaving only a little glowing space where she had stood. He closed his eyes ruled by the fancy, and when he reopened them she was at his side grinning.

'We mustn't dawdle—Otto will be quite cross if I'm late for his afternoon yoga session,' she said swinging easily into her stride again. 'Not far to go now.'

'You practise yoga?' he asked, his words almost snatched away by the wind which was increasing, as they climbed higher onto less sheltered ground.

'Have done for years.'

'Together?'

'Never apart.'

'Is that the secret—of your—eternal youth?' he shouted as the wind whipped around them.

'Part of the secret,' she laughed.

'And the other part?'

'Riotous living—what else?'

'But I thought you did—charitable works—looking after the aged and indigent citizens of Dublin—preserving our Georgian leftovers—that sort of thing—where does the time for riotous living come in, in the name of God?'

She had broken into a sprint by this time and he was finding breathing difficult, trying to keep up with her. 'Who was telling you those nice fables?'

'Our gregarious friend—back at the pub—and I don't think they are fables.'

'If it pleases you to think of me as an angel of mercy and champion of your architectural heritage, go ahead,' she said, speaking without effort as she strode along before him. 'People do tend to exaggerate, and the Irish have a positive genius for it.'

'Hyperbole is our natural pastime,' he said, trying hard not to gasp. 'Where's the fire, for God's sake?'

She looked back, puzzled. 'Fire?'

'Why this frantic blood-pumping gallop, as if the Baskerville hound was snarling and—and snapping at our heels?' he panted.

'Oh, that,' she said, laughing and slowing down a bit. 'Got carried away. I always break into a run as I get near the house.' She slowed now almost to a normal walk. 'I have this delicious dread of one day coming round the bend and seeing it go roaring up in flames.'

'You'd have to hoist in the Dublin Fire Brigade by helicopter if that ever occurred.'

'Well, here we are,' she said turning into a short overhung lane and climbing over an ancient rusty lopsided iron gate. 'Up you get.'

He looked at the gate dubiously. 'Doesn't it open?'

'Certainly it opens, if you coax it long enough and say kind words to it,' she said, taking a few steps backwards as she waited for him to follow her. 'But it's much more fun climbing over it. Don't just stand there expecting it to open—do hurry, please.'

Mindful of Otto fuming and tangling himself into solitary inextricable transcendental contortions on the hearthrug, Luke, shunning the ungracious female expedient of simply clambering over it, placed one hand carefully on the top rung of the gate and with a stern controlled intake of breath vaulted bodily into the air, doing a neat body twist in the manner of an Olympic polejumper so as to land cleanly on the soles of his feet; the gate, however, was old and feeble and under the sudden weight of him as he sprang, it buckled and collapsed, cutting him short in mid-air, and he crashed to the ground amid a tangle of twisted iron rungs and branches, sending up sprays of muck and cow-dung, and aware of a sharp streak of pain in his knee.

'Oh good Jesus Christ,' he swore softly, finding himself in a most unathletic and undignified sprawl at Sonny's sandalled feet, slipping and slithering about in squelchy mud as he strove to regain the perpendicular.

'I must say, you *do* make life difficult for yourself,' she said, contemplating him. 'It must be a dormant tendency towards excessive masochism, a form of self-mortification which I am finding increasingly peculiar to the Celtic psyche, dating back perhaps to druidic times.'

'Your—thesis—is intriguing, no doubt,' he laboured on all fours, reaching out to grasp a low-hanging tree branch to lever himself up. 'I am hardly—in a position—right now—to enter into —a—hypothetical discourse on the—the inherent peculiarities of —of my race—Balls!' he muttered as the branch promptly snapped, causing him to drop to his hands and knees again, one foot caught between the rungs of the gate.

'Oh, do let me help you,' she said, as though the notion had just occurred to her, stepping forward and offering him her hand. 'Now grab my hand while I heave—don't be afraid—I'm really quite strong—ready? One, two—what's wrong?'

'Er—my foot—it seems to have got caught somehow—'

'Ah, I see the trouble,' she said, bending and gently extricating the imprisoned limb, rubbing his ankle expertly. 'That's better? There's a good brave boy.'

He winced not so much with discomfort as with indignation at her cooing words. 'For the love of God, woman, I'm not senile.'

Her smile was almost maternal. 'Of course not, just damn clumsy. Ups-a-daisy, my Galahad!'

Her grasp was strong as she pulled him to his feet and gingerly he tested his knee, bending it up and down, but it was no more than an unpleasant ache. He looked down ruefully at his mud-splattered appearance.

'I'm not exactly dressed for dinner,' he confessed as he hobbled up the overgrown deep-rutted driveway, leaning on her arm, all masculine chagrin for the moment forgotten.

'Oh, Otto is no devotee of Savile Row himself,' she reassured him, patting his hand. 'I just want to hurry, because he won't begin his yoga without me.'

The tree branches swung so low they had to stoop to avoid being scratched; everything was grossly overgrown and entangled, an over-ripe mass of vegetation choking the very life out of the soil, swaying and undulating like the waves of the sea, a thick carpet of fungi warping the driveway, reducing it to little more than a trickle of flagstone, bleak patches of sky glimpsed through the canopy of foliage, the stench of decaying earth everywhere. Abruptly it ended and before them squatted the house listing on its side, slimy ropes of moss and ivy hanging down its stolid dull-grey walls, two debauched badly mauled stone lions with a pathetic half-snarl on their forlorn but still faintly savage faces guarding the front entrance with wan vigilance; three scarred stone steps led up to the porch and the door of massive oak chased round the edges with deep pummelled brass shaped like arrowheads, a huge brass knocker in the centre grinning down like a hyena with manic eyes. The whole house had a brooding satyr presence both melancholy and malevolent and Luke imagined he could almost hear the intake and outlet of its turgid breathing, the windows half-shuttered and a desultory wisp of brown smoke from the blunt tilted chimney as though from a half-lit smouldering pipe tipped carelessly on a ledge.

'A beautiful ghoul of a house,' said Sonny leading him across the open gravel up the front steps to the door which was swinging desolately back and forward an inch or two. 'You'll be glad to know that everything creaks.' She pushed the door inwards and pulled him impatiently into the hall, calling out, 'I'm here, Otto—Otto dear, where are you—I'm here, I'm back!' She swung through the hallway, opening doors to the left and right as she went. 'Oh now don't be childish, Otto—do come out—I *know* you're here—I've even brought something back to amuse you!'

Luke stood uncertainly behind, surrounded by pillars and recesses, hard timber floorboards, chandeliers hanging from the shadows, the peculiar cemetery cold of the place enveloping him; there was an ancientness inside the house, deliberate and remorseless in its insidious stealth, lying not merely on the skin but burrowing through to the bone, numbing the elemental quick so that he was convinced if he remained standing still in the one spot and position long enough, he would be transmogrified into one solidified piece, his blood hard and static as ice, his brain a solid frozen chunk rattling inside his skull. Uneasily he moved forward, bringing his knees high up at each step as if he were wading through glue, flexing his shoulders like a boxer in his corner, chafing his hands together and blowing on them; he was on the point of stomping them to and fro under his armpits when he saw Sonny returning round a bend at the far end of the hallway. 'I've found him!' she exclaimed triumphantly, sweeping up to him and taking him imperatively by the arm. 'Come.'

'Er—emm—where, exactly?' he enquired, hanging back against the surge of her enthusiasm.

'The meditation room!' she said, pulling him along after her. 'I'm just one exercise behind him—in here.'

She half pushed him into a long angular room absolutely devoid of furniture, one enormous curtainless window at the end, letting in a deluge of anaemic light theatrically falling upon a figure sitting cross-legged in the centre of the floor, muscular torso bare, massive head closely cropped, bullet-domed, broadboned face bland, expressionless, eyes half-lidded, hands resting passive on knees. Luke stood irresolute by the door, idly pushing his hands into the side pockets of his skimpy gabardine jacket making the few loose coins jingle, at which sound Sonny put a finger to her lips in warning. 'Ssh—quiet! He's entering a crucial stage any minute now,' she whispered as she noiselessly slipped into an adjoining room.

Luke half opened his mouth to enquire the whereabouts of the lavatory but she had already gone, and turning back to the immobile figure in Buddha-deep trance on the floor saw with some astonishment that the man was now upended on the hard-boned peak of his head, his short muscle-corded legs straight in the air revealing two severely deformed feet twisted at disparate grotesque angles as if a sculptor had started to mould something and left in a hurry halfway through. Peering tentatively from where he stood Luke could not discern any toes as such, merely unformed impressions of where toes should have been, a serrated crenellated row of raised flesh and bone at the extremities of both feet, ankles and insteps so ill-fashioned as to be almost non-existent; the feet were hoisted high as if in deliberate defiance and yet the peculiar stance of the man's body was so unselfaware as to immediately cancel out the merest hint of perverted showmanship or ostentation and render such a notion absurd and unjust. Luke stared until at last conscience overtook craven curiosity and guilty as a child watching an illicit peep-show, he backed away groping for the handle of the door—

'Don't go,' whispered Sonny, reappearing as suddenly as she had left. 'Do stay for tea.'

He watched as she sank in one flowing graceful movement onto the floor leotarded, her hair caught up behind in a single band, body lithe and supple in a boyish way, her femininity unobtrusive as she easily folded her limbs into a posture of meditative felicity, one leg resting directly under the arch of the other, hands spread palm downwards on either side of her, imperceptibly supporting her weight as she looked with intent serenity at the wall opposite, her face instantly assuming the same look of perfect vacuity and remoteness as that of her companion; whenever either of them moved it was like the subtle stirring of a shadow, not consciously perceived until it had already moved and alerted position, neither seeming to breathe or be aware of their own movements; it was akin to watching a disembodied ballet performed by ephemeral phantom figures despite the hairy solidity of the man's torso and brutelike biceps as he stood wrong end up on the floor, arms folded impassively across chest.

With a feeling of furtive guilt Luke backed towards the door, taking each step with intense care as if leaving the incense-rich precincts of a temple, and once outside in the corridor quickly made away in any direction, an illogical shame stirring in him as one who had been spying on the ultimate act of love itself. Despite its bleak nakedness he had found the room strangely oppressive and claustrophobic, and he was relieved to escape from it if only in search of another kind of relief, his bladder again sending distress signals racing to his brain, and as if guided by that imperative organ he followed the corridor until it led him round another bend down a gently sloping carpeted ramp to a door with a carved wood etching of a young boy happily engaged in performing the function of which he himself was in such dire and immediate need.

His need fulfilled, his step springier and a sense of adventure spurring him, he began going from room to room, most of them full of large grandfatherly sofas and armchairs, heavy dark furniture, and thick funereal drapes on the windows with now and then a piece of startlingly incongruous modernity standing out like a raucous beacon in a sea of wintry desolation. There was a sense of newest arrival or imminent departure hanging over everything, large wooden packing-cases standing half-opened, dustsheets shrouding chairs and tables and settees, glass book-cases full of leather-bound unopened tomes soaring to the ceiling, enormous oil paintings in gilt frames dulled with age of apocalyptic biblical scenes and depictions of famed ancient battles thrown in with gracious Gainsborough-like ladies undoubtedly bogus with rosebud features and lace shawls flowing over sun-shimmering shoulders in a setting of honeysuckle innocence. Over all there was an aura of permanent semi-detachment as though everything had been caught in a state of static suspense, only marginally lived in and for the most part put aside, unopened rather than concealed, a conglomerate heap devouring every square of available space. Exactly as the grounds outside were choked with creeping usurping vegetation, so each room seemed to be stuffed to overflowing with archaic furniture humped cheek-on-jowl like large slabs of toffee in an overblown paperbag. Prevailing disorder appeared to be the only law of the littered landscape. A gravelly patina of senile and uncharming decadence had settled upon everything, inducing a sensation of profound inertia so that the soft-breasted cooing of a wood-pigeon from the trees outside or the lethargic ticking of a clock from somewhere within seemed unspeakable intrusions into the bone-cold hiatus that stretched throughout the house.

'I suppose you'll be wanting tea and sandwiches as well, cool as you like?'

Shaking his head, Luke turned to find himself confronted by a small flame-topped turkeycock of a woman blocking the doorway, fat arms resolutely folded and a look of tight-lipped censure on her mole-pitted wrinkled collage of a countenance.

'Well—I don't know exactly—'

She nodded her head disparagingly. 'I knew it,' she said tapping her elbow with her many-ringed fingers. 'I knew it the minute I saw you creeping about the house like one of them Special Branch fellas looking for illicit arms.'

He opened his mouth. 'I'm sorry if I—'

She waved her hand. 'Don't be trying to whitewash or hoodwink me, Zozimus—sure I know your kind only too well— bending the knee and playing up to her ladyship beyant just to cadge a free meal and a few drinks gratis—oh I know your kind too bloody well.'

'I assure you, maam, I'm here as a guest—'

'Here for ham sandwiches you are, larruped with gobs of mustard and pepper and washed down with steaming mugs of tea—'

'While in no way despising the blessed bread of charity.'

'Or maybe it's fresh salad and tomatoes you're after,' the woman continued indomitably, 'with radishes and scallions and juicy slices of beetroot with a few hardboiled eggs thrown in for good measure followed by mugs of creamy porter.'

'The most blessed of all virtues, charity,' responded Luke, swallowing hard, a distinct rumble of revolt in his guts telling him it was now some hours since he had eaten. 'I freely admit a little solid sustenance would not be wholly unwelcome, maam.'

She nodded sagely, standing squat and blue-smocked in the doorway. 'You can't fool Aggie Applebud, I'm telling you,' she said, her tapping fingers making tiny musical jingles as her manifold rings tinkled against each other. 'Poor scrawny little bugger —you look like you haven't had a square meal inside you for donkey years.'

He swallowed again, pride firmly in pocket. 'Well, as a matter of fact—'

'Aggie Applebud knows an honest beggar from a thief when she sees one,' she went unstoppingly on, twitching one nostril and sniffing up it expertly. 'Oh indeed she does, and her at the catering game before your Ma was doubled up bringing you into the world—sure my God the few clothes you have on your back is hanging on you, you're nothing but skin and bone, you have the pinched blue look on your face that corpses do be wearing laid out in the habit.'

Luke's fingers went automatically to his face to feel the texture of his skin. 'I know I'm no Charlie Atlas, maam, but I had no idea my appearance was so drastic.'

She made a clucking sound, sharp duckegg-blue eyes scrutinising him. 'Aggie Applebud wasn't born yesterday—no, nor the day before either, she knows an under-fed under-nourished little scut of a fella when she sees one. Sure your hands is trembling with me talking about food—I dread to think what you'd be like if I brought you into the kitchen and sat you down at the table with a plateful of steaming pigs' feet or boiled ribs in front of you.'

Luke put out a hand and gripped the top of a chair. 'You paint images of Elysian splendour—of sumptuous prodigality.'

'But there isn't a scrap of anything left in the house except one stale crusty loaf of bread and a half can of baked beans, so you'd better skidaddle before I start screaming and have Mister Otto come and flatten you with one sweep of his hand.' She uncrossed her arms and brought one palm smacking down upon the other resoundingly. 'He'd smash you like a fly.'

'How could you let me down so cruelly after lifting me to heights of such gastronomic excellence, oh heartless Aggie Applebud?' Luke histrionically raged, throwing his arms up in despair.

A toothy smile creased her face as she almost simpered. 'I'll make you a cup of tea itself,' she said stepping back into the hallway. 'And maybe a slice or two of her ladyship's birthday cake that's been lying there for months untouched by human hand—unlike herself, I might add.'

'Aggie, you are a dark, mysterious and most delightful siren,' he announced as he hastily followed her across the echoing hall, down some steps and through the swingdoors of the kitchen. 'Into thy hands I commend my spirit.'

'Sit down and shut up,' she said abruptly, once inside the large and immaculate kitchen, bustling briskly about confident and supreme in her own earthy domain. 'I'll be put on half-pay if he finds out I'm wining and dining a stranger in here, but it isn't in the nature of Aggie Applebud to turn anyone away on a cold raw day miles away from civilisation and myself knowing the both days that were in it.'

'Aggie, I am quite overcome,' he said, managing an audible catch in his wiry throat, sitting down at the long plain wooden table, feeling the warmth from the oven stealing deliciously around his feet and knees. 'I came, a stranger to your ample hearth, an alien—'

'Ah shut that trap of yours and eat,' she ordered gruffly, shoving a plateful of sandwiches in front of him.

His eyes widened. 'Luxury unashamed! But I thought you said—'

'Ah sure we all say more than our prayers at times,' she said, cutting him short in mid-sentence as she rinsed and filled the big copper kettle and put it on the gas-ring, her every movement quick and economical. 'Sure her ladyship beyant is in the habit of bringing in all manner of stray dogs from time to time for a bite and a sup, to Mister Otto's great discomfort, I might add.'

'He sounds something of a misanthrope, does friend Otto,' he said in between hearty munching.

'I know nothing about his private life,' she said sharply, taking out the tea-caddy and spoon. 'What goes on in a man's bedroom is between himself and God, but I know this much—if he owned all the icecream parlours from here to Mandalay and back he wouldn't give you a cornet buckshee, not if your tongue was hanging down to your boots.'

'That, methinks, betokens a crass and most unchristian-like disposition,' responded Luke, biting into a thick layer of ham. 'From all accounts Otto sounds distinctly odd and unpleasant, very anti-social in contrast to his admirable sister—'

'Sister? Oh aye—his sister,' mused Aggie as she fed the boiling kettle with tea. 'Well, as they used to say in my day, there's sisters and sisters in it.'

'What happened here last night, Aggie?'

Her shoulders stiffened and she folded her arms over her bosom again. 'I always said you shouldn't try to rise above your own station in life—asking for trouble it is—sure if God intended you to be rich and idle He'd have made you so in the first place—only stands to reason.'

'Ah-hah,' Luke said picking up another sandwich. 'You no doubt refer now to the fair Karina.'

Aggie bristled. 'Karina—plain Katy Furlong she is from Booterstown that was never used to anything before but coddles and blind stews till she met your man beyant and cornered him into marrying her, the brazen rossie.'

'Ah now be fair, Aggie—be charitable,' he pleaded placing his elbows comfortably on the table. 'That act in itself took more than a little ingenuity—'

'Ingenuity—is that what you call it?' Aggie snorted derisively. 'Sure every man is a born bloody fool when it comes to dealing with women—they swallow everything we tell them if we say it to them clever enough—Katy Furlong swore till she was blue in the face that she was carrying Mister Otto's child and no matter what he may or may not be he is first and foremost a gentleman, so he ups and marries the lying deceitful scheming little bitch without a murmur out of him—the oul' eejit.'

'And was she perchance even remotely pregnant?'

'If she was it could only have been an immaculate conception,' said Aggie, taking the kettle off the ring and pouring out two mugfuls of tea. 'The poor man swore on the Bible he never as much as lifted her petticoat during the time they were courting—that was the summer before last and divil the sight or sign of a baby since. That Katy Furlong,' said Aggie shaking her head and sitting down facing him, 'if she came up on the last load itself she was the first to jump off. Going around now like the Lady Lansdowne all decked out in her fur coats and diamonds as if she was born to it and her poor Mother wearing the brass balls off every pawnshop in Dublin she went to them that much—oh it's a curse I'm telling you when people rise above their station and forget themselves.' Aggie took a thoughtful sip of tea, clasping the mug in both hands. 'Never forget your place, I always say—remember your station in life and you won't go far wrong—oh divil a bit.'

'But what exactly happened here last night, Aggie?' he persisted as she seemed about to lapse into rambling rumination about the traps and snares of mortal ambition.

Aggie grunted. 'Don't you know what happened—doesn't the whole of Dublin know what happened—sure didn't she try to kill him stone dead by putting rat poison in his whiskey when he wasn't looking, the ungrateful mean grasping little cow?' Aggie stopped and looked across the table at him sharply, screwing up her eyes. 'Why are you so keen to find out—is it a Special Branch bugger you are after all? Bejasus—I wouldn't put it past you—sitting there cool as you like pumping me for information drinking my tea and eating my sandwiches, taking advantage of my heartfelt generosity!' Aggie half rose in her chair glaring at him. 'The more I look at you the more I can see you have the dirty low cunning look of one of them Dublin Castle gits—'

Luke waved his hand. 'Peace, Aggie, peace—I'm no dread inquisitor from the dark demonic forces of the Castle. I'm just a dirty low cunning newspaper reporter git trying to make a few bob out of the mistakes and misdeeds of others.'

'A newspaper fella, hah?' said Aggie, subsiding a little, sitting down again, still not entirely mollified. 'Sure they're as bad as the police any day, if not worse—you'd hang your own Mother for a story.'

'The thought crossed my mind more than once,' he confessed wryly. 'Well, maybe I wouldn't go as far as social matricide, but the biographies of one or two of my brothers would make excellent reading if *I* could ever persuade my editor to print it anywhere else except in the Believe It Or Not column.' He put on his lost pleading martyred look. 'Don't send me out into the raw bitter light of January without a few facts, dear Aggie Applebud —you are my only unimpeachable witness to a case that may well go down in the annals of Irish criminology as one of the most bizarre and bewildering of all time, rivalling even the case of Billy the slopman and Lady Shaw's scullerymaid.'

Aggie became interested. 'I never heard of that one.'

Luke drew his brows together. 'A case of most unethical misdemeanours in the back of Billy's slop-wagon amongst the cabbage water and other assorted swill where you'd least expect a crime of passion to erupt or lust raise its demon head.'

A look of enlightenment crossed Aggie's craggy countenance. 'Would that be little Billy Gormley from Bride Street that had the short leg and the harelip? The whole family was reared in the slop trade—it was handed down you might say.'

'It might well be, Aggie, it might very well be,' said Luke, rather alarmed at the tangential turn the conversation was taking and desirous of getting back onto course. 'To return to last night, however—'

'If it's the same fella I'm not a bit surprised,' continued Aggie, 'for short leg and harelip apart, he was the dirtiest randiest little bugger you'd wish to meet in a month of Sundays—all he was short of doing was getting down on his hunkers and looking up the women's skirts—many's the glad eye he gave me, sure, and me old enough to be his Granny,' said Aggie with a proud tilt of her head before her nostrils twitched with remembered disgust. 'But the smell off him would turn the strongest stomach—you'd want the whole house fumigated after he came to collect the slop.'

'To come back to the momentous events of last night, Aggie, and our friend Katy—'

'Don't mention that one to me, the lying murderous little teasy-whacker!' Aggie fumed, finishing off her tea and rising. 'There wouldn't be a just God beyant in heaven if He didn't punish her for what she tried to do to that poor man and himself a half cripple into the bargain.'

'Ah yes, but do you know all the facts, the full facts? For instance, what *made* her try to do such a thing in the first place? Was it simply greed, avarice, or was there some darker motive—could it have been a classic case of hell having no fury like a woman scorned, do you think?'

'If you mean what I think you mean—'

'Ah, but I do, Aggie, I do indeed!'

'I have my job to keep,' said Aggie curtly putting the delf back into the cupboard, rinsing the kettle clean. 'I may think things, but it's different from saying them out loud—'

'An honest woman is a pearl of exceeding great price, Aggie,' he argued persuasively. 'Don't tarnish that pearl by being afraid to speak your mind.'

'Who says Aggie Applebud is afraid?' she flared, turning on him. 'I'm not afraid of any man, cat, dog or divil—if I see something that needs speaking out on, then mark my words I'll speak out on it without fear or favour.'

Luke clapped his hands. 'That's the spirit, Aggie—that's the spirit of true freedom, the spirit of Wolfe Tone and Emmet, of Parnell and Pearse, the same fiery spirit that made Connolly calmly face a British firing-squad as he lay slumped in a wheel-chair—hey-ho, who fears to speak of Easter week, who blushes at the name?' he cried, banging the table fervently, turning earnestly to the somewhat dumbfounded Aggie like an orator in the courtroom. 'Don't let craven fear keep you down, Aggie—let not base timidity crush the bright burning lamp of truth, but keep on waving the banner of free speech and democracy in the ancient and honourable tradition of your race unconquerable to the end—you'll not waver, will you, Aggie, you'll not accept the

Saxon shilling and hide and cower behind the shield of the foreign foe—you'll not, Aggie, will you?'

'None of my family was ever a traitor or coward, bejasus, if that's what you mean,' said Aggie recovering and drawing herself up straight. 'Sure didn't my own Father go out in Nineteen Sixteen with the best of them and got a severe injury in a very private part for his pains? And divil a penny of a pension he got out of it either and them fat-arsed buggers sitting beyant in Dail Eireann laying down the law to honest people like myself—sure they'd shit themselves yellow if you bursted a Woolworth's balloon behind their backs.'

'Democracy is in a woeful state, Aggie, a woeful state completely,' he acquiesced readily, 'which is why it is our sovereign duty as responsible citizens to speak out fearlessly on matters of grave moral significance and concern—like what happened here last night, which provides you, Aggie Applebud, with a unique opportunity of exercising your right to free speech without, as you so eloquently say, fear or favour—a right, let me add, that is not only God-given, but Irish through and through.'

Aggie again looked doubtful and confused. 'That's all very fine and grand, but what about my job?'

'Your job, Aggie, your job? Have no fear, heart of gold—should you as a consequence of speaking the truth forfeit your means of livelihood, I will use the vast media of the press to highlight the wrong done to you and you will be deluged with more offers of employment than you could possibly cope with from this to doomsday. Oh Aggie, Aggie,' he declaimed, hand on heart, 'doesn't it stir the blood in your veins to know you have the chance to strike a blow for the emancipation of the truth, the liberalisation of the press, the destruction of cant and hypocrisy and double standards throughout the whole strata of our society? Why Aggie,' he rushed forward, placing both hands on her shoulders, 'I can see you now—the little Dublin housekeeper with a Joan of Arc soul firing out salvo after salvo of truth from her embattled position deep in the dark dank dungeons of this latter-day Bastille—Oh no coward soul is thine, Aggie Applebud!' He bent close, looking into her eyes, his own shining with shrewd fanaticism. 'Shall we do it, Aggie—shall we dare it together, you and I?'

'Do what—dare what—what the bejasus hell are you talking

about?' faltered Aggie sitting down abruptly in a chair. 'Is it raving you are, or drunk, or what?'

'Drunk? Yes, let us both get drunk on truth, Aggie—you pour and I will sup every last drop with all my might—let us sing a song of truth, Aggie, let us make music with the truth, let us dance a dance of truth. Shall I lead, and if I lead will you follow? Into the waltz then, Aggie.' he dropped swiftly onto one knee by her chair, a look of anguished pleading on his face, hands tightly clenched. 'In your own peerless words, Aggie—what exactly happened here last night?'

Aggie blinked rapidly, bemused. 'I wasn't meself exactly—not when it happened—not at that exact precise particular moment of time, you understand—not exactly—I was coming up with the tea —bringing the tea up to them beyant in the livingroom—and I was outside the door just turning the handle to go in—Jesus, I have to have a drink!' Aggie broke off, panting.

'Where, Aggie, where?' he asked, jumping up.

'Up there—' she pointed, 'up there on the top shelf—behind the Jeyes fluid and the cod-liver oil.'

Luke stood on a kitchen stool and feeling expertly among the assortment of medicine bottles clustered together on the shelf, extracted half a bottle of American bourbon. 'How did this alien concoction come into your possession, Aggie?' he asked, coming back with the bottle and handing it to her. 'Product of Uncle Sam.'

'There's all manner of quare-looking bottles lying all over the kip, sure,' she told him, taking the bottle and unscrewing it, putting it to her mouth and drinking, making a face but swallowing determinedly. 'It's horrible bloody stuff altogether, but better than nothing—they keep the Powers and the Jamesons behind lock and key—' she put the bottle to her head again, her eyes rolling strangely as she drank. 'Ah now,' she said, her breathing becoming more regular, 'that's better than a belt in the ribs.'

'You were standing outside the door, Aggie, about to go in—'

She looked at him, befuddled. 'What door—when?'

'Last night—you were bringing them up their tea —'

'Oh aye—so I was,' she said, holding the bottle in her lap and stroking it as if it were a kitten. 'I had me hand on the handle about to turn it and go in, when all of a sudden there was a loud roar like someone being scalded—and Miss Sonny yelling and screaming her head off—I got such a fright I was shaking and trembling like a leaf—I don't know how I didn't let everything drop—but in I went anyway and honest to Jesus you wouldn't believe what I saw, the sight that greeted my eyes—' Aggie seemed to shiver and drank again from the bottle quickly.

'What was it, Aggie?' he urged gently, ears alert to any footsteps approaching across the hall. 'Take your time now and tell me.'

She wiped the neck of the bottle slowly with her palm. 'There was your man—Mister Otto—rolling about on the floor like an eel, kicking his legs up and down like he was doing the Can-Can only he was on the broad of his back at the time, and I thought the poor man was roaring in mortal agony, but he wasn't—he was roaring with laughing, he was, rolling about on the floor laughing his bloody head off—the tears were streaming down his face with the laughing—going hee-haw hee-haw like a demented billygoat. I never saw anyone enjoying himself so much—he was doubled up with laughing.' Aggie shook her head in wonder. 'There he was, with his poor deformed feet in the thick woollen socks, in convulsions of laughing on the floor, his face purple with the great gas of it all.'

'And Miss Sonny—what was she doing amid all this boisterous merriment?'

'What was she doing? You may well ask—she was like someone gone mad, out of her wits, doing a sort of dance around Mister Otto, clapping her hands and laughing fit to be tied, pointing over to someone in the big armchair by the window—and I didn't know whether I was coming or going—I thought I had stepped into a madhouse by mistake—and the only thing I could think of saying was, "I've brought your tea".'

'And then what?' he prompted as Aggie paused.

'That only made them worse—made them go nearly berserk with the laughing and the doubling up—and when she gathered her breath Miss Sonny turned to whoever it was in the chair and said in a spluttering voice, "Tea is served, my dear Karina,"—and I went up closer still with the tray in me hand, and there was Katy Furlong wriggling in the chair like bejasus, frothing at the mouth and her eyes lepping out of her head like someone in an epileptic fit, God bless the mark, and her face was all puffed up and blue and I thought she was choking to death—and I turned to Miss

Sonny and asked her what was wrong, and all she could manage to say was, "Miss Karina just had a rather strong drink, Mrs Applebud," and, at that, off she went into bloody hysterics again —I swear to God I thought it was up in Grangegorman I was with them all going on like they were only out for the day.'

'What did you think was wrong with Katy?'

'Now there I leave you,' said Aggie, shaking her head, 'sure you'd want to have second sight to tell just by looking at her twisting and turning in the chair, her eyes saying hello to one another and the froth bubbling out of her mouth like bejasus, but whatever it was she wasn't looking the picture of health, I can tell you.'

'Did you notice anything else, Aggie, anything that caught your eye, apart from the peculiar behaviour that was going on in the room?'

'Funny, but now that you ask I did notice that Katy Furlong was still clutching a tumbler in her hand—in both hands in fact— gripping it tight as if she couldn't let it go, and I got the impression she was trying to tell me something, but all that came out was moans and groans mixed up with the froth—she went on wriggling like someone was sticking burning needles into her—oh, it was a sight to put the fear of God into you,' said Aggie with another shiver, putting the bottle to her mouth again.

'But didn't anyone *do* anything, Aggie, after the gaiety and the stupefaction were over?' he asked sternly. 'Surely you didn't just let the poor creature go on writhing in torment?'

Aggie looked indignant. 'What do you take me for? There's no love lost between meself and Katy Furlong, but I wouldn't stand by and see a dog in pain without trying to do something to ease its suffering—'

'So what did you do, Aggie?' he pressed as she paused to take a slow dignified sip.

'Do? Didn't I do what any civilised Christian would do under the circumstances—didn't I bend down and whisper an Act of Contrition into her ear?'

Luke groaned in exasperation. 'Your concern for the state of Katy's immortal soul does you great credit, Aggie, but didn't any of you do anything a little more positive—like phoning for a doctor, for instance?'

Aggie seemed a little uncertain. 'A doctor? Oh aye—they did

get around to that right enough, soon as they could stop laughing and control themselves—Miss Sonny it was who made the call after things had quietened down a bit—'

'And how long was it before the doctor arrived?'

'Sure you have me all confused,' said Aggie aggrieved. 'With the time of this and the time of that and who said what and who did and didn't do such a thing—sure I'm not a bloody encyclopaedia.'

'Okay, Aggie, okay—a thousand pardons,' he said quickly, 'but the doctor did come eventually, I presume?'

'Certainly he came—he was a bit delayed on the way on account of running into a stray horse just at the foot of the hill and getting into an argument with them gypsies—I declare to God something ought to be done about them bloody tinkers—sure the whole country is walking alive with them—worse than rabbits they are, the way they breed—wouldn't you think the Government would step in and *do* something to protect the rights of decent citizens? I mean it's going beyond the beyonds when a medical man is held up on an errand of mercy by one of their wild horses—'

'Indeed, Aggie, indeed,' interrupted Luke, stemming the rising tide of her civic outrage. 'I'm with you a hundred per cent, but can you recollect about how long it took for the doctor to get here, give or take an hour, no doubt?'

'Well, I wouldn't swear blind to it, but the tea had gone stone cold by the time Dr McGluckan got here—'

'By which time what condition was Katy in?'

'Katy? Oh aye—well surprising to say, she had calmed down a bit by that time and wasn't tossing and frothing too much—a remarkable improvement, you might say, from when I first walked into the room and saw her doubled up in the chair.'

'And Otto and Sonny—what was their attitude by this time?'

'Oh, they were game ball by now and playing cards—'

'Playing cards? Aggie, surely you are mistaken?' he cried.

'Divil a bit mistaken,' retorted Aggie with a self-righteous preening of her head. 'I got my eyes and ears to see and hear with and they've never let me down in all the years I've had them, and I tell you they were having a game of pontoon or ponner as it's better known, and they were playing for real—you know, with real money, nothing let-on or anything like that—and Miss Sonny was winning per usual—a far superior card player in my opinion that what Mister Otto is, though she's not above a bit of cheating on the sly, especially when he's had more than a few jars on him—'

'Let me get this straight, Aggie,' he said, pacing up and down, fingers rubbing both temples ruminatively. 'You are prepared to go on record as saying that while Katy was suffering the torments of the damned a few feet away the other two were calmly engaged in a game of pontoon? Is that what you are saying, or have I got it all hopelessly muddled?'

'Sure what else could they be doing and them knowing as much about medical science as meself?' Aggie countered, puzzled and somewhat apprehensive at the solemnity of his tone, 'and anyway,' she continued, fuelled with fresh fulmination, 'wasn't it her that tried to poison Mister Otto in the first place—surely you didn't expect him to kneel down and kiss her feet after trying to dispatch him to his Maker without as much as a Hail Mary in his ear? Now that is expecting too much of human nature altogether—'

'But the unfortunate girl might have been in her death throes!' Luke exclaimed stopping in front of her. 'Didn't you stop to consider that?'

Aggie bristled. 'Don't be putting me in the dock! And besides,' Aggie asserted, vindicated, 'she was almost back to normal and sitting up in the chair when Dr McGluckan arrived with his little bag of tricks, so there was no sweet fear of her expiring on the spot and appearing naked before her Maker unabsolved—if you'll pardon the expression.'

Luke sighed in resignation. 'All right, Aggie—so be it. Mine not to reason why. And what did Dr McGluckan do when he appeared on the scene?'

'Dr McGluckan's a gentleman, I can tell you that—oh a natural-born gentleman—never married you know, but a gentleman just the same—on the wrong side of seventy if he's a day—ah, but such a gentleman—give you the shirt off his back—they do say in his young days he was a bit of a Flash Johnny—fond of the women and all that and partial to a drop—' Aggie gave a sudden high unsteady laugh—'He sowed his wild oats all over the place, you might say—but now he goes up and down the country roads in that oul' relic of a car dispensing human charity—you'd travel the length and breadth of the land before you'd meet the likes of Dr McGluckan and him with such beautiful hands—'

'But what did he actually *do* when he got here?' Luke managed to stop the flow.

'Do? He made her swallow something and got her on to her feet and made her walk up and down the length of the room and back over and over again even though she kept dragging her feet and then bejasus didn't the bloody thoughtless unsanitary bitch get sick and throw up all over the lovely Indian carpet and right down the front of the doctor's worsted suit—I was never so ashamed in all me life—a woman of her age puking like that just like a child—no respect whatsoever—and him a medical man.'

'That probably saved her life, Aggie—but never mind—what happened then?'

'Jesus, you're terrible nosey,' she said, petulant, a bourbon-bloom on her flaccid cheeks. 'Wanting to know the pros and cons and the ins and outs of everything—it'll get you into trouble if you're not careful. Well anyway,' Aggie continued wearily as though making a great effort to oblige him, 'the ambulance was called for and took her away and after I tidied everything up and Dr McGluckan cleaned his suit they all had a drink and sat down to play cards until well past midnight—'

'Didn't anyone phone the hospital to find out how Katy was?'

'How do you expect me to know—I can't be in two places at once like the Holy Ghost—wasn't I down here in the kitchen half the night making plates of bloody sandwiches for them?' Aggie sniffed and lifted a corner of the hem of her smock to wipe her nose. 'The gentry are great ones for eating, no word of a lie—Jesus, they're forever filling their gut, morning, noon and night at every fiddle's fart, gobbling up whatever comes to hand—they eat three square meals for breakfast all at once—you'd think they had an army of bloody worms inside them—they can't sit down for a chat without having something to nibble at while they're yapping—'

Just then steps echoed across the hall, a woman's light laugh, a man's deep gruff response, and Aggie's face flushed even more violently than the whiskey was responsible for and in an instant she was on her feet pushing the bottle down into the pedal-bin under the sink and clearing the remains of the tea things off the table, managing to duck her head briefly under the cold-water tap and beat her spikey hair frantically into some semblance of order as the steps and the voices drew nearer.

'Now remember,' she whispered fiercely, tying her apron-string into a big industrious knot, 'not a word out of you about what I told you, or I'll swear on the Holy Bible you made it all up—'

'Honour bright, Aggie,' he whispered loudly back, giving her the thumbs-up salute, 'honour bright'.

Still clad in her clinging black leotard, Sonny swept in making a stage entrance, twinkling on the tips of her toes, her gestures studied and theatrical. 'But Otto dear,' she was saying, pitching her voice to the imaginary upper galleries. 'I thought your balance throughout was divine, simply divine—'

'Nein, nein, mein Gretchen,' growled Otto, short, squat, middle-aged, also leotarded, hobbling in her wake. 'Two times during the meditation poses I sneezed—the fly was up my nose—almighty I tried the concentration, but the fly was there in the ointment and very hard it was to think of nothing.'

'Poor Otto,' she trilled falsetto, butterflying up to him and kissing him lightly on his broad blunt nose. 'Poor hapless Otto. But for all that you were splendid—the most exquisite buttock control, and as for the overall muscular symmetry of your perpendicular erection—well, my dear, that really had to be seen to be believed—divine, simply divine!'

Otto's ripe full melon of a face beamed and broke into creases of pride and gratification as he waddled to the centre of the kitchen, scratching the great hairy expanse of his torso and under his armpits like a pleased amiable baboon. 'You were pleased, no, my little butterfly? You were pleased with your great clumsy Otto, my little tiger moth, my little muffin-rag, my little—Mein Gott!' Otto suddenly barked, seeing Luke for the first time and halting abruptly before him, small dark gimlet eyes glittering, head thrust forward. 'Whoever have we begotten here, hah?'

'How do you do,' said Luke, formally offering his hand. 'My name is—'

Otto gripped Luke's hand in both his own and motioned Sonny furiously with his head. 'The police, Gretchen, the police call! We here have an interrupter—'

'Intruder, dear,' corrected Sonny pirouetting gracefully around them, 'do be careful with your English—I'm always telling you to form the words carefully in your head before speaking them out loud.'

'Here we have an intruder,' said Otto very precisely. 'Quick the police call before in our beds we are all murdered!'

'At half past four in the evening, dear?' cooed Sonny, giving an impromptu impression of the dying swan and draping herself sinuously at his feet. 'Hardly the ideal setting for a crime pastoral.'

'Ah, countess,' began Luke, relieved, 'perhaps you would explain to the count—'

Otto pushed his face closer to his prey. 'An anarchist he is!' he said, growling deep in his throat like a suspicious bull mastiff. 'He has maybe the bombs up his sleeve—'

'Nonsense, dear,' said Sonny caressing his lumpy woollen-socked feet, 'this is our friend Luke—'

'You *are* an anarchist, sir?' demanded Otto, his grip unrelenting.

'In theory, perhaps—' Luke struggled to say, wincing under the steely pressure.

'Hah!' shrilled Otto accusingly. 'The courage he has not to so say! You, sir,' he crowed into Luke's face, 'the courage you have not, yes?'

'Most certainly,' agreed Luke readily, trying to disengage himself as politely as possible. 'I am a theoretical hero and a very practical coward.'

'Otto dear, do listen,' Sonny said calmly. 'This is our friend Luke, here to write a nice little story about us.'

'Luke?' repeated Otto. 'I of no Luke know. The name Luke rings no bell in my head.' He turned suddenly and looked at Aggie and back again to Luke, suspicion and excitement lighting his eyes. 'You maybe attempt to contest the woman—'

'Molest, dear,' amended Sonny from the floor.

'Molest our Applebud, hah? Your intentions you fling upon her, you maybe try to carnal her with your dark wishes—you maybe try—oh mein Gott, you maybe try the rape with her—

'Oh, *Mister* Otto!' giggled Aggie, sending an arch downward look fluttering in Luke's direction. 'Sure all he got from me was a cup of tea and a sandwich—not,' Aggie continued blandly, 'that he wouldn't have taken more if offered.'

'Aggie, Aggie,' said Luke with an exaggerated groan. 'Et tu, Brute?'

'What's that he's saying, Mister Otto?' queried Aggie, greatly enjoying her prominence as a violated fawn.

'Silence!' Otto screamed. 'In my own house the silence I will have! Frau Applebud,' he said sternly, 'you shall not the sacrifice make to protect this raiding raper of women—

'Rapist, dear,' supplied Sonny, now spreadeagled on the tiled floor, drawing each leg up and down, keeping her knees unbended. 'If you're going to make such delicious accusations, dear Otto, do endeavour to get your grammar right.'

Otto growled, releasing his grip and stepping back, arms folded, legs outspread, like a mediaeval executioner minus the mask. 'Raper, rapist—I have the sure thought the Luke is a rotten apple, all wired up for evil—'

'*Wired* up, dear?' echoed Sonny, floor-prone. 'Surely you must mean fired?'

Otto stamped his foot impatiently. 'In my head I have the meaning, woman.' He gave her now the same quick dart of suspicion. 'This Luke—he is maybe your lover, hah?'

Sonny laughed, then sat up, legs crossed, chin in hand, elbow on knee, gravely contemplating Luke as he gingerly massaged his fingers. 'Hmm,' she mused, 'that had not occurred to me. He looked so lost and harmless, so under-nourished. I wanted to stroke his hair, make a fuss of him, fatten him up with good wholesome food. But maybe—' She unwound her limbs and rose, smiling, standing before the uneasy object of her speculation. 'Does the idea appeal to you at all?'

Luke ahemmed, aware of three pairs of eyes focused on him keenly, feeling like a slave standing on the auctioneers' block, half expecting the glowering Otto to come and yank open his mouth to examine his teeth and run expert fingers over his thinly distributed muscles; he was further somewhat discomfited by the proximity of a leotarded Sonny, no longer to be looked at with cool fraternal eyes; almost simultaneous with the cornered look of entreaty he gave her to deliver him from this unmanly spectacle with a kind word and a friendly touch of her fingers, he felt the slow certain rise of interest informing his loins and inwardly prayed it did not display itself too ostensibly to the concentrated scrutiny that was being bestowed upon him. Devilment danced in Sonny's eyes as she moved her hands slowly, sensuously over her trim hips, giving him a slow audacious wink which the others could not see.

Otto threw up his hands. 'Out of my hands I wash him,' he said, waddling away out the door. 'It is the good riddance, I think.

I am going to have a drink in the library—' he called back as he went across the hall, hands clasped behind his back.

'A moment, Otto, a moment,' Sonny said after him, and, aside, to Aggie without taking her cool appraising look away from Luke, 'Haven't you work to do, Applebud?'

'Potatoes to peel, carrots to scrape—'

'And beds to make, Mrs Applebud, many beds to make,' Sonny interjected pointedly, straddling a chair.

Aggie stood her ground briefly. 'But you said you wanted an Irish stew for dinner today—'

'Auf wiedersehen, Applebud,' said Sonny sweetly. 'Otherwise you will make me very cross with you—and do remember to suck a peppermint after drinking whiskey—you'll find a packet in the top right-hand drawer next to my homemade marmalade.'

Aggie's fiery face deepened a shade or two and she opened her mouth to utter something in her own defence, but found herself for once speechless and with a rigid rearing of her head and a dignified tug of her smock she flounced out muttering inaudibly.

Sonny laughed gently. 'We adore our Applebud.' She paused, scrutinising him, rubbing her chin slowly along her wrist. 'Did she tell you the full inside story of our little extravaganza, no doubt embellished with touches of native wit and whimsy?'

He nodded. 'I did succeed in extracting a few facts.'

'Do tell!' she urged, adopting a small breathless whisper.

'Well, fact one,' he began, finding it difficult to follow his own line of thought. 'Someone did try to poison someone else here yesterday evening, though exactly which way around I don't know. It was rather a mystery—I mean, a doctor was summoned, and one person, namely Countess Karina or Katy, did undoubtedly end up in hospital feeling distinctly unwell.'

'You are doing very good,' she encouraged as he stopped. 'Do go on.'

'Yes—well,' he obliged, walking up and down to get out of the range of her artillery of allure. 'The precise circumstances are confused. In fact the whole thing is a mass of innuendo and, insinuation, with not a finger raised clearly at anyone, the supposed victim becoming the suspect and go on right down through the list of dramatis personae, numbering precisely three—'

'Do you live in abject squalor?'

'What?' he said, stopping in his stride. 'Oh—er—no, not exactly abject. Sorry to disappoint you. As to the motive, the rationale of it all—'

'Do you ever want to end it all with a bare bodkin?'

'A bare bod—well, no, again not exactly, though there are occasions when I gaze longingly at the bottle of Domestos on top of the lavatory pot.'

'And have you only ravenous rats for company during the long lonely hours of creativity?'

'Oh no—my landlady Mrs Toomes adheres rigidly to the highest standards of hygiene, not a rodent for miles around, and Matt McGuggin down the hall from me is quite the raconteur, despite suffering from a deplorable stammer and being an avid reader of *Playboy,* which he receives surreptitiously from an uncle who's aide-de-camp to an Apostolic Nuncio somewhere in Bishop Auckland—but why, pray?' he asked, stopping and facing her, 'these deep analytical enquiries into the dark recesses of my private life?'

'You see, Luke,' she replied, half rising from the chair, her bottom slung out at a provocative angle, legs braced apart, semi-lidded eyes looking obliquely at him over her shoulder, cheese-caking it for all her delectable worth. 'I have this sudden all-conquering desire to find out about you—a desire that almost amounts to—*lust,*' she ended, breathing the word tremulously.

'Satan, be thou forever before me,' he said with determined heartiness, rubbing his hands together as he resumed his pacing. 'Do not mistake my discretion for lack of ardour—but with your permission, let us now return to the less perilous waters of attempted mayhem—'

'Permission refused,' she said, rising and swaying up to him, hands on hips. 'You, my friend, are an atrocious actor.'

'Oh, I don't know—I was voted best supporting donkey once in our school Nativity play—'

'You play the clown, you play Pulcinello, on with the motley,' she said, coming closer, 'but you are not unmoved by my presence—'

'Very much I am moved by your presence,' he said hoarsely, backing unsteadily away as his pupils came into direct confrontation with her pushing nipples. 'Consider your position, defender of the poor and indigent, eloquent crusader for the preservation of our historical monuments, forever to the front in public services, a tireless doer of good deeds.'

'Precisely,' she murmured placing her hands on his shoulders as he backed ultimately to a standstill against the kitchen cabinet, somewhat rickety on its ancient pins, lined with shining rows of delf. 'I see you as a victim of aesthetic and emotional—deprivation, battling bravely against outrageous fortune to make your voice heard above the roar of the rabble—'

'And Lo, an angel of the Lord appeared unto him,' he managed to croak, hearing the delf rattling as she pressed closer against him.

'Come under my wing, my little sparrow,' she purred with a slight thrilling lisp, caressing his face. 'Rest awhile in the haven of my bosom, poor storm-tossed wanderer,' she murmured, her fingers insistent on his nape. 'Do not take fright, little cockrobin —come and peck me with your little beak, peck, peck, peck—'

'Thy Kingdom come, Thy Will be done on earth,' he gasped, vile visions of a possibly avenging Otto melting away, yielding his face to her breasts. 'Verily, I will go and labour in the vineyards of the Lord.'

'Chained to a soulless task, my poor puffin,' she cooed as he nuzzled her neck. 'You with the intellect of Goethe, the spirit of Schiller, the imagination of Beethoven, the hands of—ooh,' she trembled, 'your hands, mein Lieber, are nobody's but your own . . .'

He sucked her upturned throat like a marauding bee belly-deep in nectar, 'God never closes one door—'

'Peck me,' she commanded, licking his earlobe, nipping it delicately with her teeth. 'Peck, peck, peck.'

'I—will—peck,' he panted, 'while the pecking's good.'

'Do you desire me?' she breathed, fastening around him, half climbing upon him like a squirrel up a tree. 'Do you want to take me—*now*?'

'Bring me my bow of burning gold,' he breathed ecstatic, 'bring me my arrows of desire. I will not cease from mental strife. Till I have built Jerusalem. O Jerusalem! O bold Bill Blake!' he intoned, swept away on a full tide of swooning elation. 'O Jesu, joy of man's desiring! O rare Ben Jonson, thou shouldst be alive at this hour! O fire of life anointing my loins! O blessed horn of Gabriel blasting my senses to the four winds—Oh fucking hell!' he gasped amazed as there came a sudden lurch and cracking of glass as the panels of the cabinet caved in under the weight of their ardour.

'Mutter, Oh Mutter!' Sonny screeched, scrambling away, throwing her arms up about her head as the cabinet tottered and delf came crashing down in a hail about them.

'Duck!' roared Luke, hurtling forward and catching her in a rather spectacular rugby tackle, dragging her clear just seconds ahead of total catastrophe as with a last drunken lurch the cabinet pitched forward to the floor amid a horrendous din of splitting timber and crashing glass, shaking the whole kitchen, sending the light bulb spinning crazily in its socket in the ceiling, making the very foundations groan as if hit by a minor earthquake.

It seemed an interminable time before the world regained its equilibrium and the galaxies ceased swimming crazily before his eyes and his senses came floating back to him and he looked around him, to find himself immediately staring point-blank down the muzzle of an ancient but most effective-seeming blunderbuss which Otto was holding squarely to his forehead.

'You lie, dirty dog,' Otto said very deliberately, finger primed on trigger. 'My food you eat, my drink you drink, you try the rape with our Frau Applebud, now you molest my poor bruised Gretchen, and last you bomb my house.' Otto pushed the weapon closer and Luke felt the cold iron against his brow. 'In my heart I have the mercy for you. A minute only I give you to say the Holy Mary, then you die, dog.'

Otto began counting. Dimly there was the sound of crying and looking over he beheld Aggie wailing hysterically in a corner, face smothered in her smock; with mild puzzled surprise he saw Sonny sitting casually on the edge of the table, swinging a leg languidly, a quite large whiskey in her hand, totally unscathed save for a slight discoloration on her cheek and forehead, which looked rather fetching; she was looking down at him benignly, amused, with the tired affection of a comrade in arms who had come through a major skirmish with him.

'Hello,' she said.

He scrambled to his knees and the gun travelled with him unerringly.

'Hello.'

'Are you all right?' she asked politely.

'Er—umm—I think so, yes,' he said.

She slid down off the table and knelt before him. 'Here,' she said, offering him her glass. 'A drop of this won't go amiss.'

The whiskey burned and considerably restored him. 'Thank you,' he said, handing back the glass.

'You're very welcome.'

Aggie still wailed as Otto continued to count the seconds away in a low guttural growl between formidably strong clenched teeth.

Luke surveyed the wreckage of the cabinet. 'I hope it wasn't an antique.'

'A very recent one,' Sonny said and then turned to Otto. 'Otto, you're not still holding that silly toy, are you?' she said crossly. 'Do put it away, like a good boy.'

'Eye is for eye and tooth is for tooth,' he muttered darkly.

'My eyes and teeth are perfectly intact, Otto, and besides that gun is absolutely useless. It will only make an irritating report if you discharge it.'

'A rabbit I shoot with it only last week—' began Otto in stout defence of his bellicose memento.

'You merely wounded the poor thing,' corrected Sonny. 'I found one minute pellet in its hind quarters. It limped off quite indignantly after such a clumsy attempt on its life.'

'But dead it was,' protested Otto.

'It had died of shock, naturally. You know perfectly well you have to oil the trigger for an hour before even the trigger will work!' She turned to Luke. 'This is a family heirloom, actually,' she said. 'It is quite old, at least early seventeenth century. Our great-great-great-great—oh I don't know how many greats—grandfather fought many a duel with this—he was very hotheaded and always getting embroiled in affairs of honour, usually over buxom married ladies who sat at their windows crocheting exquisite altar cloths. Really, Otto, you shouldn't play about with such delicate mementos—where is your sense of family? Now handle it carefully and put it back over the writing-desk in the library, dear.'

'I have in my heart much family, much honour,' Otto insisted stubbornly, fondling the weapon and looking rather longingly at Luke.

'Do be sensible, Otto,' said Sonny patiently, sitting back on her heels and sipping her drink. 'If you couldn't kill a poor little rabbit with the thing, how are you going to kill a strong young man like Luke?'

Otto's lips curled disdainfully. 'I think I crush him with one finger,' he said, advancing.

'I am most certain you could,' said Luke readily. 'Your marvellous muscularity evokes the highest respect in me.'

'There—your victory is complete and undisputed, dear,' Sonny soothed the squat figure as he glowered down at Luke. 'Our friend accepts defeat magnanimously—'

'Better than that,' Luke put in, 'I embrace it fervently—in fact you could say I demand it and insist on it and you can have it in writing if you like.'

'So do trot along dear,' said Sonny, rising. 'We will join you in a minute for a drink just as soon as our guest gets tidied up.'

'Maybe I get this working with much oil,' mused Otto turning the gun over in his hands. 'And then I kill him—hah?'

'We'll see, Otto dear—we'll see,' said Sonny, pushing him gently out of the door. 'Do let him tidy himself up first. He is such a child, really,' she sighed, turning back as Otto went off grunting and grumbling to himself. 'A dear gentle person at heart.'

'I take your word for it, 'Luke said, clambering unsteadily to his feet. 'I really must be making tracks—there's this dateline I must keep—'

'I can't turn you out looking like that,' Sonny interrupted, taking his arm. 'You must have a shower.'

'You make my head swim with such images of luxury,' he protested. 'Last time I had a shower was in Stoke-under-Lyme when I was sent there to cover the story of a man who had committed bigamy ten times, and I got a tremendous cold out of it, which was nothing to what your man got—they gave him ten years, one for each case of bigamy, which I thought was rather neat and made me realise how imaginative British justice can be under certain circumstances. Now had they given him nine years or eleven years it would have ruined the whole perspective of the thing completely, taken the lyric quality away, but giving the poor bugger ten gave it just that touch of poetic rightness.'

'You're talking tipsy, like you got a bang on the head,' said Sonny, leading him out. 'Take another sip of this,' she ordered, giving him her glass again, 'and then have a nice warm shower—'

'But my dateline—I must be in town by six.'

'I will drive you there myself,' she promised, leading him across the hallway and up a winding staircase. 'You will feel much better and thank me for it, believe me. Come along now—just across the landing at the top—lean on me, there's a good boy.'

He was surprised to find he had swallowed all the whiskey as they zig-zagged upstairs and a most pleasurable feeling of light-headedness pervaded him as they reached the landing and she steered him across to a white-panelled door opposite.

'In here,' she said.

Luke gave her shoulders a brotherly squeeze and started to sing softly:

> 'Wild the lovely pale lilies grow
> in fields of concrete, sand and lime,
> and their lovely magic sow
> in bleeding hearts at closing time—'

'That is a pretty song,' she said, going with him into the floral-tiled high-ceilinged room and closing the door behind them. 'You have a nice clear rounded voice—'

'And a heart of gold,' he said mawkishly, stumbling a little on the smooth marble surface of the floor. 'Did you know that James Joyce had a voice that could outrival the lark in the clear air?' he informed her, wagging a finger at her, then put his hand on his heart and declaimed:

> 'When other lips have told thee
> their tales of love divine—'

Sonny smiled at him rather brilliantly, unobtrusively loosening his jacket. 'Such pretty lines.'

'Bad eyesight and good voices,' said Luke, beholding his own slack foolish face in the mirror. 'A literary disease peculiar to the Gael.' He took up his song again:

> 'And high as God the lilies grow
> little beauties every one
> making me dance from head to toe
> from morning to the set of sun.
> O Come up from Rathangan
> Sweet Mary Mangan
> Come up you fearful girl
> and give us all a whirl

145

Unbuckle your petticoats, darling,
unabashed by lark or starling
Slip out of your finery
all fresh-limbed and winery
Strike me blind with your beauty this minute
Come, don't be a tick, love,
Come clean and come quick, love,
For the sake of the day that's in it.'

'I think that is a very pretty song indeed,' he heard her voice
say close to his ear.

'As pretty as a speckled cow,' he began, holding on to a brass
handrail to steady himself, turning around and finding her. 'Jesus
Christ,' he said, blinking rapidly, rubbing his eyes. 'What happened to your clothes?'

'Oh,' she replied, turning on the water and stretching out a
little foot to test the temperature. 'I decided to take a shower too.'

He was struggling to say something when he looked down and
discovered that he was equally as naked, without the slightest
recollection of having taken off anything.

'Do come on,' she prompted, stepping under the gushing jet
of silvery water and clasping herself with a delighted squeal.
'Oooh—it's just perfect!'

He stood rooted, mute, staring stupidly at her glistening body,
a white blur under the musical splash of water, and was still
opening and shutting his mouth feebly in an effort to speak, when
there sounded a commotion outside in the corridor and next
moment the door flew wide and Babysoft stood framed there,
rainswept and mud-splattered, her hands on her hips, a very
agitated Ranter trying to hold her back and beckoning frantically
at Luke over her shoulder, and in the background Aggie bristling
with outraged indignation, hopping up and down in fury like a
demented queen bee whose hive had been invaded.

'We came to join you for high tea,' announced Babysoft,
leaning nonchalantly against the doorjamb, looking him unhurriedly up and down, grinning. 'Jasus,' she said, extracting
from her mouth a long thin mangled dripping string of gum and
blowing it up into a bubble again, 'I'm mad about the cut of your
clobber, Mister!'

VI

'What diabolical conjunction of circumstances brought *you* here?'

Thus demanded Luke with incongruous loftiness, confronting the ill-timed intruders, an indignant affronted Caesar stamping his foot, stepping forth from the vapours of his ablutions not as much as a shred of toga between his state of Eden nakedness and the interested unbelieving stares that met him; Babysoft, blatantly interested, surveyed him head to foot and lingering middlewards, Ranter all an incredulous half splutter and behind them Aggie hysterical and hilarious peering into the swirling steam, eyes blinking and dilating, a whole seven Sundays of wonder running up and down her face.

'Is a man not to know a morsel of sweet solitude anywhere on this demented globe?' Luke cried.

'I tried to hold her back, sure as God,' Ranter attested, swallowing hard, looking studiously unaffected as Sonny swam nakedly into view behind Luke. 'I did me best to reason with her.'

'Welcome, people,' greeted Sonny placing a casual hand on Luke's shoulder, aureoled nymph appearing out of a cloud. 'I hope I didn't ask you all to tea and then forgot about it, something I do quite often, I'm afraid—'

'Holy Virgin,' screeched Aggie clapping a startled hand to her mouth. 'She hasn't got a screed on either!'

'These methinks,' said Luke aside to his smiling companion, patting her nestling hand protectively, 'are dastardly brigands and marauders come down from the Wicklow mountains with vile intentions of rape and plunder and black murder in their hearts.'

'Oh, really?' piped Sonny nuzzling her chin in the hollowy nook of his shoulder and regarding them with marvellous amity. 'I have never been raped and plundered and murdered all at once—the oddest things are happening to me today.'

'I never saw such a thing in my whole natural life!' gulped Aggie.

'Widows' memories, Mrs Ever-Ready,' drawled Babysoft resuming her laconic chewing leaning hip against doorjamb. 'Wouldn't you like to take that home for a souvenir, Agatha? Here,' she said taking a big fleecy towel from the rack and throwing it to Luke. 'Cover up your beauty spot before gaping Genevieve here has a heart attack. She's panting like a bleeding train as it is.'

'Thank you very much,' he said formally, accepting the robe, draping it around his waist and turning gravely to Sonny. 'Perhaps it would be wise if you were to follow suit—'

'Follow *suit*!' cried Aggie doubling up, holding her side as demon laughter seized her. 'Jesus, that's a good one—follow *suit*!'

'Er—would anyone like a fag?'

Ranter, nervously enquiring, all thumbs, fishing out a packet and dropping several, fumbling with matches failing to ignite.

'Maybe, if you don't mind me saying so, maam,' prompted Babysoft, putting herself between Sonny and Ranter's enslaved line of vision, 'you'd best slip into something casual like. Poor Ranter's oul' ticker isn't too dusty isn't that so, Mr O'Rourke?'

'For Jasus' sake mind me corns,' growled Ranter as Babysoft trod deliberately on his toes then glanced furtively at Sonny, pulling at the peak of his cap in deference. 'Carry on, maam,' he said quickly, finally lighting up a cigarette and puffing furiously. 'Sure amn't I a married man meself these donkey years, and in my line of business you come across things that would make the hair stand on your head—in a manner of speaking—'

'It would make something stand anyway,' Babysoft lisped toying with her chewing gum again. 'In a manner of speaking.'

'What *is* your line of business, Mr O'Rourke?' Sonny coming forward with genuine curiosity standing before him brushing back a wet gleaming swathe of hair.

Ranter struggling to speak, at least to shift his eyes from where they were dwelling glued. 'Pardon, maam?'

'I am interested in gauging the environmental pressures which our modern materialistic acquisitive society imposes on people employed in varying professions. You see, Mr O'Rourke—'

Sonny speaking with quiet animation in a normal after-dinner voice, one knee slanted at an easy conversational angle, giving him the full uninterrupted attention of her eyes, the cool white bare benefit of everything else.

'You see, I am painstakingly building up a dossier on the working habits and hazards of the different social categories as a preliminary for a doctoral thesis on the probable anthropological implications inherent in varying work-styles, and candidly you look like just the man to help me.'

'Wha—?' gulped Ranter. 'He's your man, all right,' nodded Babysoft, touching the arm of the mesmerised Ranter. 'They don't call him the demon begetter for nothing.'

'Frankly,' Sonny pursued seriously, 'you look a very forth-coming man.'

'Forthcoming?'

Another convulsive guffaw from Aggie. 'Forth—coming!'

'You look like a man with a fund of knowledge at his finger-tips,' added Sonny trustingly, laying her hand on his arm.

'Whe—where's the jacks, maam?'

Ranter mumbling, backing away, cigarette falling from power-less fingers, locked eyes still nipple-held, not daring though far gone with longing to dart downwards past her dusky pearl of beachsmooth midriff—

'Pardon, maam, but I must u—u—use your toilet—'

'Why, certainly, Mr O'Rourke.'

Sonny putting her bright face up to him, taking his arm with utmost courtesy, girl-guide resolutely leading an elderly person across a busy heedless thoroughfare. 'Let me show you the way.'

'Oh Jasus forgive you, maam!'

Ranter recoiling, pulling away as from burning tongs, raising his arms before his face, warding off her silky buttercup finger-brushes. 'And me with a houseful, maam, all steps of stairs, and old enough to be your father.'

'Steps of stairs, Mr O'Rourke?'

Sonny hesitant, drawing nearer to him, far from flaunting save only as lilies in the lilting laziness of summer.

'A joke's a joke, maam, and nobody can say I'm not broad-minded, but bejasus you must draw the line somewhere.'

'Draw the line, Mr O'Rourke? What line?'

Sonny's face full of concentration pondering and Babysoft giving a hard brittle gin-and-tonic laugh.

'It isn't the bleeding clothesline, that's for sure. Ah, Ranter me fine upstanding citizen, it's far from the smell of pissy nappies and Cow-'n-Gate you are now, and the two eyes bulging out of your head as if they were on stalks! Oh, if Gertie could only see you now,' and slapping her hip and baying forth in raucous sawdust turn-of-the-century music-hall voice:

> 'I'm only poor Dan the workingman, maam,
> I'm only the poor workingman Dan, maam,
> but though me conscience it is killing
> if you ask me I'd be willing
> to serve you the best way I can, maam,
> to serve you the best way I can.'

Babysoft with a flourish falling on one knee, doffing her imaginary top hat, fluttering her eyelids accepting the rude plaudits. 'And for my next turn, ladies and gentlemen—'

Ranter feeling his way along the wall looking from one to the other of the grinning grimacing faces that were turned on him, his eyes horrific. 'It's an effing madhouse I'm after falling into, bejasus!' he roared, as he stumbled and slithered downstairs, holding grimly on to his cap, thin face apoplectic. 'The malediction of Jasus fall on you Sheridan, for inveigling me into this hellhole of a respectable hoorhouse!'

'What a funny little man,' mused Sonny leaning over the banisters. 'I do hope he finds the toilet in time.'

'Sure there isn't a morsel of harm in poor oul' Ranter,' Babysoft spoke up stoutly. 'We've been out drinking all day and he never as much as laid a finger on me. More's the pity. Still and all, it's a change to be treated like a lady for once and not have men falling all over you stuttering and stocious with gargle.'

Sonny stopped before her, extending her hand. 'Hello. I don't think we have been introduced. I'm Sonny. Glad you could come. Are you staying for tea?'

Babysoft shook hands grinning. 'Sure I wouldn't miss it for the world. It's better than the pictures any day.'

Sonny's smile became vague, remote. 'Splendid. Maybe you'd

care for a drink while you're waiting? Applebud dear, will you see to our guest? I must finish my shower. Coming, Luke?'

'I feel definitely anti-water at the moment,' replied Luke with a dark dour look at Babysoft standing insolently by, chewing and blowing gum bubbles. 'Just give me my clothes and I'll be going, we'll *all* be going—'

'And the Lord said unto Moses—' Babysoft eyed him coolly, her close-cropped head oddly heroic, making unmalicious mockery of his puny bony-ribbed masculinity, a wary kindliness softening the city-yard glitter of her eyes.

'Don't be tiresome, Luke,' said Sonny fretfully, stooping to rub the sole of her foot on the end of his loin-draping towel. 'You practically gatecrashed your way into my heart and home. You pickpocketed my affections when I was off-guard and not looking. You are not more than a thief and uninvited guest yourself and the least I am entitled to is to ask you to stay for tea. Applebud dear, do see to our guests and lock all the doors.'

'What about my clothes?' Luke cried.

'Borrow some of Otto's,' she called back. 'Where is your initiative, my friend?'

Aggie redeyed sore-nostrilled from manic mirth looked up. 'What would Mister Otto say if he knew? He'd go berserk.'

'Dear Aggie, he *is* berserk. Everyone in this house is in a constant state of berserkdom.'

Luke tied the towel in a tight sailor-knot round his waist, patting Aggie's shoulder comfortingly as they descended, the sandals of Babysoft flapping and slapping behind them on the stairs.

'It's a quare oul' shell of a hole all the same, isn't it?' Babysoft remarked looking around her as they reached the hall. 'You'd want to be steeped in whiskey to spend the night here.'

Luke shivered as they crossed the bare hard boards. 'You haven't told me how you got here, Granuaile.'

'Divine guidance. Said a prayer to St Anthony—you know, the lost-and-found fella—he brought us here.'

'Then he must be Satan's second-in-command.'

'There's gratitude for you, and you about to have your manhood tore away from you by that little angel of mercy upstairs.'

'You ought to rinse out that mouth of yours with disinfectant!'

Aggie puffed and huffed, throwing a venomous glare at the younger woman.

'Ah now, Agatha, don't be like that. Sure that's no way to talk to a neighbour's child.'

Luke looked at both of them with new interest. 'So you two ladies know each other?'

'Sure wasn't Agatha me Mammy's handmaiden and me Da's bosom pal. And I mean bosom.'

Babysoft's cruel young laugh echoed in the bleak hallway, striking barbed at the stiff shoulders of Aggie, jaw rigid with distaste. 'It's strangled at birth you should have been with your Mother's navel-cord, bringing sin and ruination with you everywhere you set foot!'

'Jealousy is a terrible thing altogether, and you've cause to be jealous, Aggie, God love you, no longer able to prod a man into temptation and an oul' face on you that would turn back a funeral from Glasnevin. Ah, gone are the dear dead days beyond recall for the likes of you, Aggie, but let's all have a drink for the sake of auld lang syne.'

'Divil a drop you'll get in this house, Hortensia Brogan! Take yourself back to where you came from and let decent folk go about their business in peace!' Aggie swept on into the carnage of her kitchen, face mottled with rage mingled with fear at Babysoft's recalling of the indecorous past.

'Isn't that the sourpussed spiteful begrudging oul' faggot for you! You'd think she had a permanent seat at the right hand of the Lord, bejasus, looking down her nose at people, and many's the time I caught her barefaced carrying on with me oul' ram of a Da in the tenement in Brunswick Street and me poor Mammy tossing and turning in the height of her labour in the other room and meself just a chisler not knowing what it was all about but seeing Queen Agatha beyant turning up her bare arse to me Da accidental on purpose while she was suppose to be performing the corporal works of mercy for me Mammy, and the day I came in early from Jacob's and caught them at it while me Mammy was asleep—me oul' demon of a Da working away like billyo screwed into her, bejasus, under the picture of the Sacred Heart.'

Babysoft's eyes had gone strangely dark and burning, her face blanched and bitter and suddenly love-famished in the falling gloom of the great gaunt hall, standing a little away from him alone, unattached to anything in the present, her mouth twisted in a tight furious smile.

'What a traumatic experience for poor little Hortensia,' murmured Luke wanting to take her hand but then unwilling to intrude into her mood. Then, her smile loosening the hard lines of her face, 'Sure I'm not begrudging them—a bit of what you fancy does you good they say. Only I hate people putting themselves up to be what they're not and never have been and not wanting to look over their shoulders at what they were once. Makes me blood boil. And less of the Hortensia, if you don't mind.'

'Your real name?'

'Sure it's a very common name down around Brunswick Street and Prussia Street, along with Olivia and Carmelita and Marcellina. Me Mammy went to the pictures a terrible lot. Where's that Ranter till I get him to take me out of this hole and back to the pub before I pass out of me standing for a drink.'

'Patience, sweet maid. All is not lost. Behind you.'

Otto was approaching, dressed in a long flowing floor-reaching deep velvet gown, a fat cigar clamped in his mouth, carrying a tray on which reposed a squat bottle of cognac and several glasses, coming up to them ceremoniously, bowing. 'Great pleasure it would give me for us to join drinks together in the library.'

'And great pleasure we have in accepting,' responded Luke bowing in return. 'May I introduce Miss Hortensia?'

Babysoft bristled. 'Now cut it out—'

Otto came forward, took her hand and kissed it, silencing her instantly. 'It is the pleasure my own and this way please.'

Otto padding ahead of them a regal gnome in emperor robe, head held high going through a large oak doorway into a panelled room full of old leather and everywhere the sight and smell and taste of books big and small thin and fat, crooked and straight, aslant and upright, old and new, bright and faded, reaching up to the ceiling on creaking sagging overburdened shelves and books proliferating all over the floor like plants gone wild and unchecked, heaped in swaying tottering pyramids leaning drunkenly against walls, lying at haphazard angles athwart each other a yellow sleeve here a red jacket there a splash of bright vermilion on sombre brown half-opened volumes spread like easy courtesans ready for the wooing, a Fingal's cave of books echoing with the myriad voices of centuries, dusty with wisdom seen now in the dying January evening dusklight filtering through the cathedral-length windows and by the light of logs spitting forth red tongues in the immense giant's-mouth of a fireplace.

Babysoft held grimly onto Luke's arm determined not to shiver as they stood ankledeep in books, muttering to him out of the tight slanted corner of her mouth, 'I don't like it here—let's scarper.'

Luke whispered back, standing firm and straight and as dignified as his towel-wrapping would allow. 'The man is our host—it would be an act of the utmost discourtesy—'

'Discourteous me arse—he looks like Bela Lugosi—'

'Besides, there's the drink—pure cognac if I'm not mistaken.'

At this news Babysoft released her hold on his arm, clearing her throat, stoically cheerful again. 'Ah yes, I was forgetting that —might put a bit of life into me—not a bad place really, if it was dusted up a bit.'

'Please to sit, if you can,' invited Otto, pouring and handing round drinks unsmiling but enormously affable, treading his way through the chaos with easy intimacy, finding a sofa mainly un-cluttered and sitting down lifting his glass in salute. 'Your health I drink and the power to your elbow.'

'Cheers.'

Babysoft looked around her swamped with awe. 'Do you read much, sir?' she asked brightly.

'All the time when I can,' Otto replied pleased at her chirpy interest. 'Books don't go away like people. All the time I am with books. I touch them like women.'

'Is that so now?' Babysoft rejoined uncertain. 'Ah well, sure I suppose they're company for you in this big house. Tell me now,' she continued sitting down, smoothing out her skirt sedately underneath her; 'did you ever read *The Lives of the Saints* or *Old Moore's Almanac*? We had them two books at home in Brunswick Street—me Mammy had a first cousin who was a big shot in the Vincent de Paul Society in the way of getting things buckshee you know, secondhand clothes and pieces of furniture and things like that that the gentry thrun out—and one day he brought around these two books and asked me Mammy if she could find some use for them—of course me Da made a laugh of her and said they'd come in handy to light the fire with on a cold morning—shit ignorant he was, me Da—but with the gang of us me Mammy said the books would be educational like; I read them till I was nearly blind—all about the saints mortifying themselves when they'd nothing better to do, God love them, the things you have to do to be a saint, it would put you off—and the things that your man Old Moore wrote about—sure he'd put the fear of God into you: earthquakes and disasters and boiling water coming up from the ocean and wiping out the land and great big black holes opening up and swallowing everybody wholesale—if you had a weak stomach at all sure you'd have nightmares.' Babysoft dived at her drink in sudden contrition, seeing the bemused expression on Otto's face opposite her as if a loud gong had struck close to his ear leaving him deaf. 'Does he understand me, do you think?' she whispered very audibly to Luke as she continued to smile and nod over at their host.

'I very much doubt it.'

Babysoft nodded sagely. 'Ah, it's on account of him being foreign, I suppose, the poor man. Don't be letting me do all the talking,' she said growing irascible. 'Don't just sit there like Ben Hur with a towel wrapped round you—recite him some poems or something and keep the ball rolling.'

'We don't have to do anything except be polite.'

A storm grew in Babysoft's face. 'Polite is it? Where's the politeness in sitting around half-naked guzzling gargle and not opening your mouth? Are you accusing me of not being polite? Let me tell you I was brought up on good manners, they were bet into me since I can remember, we were never allowed to touch a crust of bread off the table till our Da and Ma had theirs first, it was always 'yes, sir' and 'yes, maam' 'no, sir' and 'no, maam' in our place, I'm telling you. We knew our manners and don't you go all high and mighty and say I'm sitting on them now.'

'If perchance that should be so, then I assure you they are the most exquisite of manners and greatly to be envied and admired.'

Babysoft tossed her drink down contemptuously waving him away as the stupefied Otto looked on uncomprehending.

'You and your smarmy talk cuts no butter with me. You're not dealing with poor gormless Rosie now and she so easy taken in by you that night that she went around singing next morning like a bloody thrush gone mad.'

A fine rush of blood had warmed the pallor of her cheeks, her eyes dark and hot snapping at him like whips, he thrilling and tingling at her superb anger, swinging his glass aloft in the air as though conducting an orchestra spurring her on to higher scales of wrath, leading her through more intricate loops of disdain—

'Effing men only good for one thing, get in and out like a flash thinking the only natural state for a woman to be in is flat on her back, thinking she does all her best talking that way, thinking she's giving him all she's got, his little hour of kingdom come, and all the while she's lying there under him she's thinking what a poor eejit he is whooping and squealing like a little boy on a hobbyhorse, tuppence for a ride, sir, tuppence for a ride—'

'A little drink we have, Fräulein, ja?' Otto's coarse guttural voice strangely paternal stemming her low-humming rage, the glowering mist lifting from her eyes, turning to him with a glad swift motion of her head holding out her glass—

'Sure you're a gentleman born, sir, a gentleman born. Don't be minding me—I don't know what I do be saying from one minute to the next, truth of God. Ah, thanks, sir.' A high lilt of a laugh as she held her glass up seeing flames leaping in the amber depths. 'That stuff would make the poor corpses beyant in Glasnevin lep out of the ground and start doing a four-hand reel and the high-caul cap.'

'You make the joke, ja, Fräulein? You dance for me, ja? You do the Salome for Uncle Otto, ja?'

Babysoft arch and puckish preened herself, sipping her drink with delicate decorous little sallies. 'I don't know any fancy stuff, mind you—but I did win a few cups and medals and a weekend down in Butlins for the jig and the hornpipe when I was with the nuns.'

Turning brighteyed, cherrylipped, to Luke, jumping up, one hand on her hip the other above her head poised and waiting.

'Do you know "The Wind That Shakes The Barley"?'

'Like the back of my hand.'

Luke began humming the repetitive gambolling heathery tune, tapping his glass on a tabletop, and Babysoft taking up the rhythm with voice and feet clear and light as Otto swept books aside making a space for her, clapping his hands in broadbeamed delight.

'Dance, Fräulein, dance the jig, ja, and the hornypipe!'

Babysoft turning and twisting, agile slimwaisted highflown in the dance, twirling in swift circles of rapture, sailorboy countenance lit by the logflames, short skirt riding up her strong coltish legs beating out a chaotic anthem of merriment in the tangled mist of musty leathery learning.

'Mein Gott, Fräulein—gut, gut, oh ja!'

Otto flung books wildly about out of her way to widen her stage, bellowing out encouragement an amiable satyr stuttering and stumbling in the wake of a sturdy-limbed gazelle dancing bright rings round him in the firedance, floundering and tottering after her, chortling and lavishing her with praises unintelligible as Luke faltering on the edge of the charmed circle tried to keep pace but falling behind in the dance, watching Babysoft spinning past on and on faster ever faster, blurring crazily before him—

'Oh Mammy!'

A sudden injudicious moment tripping over a protruding corner of a book sent her slewing against Otto and the two in a tangle of limbs crashed backwards over the sofa into a precarious pyramid of books starting a landslide.

'Oh Jasus—me effing back is broke!'

Babysoft upended, legs flailing flung ceilingwards, black triangle of knickers taut over writhing buttocks, squealing with shrill girlish laughter, thrashing about and Otto likewise scuttled, thrown across her convulsed with gaiety and then her reproving delighted laugh pealing in discovery—'Oh, Uncle Otto!'

Otto squealing hysterical under her brash mocking marauding fingers slipping beneath his loosened robe—

'Oh Fräulein, ja, ja, oh please, ja!'

Babysoft half pushing him off sitting up crude and friendly tickling him playfully in the ribs.

'I'll ya, ya, ya you, Franz Josef, and you with not a stitch on under your Alice-blue gown!'

Otto twisting about giving little guttural snorts of ecstasy under Babysoft's murderous finger-jabbing and tickling poking and pinching him as though playing with a giant teddybear squirming in agonised transports of pleasure, the books slipping and sliding underneath them as sand-dunes demolished by wind, she catching his ear, yanking it towards her, whispering something into it, sending him off on new spasms of imbecilic laughter, her fingers unmerciful ribbing his flesh, her skirt riding waist-high, plump thighs careless and free, and Luke a little marooned, beholding their animal antics wistful and weary, an obscure regret working in him.

Babysoft struggled to her feet laughing, unhurriedly, wriggling her skirt into place, coming across the room wavering, putting her arms around Luke's neck fondly rubbing noses with him, the brandy strong and pungent on her breath.

'Ah, don't look all sad and left out in the cold, Lukey love. Sure don't you know you're the apple of my eye, even if you're a bit sour. Com'ere to me now and I'll sing a little song for you.'

Babysoft's mouth close to his own crooning only for him:

> 'I know where I'm going
> and I know who's going with me,
> I know who I love
> but the divil know who I'll marry.'

Her voice was soft and heavy, trickling into his ear. 'Do you like that, Lukey, do you? Ah listen.

> "He buys me stockings of silk,
> shoes of fine green leather,
> combs to brush my hair
> and a ring for every finger."

Take that sad look off your face, Lukey love, sure amn't I singing me bloody heart out for you?

> "Some say he's black
> but I say he's bonny
> and I would leave them all
> to go with my love Johnny
> yes I would leave them all
> for my handsome winsome Johnny." '

Babysoft nuzzled his neck with odd tentative gentleness and sad little flurries of kisses down his neck and along the bony ridge of his shoulder.

'How can you be downhearted with such a beautiful song? Lift up your heart and praise the Lord.'

Cocking her head to one side, rushing round singing to herself, all the pub-bedlam of the land ringing in her ears:

'I took me mot up to the zoo
to show her the lions and the kangaroo
and she asked me to show her me oul' cockatoo
outside the zoological gardens.'

The fire warmly licking Luke's bare bumcheeks as he stood before it, Ranter appeared in the doorway, cap at a fighting angle over one eye, beholding the scene with monkish disapproval as though by mischance wandering into a temple of profane pagan rites. 'I can't find me way out of this effing place.'

'Ah Ranter, friend tried and true, there you are. You're puce with the cold. Come in and have a gargle for the love and honour of Jasus, sure we might all be dead and buried tomorrow. We never know the hour or the minute. Take off your cap itself before you're got dead in it.'

Babysoft caught hold of Ranter's hands, dragged him over the threshold, putting a glass before him, splashing brandy into it, pulling him over to Otto still half submerged in books nodding and smiling, in vigorous bonhomie stretching forth a hand.

'Isn't he a tonic? Mad as Mulligan's effing donkey, but a scream just the same.'

Otto looked up at them bemused, trying to convey his goodwill plus the state of his prone predicament and Ranter touching his cap-peak bent to offer his own hand.

'How's it going, oul' son?'

'Ja, up with me, nein? Gut, ja, gut. My hand you pull?'

'What's that again, chiner? What's he trying to say?'

'Give him a hand up,' said Luke coming forward.

'Oh, certainly so, oul' son. Sure I had an uncle meself and he used to suffer terrible from the oul' arteritis.'

Ranter clasped the other man's hand in a firm brotherly grasp, and pitching promptly forward as Otto attempted to hoist himself up, grunting loudly under the impact of Ranter's head butting him in the abdomen, taking the wind out of them both, and Babysoft's high hoarse chortle of gaiety.

'Mind yourself Ranter or you'll damage Gertie's pride and joy!'

Ranter gasped on his knees face red with exertion, retrieving his cap. 'He has a pull on him bejasus like Johnny Weissmuller—near took me arm out of its socket! Get behind me can't you and give us a lift.'

The three of them joined forces, hauling Otto crane-like to his feet, setting the teutonic cavalier on the perpendicular where he stood splayfooted holding hands with the puffing redfaced Ranter, covering all three of them in a benign glow, nodding his wrestler's head vigorously up and down muttering thanks—

'Danke schön, meine Brüder, danke schön! A drink we toast for the old sake of time!'

Babysoft gone again on a high giggle flounced about holding hands, skipping once more on a singing pavement in quayside shadows:

> 'Ring-a-ring-a-rosie
> a pocketful of posie
> asha-asha we all fall down!
> Skinny-me-Link melodeon legs
> umbrella feet
> went to the pictures and couldn't get a seat
> When the pictures started
> Skinny-me-Link farted
> That was the end of poor Skinny-me-Link
> and his umbrella feet.'

'Jasus,' she turned on Luke, 'you'd think all belonging to you had just died! Will you take that long face off you before it cracks every bloody mirror in the house.'

'You are the last and only wonder of the world, Hortensia, lily fair and beautiful, gilding the shallow rock of my existence—'

'Less of the bloody Hortensia—I warned you before about calling me that—don't think I'm here to be made a laughing-stock of—I saw the time I wouldn't pass the time of day with the likes of you.' Babysoft hardeyed and brittle again measuring the size of him disdainfully. 'Hortensia bejasus! I never forgave me Mammy for calling me that, and I won't stand the likes of you saying it to me face.'

'I meant no disrespect, O maid of many moods—'

'Then stop talking like someone out of a bleeding play and act your age.'

'Do not I implore ask so cruel a price, madam, for if I am to indeed act my age I would have to revert to rompers and a teating-bottle, and then would I truly be unmanned.'

'Ah, you're not half bad after all—a bit of a thick, mind you, oh yes definitely, a bit of a gobshite in spite of all your grand talk but not half bad at the back of it all.'

Ranter eyes twinkling under the peaked cap face slowly flushing with fraternal fervour and brandy placed a comradely hand on Otto's shoulder and his voice uneven but ardent:

'Brothers all beneath the skin
onward let us venture and win
and free from vain pride and foolish hate
I wait for you, brother, at the pearly gate.
Yellow, black, red or brown
it matters not when the chips are down
and we stand trembling before the throne
of Judgement, each one of us alone.
O before that last eternal rest
I clasp you, brother, to my breast,
mother and child, man and woman,
in certain hope of the Second Coming.'

Otto crying freely, tears flowing fast, thumped his chest in an agony of brotherly response and to Ranter's abrupt dismay clasped him impulsively to his bosom amid spluttering protestations of undying fraternity as Ranter struggled trying to dodge the huge moist kisses raining down upon him.

'Ah now for Jasus' sake oul' son, hold on—'

'Mein Bruder, ja, mein Bruder!'

Otto convulsed with manly concord and deepwelling tearful affection gurgling incoherently, bear-hugging the recalcitrant Ranter thumping the thin tweeded shoulders of his companion.

'Myself it is I kill for mein Bruder—oh ja, ja! A drink I toast for the liberty, ja, the equality, ja, and the maternity, oh ja, ja!'

Ranter panting perilously close to apoplectic explosion: 'Will someone get this fucking maniac off me before he smothers me to death? Oh for the love and honour of Jasus lay off, will you— a man of your age—is it quare he is, or what?'

Ranter getting one hand free desperately clung on to his cap, twisting his head around to the languid two at the fireplace in a furious signal of distress as Otto half lifted him off the floor lost in ecstasies of platonic fervour, and Babysoft going to the rescue of Ranter, her rough musical laugh stepping between them, separating the reluctant and the fervent with a gay push sending Otto tottering but smiling still through great splashing tears.

'Give him air before you crush the poor sod. Sure he's only being friendly, Ranter—he meant no harm—did you, Uncle Otto love? Ah, there now, look at him, smiling all over like a baby, all snots and tears, not a bit of harm in him—You wouldn't want to mind these foreigners, Ranter—they do get all worked up over bugger all—give him a bar or two of Mother Machree and he'll fall asunder altogether bejasus—Mind the holy water, Uncle Otto —ah, don't be spilling it all over the place—here, give it to me for safe keeping, you effing oul' eejit—When you're smiling, Keep on smiling, for the Whole World Smiles With You—'

Taking a decanter from the tame obedient fingers of Otto, putting it to her lips taking a quick sip. 'You can say what you like but you can't beat rich friends, even if they do look like first cousins to Fu ManChu and the Hunchback of Notree Dam!'

Putting out a hand to steady the wavering Otto, pursing her lips, stooping forward to plant a large moist resounding kiss succulent on his bald shining pate and proceeding to prattle forth prettily:

'Come to the grotto, Otto,
let's say an Ave together.
Let's have fun as our motto, Otto,
and roll in the hay together.
We'll say a decade of the Rosary, Otto,
while I take off me hosiery, Otto,
and when the Angelus chimes at six
we'll be up to our eyes in all sorts of tricks.
For as the holy man said
sending sheep's eyes towards the bed—
them that do pray together
with themselves do play together.
Oh I love the man who's heaven-sent
strong and upright and not a bit bent.

So come to the grotto, Otto,
let's say an Ave,
we'll go to the grotto, Otto,
and come like bejasus all day—'

Ending on a high hoarse-throated giggle, tweaking Otto's blunt wide-nostrilled nose, skipping away waving the decanter up and down like a beacon as Otto tottered after her, deep-bellied grunts of pleasure coming from him drawing a wet anticipatory wrist across his mouth ogling her owlishly.

Sonny came into the room soft-sandalled in a plain white satin gown, small pert highcheeked face unsurprised, calmly smiling, trailing a long black ebony cigarette-holder behind her in languid fingers frail smoke wisping from it, now and then lifting it dreamily to her lips inhaling, imperceptibly strolling around the room as if wandering through a stage setting, flicking flurries of ash, patently remote and ephemeral walking ghostlike up to Luke, cool and amused, 'You, my rugged Adonis, my endearing Endymion, are wanted rather urgently on the telephone.'

'Ah, my esteemed friend Mulligan, no doubt, wondering what the hell happened to my deadline.'

'He uses the most ingenious profanities emphatically enriched by an accent as indigenous as the smell of the Liffey.'

'My friend Mulligan, indubitably. I wonder what did happen to my deadline?'

'I did.'

'Of course. A drop of brandy now to fortify myself against Mr Mulligan's broadsides. And where may I take the call?'

'All manner of places, but I would recommend the room immediately to your right as you leave here, a few paces up the hall. There you will enjoy absolute privacy and a wine cabinet besides.'

'Arcady revisited. What did you tell Mulligan, by the way?'

'That you were still delving deep into the murky waters of our little scandal, entirely in possession of all the salient facts.'

'The only salient fact I am in total possession of right now is that I am distinctly close to inebriation—Mulligan has a most disagreeable knack of smelling one's breath even over the telephone, as if endowed with one of the least attractive aspects of ESP.'

'I am ready to drive you into town whenever you are,' said Ranter.

'I'd better take the call first.'

'Me heart bleeds for you, but I must go and have a piss.' Ranter pulling his cap forward again shambled off across the hall, hands thrust into overcoat pockets, whistling forlornly to console himself and Luke entered the indicated room, to be greeted by the verbal tirade already erupting from the dangling telephone on a table beside a huge canopied fourposter bed.

Luke drew apart the doors of a charming insignificant little cabinet directly under the table, merry with bottles, choosing one for its bright warm cherry-red cork, opening it, catching the escaping musk-rich odour sweet in the nostrils, a drop of dark purple fullness on the tongue spreading serene down the throat, sitting cross-legged on the floor slanting an ear to the vibrating mouthpiece, drawing back a little in distaste from the vocal fusillade—

'. . . not paying you to go on a screwing spree out there in some Gothic hoorhouse in Howth laughing up your cuff at me—What's going on—is it deaf you are or what? Hello, hello,—am I talking to myself? Sheridan, you hoor's melt, can you hear me?'

'This is the Fustenhalter residence—who's speaking, please?' Luke spoke drowsily into the slightly swaying phone, rolling the wine sensuously about on his tongue.

A bull-like bellow of futile rage blasted into the room. 'Sheridan! You conglomerated shit of a hoor! Don't try to hoodwink me. I know your snakey sub-cultural voice!'

'Ah, Matthew. How strange. Just as I was about to contact you.'

'Contact my arse. I've been trying to ring you all afternoon till I'm blue in the face!'

'Just this instant, Matthew, I was seized with a sudden overwhelming impulse to hear your voice.'

'What's so sudden or overwhelming about that? You're working for me, remember. You're supposed to be out on a job.' An abrupt pause. 'Ah. So that's it, is it? You've been on *the* job again, have you—and on my shagging time?'

'This is psychic, Matthew, you ringing me just now. As I entered the room you were the only single thought in my mind.'

'Where are you—in the jacks?'

'As a matter of fact, Matthew, I'm in a rather nice bedroom—'

'And *I* was the only one on your mind? Have you been hiding your true nature from me all these years, Sheridan?'

'My true nature. Funny you should bring that up, Matthew. That is precisely what I should like to talk over with you—'

'We'll be talking over your social security cards if you don't come up with the story I sent you out to get. It will only be fit for the mortuary by the time you bring it in.'

'Now, now, Matthew—don't lose control. Things are working up to a nice climax, actually—'

'That's good, that is—that's bloody good—working up to a climax. Is that what you've been doing all day, Sheridan—working up to a climax? How many times, you get—how many times, eh?'

'I have been struggling with dark imponderable forces all day.'

'I bet you have—trying to keep your trousers on. Now listen to me, you consolidated shit—I ought to see a psychiatrist, I know, but for old time's sake I'm going to let my heart rule my head just one more time.'

'Matthew, thy name should be Brutus, the noblest of them all—'

'Shut up and listen. It's too late now to make the evening edition—there's a rumour about some millionaire ex-Jesuit setting up a secret French-letter factory somewhere in Mallow.'

'Sounds somewhat esoteric.'

'They say he escaped from a Swiss lunatic asylum last year but has already filed exclusive patent rights to his product—'

'Matthew, if you will but lend an ear—'

'It's probably a hoax got up by one of his ex-mistresses or else a frustrated daily communicant who feels he's missing out on something, but I'll use it as a filler—'

' "For we are born in others' pain and perish in our own".'

'What's that you're mumbling out of you? Never mind. Now listen, Dostoevsky, I want you to bring in that story for to-morrow morning's early edition—get it? I want you here in this office by ten o'clock this evening—ten o'clock sharp, or so help me Jasus you'll be walking on your uppers tomorrow.'

'Matthew!' A high imperative moan mounting almost to a screech.

'What's going on—what the hell are you moaning about? You sound like someone with a hot poker up his arse.'

'I have been wrestling with my soul all day, Matthew.'

'What? What's that you said?'

'All day, Matthew. I have been engaged in a titanic conflict all day with the dark centrifugal forces of my inner self.'

'Now don't come the hound with me, Sheridan Le Fanu.'

'And I have come to a certain conclusion, Matthew.'

An enraged spluttering roar goaded into incoherence, and behind eyes serenely closed Luke easily visioned the veins standing out thickcorded on that bloated bullfrog throat, plainly caught the splash of whiskey in a glass lifted to jerking foaming mouth. 'You skinny runt-arsed shit-yellow little bastard.'

'My life up to now has been an astounding failure, Matthew.'

A gasp incredulous overtaken by a quick sigh of relief, the gurgling of more leisurely whiskey-slugging, a patronising purring snigger. 'Are you only realising that now?'

'Mine has been a protracted odyssey, a stationary journey in search of my Father.'

Uncertainty creeping into the bluff blustering voice. 'Am I on the right line? Is that you at the other end, Sheridan?'

'Who am I? I am Orestes.'

'Who?'

'I am Telemachus.'

'I can't hear you properly.'

'I am Jason.'

'Jason who, for Jasus' sake?'

'I am likewise Stephen Dedalus.'

'You are likewise fucking mad.'

'Wandering the earth forever. Lonely as a cloud. In perennial pursuit of my Father.'

'Look, you haven't got a Father. The poor man's been dead and gone this many a day. Rheumatic fever, wasn't it? Now less of the guru caper, Sheridan. What have you found out so far?'

'Many things, Matthew. Even in the sojourn of a single day I have found out many things.'

'Good, good. Now you're talking. Shoot.'

'Yea and verily I say unto thee, in the fall of a single leaf there reposits a boundless universe of knowledge and truth.'

'Forget the poetry, Percy Bysshe—just give me the facts.'

'I am strangely joyful and full of peace, Matthew.'

Again the baited baleful bellicose bellow causing the swaying pendulum of the mouthpiece to vibrate visibly. 'Listen, I don't give a fiddler's fuck if you're breaking bread with Columcille himself in his rowingboat. All I want from you are the facts.'

'I have reached journey's end, Matthew.'

'Which is at the head of the dole queue rapid if you don't come across with some *facts*,' Mulligan's voice lifted suddenly as he flung the last imperative word over the humming rural distances.

'I have found my Father, Matthew.'

'You've found your oul' fella, have you? Give him my best regards. A right fucking state he must be in by now, the poor bastard. Now you bleeding well cock your ear to me—'

'I am! Yet what I am who cares or knows?
My friends forsake me like a memory lost
I am the self-consumer of my woes—'

'Listen, head of shit—'

'Ah, but not anymore! I was lost a little while, but now I am truly restored to my rightful estate—'

Again the bull-like roar faltering at its maddened pitch to a worn-out ragged whimper of petulant entreaty, 'Jesus Christ, what did I ever do to deserve you, Sheridan? Why do you pick on me—why do you taunt me like this? Haven't I always played the game with you, treated you just like a son?'

Luke soaring triumphantly to the celestial cue cried, 'Father!'

Mulligan stymied, befuddled, staring stupefied at the phone, whiskey hand for a moment stayed in the solemn act of pouring. 'What's that you said?'

'Clash of cymbals. Roll of drums. Father!'

Mulligan, blinking tired redrimmed woman-famished eyes, missed the discreet eau-de-Cologne presence of sedate succinct Miss Springett teasing his print-weary senses with her prim maidenly fortyish nunnery allure, long since gone to her suburban pigeonloft. 'Look, Sheridan, I've had a long day. I'll say a prayer for your poor Father's soul, if that makes you feel better.'

'You *are* my Father, Matthew.'

'Father Matthew? What's he got to do with all this?'

Luke allowed himself a soft comfortable truant chuckle, lazily scratching his snugly drowsy genitals eyes half-lidded. 'You misunderstand, Matthew. What I meant to say was, you, Matthew, are my Father.'

'I still don't get you. It's a terrible line.'

'You, Matthew. The Father I have been searching for all these years, Matthew, all these lost heartscalding years.'

'Who is it you're raving about now, in the name of Jasus?'

'You, Matthew. True Father of my innermost psyche.'

Mulligan, whiskey-renewed, growing bellicose once more, barking furiously over the airwaves, thumping the desk with mauling inkstained fist. 'Cut it out, you mad fucker, I'm warning you—'

'You, Matthew. My true spiritual indivisible alter ego. All these years.'

'Ego is right—you're shitting the stuff.'

'The primordial godhead of my buried life. What a strange karma ours is, Matthew! To think we have travelled such a long long road together, and never once did it enter my dull work-weary head that you were the Father I never knew.'

'I amn't my jumping bollocks.'

'Father all-bounteous and forgiving, thy Prodigal Son returneth. Rejoice, Matthew. Our morning is nigh. Such a long weary travail but I have found you at last.'

Mulligan audibly sniffing raised his quivering nostrils closer to the phone poised to pounce stiff with suspicion, giving the desk an extra wallop. 'You're pissed, you curse-of-God bastard, pissed as bejasus! I can smell it off you from here.'

'This is an epiphany which Joyce was wont to celebrate, a moment of sudden overpowering revelation. One is abruptly startled out of one's ordinary senses with mystical awe at the inexplicable uniqueness in the minutest granule of mortal existence, opening up to us for the splittest of split seconds a whole new world of which ordinarily we are abysmally ignorant. "Turn a stone, start a wing. 'Tis ye, 'tis your estranged faces, that miss the many-splendoured thing . . ." '

'As drunk as Tim Finnegan's fucking ghost.'

Luke, wounded by such flippancy, held up his hand in unseen admonition, chastising the dangling telephone. Shame on you, Matthew. Where is your sense of the mysterious, the unexplained, the occult? Even in your philosophy there must be more things in heaven and earth . . .'

Mulligan regaining a shred of composure, sniggering grotesquely at the sad state of Luke's non-prospects ahead. 'What's so fucking occult about being kicked out of work on your arse, eh, Sheridan? Answer me that one, Cassandra!'

Luke patient as the waiting grave. 'Ah, Matthew, Matthew! Don't you feel even the tiniest quiver of mystery? Don't you experience anything at all even remotely mystical—a certain, shall we say, extraterrestrial exaltation at this precise point in time, when you—not the fat slovenly perspiring obnoxious you, of course—but your inner self, your most singular and unique Id, have come at last into absolute parallel conjunction with another metaphysical entity—to be precise, *my* most singular and unique Id?'

Mulligan all composure crumpled, venting a gasp of paralytic verbal impotence, bellowed finally spluttering half-sobbing fulminations, enraged and lachrymose at once, gripping the sleek phonepiece as though it were Luke's stringy windpipe. 'That's it, you hoor's spawn—that's the straw that broke the elephant's fucking back! In less than nine shakes of a cow's tail I'll be hotfoot out there to give you your bleeding cards in person!'

Luke lifted reed-thin quavering choirboy tremolo lisping moistly into the phone:

> 'You nursed me from the cradle, Father mine,
> and leathered me with the ladle, Father mine,
> but I forgive you from the heart
> you drunken fornicating oul' fart,
> before I belt you with the table, Father mine—'

'You bastard—you—you ingrate—you'll not walk through the door of this office again! You're fired, Sheridan, you hear me—F.I.R.E.D! You can walk the length and breadth of Dublin but you'll not get onto any other newspaper—I'll see to that!'

'So soon estranged after so brief a reunion? Am I once more to go out into the world alone and fatherless after so idyllic a marriage of true minds? Ah, Matthew, I say unto you verily, you cut me to the quick!'

'You've played your last con-trick on me, Sheridan. You'll have all the time in the world now to write that fiddle's fart of a book, sitting on your arse up in that dogbox of a flat in Ballsbridge, eating baked beans for breakfast, dinner and tea, going mad for the want of a pint, never mind a woman. Oh, you'll starve in a garret all right, Clarence Mangan—I'll make sure of that—you'll get your bellyful of hunger, mark my words—'

Luke manfully choking back a cry of filial devotion reached out and held the phone tight to his mouth with a lover's ardour, the choirboy from remote organ-and-candlewax days once again quivering uncertainly into voice:

'I hear you calling me.
You called me when the moon had veiled her light,
before you went from me into the night—

No, no, I cannot go on—you fill the cup of my sorrow to over-flowing, Matthew—Gone, gone, and never called me Son!'

'I'm on my way, Sheridan—I'll find you wherever you are, you ungrateful little bastard, you—you *venereal* beast!'

'Oh Matthew, that's beautiful, that's inspired—your eloquence takes my breath away. Say it again.'

Mulligan threw the last of the whiskey down his throat. 'That will be your lot, Sheridan—you'll die roaring in agony with the pox—you'll get a dose from some oul' hoor one of these days, as God is my judge—you'll double up and wither away with the pox—'

'Being the supreme expert on the subject, Matthew, I would not dispute your prognostication for a moment, though it would sadden me if I were to outlive you and see you die such an ignominious death after a lifetime of such miraculous escape.'

Mulligan at last speechless, sprawling across the desk, knocking the phone to the floor, crying helpless as a thwarted baby-bully, moisture streaming from eyes and nose as Luke serene as sunset sat cross-legged contemplating with amused compassion the still swaying phone dangling from the table in front of him as though it were Mulligan the harassed bloated buffoon himself before him, all clammy blusterings gone, denuded of pride and authority, a cardboard Colossus fallen soggy with futile rage, no sad lust of Springett now to give his veins imaginary fire, only a tired longing for camphor and starch and elegant mother-things held in her frosty look and long decades of whiskey gone sour in his guts rancid like the rest of him slewed across the desk fuming and wailing, enmeshed and snared in the long useless tangle and coil of his life.

'Poor Yorick, alas,' sighed Luke with closed eyes.

'May I come in?'

Sonny holding a rotund brandy goblet in both hands close to her midriff as a bride would clasp her bouquet, smiling gravely down at him. 'Did you receive your call, and was it Mr Mulligan?'

'It was indeed poor Yorick, yes, and a thousand alases.'

Sonny stooped and replaced the receiver in its snug little cradle, kneeling on the floor in front of him, her smile glimmering and the idea of a Japanese print came floating into his mind, an image of stilted formalised adoration as though she might the next moment lean forward with lowered lids and offer the cool honeyed milk of her breast to sweeten the cup he was lifting to his lips.

'I think I am out of a job,' said Luke taking a noisy swallow of wine.

'Then you can grandly starve at last while you put your whole mind to your book!' cried Sonny hugging the goblet happily to her bosom. 'I'm so happy for you!'

'Your enthusiasm for my coming destruction is deeply touching,' said Luke leaning back and balancing the bottle on his ankles. 'I shall probably become a ponce. There's always room and work for them, as any true Dubliner knows, though it's probably a closed shop. Any suggestions?'

'Become my lover and be a very well kept man,' Sonny said rather dreamily sitting back on her heels. 'The more I think about it the more it seems that would be the best and most logical solution to everything. Yes,' she said, decisively nodding her head, 'you really should become my lover. Pay and conditions will be as you dictate them. Don't you think that a reasonable proposition?'

'Eminently reasonable. Prodigal, in fact. But haven't you got a lover already?'

'Oh, several. Isn't that rather irrelevant? I have several changes of clothes too, but I can never pass a well-stocked fashion store without going in and purchasing more. The same with shoes, hats, handbags, gloves, dogs, earrings, all manner of things——'

'And lovers?'

'And lovers, certainly, though not always strictly in the purest sense of the term, you understand.'

'The purest sense? Ah, you mean mind, intellect, spirit, companions thereof?'

'Exactly. I think the word "lover" is for the most part a complete misnomer anyway, since one's lovers are invariably neither very loving nor lovable and are usually equipped only to fulfil a strictly functional requirement. Friends of the boudoir would perhaps be a more apt description, though even in that context "friends" is more hopeful than accurate.'

'You seem to speak from considerable experience, dear countess.'

Her silvery smile grew. 'One gathers admirers as little girls make daisy-chains. The reasoning behind the two processes is remarkably similar.'

'And you would like me to become part of that chain?'

'You are the most improbable-looking daisy I have ever seen, but maybe that's why I like you.'

'To add to your collection?'

'Why not? Does the idea offend your sense of your own worth?'

'Not in the least. Most of us are little more than collectors' items anyway, and there's nothing wrong with that. There's even a certain honour in it, a certain flattery, depending on the taste of the collector, of course.'

'And you think I have good taste?'

'Oh, the best, the very best, if you seek to include me in your little collection. You see, my sense of my own worth is quite sound. What would Otto say to this very engaging little tête-à-tête we are having, countess?'

'What would Otto say? Do you very much care?'

'Frankly, yes. I'd think twice and then twice again multiplied before falling foul of him. His musculature is very intimidating.'

Sonny laughed. 'You're not afraid of Otto, surely?'

'Oh, but I very surely am. Already I can distinctly hear my bones cracking like twigs.'

'He is basically non-violent.'

'And I am basically a coward.'

'Does that mean you turn down my proposal?'

'It means I respect Otto very much, and my neck a whole lot more.'

'Cowards have always had a fatal fascination for me. All the world applauds a hero, the more stupid and foolhardy the better, but nobody admires a coward, however wise and judicious his cowardice. Am I just being contrary, do you think, going against the accepted norm?'

'Perhaps, but I wouldn't worry about it. True eccentricity is very hard to come by, in any shape or form. Otto didn't strike me as being particularly cowardly.'

'He's terrified of mice, would you believe, his nerves seize up solid at the sight of one, and the most innocuous of insects give him Saint Vitus convulsions. And of course he leaves his bedroom light burning all night. He is what I call a petty coward. I like my cowards to be afraid of strange and unusual things and to be absolutely terrified out of their wits by the things they are afraid of. I hate it when they pretend they are not afraid and try to hide their trembling hands behind their backs. It's so childish to pretend you are not afraid when you're actually dying to scream out loud with terror. Men *are* such children anyway.'

'I'm sorry to say all my fears and phobias are little ones and very unoriginal,' Luke confessed, mournfully picking up the bottle and swinging it gently in the concave space between his knees. 'I mean, what could be more unoriginal than my fear of being throttled to death by Otto if he happened to come through that door right now and saw us together like this?'

Sonny sipped slowly. 'I did not think our position was particularly compromising. Certainly not one to inspire such an exotic occurrence as a crime passionnel. And anyway Otto hasn't the imagination for it.'

'It doesn't require a brilliant imagination to guzzle somebody to death.'

'Why are you so sensitive on the subject of Otto?'

'Well, he's leader of the daisy-chain, isn't he?'

Her dusklit smile deepened. 'Is that what you think?'

'Well—isn't he? You aren't exactly brother and sister in your attitude to each other on the evidence of my eyes at least.'

'Of course we are brother and sister.'

'Oh. Oh well, in that case pardon me. I must admit the evidence of my eyes is not always infallible.'

'Oh, you have been seeing perfectly all right. I'm sure whatever conclusion you have arrived at is the absolutely right one.'

'You're either very frank or very devious. Possibly both.'

'Possibly. Otto and I are lovers, of course. Have been for years.'
Sonny was holding her goblet once more in a reverential fashion,

gazing into it as if it were a chalice containing the holy wafer of communion.

'I see. And you have been—er—brother and sister for an equal number of years?'

'For as long as I can remember.'

Luke whistled softly and began to intone:

> 'Over Erin's holy isle so sweet and fair
> came the sweet smell of incest on the air—'

Sonny was still smiling, but it was a sad faded forlorn waif of a smile now. 'Sorry to disabuse you of such a lovely fantasy, but we are not at all embued with the Borgia strain. We are of the platonic persuasion. I am Otto's soul-sister, as he is my soul-brother. The vile question of blood does not, happily, arise.'

Luke sighed. 'Brothers and sisters all under the skin, eh? A spiritual consummation only, and one I am sure devoutly to be wished. And there I was saying to myself as I mentally licked my chops, "What have we got here, eh—a subterranean hive of dark forbidden desires steaming in the catacombs of this monstrous Gothic folly overlooking Dublin Bay . . ." And already I was committing the black delicious story to immortality when you had to ruin it all by confessing that you and Otto the ominous are nothing more horrific than soul mates. Such as the paper dreams of fledgling authors.'

'You are a good man, Luke. I am glad poor Katy tried to poison Otto otherwise I might never have met you.'

'Ah, strange, nay, passing strange are the paths of human destiny. Jesus, I wish I hadn't said that. The very sound of it leaves a bad taste on my mouth.'

He drank deep from the bottle, the slim elegant neck of it fitting snugly into his mouth, the wine cool and knowing sliding smoothly down his gullet, fruit of the earth and sun coming together in a bittersweet collusion, the seasons combining to please him sweetly and good it felt to be on earth at that one moment in time, all others past and future forgotten and unthought-of.

'I wish I knew you beyond the words you speak,' said Sonny out of the silence as if raising a shutter and looking into the lazy chaos of his thoughts. 'Or is that altogether too audacious of me?'

'Dear countess, do not be deceived. I *am* the words I speak, I *am* as I sound. There is no beyond to me, no mysterious behind ness. Don't fall into the folly into which I am continually falling, don't invest me with unknown qualities I don't possess, don't put three sides where there are only two. It is a most unfair practice, for then we start expecting these poor souls to live up to our own fantasies of them and feel cheated and deceived when they do not, because of course they cannot, being who and what they are and not as we see them.' Luke halted and looked both surprised and suspicious. 'I beg your pardon. I am committing the cardinal error of sounding wise, which is inexcusable and a sure sign that I have not yet reached an acceptable level of inebriation. And that,' said Luke finishing off the bottle and sliding himself upwards along the wall until he was on his feet, 'is something that must be remedied if I am to be in any fit state to withstand the maudlin onslaughts of Matthew Mulligan, Esquire, who will drown me in a flood of paternal tears and reproach if he catches me even quarterways undrunk.'

Sonny was on her feet before he had noticed. 'Are you still worried about that deadline of yours?'

'Deadline? What deadline? The only deadline I am worried about now is getting to the unemployment exchange on time on Monday morning. "Shoot me like a soldier, do not hang me like a dog".'

The branches outside the window moved and swayed and through them the stars were beckoning in their cold remote yet oddly friendly fashion and he weaved his way across the room to return the salutation. Then the loosened towel slipped from his waist coming between him and his good intention, causing him to stumble and trip and rather to his surprise he found himself on the virginal eiderdown looking confusedly up at the ceiling and then at Sonny's face swimming distantly into view above him.

'You look just like my little brother used to look when I would come and tuck him into bed at night after he said his prayers.'

' "For Thine is the Kingdom, the Power and the Glory".

> Oh, Show me the way to go home,
> I'm tired and I want to go to bed,
> I had a little drink about an hour ago,
> And it's gone right to my head . . .'

'Just like little Wolfgang back home in Baden-Baden.'

'Did Wolfgang every cry, countess?'

'If he cried I would tousle his hair and kiss his tears away.'

'Lucky snotty little sod, Wolfgang. He probably pissed in his sleep too, to add to his elfin charms.'

'Wolfgang was an angel. He drowned in the swimming-pool. Dare you insult his memory?'

'Jesus, I'm sorry. Wolfgang alive is bad enough, but I can't cope with a drowned Wolfgang. I'll say a prayer for him as soon as I can get onto my knees.'

Luke, spreadeagled, tried vainly to rise from his position like a newborn puppydog scrambling weakly to get onto all fours, and then the next moment the soft cloudy weight of Sonny descended upon him, pinioning him back against the mattress, an image swimming into his befogged yet lightsome mind of a butterfly starfished for dusty decades between the pages of a desiccated unread volume, her fingers roaming over his face as though tracing the graven lettering on a tombstone, finding the thin line of mouth and jaw, her tongue busy licking him kitten-warm and decorous rubbing her nose against the furry edges of his beard, a little seaside urchin eating candyfloss.

'Methinks I hear the angry approach of friend Otto—'

'Nonsense, darling—relax, savour this little snatched moment—'

'I'd savour it with a heart and a half if I knew Otto was miles away, taking a long walk in the Black Forest.'

'Man of little faith.' Her mouth made quick furtive little sallies upon his own. 'Otto *is* miles away, dancing Irish jigs with your funny little gypsy girlfriend—'

'Do not malign Babysoft,' Luke counselled speaking with difficulty against the rush of her caressing mouth. 'She is no stray waif of the wayside, but a lady of highminded resolve—Dark Helen of the Quays and dockside, inspiring heights of volcanic passion in the most mundane and meagre of souls—'

'A female Heathcliff, dark-browed and devilish and dangerous to simple men—I like her. But not at this very moment.'

Sonny all a ferny weight lying upon him her tongue roving, kissing closed his wine-heavy lids, her fingers moving over his goose-pimply skin engulfing him in a snug satiny little envelope of warmth, foiling his inept halfhearted attempts to rise with the competent firmness of an elder sister of wise knowledgeable ways resolutely serenading him to semi-slumber.

'I am drowning now, like little Wolfgang, the poor unfortunate sod.'

'Be quiet, darling. Wolfgang was an angel. So are you. I like my victims to be angels. There is a certain delicious element of perversity in seducing angels. It adds relish to the act.'

'Couldn't he bloody well swim, little Wolfgang?'

'No man can swim for long in my pool.'

'I learned to swim in the Grand Canal when I was a kid. I learned fast. I had to. They threw me in.'

'Who threw my angel in?'

Her strangely trite conventional tone was cool and clearly enunciated close to his captive ear as if she were holding a midday chat on the telephone while waiting for the coffee to percolate.

'Oh, Sammy Jordan, Ollie Lynch, Pig-eyes Kelly—my happy little playmates. They took strong objection to the fact that while they fished for pinkeens I sat on my arse reading *Mein Kampf*. So quite rightly they baptised me headfirst in lovely shit-slimey canal water, clothes and all, and Hitler after me.'

'Poor angel. You might never have come up again. Like my poor little Wolfgang.'

'I very nearly didn't, like your poor little Wolfgang. Unlike Wolfie, all I did was swallow a bellyful of duck's shit, but I did learn to swim. I don't want to interrupt you, countess, but I'm certain my ears detect the heavy breathing of Otto immediately outside the door.'

She put her mouth decorous upon his, the firm warm tip of her tongue wriggling inside. 'What ignoble suspicions you harbour about poor Otto. He is the most naïve and openhearted of men. Do please be quiet, darling.'

'Quiet my arse, my lady, if you'll pardon my crude vernacular. A gentleman he well may be, and far be it from me to say otherwise, but I must admit I don't exactly relish being crushed like a frankfurter in those mighty teutonic hands of his.'

'Otto is all wind and bombast. He hasn't it in him to hurt a fly. Am I too heavy for your slight aesthetic frame, darling?'

'You'll slip into Brahms' Lullaby any minute now.'

'Do be quiet.'

'As the grave. Oh Jesus—who said that?'

'Ssh. Quiet . . .'

Lying lamb-sacrificial beneath her, his ears muffled now by the sweep and commotion of his blood. 'Countess, I beg you, while time is still with us, consider your position.'

'What is there to consider, darling? I like my position.'

'I seem to recollect being here before, the moment before last or a year ago, and there was this loud report—'

'You do talk . . .'

There or most probably somewhere else half-awake or dreaming, unsure and uncaring of either Luke felt himself slide slowly down the man-smooth slope of perdition with a sigh of courageous resignation, hearing the svelte discreet apologetic little sounds she was making as if otherwise engaged in some innocuous diversion demanding the utmost attention to detail, but at the same time her suddenly strong workmanlike hands gripping both his ears like the reins of a horse urging him forward, prodding him into a gallop faster and faster rising and falling uphill and downdale guiding him onward with knee and heel forward over diminishing ground holding a straight furious course to the first exhilarating flight—

'Into Thy hands O Lord—'

The room was flooded suddenly with searing light as if a gigantic arclamp had been turned on them, caught petrified upon the quilt humped in a pose of arrested ardour, a lithe ambitious piece of statuary begun in haste and abandoned in panic, static like Pompeii sculptures carved into each other, as three hobgoblin forms ran prancing and dancing around the bed holding hands in a fiendish ups-a-daisy foray, swinging glasses high faces sunbursting with wide smiles, sweeping everything irresistibly into the swirling vortex of their gaiety:

> 'As I went down to Dublin city
> at the hour of twelve at night
> who should I see but a Spanish Lady
> brushing her hair by broad moonlight.
> First she washed it then she dried it
> over a fire of amber coal,
> in all my life I ne'er did see
> a girl so neat about the soul—'

The three demented choristers handlocked and capered, faces ablaze, and rising overhead like a ragged lark the hard bruised oddly melodic notes of Babysoft a child at a circus for the very first time shorn of all meaner masks and devious disguises, her head rocking furious from side to side her bare brown heels swung aloft in the dance:

'Whack for the toora-toora-rally
Whack for the toora-toora-lay—'

Ranter his harvest-moon countenance grinning, a dazed merry-hearted captive flying out through the suddenly unlocked doors of his cell, for once freed from merciless cares that time had grown like a hideous carbuncle over his hidden truant schoolboy soul, winking at the two immobile upon the bed:

'As I went out from Dublin city
at the hour of first dawnlight
Who should I see but the Spanish Lady
weeping hot tears over love's swift flight—'

And wedged like a squat stolid foreshortened Samson between these two horrendous Hibernians the bemused Otto, an ever valiant satyr, large florid face liberally awash with tears and perspiration, breaking from the dance and falling on his knees at the canopied couch of near betrayal, flinging his arms wide as if to engulf the teeming thieving vainglorious conniving mass of mankind into his immense embrace, all the shorn straying lambs and blackest most obdurate of black sheep that ever wandered lazy upon the earth bringing heartscald to large simple hoof-footed souls like himself, proclaimed with hoarse quavering voice and swelling throat—'I love you all, meine Brüder, all you I, Otto, love!'

VII

'Coitus interruptus,' croaked Luke bravely essaying a flippancy made none too convincing by the distinct chattering of his teeth as he tried inadequately to cover his exposed more vulnerable parts by twisting his limbs into contorted defensive angles. 'In flagrante delicto—'

'That's all very well,' rejoined Babysoft when their frenzied frolics had subsided somewhat, 'and well spoken, but the fact remains, I never clapped eyes on such a shower of bare arses since the crèche caught fire beyond in Summerhill!'

'And him trying to bamboozle us with them foreign words!' said Ranter with goodhumoured objection, pushing the cap back on his head. 'He must think we never went to Mass.'

Sonny coolly gathered up her gown, kneeling and holding it in front of her a picture of outraged decorum. 'Really, Otto, I must protest—you could at least have knocked.'

'Ah, mein little Gretchen.'

'It really does display an appalling lack of good manners to simply come barging into one's bedroom like werewolves on the rampage.'

'Ah, sure he was only looking for his mate, maam,' said Ranter coming to comradely defence. 'You know, like Tarzan.'

'We just got carried away, sort of,' Babysoft explained, quite composed herself now. 'We wanted to share our high spirits with you—isn't that so, Uncle Otto?' she added, planting a moist daughterly kiss on the gleaming dome.

'Oh, ja, ja, mein liebes Fräulein,' Otto responded gratefully, on his knees and fumbling in faltering hope for the hand of Sonny proud and remote and inaccessible as Isis upon the bed. 'We sing the songs and we dance the jigs and the hornypipes so much till we cry with the tears so happy, and we look for you Gretchen, and the good fellow Luke here, to sing and dance with us also, all the Brüder and the sisters, ja? But nowhere do we find you, Gretchen, all the place over we look for you, and so—' Otto paused and looked about in confusion—'and so we find you. Here.' He blinked and repeated greatly puzzled, 'Here.'

'Nice to see you again, Otto,' said Luke heartily putting out his hand as if meeting a friend on a street corner. 'So nice of you to have us, but we really must be going—we have imposed on your hospitality too much as it is.'

'Ah, there's nothing like it,' mused Ranter, hands clasped together and eyes raised upwards. 'Hospitality.'

Babysoft put protective arms around Otto's broad velvet-clad shoulders. 'You'll have him all snots and tears over again, I'm telling you.'

'The poor eejit,' intoned Ranter with feeling.

'Don't forget, Ranter,' reminded Babysoft. 'Blessed are the pure at heart.'

'Lamb of God, meek and mild,' Ranter replied sighing, 'but this takes the biscuit.'

'For they shall see God,' continued Babysoft. 'Ah, isn't innocence a lovely thing, just the same, especially in a grown man?'

Otto still gazed at the pair on the bed with clouded confusion. 'Why do we find you here, Gretchen, with the good fellow, Luke, and dressed like that with no clothes on?' He shook his great animalian head. 'It is much of a puzzle to me, mein Gretchen.'

Babysoft swooped to the rescue. 'Ah, they were only playing fathers and mothers, Uncle Otto,' she said bending to nibble at Otto's sausage-succulent ear. 'Sure we play all sorts of little games in Dublin—especially *that* one—don't we, Ranter? Not a morsel of harm in it—is there, Ranter?' said Babysoft smiling steadily and kicking the uncomprehending Ranter soundly on the shins. 'Say something, for Jasus' sake,' she hissed.

'Wha'? Oh!' Ranter winced. 'Oh aye—that's right, Otto oul' son. Divil a bit of harm in it, oh divil a bit. Just something to pass the oul' time, you might say.'

'I wouldn't,' Babysoft giggled.

'You wouldn't what?' asked Ranter blankly.

'I wouldn't say that, you gobshite.'

'Oh aye—I see. Well, Otto me oul' flower, there's nothing in it that Our Holy Mother Herself wouldn't look down upon and smile from her golden throne at the right hand of Our Lord and Saviour.'

'Don't run away with it altogether, for Jasus' sake,' interrupted Babysoft, snipping the tenuous thread of evangelical rhetoric just as Ranter was gathering steam.

'Sure we're all boys and girls together, aren't we, Uncle Otto?' she said, resuming her pecking on his earlobe. 'All lads and lassies together, eh?' She kissed again the broad hairless expanse of glittering cranium slightly below her. "Course we are!'

'Here, for Jasus' sake,' said Ranter stooping and picking the towel up off the floor, throwing it to Luke who had been trying to burrow a hole for himself in the sumptuous eiderdown. 'You look so fucking foolish there shaking like a newborn foal. Get up and put something decent on before Attila there catches himself on, or it's the knacker's yard for you, chiner.'

'I suppose it does appear somewhat sinister,' admitted Luke draping the towel around him. 'I suppose at times I do tend to push my faith in the innate goodness of human nature a little too far.'

'I wouldn't know about that, but a blind man could see it wasn't a game of Ludo you were getting ready for.'

'It is a great puzzle to me, Gretchen,' insisted the genuflecting Otto with the same pondering uncertainty, his happily befuddled brain trying still to grasp the shrouded implications swirling about him, only peripherally distracted by the determined advances of Babysoft and her nibbling teeth. 'I find you in here bare with Luke, and no words you have for me.'

'My dear Otto,' began Sonny kneeling up straight on the bed holding the gown before her, regally composed, 'if you do not possess the ordinary courtesy of knocking first before you venture to enter a lady's bedchamber, you really should not expect to receive an explanation for whatever you may possibly discover once you are inside that bedchamber.'

'Ja, ja, mein Gretchen, but—'

'Let me continue,' commanded Sonny, uncurling herself unhurriedly and sliding into her gown once more. 'I really am quite cross with you, Otto, most definitely quite cross with you. I had naturally expected you to behave like the perfect gentleman I always took you to be, but instead, what happens?'

Otto made several inarticulate entreating sounds.

'No, Otto. You come thundering in unannounced through my bedroom door like a one-man charge of the Light Brigade, and worse, a vulgar caricature of a bloated Bavarian beerswiller, and you expect explanations, no less!' Sonny's fragile bosom seemed to throb with refined indignation. 'Really, Otto, it is altogether too inexcusable—where is your sense of decorum, and what must our new friends think of our proud Teutonic propriety?'

Otto stupefied and shaking his head, looking endearingly foolish, heaved himself ponderously to his feet and stumbled over to where Sonny stood arrayed in iridescent ire, fumbling for her hand, lifting it to his lips and kissing it profusely. 'Ah, mein Gretchen, so right you are—hah, I am such a stupid Otto!' He raised his clenched fist and smote himself hard on the forehead. 'Myself it is I could kill, so stupid I am—say you have the mercy for me, Gretchen.'

'There, there,' soothed Sonny patting his hand and extricating her own. 'You are forgiven. Now go and apologise to Luke for being so rude. Go on now, like a good fellow,' she said turning him around by the shoulders and pushing him gently in the direction she wanted him to go. 'It is the very least you can do to show there are no ill feelings.'

Luke whistled softly. 'Bravo, countess, bravo.'

Ranter tipped the cap back on his head and surveyed Sonny with respect and awe. 'The cool neat way she put the poor oul' bugger in the wrong all unknowst to himself, as if he'd just beheaded somebody, bejasus.' He swept off his cap and doffed it at her. 'Fair play to you, maam. You're a credit to your sex and one in a thousand, though I wouldn't want to be married to you for a day, no, bejasus, thank you maam, not for all the stones in Connemara!'

'Watch your marbles now,' cautioned Babysoft as Otto came up to Luke and began shaking hands. 'A quick throw over his shoulder and we'll be picking you up off the floor—bit by bit.'

'I don't like the way his ears are twitching at all,' declared Ranter. 'And his nose is not much better. Like a bulldog closing in on a cornered hare.'

Babysoft sniffed ostentatiously. 'It was a good life while it lasted Luke. What more can we ask for?'

Ranter saluted. 'We'll never forget you, Luke. Word of honour. Every time I borrow a tenner in Mooneys I'll remember you—'

'Stop it, Ranter,' pleaded Babysoft. 'Sure you're spoiling me eye-shadow with the tears.'

Otto wreathed in smiles, pumping Luke's imprisoned hand vigorously up and down, showing his hard level molars. 'Luke, the good friend, you have the feelings, they are not hard, no?'

'Why, Otto, dear friend, not at all,' replied Luke repressing a wince.

'The feelings, I do not hurt, Luke, no?'

'Not at all. Whatever gave you that idea?'

Otto purring with gratification, increased the earnest pressure, yanking Luke's whole arm up and down as if bent on absolving himself of all former heinous suspicions. 'Ah, Luke, you are the good friend, ja, you are the true Bruder, ja?'

'Would I not ride with you into the valley of death itself?' Luke said grimly continuing to smile in an agonised way. 'Brothers to the—the death.'

'Sorry I am if I pained you in any way,' Otto said with the heady enthusiasm of contrition, not a fraction lessening his grip.

'Pained me?' gasped Luke. 'Think nothing of it, friend—a little misunderstanding, due no doubt to the barriers of language.'

'Then we are the friends still, ja?'

'Oh, ja, ja, a thousand times ja,' muttered Luke. 'A fine manly grip you have there, Otto.'

'You like my grip, ja?' cried Otto delightedly, a certain cunning expression showing on his bland goodnatured face.

'What say you we let bygones be definitely bygones, Otto, dear old comrade, eh?' Luke said swallowing and trying to wriggle away his fingers by now quite numb away but sharp little slivers of pain darting the sorry length of his arm. 'Revenge is—such an unmanly emotion, don't you think?'

'With all my heart, friend Luke,' responded Otto following after him, keeping deadly pace, a fixed mad child's grin on his face. 'With all my heart!'

'Nothing like brotherhood to keep the heart going, eh, Otto?' said Luke valiant, still backing futilely away. 'The tears you see

brimming in my eyes? Tears of fraternal fervour, I assure you—'
Luke with buckling knees forcing himself upright against the wall,
throwing back his head in defiance.

'Though cowards mock and traitors sneer
We'll keep the Red Flag flying here—'

'Me life on you, Luke!' shouted Babysoft jubilant clapping her
hands. 'A few more like you and we'd beat the world!'

Luke eyes fast closed, jaw muscles aching with the effort to blot
out the pain, back truly against the wall now, fiercely thinking of
anything; reflections of sunset in dark canal waters and clouds
scudding like foam overhead, a girl's broadbrimmed summer hat
floating transparent as smoked glass, a bedraggled swan drifting
forlorn in the green shade of weeds, black tankards of porter
ringed with thin white clerical collars, a frail patina of yellow
round the edges, a soggy ball whizzing moistly through the air,
heading erratically towards the goalpost made of bundled jerseys,
and a church spire in the smokey distance rising like a withered
finger against bland sabbattical sky; Luke thought fiercely also
of smells and sounds and the feel of things, shutting out the bone-
crunching by sniffing up his nostrils once more the clean good
whiff of fresh horsepiss splashing and hissing on hot tarred roads
or on dark glowering evenings sizzling in the snow, leaving deep
mudyellow puddles, and the bathtub on Saturday nights scalding
and carbolic-thick, the scrubbing-brush raking his back hard and
brutal in his Father's hand, a figure splendid and awesome tower-
ing over him redolent of stale beer and tobacco, Oh yes and the
frying-pan on the squat ugly pantry stove hopping with sausages
and rashers and rings of white pudding and—

'Otto dear, kindly desist from this ridiculous circus act and give
poor Luke back his hand. At once, Otto!'

Sonny's crisp tone peremptory and decisive was music unimaginable to his ear and still he did not know that Otto had
obeyed until he slowly opened his eyes and saw the broad friendly
rather sheepish grin on the pugilistic face and looked down surprised at his hand still five-fingered, static in front of him, sticking
out like the claw of a stuffed animal, blue-jointed and frozen
hanging there.

'He didn't really hurt you, did he?' Sonny enquired coming up and turning her back towards them. 'Zip me up, Otto. He can be so clumsy at times, but so gentle behind it all—'

'Mein liebes Gretchen, my poppy.' Otto going about his lady's bidding, his fingers agile and rarely gentle now pulling up the zip of her gown between her shoulders, kissing her smooth white nape as tentatively as he might touch the wings of a butterfly.

'Stop being maudlin, Otto,' said Sonny in a bored voice once more turning round to Luke. 'You are quite sure he didn't hurt you?' Luke shook his head, the same set grimacing smile on his face as though it was pasted on. 'Who—Otto? He wouldn't hurt the littlest fly, as you keep reminding us.'

'Precisely,' agreed Sonny lightly brushing her hair with her fingers. 'Though, on the other hand, you—are not a fly.'

'No,' he concurred slowly stretching his fingers. 'Just an ordinary common or garden insect with certain refined sensibilities of self-preservation—Jesus jumping Christ!'

The static bonechilled limb came fitfully back to life as the blood pounded once more into circulation, leaping the veins with startling voltage, slamming him back against the wall, opening up his arm again to sensation and he could distinctly hear the bones click and clack as he squeezed tight and spread wide his fingers in a warm wild surge of relief that he could do so with diminishing discomfort.

'A little case of pins and needles,' Sonny assured him flicking the corner of her mouth delicately with her fingertip. 'I always find it a pleasurable sensation.'

'Ecstatic,' agreed Luke as the pain receded slowly to a tingling pleasant ache. 'I must ask Otto to do it more often—he'd be delighted to oblige me, I'm sure.'

'I hope that's not your drinking hand,' Ranter said with genuine concern, drawing near and inspecting the afflicted limb closely. 'If so, you're bollocksed—I wouldn't want to wish that on me worst enemy, bejasus. Sure it would destroy a man's whole social life.'

'You took it like a man anyway,' consoled Babysoft coming up and putting out her glass to him. 'Here, there's still a drop left in it—take it and welcome, me fine fighting cocksparrow.'

He accepted the glass bravely and turned to Otto, hulking rather gloomily in the background. 'I salute you, noble gladiator. It was a fair and honourable contest—a little onesided perhaps, but fair and honourable and in intent at least, scrupulously clean—'

'For the love of Jasus,' Ranter broke in exasperated, 'will you listen to him—you'd think he was after going fifteen fucking rounds with that Ali fella himself!'

'Still and all,' said Babysoft, loyally linking her arm through Luke's, 'it made me heart thump on me bosom to see the proud way he kept from breaking down and crying. Sure they don't breed men like that anymore.'

Luke looked fondly at her. 'You turn my head, Babysoft, with those glittering panegyrics.' He clutched at his waist as the towel once more started to slip. 'I really must go now and put something on.'

'After that,' Sonny interposed plucking imaginary specks of dust from her sleeve, 'I suggest we all go into town and pawn our flesh for a Tinker's song. I am suddenly densely bored with this Gothic mausoleum that is crumbling all around us. Let us go and lose our souls in the mad throbbing metropolis of Dublin.'

Babysoft became wistful. 'Poor Rosie.' She gave Luke a reproachful look as she tightened her grip on his arm. 'She's mad about you, God help her.'

'Amen to that,' replied Luke prising himself away. 'I'll throw discretion to the wind and buy her a large gin and tonic when we get there. First, I must put some clothes on—excuse me.'

'Poor Rosie,' repeated Babysoft putting a hand to her mouth to stifle a yawn. 'She comes out with such foolish things at times. This morning, for instance—ah, but maybe I shouldn't tell you. It was kind of a secret, like—anyway,' she went on without pause still looking at Luke, 'it was about you.'

'What about me?'

'Sure you wouldn't want to mind poor Rosie—spends half her time daydreaming if you ask me—terrible innocent for her age, you know. Still and all, she said something very funny this morning. About you.'

'So you said. What did poor innocent daydreaming Rosie have to say about me?'

'Do you really want to know? No,' said Babysoft as if battling with sombre second thoughts. 'I don't think you ought to know. I never expected to hear such a thing, not even from Rosie.'

'Okay, Babysoft,' sighed Luke. 'I'll buy you a large gin and tonic too tonight. Or would you prefer brandy?'

'Are you trying to bribe me or something?'

'Yes.'

Babysoft lifted her shoulders. 'Oh well, that just shows what type you are, trying to squeeze a secret out of me with gin and tonic.'

'Large gins,' Luke prudently reminded her.

'As if I wasn't used to blokes buying me drinks, large or small. As if I could be bought and won over by a couple of drinks.'

'I do beg your pardon most humbly,' said Luke with a bow and a reversal of tactics. 'I should have known better than to imagine you would succumb to so base a proposition.'

'That's better,' said Babysoft blowing on her fingernails and rubbing them against the lapel of her blouse. 'One thing I hate is being taken for a common hoor.'

'She being an uncommon one you see,' Ranter pointed out. 'They have standards of their own too, don't forget—'

'Certainly they have,' said Babysoft with an emphatic nod.

'What you might call a hierarchy of whores.'

'That's a lovely way of saying it, Ranter,' enthused Babysoft. 'You have a nice way of putting things—as I am sure Gertie knows only too well.'

'Anyway apologies again,' said Luke turning towards the door. 'Let's just forget about the whole thing.'

'What's your hurry—don't you want to hear what Rosie said?' cried Babysoft going after him.

Luke paused. 'Not particularly, but since you're dying to tell me I may as well hear it now as later.'

Sonny put her hand on Otto's arm. 'Come, Otto—some confidences are best left unheard by strangers.'

'And I must be going about me Father's business again,' said Ranter. 'Er—second door across the hall you said, maam?'

Luke held up his hand. 'Please stay, ladies and gentlemen. I am sure you are all breathless with suspense as I am to hear what damning inflammatory words are about to fall from Miss Brogan's delectable lips.'

Babysoft bristled. 'I didn't come here to be laughed at.'

Luke waved an apostolic hand. 'Peace, Babysoft, peace. I didn't mean to be flippant, no offence meant at all. But while you are embroiled in a moral debate within yourself as to whether to spill Rosie's beans or not, the odds of me catching double pneumonia must be down to evens or money on, not to mention Ranter. So will you kindly relieve us all by telling us what exactly Rosie said to you this morning?'

'I'm not one to carry tales, mind you—'

'The only tales you'd carry would be ones of enchantment, I'm sure,' said Luke promptly. 'I'd tell you things nobody else would squeeze out of me with burning tongs. But do go on.'

'Oh, it was nothing much I suppose, now that I come to think of it. You know Rosie.'

'Not very well.'

'Well, she says the most stupid things be times.'

'So you said.'

'Well, this morning for instance—she was just wondering to herself, I suppose, out loud you might say, about what sort of father you would make.'

Ranter gave an explosive sneeze. 'Holy Jasus.'

Sonny's eyes played on him with silver malice. 'I really ought to break into Brahms' "Lullaby" now, dear Luke.'

'Vat is happening?' asked Otto with ogling eyes.

Sonny pushed him forward again. 'Go and congratulate our friend Luke, Otto. He is about to become a father.'

'While the question of my extremely problematical fatherhood is being sorted out,' said Luke resolutely putting his hands behind his back; 'you don't mind if I don't shake hands, do you, Otto?'

'Hah—you are now to be the Vater!' cried Otto in quick delight. 'That is very, very gut. Oh ja, that is very gut. All my life I want to be the Vater, oh ja. And now the Vater is you.'

'I wish you'd curtail your enthusiasm, Otto,' sighed Luke, 'at least until the death sentence is confirmed.'

Otto chuckled. 'You make the little joke, ja?' He spread out his arms to embrace him. 'Luke the Vater is—' Otto stopped in sudden confusion, his trusting face a creased study in comic bewilderment. 'Very gut, ja,' he faltered, 'but if Luke the Vater is, who then is the Mutter?' Otto turned imploringly mystified eyes to Sonny. 'Gretchen? My little poppy? My honey-pot? My little orange carrot—nein, nein?'

'Orange carrot?' echoed Babysoft and Ranter together.

'He adores raw carrots,' said Sonny turning to Otto with weary patience. 'Don't be absurd, Otto. I waive all claims at aspiring towards an Immaculate Conception, which I definitely would have to have in order to attain to the state of potential maternity via our friend Luke or any other vehicle of God's holy will.'

'And you are not with the child, no?' Otto persisted from a great painful urge to convince himself.

'I am most decidedly not with the child, Otto. Do be quiet.'

'But I come here, Gretchen, and find you bare with Luke,' mumbled Otto miserably.

'I heard it said we're all bare in the sight of God,' Ranter put in helpfully, adding, 'Never could twig on to it meself, mind you. I mean to say now, if we're all that bloody bare all the time, what's the use of spending on clothes in the first place?'

'Shut up, Ranter,' spoke out Luke, giving the towel a more decisive twist round his waist. 'And quit yelping like a whipped cur, Otto. Sonny and I might have been Hansel and Gretel for all that didn't happen between us.' He turned to Babysoft who was calmly examining her hands and suppressing yawns in a theatrical way. 'So, if I understand you correctly, Rosie expressed to you certain inklings that she might possibly find herself in an interesting condition. Right?'

'Pardon? Oh, poor Rosie. Well, I told her not to be such an eejit, that it was probably just constipation. She's very subject to constipation, Rosie is. Now me on the other hand, I'm just the opposite—'

'Babysoft, can't you keep the conversation on a straight line?'

'Course I can—what do you take me for, a thick or something? Anyway, I'm forever telling her to take precautions.'

'Against what—constipation or pregnancy?'

'Don't be smart, you—it makes you look more like a monkey playing tricks. Anyway, in our particular line of business—'

'Skip the trade manual, Babysoft. Take it up with your local shop steward. Now the fact is,' said Luke rubbing the side of his nose as he had seen many lawyers and other legal gentlemen do; 'I had never laid eyes on Miss Rosie Hand before that night, and while I am the first to admit that I am gifted in many ways—'

'Jasus, you hate yourself, don't you?'

'I really must in all modesty refuse to believe that my undoubted prowess could manifest itself with such remarkable celerity.'

Babysoft patted her hair. 'Oh, believe it or believe it not, like that cartoon thing in the papers, but why else should she want to know if you'd make a good father or not? I mean, why should she bother her arse anyway one way or another, if she wasn't interested herself, personal like?'

'She has a point there all right.'

'Shut up, Ranter.'

'Ah, but you have to admit it's as fishy as a barrel of stale herrings.'

'Shut up, Ranter, for Christ's sake. I refuse to be flustered,' said Luke rubbing a hand over his mouth and pulling at his beard very flustered indeed. 'The whole thing defies logic.'

'As the sailor said to the girl, looking at her belly sticking out a mile—'

'Let's have a resumé of what happened,' Luke went on, stoically ignoring the wasp-like nuisance of Ranter. 'I find my way to Madame Lala's lonely and dispirited, my best girl had just left me. I am in need of convivial company. I find it, at a price. Fair enough. I pass a pleasant evening in that hospitable hostelry. I drink a fair bit, needless to say, but I am not, repeat, not drunk when the evening's festivities come to a close. After much stumbling down dark unlit corridors I finally lay my head on the pillow—'

'Next to Rosie's.'

'Fair enough, Babysoft,' agreed Luke amicably. 'Next to Rosie's, after first putting up a herculean battle against your own sultry seductive blandishments—'

'Now lookit here, you—' began Babysoft before she reconsidered and smiled. 'Thank you very much said the Mistress unto Dan.'

Luke returned the smile. 'You're welcome. Now, despite her air, one might say her aura, of charming pristine innocence and trust all beguiling, I find it hard, nay, impossible to believe that I was the first even remotely full-blooded man to lay my head next to hers and go to sleep with her fragrant breath in my face.'

'Oh, granted you may have toddled off to sleep, right enough,' conceded Babysoft magnanimously once again studying her nails. 'After you did it.'

'After I—*did it*?' echoed Luke allowing a certain note of ridicule to creep into his voice. 'After I—*did* what?'

'Said the Rosary,' prompted Ranter. 'Hey—that's good. Do you get it? After you said the *Rose*-ary. Can't you see—your woman's name was—'

'Ranter, will you do humanity a favour and jump off Howth Head? Now,' he said turning to Babysoft; 'could you be more explicit?'

Babysoft flared. 'Ah, explicit me arse! Do you want me to draw you up a diagram or what? You're not going to stand there and tell me you said your prayers like your Ma always told you and then fell off to by-byes, surely to Christ?'

'No,' said Luke, rubbing his hands together. 'No, I am not going to say that, Babysoft. Perjury is abhorrent to every instinct of my being. No,' he continued, beginning to take measured paces up and down relishing the fact that he had the undivided attention of his audience. 'No, the simple truth is I gratefully partook of the —er—delicacies which the lady so kindly offered me. For which,' he waved his hand lightly in the air, 'for which I offer no apologies, since none are needed. To decline would have been tantamount to an insult to her—er—her exceeding generosity and good nature, and in any case I have always tried to follow that excellent if sometimes difficult advice from Shakespeare, "To thine own self be true".'

'Bejasus, isn't he bursting with brains all the same?' said Ranter admiringly, hands on knees, looking at the orator.

'All this, ladies and gentlemen,' Luke went on holding up his forefinger in a quivering histrionic manner as though out to convince a particularly sceptical jury; 'all this I admit freely and openly and under no duress whatever. But,' here he swung around to confront Babysoft with a dramatic flourish that was somewhat spoiled by the fact that he stubbed his big toe hard against the leg of a chair—'Fuck it—' he gulped and swallowed rapidly and grinned winningly at everyone, 'A slight—er—ahem —But,' he declaimed picking up the oratorical reins again—'and this, ladies and gentlemen, is indubitably the leading question— was I the very first living male to have so partaken of the selfsame —erd—elicacies? Can you in all honesty claim that I was, Miss Brogan—*can* you?' he finished slightly out of breath but bending forward intently for her reply.

Babysoft looked at him with a mixture of pity and hilarity. 'If I knew half of what you were bleeding well saying, I might be able to answer you yes or no.'

'Ah!' shouted Luke triumphantly raising his hand higher. 'That is precisely what we want from you—yes or no!'

'Who's we?' Ranter not unreasonably wanted to know. 'Personally, I don't give a fiddler's fart. All I want to do is—'

'Shut up, Ranter. Which is it to be, Miss Brogan? We are all hanging upon your answer.'

'What are you on about, with your Miss Brogan this and Miss Brogan that?' asked Babysoft peeved. 'And who the hell do you think you are anyway, bleeding Daniel O'Connell? Waving your arms in the air like an escaped lunatic—' she suddenly giggled. 'Jasus, you'd look a quare sight, with just a wig on and your bare credentials for the whole world to see! The Hanging Judge is right, bejasus!' and off she went into peals of gusty mirth.

Ranter sat down on the bed to take the weight off his once-more overloaded kidneys. 'I wish you'd hurry up with the inquisition and let me go to the jacks before I disgrace meself.'

'Yes, do accelerate the proceedings, Luke,' said Sonny. 'It seems such a simple straight-forward matter, really. I mean, do you wish to contest the paternity issue or not?'

Luke jerked as though he had trodden on a live electrical current. 'You do have such an incisive mentality, countess. You do love putting things into nutshells. However, I don't like this particular nutshell very much, so if you will allow me—' he turned his attention to Babysoft once again. 'In other words, Miss Hortensia—'

Babysoft abruptly stopped laughing. 'Now lookit, hedderball, I warned you about that before.'

'I stand corrected. Let me put it this way to you—'

'As the soldier said to the—'

'Shut bloody up, Ranter, you under-nourished lump of ecto-plasm.'

Ranter sniffed complacently. 'I like being called poetic names.'

'Are you saying, Babysoft, that I am the first man that ever slept with Rosie?'

'Well, I don't know about sleeping—'

'Touché. Let me put it—no, no—let me ask you, am I the first man she ever went to bed with?'

Babysoft sighed and shook her head. 'Ah no, I can't say that, no, I can't say that a'tall. Sure that would be a mortal lie. And anyway,' she said angrily as the implication sank in, 'you know as well as I do there's no room for effing virgins in Madame Lala's.

Oh, maybe to start out with, yes, but if you're any good a'tall you soon get your stripes.'

'Let us not confuse the issue—'

'The paternity issue?' echoed Sonny hopefully.

'With professional technicalities,' pursued Luke slipping into a role again sticking his thumbs under non-existent blackrobed lapels. 'So you admit, do you, that the lady in question—to wit, one Miss Rosie Hand—'

'Oh Jasus,' groaned Ranter crossing his arms tightly over his abdomen. 'Here we go—to wit to woo. Get on with it can't you, before me bleeding bladder bursts.'

'To wit, one Miss Rosie Hand has made what one might legitimately call a practice of entertaining gentlemen in her chambers at night?'

'And during the day too, if the money's good,' volunteered Babysoft unbidden. 'Sure we're not superstitious.'

'So therefore you must further admit that I am far from being the first gentleman to be so entertained by the aforesaid Miss Hand?'

'You're not the first fish to be hauled in, if that's what you mean. Nor the last neither, with the help of God.'

'Amen again. So,' said Luke as he scratched his beard, 'taking into account all her past experience, or lack of it if you like, might one not reasonably assume that Miss Hand had on more than one previous occasion ample opportunities for finding herself in "an interesting condition"? In other words,' he pressed, drawing quite close to the blithely unimpressed Babysoft, 'and to be quite blatantly crude—if it has happened now why the hell didn't it happen before?'

'Now you have a point there, Sylvester—' Ranter started.

'How the hell do I know?' retorted Babysoft. 'Maybe you were just lucky.'

Ranter raised his cap towards her. 'On the other hand—she has a point too. Can I go now?'

'A moment, please, a moment,' said Luke joining his fingers together and cracking the joints. 'Did Rosie say positively to you that she *was* pregnant?'

'No, but Madame Lala says she is.'

Ranter momentarily forgot his own pressing discomfort and looked at Luke with disbelief. 'Holy divine hand of Jasus—you

haven't gone near that poor oul' creature, surely to God? Ah no
—tell me it isn't true—I know you'd get up on anything, Sheridan,
but a poor decrepit oul' woman like that, old enough to be your
Granny and just waiting for God to call her any day now—now
I'm not religious be any manner or means but I draw the line at
that—'

'Shut up, Ranter, and stop looking at me as if I was Boris
Karloff in drag. You have completely misconstrued Babysoft's
meaning.' He turned to her: 'I take it Madame Lala herself is
quite well and not in the least pregnant?'

Babysoft spluttered. 'Jasus, what a thing to say! Now that
would be a miracle and the state of poor oul' Freddie—' she became
serious again and lifted her chin indignantly. 'I never in me life
heard of such a low obscene thing, talking that way about
Madame Lala as if she was a hoor or something.' She flashed her
eyes at Ranter. 'You should know better, Ranter O'Rourke, a
man of your age speaking like that about a lady—you should go
and wash out your mouth with carbolic!'

Ranter flared back. 'It's not me you should be picking on, but
your man there—the man with the magic flute, bejasus, the only
man I know who walks about on his middle leg!' Ranter as
quickly subsided and touched the peak of his cap rather mournfully. 'Begging all of yous pardon, naturally.'

Luke rubbed his palms together peaceably. 'I'm sure you meant
no disrespect to anyone, Ranter, and the toilet is exactly where it
was the last time you were there.'

Ranter got up huffily. 'Sometimes you break me bleeding heart,
Sheridan, you're so kind,' he said as he shuffled out.

'So, Rosie doesn't feel well and goes to Madame Lala—'

'I'm gasping for a drink,' Babysoft sighed. 'Talking always
makes the gargle go stale in me.'

'I'm sure we could all do with one,' said Sonny going to the
cabinet and taking out a bottle. 'After dear Luke's tortuous
excavation in search of a very unimportant truth I feel quite dry
myself. I'm afraid we've only wine left—all right, my children?'

'Better than a dose of Epsom salts anyway,' said Babysoft
charitably accepting a glass. 'Never could work up a taste for this
stuff. Still—' she tipped the glass and almost emptied it. 'Now
lookit here, I didn't say anything positive, did I? All I said was
that Rosie told me what Madame Lala told her—'

'Which was—precisely what?' Luke prompted.

'Well,' said Babysoft filling her glass from the bottle on the bedside table, 'she goes to Madame Lala and tells her the way she's feeling—'

'She was not feeling well, poor dear?' Sonny suggested sipping at her wine.

Babysoft looked at her surprised. 'Who—Rosie? Not a'tall—she was feeling great. Didn't I tell you she was flying around chirruping like a bleeding nightingale? She was—well, different, that's all. She's usually so effing grumpy in the mornings, a face on her as long as a late breakfast, but this morning she felt so good she knew something drastic must be wrong with her system or something. So she goes to Madame Lala—sure we all go to Madame Lala when we don't know what's wrong with us—and that was when she knew.'

'When she knew what?' asked Luke.

'When she knew she was going to have a baby. Or so she said.'

'Who said?'

'Jasus, are you deaf or something? Madame Lala said. She told Rosie she was—that way.' Babysoft made a vague indefinite movement of her hand towards her stomach. 'You know—that way.'

Sonny began to hum Brahms' 'Lullaby' dreamily and as if on cue waking from a trance Otto clapped his hands loudly and advanced. 'Hah—Luke the Vater is—we sing now the song, ja?' and started capering clumsily about in a circle:

'For he is the jolly gut fellow
ja, he is the jolly gut fellow
oh ja, Luke is the jolly gut fellow
and so we all of us so say!
We all of us so say
we all of us so say—'

'For the love of God, Otto,' said Luke ducking out of reach as Otto tried to embrace him, 'it's too soon to start dancing on my grave, as much as I appreciate the kind thought. Drink up and sit down.'

Otto stopped and looked at him in consternation. 'But understand I do not—you the Vater are this night—nein?'

Luke shook his head emphatically. 'Nein, nein, nein, a thousand times nein! I the Vater am not this night or any other bloody night.' He faced Babysoft accusingly, 'How the hell could Madame Lala know Rosie was "that way" just by looking at her?'

'I didn't say she *just* looked at her,' Babysoft told him with fine-edged scorn. 'Didn't she know by her hands?'

Luke stared. 'Her—hands? Whose hands, for God's sake?'

Babysoft threw her eyes ceilingwards. 'Madame Lala's hands of course—who else's? She just lay them on Rosie's belly and knew straight away. She always does. You'd need go no further than Madame Lala's hands if you want to know anything.'

'Ah,' said Luke enlightened, 'you mean there was a laying-on of hands at the establishment this morning?'

Babysoft frowned. 'I don't like the sound of that.'

'I mean, by laying her fine sensitive hands on the—er—the affected part, Madame Lala immediately divined the exact state of Rosie's health?'

'Up the pole you mean? Yeah—something like that, I suppose,' agreed Babysoft laconically. 'Oh, it never fails, take it from me. Madame Lala says her hands is—let me think now, what way did she put it? Oh yeah—infallible. That's it,' said Babysoft satisfied, 'her hands is infallible. That means they can never lie,' she added challengingly. 'Never. Like the Pope you know—infallible.'

'It would seem,' Sonny interposed serenely, 'that your fate has been ordained and sealed under the edict of Papal infallibility itself, dear Luke.'

'The Pope isn't being accused of clandestine fatherhood, at least not in this instance, as far as I can make out,' Luke retorted. 'His paternity is strictly of the spiritual variety, the fortunate old maharajah. He won't be sued for child maintenance, as I will be if I don't unravel this mortal coil before it chokes me.' He turned to Babysoft. 'Are you saying that Madame Lala is some kind of faith-healer among her other accomplishments?'

'Baby-diviner would be a more apt description, don't you think?' said Sonny sweet as honeyed arsenic.

'Lookit,' huffed Babysoft annoyed, 'I'm not saying anything I don't know about. All I'm saying is, if you've as much as a pain in your little toe Madame Lala can tell just by putting her hands on you. There's no use hiding things from her. She knows you've got things before you even know it yourself.'

'In her capacity an invaluable asset, surely,' said Luke sourly. 'That's all I need—a brothel-keeper gifted with extra-sensory perception.'

'What's that you said?' Babysoft asked quickly, her hackles rearing. 'What do you mean—a brothel-keeper? And what do you think you're calling a brothel? Madame Lala runs a respectable premises, in case you didn't know, and she's choosey who she lets in, never mind who she lets work there,' hand on hip she scrutinised Luke up and down. 'How she ever let the likes of *you* in I'll never know—you must've snaked in through the backdoor.'

Luke held up a peacekeeping hand. 'Mea culpa, Miss Brogan—an unforgivable lapse on my part. I don't normally possess the awful ill manners of looking a gift horse in the mouth or the still more deplorable habit of calling a spade a spade—put it all down to the tidings of dire foreboding which you in all innocence I am sure have just sprung on me, rendering logic difficult and propriety a positive effort of will. You've unsettled the usual calm tenor of my thoughts—'

'If you put your clothes on it might be better,' suggested Babysoft refilling her glass.

'How would that improve my mental processes?'

'I don't know about any processes, but it might help you to think better,' replied Babysoft. 'Do you know something?—you can catch a chill on the brain as easy as a chill on the kidneys. Did you know that now?'

'No, I must admit—'

'Oh yes—as easy as that. Sure isn't that what happened to my poor oul' Mongoose, the pet?'

'You mean you really have a mongoose as a pet, Miss Brogan?' enquired Sonny with happy interest.

'What's that? Oh yeah. Yeah—I suppose you could say that, right enough,' said Babysoft looking at her with puzzled suspicion.

'How delightful. I once had the most divine little ferret back in Baden-Baden. I christened him Leopold. We were inseparable. But a mongoose—now that *is* original.'

'A slight confusion of species, I think—' began Luke.

'Sure poor oul' Mongoose is a real pet,' added Babysoft with a hiccup. 'Pardon. Ah yes, a real oul' pet is poor Mongoose. Couple of marbles missing, mind you, but harmless. Ah yes, indeed,' she sighed, 'harmless is poor oul' Mongoose, in or out of bed, I'm sorry to say.'

'Oooh!' exclaimed Sonny in a little rush of excitement. 'I used to take my Leopold to bed with me too. He insisted on it—'

'Yes—Mongoose can be like that at times too—'

'He would curl up into a little ball at my feet—'

'Now Mongoose is a bit big to curl into a ball, mind you—'

'Well, yes, of course—I should think such a posture *would* be rather difficult for a mongoose to adopt—they are somewhat large—'

'It's his feet, mostly, you see—sweaty acres, I do call them, and Jasus, the stink when he takes his socks off—'

'You mean you have trained your mongoose to wear socks?' said Sonny intrigued.

'Trained him? Sure he always wore socks, as far as I can make out. And as for postures—well, you should see the positions my poor oul' Mongoose gets himself into betimes, especially with a few jars in him—'

'An imbibing mongoose—delicious! But, tell me, Miss Brogan,' said Sonny moving forward with genuine interest; 'how did you manage to acquire such a creature in the first place?'

Acquire him?' Babysoft echoed. 'What in the name of Jasus do you mean, "acquire him"? Do you think I picked him up in a bleeding jumble sale or something?'

'Naturally not, but aren't such creatures rather rare in these climes? I mean—'

'Rare? Sure the only thing rare about Mongoose is that he never comes to me on holy days or days of obligation. The rest of the year I can't get shut of him.'

'Such a faithful creature, too.'

'And don't keep calling him a "creature"—he's a terrible oul' eejit, granted, but he's still flesh and blood like me and you.' She turned to Luke for confirmation: 'You met him yourself.'

'Ah yes. He was regaling us with a few bars from "Speak To Me, Thora" if I remember correctly.'

'His effing national anthem,' said Babysoft gloomily. 'If you ask him a question, anything a'tall, he looks at you with that stoopid grin on his kisser and breaks into "Speak To Me, Thora". I swear to Jasus, if he was on his deathbed and the priest asked him if he had anything to confess before he met his Maker, the oul' gobshite would break into "Speak To Me Thora".'

'Now I am really confused,' said Sonny. 'A real-live genuine mongoose that drinks and sings and wears socks and—' She stopped. 'Oh, dear. The mist clears. Do forgive me, Miss Brogan. How can one be so dense? All this time you have been referring to a gentleman friend whose affectionate pet-name I took too literally.'

'Sure it's no matter a'tall—mistakes will happen. As poor Sadie Lundy said up in the Rotunda when they brought her in a little black baby. Anyway,' she continued turning to Luke, 'I was telling you how Mongoose got a chill on the brain—'

'Another time, Babysoft,' he said going resolutely to the door. 'I'm sure it's an intriguing story, full of warm human interest, and you must promise to give me the full unabridged unexpurgated account sometime and we'll both make a fortune from the Sunday papers. But it is a far far better thing that I do now—'

Ranter returned, still rather glum, hands sunk deep in overcoat pockets, shoulders hunched together, one eye open peering truculent and red-rimmed around.

'Ah good Horatio,' greeted Luke, clapping him fondly about the shoulders. 'Art thou relieved of thy fearful burden? What say'st thou? Fleet'st thou with me, good marry, onward through night's dread canyons to where good ale and logfire and the laughter of merry servant wenches await us?'

'Get fucking stuffed, Sheridan.'

'All I meant to say was—how soon can you get rolling?'

'You're ready to piss off outa here, you mean?' said Ranter brightening visibly.

'I'll just slip into something more comfortable,' lisped Luke giving Ranter's nose a playful tweak as he skipped out stumbling and clutching at the towel as he went, thus spoiling that unremarkable little exit, muttering as he went, 'Fuck it again . . .'

'Thanks be to Jasus,' said Ranter rubbing his hands heartily together 'I thought we were here for the duration. No disrespect to you, maam,' he added to Sonny. 'A fine gaff you have here, without a doubt,' he went on looking about him with a new respect and admiration now that the moment of departure was imminent. 'Sure I never saw so many jacks in me life. You might say there's jacks all over the kip, and everything that clean you could ate off the floor. And the gargle now—oh no damper on the gargle. Sure you couldn't be kinder and that's a fact. But as true as God, maam, if I go further than Castleknock I get homesick.' He appealed to Babysoft. 'Is that a word of a lie I'm telling?'

'True for you, Ranter, true for you. Sure as far as Ranter is concerned the Liffey might as well be the Nile and the Wicklow mountains the bleeding Alps. He's not too sure of his way even when he steps outside of the Liberties—'

'Ah now don't run away with it altogether,' said Ranter, a little perturbed to have such claustrophobic insularity ascribed to him. 'Be reasonable now. Sure amn't I a taximan and I must know the lie of the land in the line of duty if I'm to earn a few bob a'tall. Still and all,' he said sniffing noisily, 'if you ever wanted to get rid of me in a hurry you'd only have to exile me to the likes of Monkstown or Malahide and I'd wither away in no time.'

'You are a lovely man, Mr O'Rourke,' said Sonny stepping up and kissing him fondly on the cheek. 'I could easily fall desperately in love with you.'

'Oh Jasus, Ranter, be careful!' murmured Babysoft with mock fervour. 'I don't think you'd take too well if you were transplanted to Baden-Baden. Poor Ranter—you'd wither on the stem, like the last rose of summer.'

'Can't a person be—be friendly, for the love of God,' stammered Ranter backing away, 'without you making carnal remarks like that?'

'Oh, Mr O'Rourke,' cried Sonny taking hold of his hand and pressing it to her bosom, 'dear Mr O'Rourke, let us all go and sample the nocturnal beatitudes and benedictions of your beloved city.'

'Careful, Ranter,' murmured Babysoft making soft purring feline sounds. 'I don't like the way your man is looking at you.'

'Sure you're not dressed for it, maam,' said Ranter casting a wary eye in Otto's direction. 'You wouldn't want to be venturing out on a night like this, raining cats and dogs—'

'I love all animals,' answered Sonny brushing the tips of his fingers with her lips; 'especially cats and dogs.'

'Why don't you stay and play cards or something, maam?' Ranter said puffing heavily and trying gently to extricate his hand from hers. 'Sure you can't leave poor oul' Otto here alone, all by himself.'

'I just love venturing out on nights like this, Mr O'Rourke,' Sonny replied, 'and as for dear Otto—I would not dream of leaving him behind. Would I, pet?' she cooed and to Ranter's immense relief relinquished his hand and returned to Otto's side. 'You want to come to Dublin's fair city too, don't you, my lamb?'

Her voice being addressed exclusively to him made Otto's face light up like a flare, eyes agleam, and she suffered his impulsive compulsive bearhug.

'Ja, ja, mein Gretchen, oh ja, to Dublin city the fair we all go,' and holding his hand aloft thundered forth:

> 'In the fair Dublin city
> where the Fräuleins they are pretty
> my eyes they go after the Molly Malone
> and she sits there in her barrow
> and the streets they are narrow
> guten Morgen guten Morgen for the Molly Malone—'

'First time I ever heard that sung in German before,' Babysoft remarked. 'I heard of broken English, but that's in smithereens, bejasus.'

'Give credit where credit is due now,' reproved Ranter, 'He made a brave stab at it.'

'Stab at it? He knifed it,' said Babysoft finishing off her glass. 'He axed it to death.'

'It must be powerful to speak a foreign language all the same,' said Ranter with respect as Sonny dutifully congratulated the beaming Otto with a chaste kiss. 'I wouldn't mind speaking broken German, bejasus.'

'Ah, you're like meself, Ranter. The only other language you know is effing and blinding.'

'You're laughing at your man there for the way he sang "Molly Malone",' continued Ranter, his mind at rest now fixed on a certain target and ready for amiable argument. 'But who are we to mock and jeer when we can't speak a dickybird in *his* native tongue?'

'Speak for yourself—I read every story that Hans Christian Andersen ever wrote.'

Ranter looked at her with immense pity. 'Hans Christian

bleeding Andersen? Isn't that wonderful now? And what was Hans Christian Andersen but a fucking Dane?'

Babysoft tossed her head. 'Danes, Dutchmen, Swedes or Germans—sure they're all the same, aren't they, foreigners the lot of them, for Christ's sake—they're all tarred with the one stick. And anyway,' she challenged with jutting chin, 'what are *you* getting up on your bike for? Did *you* ever read Hans Christian Andersen?'

Ranter scornfully dismissed, 'Jasus bless your innocence—do you think I have nothing better to do with me time than sit on me arse reading some bleeding foreigner writing about inchworms and invisible clobbers and magic windmills and all that bullshit?'

'Ah, you've seen the picture!' cried Babysoft accusingly. 'You've seen the effing picture—it had what's-his-name Danny Kaye in it skipping and hopping like bejasus all over the place galloping into song if you as much as gave him a crooked look.'

'I didn't me arse see the picture,' said Ranter indignantly. 'When have I the time to go and see pictures and me up to me neck in bawling shitty-arsed kids? The last time I saw a picture was *The Jazz Singer,* and that was the first talking movie and the very first film that your man Al Jolson was in.'

Babysoft's eyes widened. 'Jasus, Ranter, are you that ancient? Sure that was before the Flood. Where did they dig you up from a'tall?'

'Old wine is the best, Mr O'Rourke,' consoled Sonny her hand clasped in Otto's. 'I go always for vintage models myself.'

'Thank you kindly, maam,' said Ranter, his ire only slightly mollified. 'But to hear Shirley Temple there talking,' he returned the hard look that Babysoft had given him, 'you'd think I was laid out in the habit already and them all shedding crocodile tears over me.' He gave the peak of his cap an extra forceful twist. 'Sure a man isn't ready to be nailed down and coffined at fifty-two, surely to Jasus!'

'May I,' said Sonny graciously, 'return the compliment you paid me a few minutes ago by saying that you, too, are a credit to your sex, Mr O'Rourke?'

'Oh, it's not just age, maam,' Ranter affirmed with a nonchalant wave of his hand. 'Sure age means nothing to me, maam. It's childish to be touchy about age. Only,' he said turning a still rancorous eye to Babysoft, 'I don't like people making disparaging remarks about their seniors and giving sly snaky little hints when they don't know what they're talking about!'

'Ah, you're not cross with me, Ranter, are you?' said Babysoft crossing over and putting her head trustingly on his shoulder. 'Sure don't you know if it wasn't for Gertie I'd drop everything for you?'

'Leave a man alone, can't you,' grumbled Ranter shoving her gently off. 'Don't be putting me in the way of temptation, girl, or I might have a great fall like Humpty Dumpty and I doubt if Gertie would want to put me together again.'

'Ah, Ranter, Ranter,' cried Babysoft taking the stage again, throwing her arms wide. 'Don't be a fool, Rhett Butler—don't you know this thing is bigger than both of us?' She started to giggle. 'As the girl said to the greengrocer when she asked him how much were his cucumbers.'

'It breaks me heart,' said Ranter shaking his head, 'it breaks me bleeding heart to see a fine fresh young mayflower like yourself going down the thorny path of perdition.'

'Cathleen Ni Hounihan,' dramatised Babysoft arms outstretched contemplating the ceiling, 'your way is a thorny way,' she slapped her thigh resoundingly, 'and more power to your fallopian tubes, Cathleen alanna!'

And swinging imaginary top hat and cane swirling and twirling into pantomimic revelry once more:

'Oh darling Sylvester
let's you and me sequester
down among the sand dunes at Dollymount.
Oh wouldn't it be Utopian
if you fondled my fallopian
down among the sand dunes at Dollymount.
Oh silvery Sylvester
don't let your passion fester
but come and be my jester
down among the sand dunes at Dollymount.
For there's no fool like an old fool
as I found out in my old school
as our Master gave us sums
and pinched all our little bums.

So get up on your bike Sylvester
and do what you bloody like Sylvester
down among the sand dunes at Dollymount.'

'Bravo, Miss Brogan,' said Sonny clapping politely. 'Did you
ever contemplate going on the stage? You seem to possess a real
talent for the impromptu performance.'

Babysoft gave a high contrived tinkling laugh and threw back
her head after taking several mythical encores, looking beyond
Sonny to where shone for her at a precise point between the
curtain-rail and the ceiling a glaring archipelago of dazzling
stagelights. 'Me on the stage, is it? You may well ask, Miss Otis,
oh you may well ask! Sure amn't I blinded with all them bleeding
footlights burning up into me eyes night after night and nearly
deaf with the crowd cheering and clapping like mad? A star was
born, I'm telling you, when I first saw the light of day. In a cakebox it was, a Bewley's cakebox of course, under the stage of the
oul' Royal in Hawkin's Street! Sure wasn't me poor Mother, the
light of heaven on her, second cousin removed from the great
Gerty Gitana? And didn't me oul' Da, may he roast in hell, often
got locked beyant in Phil Reilly's with none other than the
Chocolate-Coloured Coon himself, G. H. Elliott? Oh yes bejasus,'
affirmed Babysoft preening, 'I come from a long line of
theatricals.'

'I must confess I am not familiar with any of those names,
frankly,' said Sonny, 'but it all sounds fascinating.'

'The age of innocence is with us yet,' said Ranter softly.

'Ah, don't be minding me,' sighed Babysoft, dropping the mask
reluctantly and sitting down on the bed. 'Sure I'm just having
you on.'

'You mean there was no cakebox under the stage?' asked
Sonny.

'There might've been a shower of cakeboxes under the stage,
but I wasn't in any of them. Sure the closest I ever got to knocking
poor Judy Garland off her pedestal was when we put on Snow
White and the Seven Dwarfs beyant in the Father Matthew Hall
in Church Street. I was eight at the time.'

'But you did play Snow White?' pressed Sonny hopefully.

'Well—no, not exactly,' admitted Babysoft. 'Snow White was
played by a little bitch from Sherriff Street called Bridie Maguire

—she had spots all over her and nits in her hair, not to mention dirty big warts on her fingers.'

'A right bleeding Snow White she must've made,' said Ranter.

'Red tape,' informed Babysoft haughtily. 'Corruption in high places you might say. Sure wasn't it her uncle Father Columbanus who put the show on in the first place?'

'So you never quite got to play Snow White?' Sonny commiserated. 'How sad for you.'

'Oh, I had a very important role just the same,' Babysoft answered with pride. 'It was what you might call a supporting role. You see, your woman Snow White always had a great big star hung over her head—it went with her whenever she moved. Well, in our panto I was the one that had to hold that star and carry it everywhere.'

'Like the bloke that carries the flag at the head of the cavalry,' put in Ranter.

'A bit like that, I suppose, except that nobody ever saw a bit of me, on account of I had to hide behind your woman Bridie Maguire—the one that was Snow White you know—who was wearing one of them big huge old-fashioned dresses that sweep out for miles, but it was a very important part just the same. I mean to say,' Babysoft went on with supreme vindication, 'what good would Snow White have been without her effing star?'

'Did I hear someone mention my name?' said Luke in the doorway. He stood smiling at them, dressed again after a casual freehanded haphazard fashion, shirt widenecked and loose jacket slung over shoulder, one foot minus a sock, but keeneyed and readymouthed, fit for the fray once more. 'Are we ready to fold up tents and silently steal away?' he asked coming in. 'I have now another sort of dateline to keep.'

'You said it, Hornblower,' said Babysoft, getting off the bed and weaving an unsteady but determined path towards the bottle half full on the cabinet. 'It's the sweet smell of pissy shitty nappies for you from now on. You'll be a great loss to us hard-working girls in Madame Lala's, but you're getting a good woman.'

'Well,' said Ranter with simple good sense, 'from my position on the sidelines, I would say it's neither a man lost nor a woman thrown away.'

'There's nobody going to say anything funny about Rosie in my presence, let me tell you,' said Babysoft tipping wine over the side of her glass and giving them all the benefit of a defiant look. 'She may be a high-and-mighty bitch betimes, turning up her nose at whiskey and looking for Napoleon brandy, but more power to her if she can get the eejits to buy it for her, and anyway Rosie's my friend.' Her eyes that constantly had the quality of hard dark polished marble momentarily misted over as another loud hiccup surfaced unchecked. 'That's right, ladies and gentlemen—Rosie's my friend, my sister in adversity you might say, a pal tried and true, pinned down like meself on the rack of life.'

'Your loyalty does you credit, Miss Brogan,' said Sonny warmly. 'Loyalty is one of the greatest qualities in life.'

'Ah loyalty me arse,' retorted Babysoft with scorn, licking her wrist after drawing it across her wine-wet chin. 'It's human nature, that's all it is—human nature. Sure them bleeding politicians and clergymen with nothing better to do are always on about loyalty—loyalty to your country, to the government, to the holy Catholic church, loyalty to this cause and that cause and every bleeding little cross-breed of a cause under the sun. And where does it all get us?' she demanded looking at each of them in turn with belligerent contempt. 'Bleeding nowhere! We're stuffed with all kinds of loyalty from the day we're born like Cow-'n-Gate! To hell with loyalty,' concluded Babysoft managing finally to fill her glass without mishap. 'It's human nature, that's all it is—just human nature.'

'Amn't I a trade unionist meself?' Ranter broke in. 'Don't I know what the spirit of brotherhood is meself? Sure aren't we all united against the common foe?' Ranter held up his fingers and began counting on them. 'Rising prices, falling wages, working conditions only fit for muck-savages, bleeding managers and bosses left over from the Penal days, little fucking Cromwells in boilersuits or Lord Lieutenants with derbies and brollies and pinstripped clobbers sipping wine and sherry in the Shelbourne and telling us how much we are worth—they should be lined up against the wall of the nearest public pisshouse and shot, the whole poxy lot of them.'

'Mind your blood pressure, Ranter,' cautioned Babysoft. 'You're getting a lovely shade of scarlet round the gills.'

'Don't be minding me blood pressure or the coloration of me mincepies,' snorted Ranter continuing to enumerate on his fingers.

'It's diabolical what the worker has to put up with in this city where Jim Larkin spilt his rich red blood for us—'

'I was under the impression,' observed Luke, 'that he passed away rather comfortably in bed somewhere in the States—'

'Taxes as high as Finn McCoole's nose,' Ranter went on stoically ignoring such unmanly jibes; 'never a bloody rebate to talk about, and what they give you on the Labour wouldn't keep a midget in salt and pepper, never mind a man with a houseful of nippers.'

'If you only knew,' mused Babysoft wandering around the room feeling the walls, 'if you only knew what me and poor Rosie have gone through. It's not all sunshine, I can tell you, it's not all gargle and giggles—ah, bejasus it's not! The things we have to put up with just to make a decent living—it would make your hair stand on end—not to mention anything else.'

'Sure the conditions for the workingman in Dublin is deplorable altogether,' Ranter said vehemently and added as a solicitous afterthought, 'or the workingwoman, for that matter. What we want in this city is democracy for all, but the only democratic thing left in life is death.'

'Now I'm not saying anything bad about Madame Lala behind her back,' Babysoft emphasised, taking time and care with her words. 'Sure everyone knows it's one of the most respectable and best-run houses in Dublin.' She paused as though to allow the significance of her description sink duly in. 'Pleasure-house is what I said, exactly what it is.'

'An abode of endless delight,' Luke concurred, 'and, I might add, endless corridors.'

'Pleasure-house *is* what I said,' reiterated Babysoft highly pleased with her inventiveness and then frowning. 'But not even Madame Lala can see and hear everything at once like God or the Virgin Mary, see and hear everything that's going on in the world all at once—upstairs and downstairs, you might say—'

Otto suddenly and without preamble erupted forthwith into a spirited rendition of a folk-ballad sung or more correctly blared out in his native tongue.

'Oh dear,' said Sonny fondly, 'Otto is on parade again.'

'Does he often take turns like that?' enquired Luke.

'Only when he's reminded of his illustrious past.'

'Did he have an illustrious past?'

'Oh quite. I wonder who is taking the salute this time—fat Hermann, jolly Martin, fanatical Rudolf, or the funny adorable animated little robot himself?'

'He knew them well, did he?'

'Oh intimately. They were his familiars.'

'And what illustrious rank did he hold in those great and glorious days of the thousand years? Did he have Adolf's pearly ear?'

'Otto played a Trojan part in the war,' replied Sonny, 'directing the intricate operation of the annual grape offensive in his vineyard at Baden-Baden. Every third barrel was set aside for the enlightenment and moral edification of the Third Reich. Each year he conducted a tremendous counter-attack from the ramparts fighting off the troops on their way to the Front. He claims he should have got the Iron Cross for that alone.'

'They also serve who stay at home and squish grapes,' murmured Luke, taking the bottle from the unresisting hand of Babysoft and putting it to his mouth.

'What we want in this city,' said Ranter valiantly, 'is less bullshit and more concrete action—I mean, it's no fucking good putting down motions if you're not going to put up actions, is it? And as for the unions, well, there again, you have all the wrong men—'

The door was pushed open of a sudden and the squat dumpling somehow oddly malevolent figure of Aggie filled the threshold, arms crossed and hair in frantic disarray confronting them, her whole face glowing like a roaring logfire. 'Dinner is served, me lord, ladies and gentlemen,' announced Aggie with heavily slurred voice, 'for them that's able for it, and them that's not know where the front door is!'

'Don't be absurd, dear Applebud,' said Sonny sailing up on a cloud of satiny gentility. 'You couldn't have dinner served, since there is no food of a remotely digestible or edible kind to serve dinner with, unless you have wrought unimaginable miracles in the kitchen, and anyway we have all decided to go out.'

Aggie's face became a deeper more unequivocal red as she stood like a female Samson in the doorway. 'All going out, are you?' she panted, her fingers taking up their agitated tipping and tapping tattoo on her stout forearm. 'Just like that you are all abandoning ship, and me after sizzling me gizzards over the stove for you this last bloody hour—Mother of God!' she cried suddenly succumbing to both grief and wrath, flinging her smock before her eyes and stamping her dwarfish slippered foot. 'Where is the justice in the world, where is the justice, I ask you?'

Otto came forward, click-heeled saluting her with grave courteous concentration. 'Frau Applebud, the red apples they dance in your cheeks, ja.'

'Oh, Mister Otto, nobody wants me beautiful stew that I'm after crucifying meself over for the last hour.'

Otto all one brilliant uncomprehending gargoyle smile caught hold of Aggie and swung her around and around in ever widening and erratic circles.

'Oh, Mister Otto!'

'Bejasus,' said Ranter, beholding with interest and not a little awe Aggie's fulsome bosom tossing aloft, 'they'll effing well fall off her if he swings her about like that much longer.'

'Otto dear, do desist,' ordered Sonny taking hold of his arm. 'Let Applebud go before the dear lady disintegrates in a purple shower of exploding molecules. One must have reasonable respect for age, after all.'

'Isn't it a wonder now,' said Ranter sidemouthed to Luke, 'that your man there, the mad count, wasn't put down years ago? A bloke like that is a walking menace to society, going around like Genghis Khan in the height of delirium.'

'Charity, Ranter, charity,' counselled Luke, passing the dwindling contents of the bottle to him. 'Forget not the multitude it covers. Friend Otto is nothing if not a gentleman, despite his slightly unorthodox appearance.'

Ranter shuffled his feet uneasily as he took a swig. 'Are we carting all that shower back to Dublin with us?'

'Surely it is the least we can do to show our appreciation of their hospitality?' reasoned Luke.

'Couldn't you just send them a postcard of O'Connell Bridge or something with a few words on it,' said Ranter feebly, 'you know, just to take the harm out of it?'

The bed shuddered as Aggie flounced down upon it, smock and apron shooting upwards revealing black elastic garters sunk into layers of lard-like flesh.

'Jasus—I'm bet!' puffed Aggie her hand fluttering to and fro in front of her face in a vain attempt to fan herself. 'I saw the time

—the time that I could dance—dance the buckles off the shoes of the—of the best ceili dancer in Leinster!'

'That was before the rebellion, Agatha,' lisped Babysoft tottering up and waving a reproving mocking finger. 'When Adam was a highlander and Cormac MacAirt was plucking the Jewish-harp in Tara's halls.'

Aggie's eyes grew quite dark as her malevolence flared again. 'Take the likes of yourself across the threshold of an honest man's house, Hortensia Brogan!' she breathed in a series of aggrieved and aggravated snorts. 'You're not fit to lick Mister Otto's boots.'

'He's not wearing any bleeding boots,' Babysoft pointed out, stooping forward to make sure. 'Are you, Otto love? 'Course you're not, silly 'oul cow, and anyway, Agatha,' she said straightening perilously up, 'I'm sure you could do a far better job at licking than me, whether it's his boots or his arse.'

'Mister Otto—Miss Sonny,' stammered Aggie gulping down her dismay, 'how could you let a—a creature, a—a *thing* like that wan into a respectable abode, polluting the very air with her—her filthy language, and the smell of drink off her—'

Babysoft returned to the offensive with already the pronounced swagger of the victor. 'Drink she says, and her oul' kisser lit up like hallowe'en with the whiskey! Don't go within a yard of her with a lighted match, or we'll all go up in flames.'

Aggie was finding coherent counter-attack rather difficult. 'You —you little—little—' she paused struggling for the definitive expletive, then her inflamed eyes narrowed and her nostrils twitched as she spat it out with venom. 'You *pro!*'

Babysoft strutted before her hapless empurpled victim heavily seated on the bed. 'Ah-hah,' she said putting on a softer more intimate tone of voice and wagging her forefinger, 'I know your little secret, Agatha—I know what you've been up to while your master and your mistress were away.' Babysoft bent forward slightly swaying but maintaining an air of schoolteacherly reproach, 'You've been doing naughty things to the cooking wine again, haven't you, Agatha?'

Strange gurgling noises were coming from Aggie as she almost cringed and cowered back on the bed from this merciless finger-wagging inquisition.

'Really, Agatha,' continued Babysoft crossing her arms as she took a step back and looked down with a sorrowful shake of her head. 'Whatever are we to do with you?' Her voice took on an accent of stilted gentility. 'We cannot, repeat, can-*not* go on giving you one—a—more—a—chance, Agatha. I'm greatly afraid we must send you packing again on another Retreat to the Carmelite Fathers in Foxrock—' she held up her hand as the anguished sounds from the bed grew louder—'No, no, Agatha, it's no use appealing to my good nature—it's for your own good!'

'You really do have a most remarkable theatrical bent, Miss Brogan,' complimented Sonny with renewed admiration. 'What a shame you were not found in a cakebox under the stage, after all.' Sonny began to rub her chin. 'Now who do I know in a position to promote and facilitate aspiring young Bernhardts?'

Aggie at last found voice, struggling thickly through her rage. 'Like your fornicating oul' Da before you!' she cried, her small pudding fingers working in fury on the eiderdown. 'Puffed up with deceit and lust, dragging decent folk down into the gutter with you.'

'Ah now c'mon, Agatha,' said Babysoft circling the bed with arrogant swivelling hips. 'That's no way to be talking about an oul' sweetheart. Be charitable to the dead, Agatha, for Jasus only knows you were charitable enough to him when he was in it!'

Apprehension swept across Aggie's face even as her defiance briefly glimmered. 'What are you insinuating, Hortensia Brogan? Don't you be trying to take me good name—'

'Take what was took years ago? Ah now c'mon, Agatha, what do you take me for?'

'I can hold me head higher than anyone in this room.'

'I'm not one to rub salt and vinegar in, Agatha oul' flower,' said Babysoft, resting both hands on the bed and leaning towards Aggie, 'but I distinctly remember the colour of your drawers that day.

Aggie's face seemed to crumble and dissolve away like a mound of treacle melting. 'I never did, Mister Otto,' she wailed tears of utter misery making a reddened soggy mess of her eyes. 'I never did, Miss Sonny, as God is my judge.'

'Here now, Aggie, take a snort of this,' said Babysoft, suddenly relenting, urging the wine upon the other woman. 'It's only wine, I'm sorry to say, but take a sip, it'll do you good.'

Aggie, resigned and passive, let the bottle be put to her mouth, the wine making a crimson furrow down her creased hairy chin, her eyes misted strangely old and rheumy staring out beyond them. 'I meant no harm, no harm at all. I liked poor Nellie Peabody. A kind harmless poor soul. We were brought up together, sure, the same age and all. I was only trying to do me duty as a neighbour and a Christian, helping out and lending a hand when she took bad with the child coming. There wasn't a bad thought in me head when he came in early that day, when Jamesy Brogan came in . . .'

'Will somebody burst into song or something?' implored Ranter.

Sonny released Otto whose arm she had firmly been detaining in hers. 'I must say it *is* somewhat indecent of us,' she declared picking up a silver-handled hairbrush off the dressing-table and stroking her head vaguely, 'standing here as if ranged round the catafalque of someone lying in state, listening while poor dear Applebud makes a tortuous excursion back into her torrid girlhood. We should all feel thoroughly ashamed of ourselves.'

'I can't bleeding well gag her, can I?' whispered Babysoft.

'I vote we all post-haste vacate these dismal premises,' proposed Luke, 'and sally forth with a loud tally-ho on the slightly uneven road to Dublin.'

'All in favour raise their hands or, failing that, show the whites of their eyes,' said Ranter.

Sonny stepped forward. 'Come along, Applebud dear,' she said taking Aggie firmly by the hand and raising her from the bed. 'I will take you to your room for a little nap.'

'I didn't mean any harm.'

'A little nap now, Applebud. I absolutely insist on it. I have a nice little bottle of Jack Daniels put by specially for you, there's a dear.'

'Men is a curse,' muttered Aggie allowing herself to be led tamely away, moving sluggishly and shaking her head bemused and jaded. 'That's what they are, the bloody curse of the world . . .'

'You were right, Ranter,' acknowledged Babysoft getting to her feet. 'I shouldn't have gone on at her like that, and she not knowing if it was today or tomorrow. I didn't think she'd feel that way about it, and all that time in between.'

'What I suggest is,' said Ranter as he pulled the cap more firmly down on his head, 'that we all get the hell out of here before we end up screaming for the Holy Ghost to help us. Sure there's saner locked up beyant in Portrane.' He stopped halfway across the cold expanse of hall as the others filed after him. 'Hey, hold your horses a minute,' he said as a dark thought loomed. 'What happens if we're stopped by the law on the way back?'

'No bother,' said Luke waving airily. 'We'll say we are either coming from or going to a wake. Wakes are the only social functions left in Ireland today that have any aesthetic status. Even the most bovine-minded policeman—which only the best are, by the way—understands the mystical significance of a wake. You might say that at a wake we are in the midst of life.'

'That may or may not be, Einstein,' said Ranter stubbornly sticking to his guns,' but one look at your man there, and we'll all be fucking impounded!'

'Be not blinded, Ranter, by the foibles and baubles of the passing parade—for lo

> Show me a beggar and I'll show you a king
> said the blindman unto the dandy—'

Luke declaiming sprinted past them to the great heavy oak front-door with its massive black iron bolts, prising it open and standing in an attitude of profound meditation at the top step framed in the portal haloed in the overhead light.

> 'For the straightest of creatures is the ape
> though he be crooked-arsed and bandy—'

'Poetry, that is,' said Babysoft as she swept gaily across the hall with the martial-stomping Otto in tow. 'Ah, Lukey love,' she cooed, sliding a serpentine arm round his neck, her upturned yellow-lit face piquant and oddly mannish in its vulpine response, 'I'd run away meself without benefit of priest or vicar if you didn't have to stand by poor Rosie!'

'I do wish you wouldn't keep insisting on me carrying out my obligations as a gentleman,' Luke said in a vexed way. 'It is a role that ill befits my other sterling qualities, such as my cherished cowardice which I guard so zealously against those who would cruelly dispossess me of it.'

'Surely to Jasus your man there, Kaiser Willie, could put something decent on?' Ranter complained pointing to Otto who stood grinning and saluting as he meanwhile conducted himself through the stirring strains of war. 'He looks like a leftover understudy from *The Great Dictator*.'

Luke held up his bottle hand in emphasis. 'Clothes, my friend, do not the true man make, unless he be construed of folly and fake—' he struck his forehead with open palm—'Hah, it rhymes, it rhymes! Now I know that my Redeemer liveth—Ahoy!' he shouted exultant leaping down the broad stone steps. 'Verily I say unto you, I shall go out from this place and become a legend in my own lifetime!'

'And why wouldn't you?' yelled Babysoft, throwing up her hands and running after him. 'Sure it's better than sitting blowing your fingers by the fire!'

'Yes, indeed,' said Luke raindrops falling on him as he grabbed hold of a low treebranch and shook it, 'I will definitely set out to become a cult.'

Ranter came up raggedly cap askew, blowing heavily. 'You were always that, bejasus!'

'No, no, Ranter,' shouted Luke dancing round in widening circles in and out of the trees, 'you misinterpret. The word in question is cult. C.U.L.T.—emphasis on the L, Ranter my soulmate.' He raised his head to a chipped incomplete moon racing harelike through sullen bileful clouds. 'My senses reel with wine and poetry!'

'Ah—will you listen to that!' sighed Babysoft. 'Poetry that is— pure poetry!'

'Pure bullshit,' growled Ranter grimly holding on to his cap as the wind slewed him around. 'Where is me bleeding car gone?'

'Where you left it,' Babysoft told him.

'And where's that, might I ask?'

'How the hell do I know? C'mon and dance out of that!'

'Ah g'wan and leave me be, can't you?' said Ranter impatiently pushing her away. 'We'll all have to walk it back unless I find the car, and the smile will be on the other side of your kisser then, I'm telling you!'

'I don't care!' cried Babysoft throwing herself down on the wet abundant grass and kissing it. 'You haven't got a soul, Ranter,' she panted rubbing her face in the grass and tearing at it with her strong virile teeth. 'That's *your* trouble, Ranter O'Rourke —you haven't got a soul!'

'Never you mind about me soul, girl—just let me find me curse-of-God car!'

'Oh Ranter, c'mon and taste the beautiful grass.'

'Where's me bollocking car, you mad hooring bitch? You'd think you were a cow, bejasus,' said Ranter his words swept away by the wind. 'Eating the fucking grass like that.'

Otto with robe flapping wildly about him doing a demonic cavort up and down the driveway:

> 'In Dublin fair the city
> and the Fräuleins they do be pretty
> in their barrels and their barrows
> my eyes they are seeing die Molly Malone—'

Luke with an elaborate bow extended a hand to the earth-prone Babysoft, every ungainly inch the debonair cavalier—'Arise, my Lady Greensleeves, and take the arm of he who would gather together the sun, moon and stars and wrap them in a little scented handkerchief to give to thee, Oh sweet dispenser of endless charm—'

And unprepared for the vigour with which the lady responded keeled over and promptly tumbled on top of her in the grass.

'Jasus, you're only skin and bones, God love you,' squealed Babysoft, gleefully balancing his lightweight frame upon her as though he were some fragile plaything designed exclusively for her pleasure. 'Stop wriggling—sure I won't bite you.'

'Be good, sweet maid, and let who will be clever.'

Babysoft pulled his face down to hers. 'Ah can't you shut up for once in your life and give us a kiss for Jasus' sake!'

'Do noble deeds, not dream them all day long,' mumbled Luke, his mouth slipping and sliding over hers.

Babysoft sucked hungrily at him. 'Oh, this is gorgeous—don't mind who's looking—put your hand there, darling—*there* . . .'

'And so make life, love, and the vast forever—'

Babysoft wriggled frantically beneath him, manoeuvring him between the widening arc of her legs. 'Oh would you ever shut up and do what God gave you the power to do.'

'One grand sweet song—'

A sudden deluge of swollen raindrops from the overhanging

branches in a wild gust of wind, drenching the entangled couple below in a muddy cascade.

Babysoft baulked and shrieked, unceremoniously dislodging her lethargic Lothario. 'Jasus, I'm bleeding drownded—would you ever get up off me, you stupid omadhaun, and me covered in mud and muck!'

'You cut me to the quick, Guinevere,' said Luke springing lightly to his feet. 'But never let it be said I was found wanting in chivalry—' he flung his jacket to the ground making a small carpeted causeway from lawn to driveway—'The spirit of Raleigh lives.'

The truant vehicle was rediscovered at length nosedeep in tangled clutch of shrubbery, inhabited by a pair of busily interlocked rabbits on the back seat startled from their amorous labours into chattering flight, a blur of fur flying past headlong into the brambly sanctuary of woodland—

'Nowhere is safe,' said Ranter woefully, 'from the fornicating influence of foreign infiltration, bejasus!'

Into the dark musty interior of the car went a pitch and tumble of bodies. The engine began to tick over, exuding life, yielding a slow evasive warmth.

'Halt, halt!'

Otto tangled up in his robe, struggling to scramble out as the car started to move under him, gesticulated wildly towards the house. 'Mein Gretchen—in with the Applebud she is!'

'Will you keep that fucking Attila quiet in there before he goes berserk?' barked Ranter, testily reversing up onto the driveway facing the lighted entrance of the house.

'In with the Applebud she is, mein Gretchen!' cried Otto distraught as he struggled with the doorhandle. 'To the moon I will not go without mein Gretchen, nein, nein!'

'Nein fucking nein yourself!' retorted Ranter wrestling with the steering-wheel, his face a shade of mottled purple from his exertions.

'C'mere to me, Otto me oul' cockatoo,' cooed Babysoft taking his hand and placing it firmly between her knees. 'Sure we wouldn't dream of scarpering without your little bit of mortal comfort—would we, Ranter? Jasus knows we're not without feelings.'

Ranter pushed the cap further back on his head as he rested

from his labours. 'What's keeping your woman in the name of Jasus? I'm gasping for a good pint.'

'Self-torture, my friend,' counselled Luke, nursing the last of the wine. 'The masochistic tendency that would appear to be endemic to the Celtic psyche.'

'Fuck off, Brinsley Sheridan,' interrupted Ranter sourly rubbing his mouth with the back of his wrist. 'It's all that hooring wine that has me as dry as me dead Granny's paps. I felt like a fucking altarboy in there with all that wine around me.'

'You lack sophistication, Ranter. Allow me to enlighten you as to the aesthetic benefits to be gained from a proper appreciation of the fruit of the vine—when you are nodding half asleep on the taxi rank in O'Connell Street admiring the potted plants and waiting for our rich gaudy American cousins to come streaming out of the Gresham.'

'That bleeding stuff isn't a gargle at all!' broke in Ranter with disgust. 'It's vinegar with a bit of sugar added. It's only fit for hoors and queers. Sure I often pissed better gargle than that!'

Otto meanwhile had grown calmer under Babysoft's stroking fingers. 'The soul very good you have, little Softbaby.'

Ranter spluttered. 'Softbaby, bejasus!'

'Shut up, Ranter,' said Babysoft huffily, 'and let the gentleman speak.'

'Und very much it is I like you,' continued Otto in a thick lugubrious tone as he in turn patted her hand fondly. 'But the heart is here in me,' he thumped his chest hard, 'very much clippity-clop-clip it goes for mein liebes Gretchen—very much it goes boom-bang-boom for Gretchen, and nowhere,' he thumped the back of the seat resoundingly, 'nowhere do I, Otto, go round der face of der world without Gretchen—nein, nein, Fräulein Softbaby!'

'That touches me, that does, that really touches me,' said Babysoft sniffling loudly. 'Not a bloody inch will he stir without his Cathleen alanna. Now that makes me want to cry, that does. It's just what Cary Grant would do for Ingrid Bergman, or Clark Gable would do for Ava Gardner, or—'

'Or what Cocky Roche would do for Kitty Geraghty if he caught her up a back-alley after closing time,' Ranter interposed with prosaic finesse.

'The men of Dublin haven't one iota of romance in them—you'd get more out of a bleeding Zulu!' Babysoft turned on Luke irritably—'Is there anything left in that effing bottle itself?'

'The thirst that from the soul doth rise,' he intoned as she snatched the bottle from his hand. 'I think we would all agree,' he went on leaning back comfortably and stretching his legs over the top of the front seat with a slight self-satisfied belch, 'that this has been a rather eventful day crammed with nerve-tingling mind-blowing happenings.'

'Like you getting the bullet,' said Ranter.

'Yes,' nodded Luke meditatively. 'Yes, that was without doubt a revelatory experience. All in all, I think a little celebratory acclamation would not be amiss—or, so as not to put too fine an edge on it, a ballad—'

'You'll fracture your vocal chords if you don't restrain yourself,' warned Ranter.

'Sure you never had what you might call an ear for music, Ranter,' mused Babysoft, absently fondling Otto's hand again. 'Whenever you breaks into song, once in a blue moon thank God, it's like the poor souls in Purgatory being released all together. But give us a few oul' bars anyway,' she encouraged. 'Nothing like a song to loosen the tightest garter, I always say.'

'Not so much a song,' explained Luke. 'More, shall we say, an extemporaneous emission of irresistible exultation—'

'Exactly,' said Babysoft with an emphatic nod. 'That's exactly what I had in mind.'

Luke for fully half a minute lapsed into a Buddha-like trance, eyes shut and every limb rapt, before he cleared his throat and placing his hand half-way over his mouth put a finger in his right ear and inclined his head to one side turning to straight recitation whenever the tenuous line of melody ran out:

'Lush grow the Lilies see how wild they run
upon the bright plains of Galza and Ballymun
thro' the sweet glades of Drimnagh and Walkinstown too
the lovely Lilies run riot for me and for you
But hark! in the wastelands of Malahide
all the true Lilies that have withered and died
The same can be said for Foxrock and Sutton—
the poor Lilies there are not worth a button

in Sandymount, too, Castleknock and Dalkey
the Lilies are maggoty pale and stalky
and their poor pale sisters can be seen
parading on the guinea side of The Green
caked with powder to hide wrinkle and blotch
tho' if you get near you cannot but peer
at the sorry sight in broad daylight
of false tits and rubberoid crotch—'

'You've a very good singing voice, you know,' Babysoft told
him seriously. 'You ought to get it trained. I knew a fella once,
and his voice took him all the way to Italy. That's where they all
go to get trained,' she added. 'To Italy. They do marvellous
things with the voice over there.' She thought a moment. 'Maybe
that's why the Eyetalians are so bleeding noisy.'

'Thank you for your critical advice,' said Luke. 'But the surge
of inspiration continues unabated:

'And saith the Good Shepherd to his flock
in thy collective mouth do put a sock
and follow my dictates without murmur or question
be thankful for thy daily bread
and thy orisons say before going to bed
and there with your wife duly copulate
and never once pause to speculate
on the thorny subject of contraception—'

'People long ago had no idea all the same, had they?' Babysoft
said. 'I mean, about French letters and things like that. God love
them, they thought that kind of letter only meant it came from
France. Still,' she added sighing, 'as me poor Ma used to say—
what's the point of joining the army if you don't soldier?'

'An admirable sentiment,' said Luke ever the gentleman en-
during another interruption, thrusting his finger deeper into his
ear. 'Grotesquely naïve, but admirable. To conclude my little
elegaic ditty:

Rise up my haggard brothers and with me follow
thro' fragrant glade and hallowed hollow

our glad-eyed sisters of concupiscent sin
for Roses are Shining in Perfidy
for well-hung stallions like you and me
and you don't have to pay to get in
See the lovely Lilies grow in concrete and stone
and where there's a Lily you're never alone
And so I say unto you without hesitation—
You're the most luscious Lily in all Procreation!'

'And they all sang God Save Ireland,' said Luke after a suitable pause when he had done. 'As if Ireland had ever wanted to be saved, a presumption that has led us into all sorts of diabolical trouble long before the minstrel boy ever plucked a harp.'

Ranter clapped his hands. 'The British are coming, aroo, aroo, they aren't Mr Bollocks said Brian Boru. I always thought that song was the height of patriotism—the ancient battlecry of the Gael streaming out of the boozers on Saturday nights.'

Babysoft handed what remained of the wine to the balladeer. 'That song now—what was it about, exactly?'

'Oh, bountiful lady, you disappoint me,' answered Luke draining the dregs. 'Surely you are not one of those disagreeable people who seek a logical explanation to the sweet mysteries of life? Besides,' added Luke darkly, 'there are some things that are best left in the limbo of probability.'

Babysoft suddenly screeched in unfeigned fright as something white hovered up near the windscreen. 'Jesus, Mary and holy St Joseph—'

'I'm afraid I kept you waiting,' apologised Sonny as she got into the front seat. 'Poor dear Applebud insisted on telling me the second part of her life-story before the Jack Daniels finally sent her off to sleep.'

'You put the heart crossways in me,' said Babysoft, 'appearing like that out of nowhere, like an apparition.'

'Let's get back to heart and home anyway,' said Ranter as he swung the car around and started back down the avenue, 'before I forget what a pint tastes like.' He revved up the engine and in reverse started down the tunnel-like avenue of trees.

'You can have Otto back now,' said Babysoft moving closer to Luke and taking his hand. 'He was as good as gold, I'm sorry to say.'

'How kind of you,' Sonny replied, reaching across and patting Otto's hand in the close dark of the car. 'I had no idea I would be detained so long hearing confessions. And you behaved yourself reasonably well, Otto?'

'Oh ja, ja, mein Gretchen,' he answered eager as a child accepting sweets. 'All the time I was good and watching for you in the night.'

Sonny kissed his hand indulgently. 'You are an adorable brute, dear. I had no idea poor Applebud was labouring under such a secret tragedy of lost love—'

'Take the secret tragedy out of people's lives,' said Luke, 'and you take the secret grief, and people can't survive without that.'

'That is a cynical philosophy, and quite heartless,' Sonny told him. 'Only the young can afford to think like that. I'm sure poor Applebud doesn't willingly want to live a life of such dismal dimensions, eaten up by remorse and scarred by failure.'

'Don't be deluded into imagining she feels anything of the kind,' retorted Luke. 'Give her the opportunity to re-live the past and she'd take off like a hare pursued by frothing greyhounds, as any sensible person would. Nostalgia, like charity, covers a multitude of sins.'

'I refuse to believe you are as cynical as you sound, dear Luke,' Sonny said calmly. 'I think you simply like the sound of saying clever, epigrammatical things. Tragedy is the only real triumph of the human spirit—things like that, which sound wise are really very silly. And anyway, Wilde was much better at it, though of course it ruined him as a writer.'

Luke smiled. 'By what circuitous process of feminine non-logic do you arrive at that conclusion?'

'It's really too simple. Take away poor Oscar's epigrams and what have you got? A pompous self-indulgent bore writing his dreary little notes about fashionable society while he sits at a side table sipping Pernod. Far from being his downfall and his nemesis, the affair with Lord Alfred brought out the best in him as a writer —whatever would he have written about if it had never happened? He was already running out of epigrams as well as Pernod.'

'Truth always has two sides, and an epigram is merely something that shows us the other side. That's all Wilde did, and you can't just wrap him up in an epigram and throw him away.'

'Why not? That is precisely what Mr Wilde tried to do with

life, until it caught up with him, and then he found himself at last as a writer instead of a foppy dilettante going about Chelsea wearing absurd carnations in his open buttonhole, another one of his pathetic affectations which he was only beginning to shed and disown towards the end of his short unhappy life.'

'Is it your man Oscar Wilde you're talking about?' asked Ranter as they wended through black narrow country lanes leading to the main road. 'Begging your pardon, maam, but wasn't he something of a queer?'

'He had certain predilections of that nature, yes,' Sonny replied. 'I am almost tempted to be unkind and say that that aspect of his life was also an affectation, except that he wrote so movingly of it, which redeemed matters somewhat.'

'If my information is correct,' said Ranter as if discussing something pulsatingly topical, 'he ran after young boys and the like, which is going beyond the beyonds altogether, if you ask me —I mean to say,' he continued as they jogged and bumped round sudden unexpected bends, 'I mean to say, every man to his liking and all that, and I'm as democratic as the next man, but there's limits to everything, isn't there now?'

Babysoft yawned, making tired cosy little noises. 'I don't know what you're all on about, with your diagrams and carnations and blokes wandering about with their buttonholes open in Chelsea.'

Ranter shook his head. 'Don't tell me you never heard of Oscar Wilde?'

'Of course I've heard of Oscar bleeding Wilde!' said Babysoft sharply. 'Do you think I'm shit-ignorant or something? Sure your man Oscar is as well known as Golden Miller—'

'Suffering Jasus,' muttered Ranter grimacing over the wheel, 'Golden Miller was a bleeding racehorse!'

'Don't I know he was a racehorse—did I say he wasn't a racehorse?' Babysoft sat up straighter. 'He won four Grand Nationals in a row—'

'It was five Gold Cups he won in a row,' Ranter told her with a sigh. 'He won the National once, that's all. You can't talk about Oscar Wilde and Golden Miller in the same breath.'

'Why—because one of them was a racehorse?'

'Do you know which one?' growled Ranter.

'I don't see why you can't talk about them in the same breath anyway—they were both good at their jobs.'

'If that's the case,' Ranter interjected, 'you could say there was comparisons between Jesus Christ and bleeding Bluebeard or Casanova if all you can say is "they were both good at their jobs".'

'And why not?' Babysoft wanted to know glaring at the back of Ranter's head. 'Why can't you compare them just because they did different kinds of work? Golden Miller was good at his job, so was Oscar Wilde, and I don't see why one should be put above the other.'

'Did Oscar Wilde ever win five Gold Cups in a row?' Ranter shouted, in his agitation pressing harder upon the accelerator. 'Did Golden Miller ever ever walk upon the hooring water or feed thousands with only one bleeding loaf of bread?'

'How the effing hell do you expect me to know?' retorted Babysoft. 'I wasn't there, was I?'

'Women are bleeding thick,' Ranter said contemptuously. He cast a sideward look at Sonny. 'Not all women by no means. Now take yourself maam, sure you'd know better than to couple Oscar Wilde with a bleeding racehorse.'

'Perhaps,' smiled Sonny, 'though I am not at all sure who would suffer most by the comparison.'

'There you are!' cried Babysoft with glee. 'What did I tell you? There's a quare kick in the arse for you now, Mr Brainstrust! Your woman here is educated as bejasus, and even she says you can compare Oscar Wilde with Golden Miller.'

'She said nothing of the kind,' Ranter affirmed. 'She was only talking in a general roundabout sort of way.'

'I heard her distinctly,' Babysoft replied adamant, settling back satisfied. 'What was so bleeding high-and-mighty about Oscar Wilde anyway, I'd like to know? You said yourself he chased after young boys, the dirty bugger. People like that should be shot.'

'The chiner's been dead and buried for years, for fuck's sake,' said Ranter pushing his cap with an angry swipe as it fell forward over his eye.

'That's no excuse—molesting young boys like that—going against nature. That sort of person should be castrated for their own good.'

'You'd even castrate the dead, bejasus!' growled Ranter.

'Now I wouldn't go that far,' corrected Babysoft in a pensive way after a pause. 'No, I definitely wouldn't go that far. Sure what would be the point—what good would it do them if they were dead? But young boys and little children should be protected from people like that—if they can't have it the same as me and you and other normal people, then cut the bleeding thing off, that's what I say, or else round them up and put them all together in a monastery or something, out of harm's way.'

'A very humane suggestion, if I may say so,' spoke Luke gnawing meditatively at a broken thumbnail, 'and one which I am sure would gain unanimous support from the gentlemen concerned, though the monks might possibly voice some mild objections to their premises being commandeered for such sociological purposes.'

'Oh, I don't know,' Ranter responded in a more amiable manner. 'It would be company for them, it would give them a break away from all that winemaking, for one thing, and for another it would give them something real to pray for, for a change, something positive, you know, for them to do penance for.'

'That, also,' said Luke, 'is a very humane and charitable way of looking at things. You might as well enjoy the things you are doing penance for, I suppose, and I was always rather suspicious about Anchorites doing their thing out there in the desert—seemed an inexcusable indulgence on their part if they were merely doing penance and mortifying themselves for infantile misdemeanours committed by others.'

'I knew a monk once,' went on Ranter bending forward to rub his chin against the steering-wheel, 'well, when I say I knew him what I mean is, I knew a bloke who knew him—and you'd hardly credit the things he told me they get up to.'

'I'm sure I wouldn't credit them at all,' Luke replied chewing on the piece of nail he had managed to bite off. 'It is invariably an ill wind.'

'Now I'm not saying I believed everything he told me, am I?' said Ranter defending himself. 'I'm not gullible. Still, you get funny ideas knocking around in your oul' loaf when you're shut up all on your tod—the devil moves in strange and mysterious ways too, you know.'

'True,' agreed Luke. 'I don't suppose he can afford to be less inventive and ingenious than his more illustrious opponent.'

'Anyway, your man was telling me that the monks develop some peculiar habits. One fella he knew had a brother a monk, and he used to breed pet earwigs in his cell—used to train them, so to speak, to do certain things at certain times of the day.'

'I must say,' remarked Sonny, 'it sounds a highly specialised and esoteric practice.'

'Devotional earwigs,' marvelled Luke.

'Of course,' Ranter elaborated. 'You'd have to catch your earwig in the right mood, so to speak, before he'd do a bleeding thing at all—your man was telling me that the monk's brother was telling him that earwigs were very stubborn little effers altogether—wouldn't budge an inch if they weren't in the humour, and I believe the monk ended up by saying more effs and bees than Hail Marys if they wouldn't obey his orders.'

Babysoft abruptly. 'What have you got against horses?'

'Is it me you're talking to?' enquired Ranter squinting at the overhead mirror.

'It's not Oscar Wilde.'

'I have nothing against horses.'

'Why do you hate them then?'

'I don't hate them—I didn't say I hated them.'

'You didn't say, but you prefer effing Oscar Wilde to horses, and sure everyone knows they're the most beautiful creatures under the sun. I'm sure God prefers horses to human beings any day of the week.'

'In that respect at least,' said Luke, 'I can safely say I have a close relationship with God.'

'For Jasus' sake,' said Ranter, 'don't keep on about Oscar Wilde—let the poor bastard rest in peace, didn't he pay for his fornications?'

'Then you should let poor Golden Miller rest in peace,' Babysoft countered. 'He never did you any harm when he was alive, did he?'

'I never even met the hooring horse!'

'At least Golden Miller never chased after young boys.'

'In his case it would be young colts, wouldn't it?' said Ranter.

'If I ever owned a horse,' persuaded Babysoft relentlessly, 'I swear to Jasus no man would throw a leg over it.'

'In that case you should inveigle one of the gentry into marrying you,' advised Ranter. 'Some oul' retired English major with a big house in Kildare, a high insurance premium and a bladder rotted with whiskey.'

'I could only marry for love,' averred Babysoft with fine resignation. 'Me destiny is ruled by the stars.'

'You'd have all the horses you want then—the gentry think about nothing but horses morning, noon and night. It's a sort of religion with them.'

'I always wanted to go to one of them riding schools.'

'You're working in one now, aren't you?'

'Don't you say anything derogatory about my place of employment!' Babysoft flared. 'You're bleeding glad of it when Gertie turns her face to the wall at night!'

'I only go there on business.'

'That's what I meant!'

'Taxi business.'

'You're like all men—when your missus puts up the no-go area sign you turn to us for succour.'

Then suddenly she laughed and leaned over the seat kissing the back of his neck and hugging him as she warbled:

'When Ranter breaks into a canter
let the women of Dublin take flight
For when Ranter breaks into a canter
his oul' cock will stay up the whole night!'

'Restrain your ardour, woman,' said Ranter, 'and kindly stop biting me ears while you're at it.'

'That's what they do in the pictures, you know, when they're burning up with passion, God love them, and can't control themselves—' she twisted her face round to Luke—'Isn't that right, Lukey love—don't they take lumps out of one another in the heat of passion?'

'Cannibalism runs deep and dark through the whole spectrum of human emotions,' replied Luke. 'Man is the fiercest predator of all the beasts on land and sea.'

'You could sing that if you had an air to it.'

'Don't be distracting me,' cautioned Ranter loudly as the car slewed and swayed, brushing past overhanging branches. 'Out here you're liable to run into some oul' farmer taking his ease in the middle of the road reading the cattle market report.'

Warm bodies cosily touching companionable in the dark of the car, twin arcs of headlamps slicing the night air, caught in the glare frenzied swarms of moths mashed upon the windscreen brushed aside by the purring strokes of the wiper, the luminous blurred sheen of leaves rushing past, stars glimpsed among the trees frail and inconstant, the ominous stillness of woodland alive with furtive life animal eyes showing suddenly on the edge of teeming darkness, glowing yellow, the stir and raw smell of earth awakening torpor bitter and keen.

At last they swung out to the open road, and suddenly out of the night, advancing with apocalyptic suddenness stamping and pawing the wet gleaming asphalt, a snorting fettlesome steed reared angrily to a halt in front of them, dazzled by the headlights, massive maned head flung back and great startled eyes ablaze.

'What in the name of Jasus is that?'

Ranter rammed hard on the brakes, the jolt of gravity pitching them all forward and then back.

'Oh Jasus, we're all killed.'

'I suggest we all keep calm.'

'Calm, me bollocks,' roared Ranter, catching his cap as it fell forward.

Luke drew down his window and stuck out his head. 'Excuse me, but are we on the right road to Damascus?'

Sonny sat up and finding her handkerchief dabbed at her forehead where a dark thin streak of blood showed.

'What an extraordinary thing to happen! I do hope the poor animal hasn't been hurt.'

Otto bent over her and bellowed, 'Mein Gretchen, mein liebes Gretchen! Assassins!'

'Do be quiet, Otto dear.'

'Quick—the police call, the ambulance call, the fire-engine call —mein Gott, someone call, quick, or mein Gretchen is utterly dead!'

'Do be quiet, Otto.' Sonny put her hand on Luke's arm. 'Do please go and see if the poor horse is hurt in any way.'

Luke bowed his head. 'In this sad murderous world let us hope that Pegasus, at least, continues to enjoy his winged state of grace.'

He opened the door and unwinding his legs stepped out.

Ranter passed a hand none too steady over his face. 'It come out of nowhere, bejasus, and there it was, staring me in the face like the Hound of the Baskervilles.'

'What was it, in the name of God?' asked Babysoft, teeth ajitter. 'I never saw anything like it in all me born days, truth of God.'

'Assassins!' roared Otto anew with a discernible catch in his voice as he surveyed Sonny's brow. 'Foul assassins of mein liebes Gretchen!'

'It is a mere scratch, Otto dear, and if it looks dramatic enough there it shall remain.'

'But mein lovely petal—'

'It is probably the nearest I will ever get to a properly attractive disfigurement, and I shall regard as totally irrelevant the fact that it was caused by a dear old wandering Irish stray, most probably one-eyed, on a wet wintry night in the hamlet Howth rather than in the bedroom of a jealous woman whose lover I had enticed away.' She dabbed at the wound delicately and looked at the slight smear of blood with interest. 'At least it happened by the sea, which is always good for a touch of mystery and romance.'

'I have to admire you all the same,' conceded Babysoft. 'It didn't take a corner out of you. I could never stand the sight of blood—especially me own. Jasus,' she exclaimed as she felt her knee gingerly, 'I think I'm after breaking me tibia or femur or whatever the bastarding hell it's called!'

Luke came back and leaned through the window. 'Pegasus lives, but of even greater curiosity value is the rider.'

'Get out of me fucking way, Sheridan, you bollocks!'

Luke moved aside as someone barged up behind him. 'May I introduce a gentleman I have known and revered for many years and until quite recently in whose esteem and employ I once delighted?'

'Fuck off, you little shit, before I kick the balls out of you! Oh good God,' said the gruff voice faltering. 'I didn't realise there were ladies present—I do beg a thousand pardons.' The large balding man stepped forward into a pool of amber street light, flushed face florid and confused but instantly assuming an unctuous ingratiating smile. 'Mulligan's the name, ladies—Matt Mulligan, and I would doff my hat to you if I had one.'

Luke grinned standing against the hard sea-stiff wind, hands pushed into the narrow pockets of his jeans. 'You see, it really was the Damascus road.'

Part Three

VIII

'I lent your man Rambler when he said he was a mate of yours and his car had broken down,' said Octavius to Luke at the bar setting up the drinks. 'In this trade the less questions you ask the better—what you might call a vow of knowing silence, if you get my meaning?'

'I do indeed, Octavius, I do indeed, and well met once more.'

'Gathered once again, you might say, in the sight of John Jameson and the other household gods of the Irish hearth.'

'Indeed you might say that, Octavius, indeed you might.'

'Put your money away, man, this one's on me.'

'You are too kind, Octavius. You'll never hold a business together at this rate.'

Octavius pondered awhile. 'Businesses, like love, were meant to be won and lost.'

'And won over again, we hope.'

'Aye,' rejoined Octavius gazing mournfully down at the tray of drinks. 'Aye, we can at least hope that, though once lost it's bloody hard to win either back, business or love.'

'Octavius, you are a philosopher, albeit a melancholy one.'

Octavius brightened as he turned and rang the till. 'Anyway, I see you brought your bit of German cheese back with you.'

'Savoury as ever, Octavius.'

'Along with the bold count himself, too, I notice.'

'A gentleman born, I'm glad to say.'

'He didn't dislocate any of your vital parts?'

'You can now take it on good authority that the state of Irish–German relations was never better.'

'I did Rambler a disservice, letting that big fat heap of cowshit up on him. Oh, sorry—I forgot he was a friend of yours.'

'I had of late worked under him—a subtle difference.'

'All the difference in the world, oul' son. And from the way he's looking at your lady friends I bet he wouldn't say no to either of them working under him and all.'

'You possess truly remarkable powers of clairvoyance, Octavius.'

Octavius sighed. 'It goes with the job.'

'Anyway,' said Luke picking up the laden tray, 'thanks again for your hospitality, and my respects to Rambler and your Missus.'

'I'll pass them on—in that order.'

'No offence meant, Octavius.'

'And only pleasure taken. A man who gets his priorities right. Come back when your glass needs refilling.'

'It will be but a short adieu, Octavius.'

Luke ensconced himself again by the wide hearthstone glowing under the smoky rafters, turf-and-tobacco odours thick in the air, the slurring lift of voices and glasses clinking making a cosy nest of noise in the front parlour, the scrape of solid country boots on the stone floor moving to the bar and through the haze the clang of the cash register like the buzz of an ancient tram conductor's bell. Octavius sat erect and convivial behind the counter in shirt-sleeves, snapping his thick elastic navy-blue braces afloat on a bellyful of prime malt whiskey, bland and beatific, swaying back and forth on the soles of his woollen-stockinged feet as though poised on the axis of the globe spinning benevolently beneath him—

'Where's the Cork Dry Gin, Father?'

'What's that, boy?'

His son lithe and diligent stood at his side in the narrow bottle-necked aisle of the bar, full of sapling promise and too early wisdom, dreamy rebellion stirring deep in the dark discerning eyes, sensuous mouth, drooped a little with fatigue of grownup company, slim pianistic fingers adept for the knowing of bottles, this bramble-headed son of his upon whom Octavius looked ever more fondly with each fall in the spirit level of the private bottle hidden within reach under the middle shelf. He fed himself with lies about the boy being the true indivisible and better shadow of himself the more to hush the sense of awe and occasional dread that such a wonder as Ultan had come from the slobbering drunken groping and plundering of the lost middle years upstairs in the sprawling bed where his woman had lain rigid and tight-lipped beneath him as he emptied his comic rage and tawdry pride into her. And ages later after the hiatus of childless merry-making the eight other infants had come filling the house and himself with commotion and truculence and yet at odd moments frightening him with soft new feelings unanswered in the bitter accusing eyes of Ethel-May staring past him into a life of greener gentler things that love of him once had made her renounce, the selfsame love that the years had turned to a bitter bile burning inside her and stunted now to a screeching clawing malignant shrew of a thing.

'The Cork Dry Gin, Father.'

'To be sure, son, to be sure—here you are.'

Octavius reached up and handed the bottle to his son and for a moment his hand hovered over the bright red head trembling with the fierce urge to touch it just once without making a tired pale joke of it, but Ultan had already turned away to tend to the customers and with a broad heave of not inconsolable resignation Octavius picked up his glass and lifted it to his lips.

A black pipe was lifted out of a beery gum-soft mouth. 'A fine boy you have there, Octavius.'

'Aye, a fine enough young bugger, right enough.'

The gums broke in a wide grin. 'Isn't it a great wonder all the same that a ugly oul' renegade like yourself should produce such a fine sample of young manhood?'

'Oh, sure it's one of the wonders of the world, Patsy,' replied Octavius leaning on the counter. 'One of the wonders of the world.'

At the table by the blazing hearth the red-rimmed gimlet eyes of Matt Mulligan regarded the two women sitting opposite him with nervous rapacity. 'I couldn't believe my eyes,' he was saying leaning forward heavily arms folded, 'when Luke here stepped out of that taxi large as life—"a mirage," I said to myself, "a mirage!" And then when I looked closer and beheld these two magnificent females—well!'

'Things grew curiouser and curiouser, eh, Matt?'

'Not only that—the more I gazed in wonder the lovelier they seemed to grow. Why, even now as I look at them their faces become more lovely and their—forgive the familiarity, but I must say it—their figures become more fabulous, more entrancing, more—'

'Desirable, Mr Mulligan?' suggested Sonny in a voice like a thin blade of ice crackling in the heat.

The sweat glistened more feverishly on Mulligan's brow. 'You took the word right out of my mouth, maam, loth as I was to be so bold as to say it myself.' He raised his glass 'Your very excellent health, ladies—not that you need it, ripe as you both are—'

'I will admit it was rather a surprise,' broke in Luke, 'to see you perched up there on top of the horse, like a slightly disorientated Genghis Khan trying to find his way home after the latest orgy.'

Mulligan's eyes became infused with a more pronounced redness. 'An orgy! Now that is something that has been missing from my bleak bachelor existence—do you know of any good ones going at the moment, Luke? You're such a worldlywise bloke geared to the latest social extravaganzas.'

'An underpaid voyeur would be a more accurate way of describing my working status as of late.'

'And now you must venture out into the rude world, Mr Mulligan,' said Sonny, 'and gather your own sordid material. You will then become, I expect, a considerably overpaid voyeur.'

Mulligan's queasy smile remained. 'I like humour in a beautiful woman. So many beautiful women are lacking in a sense of humour—it spoils everything when they open their gobs and nothing but dry words come out. Like peacocks—ornamental birds until they start squawking.' Mulligan leaned further across the table. 'What did you think of my horsemanship anyway, maam?'

Sonny studied him with cool-eyed interest, her fingers entwined in Otto's on the table.

'My admiration for the horse knows no bound.'

'Ah! but where would the horse be without the jockey?' asked Mulligan.

Sonny sipped her drink. 'I am sure it is far from being the accepted norm for an employer to arrive on horseback to serve a dismissal notice on an employee. Even in Ireland I would imagine such behaviour to be slightly quixotic.'

Mulligan beamed. 'Quixotic! You have a genius for using just the exact phrase, maam. That is a word I would definitely use to describe myself. Quixotic could be my middle name, for my old colleague and erstwhile friend Luke here will vouch, I am a most quixotic individual, to a drastic degree in fact, and much given to impulses and flights of imagination that sometimes take even *me* by surprise.' He turned to the younger man with pink-jowled joviality, 'Isn't that so, Luke?'

Luke stared at the glass in his hand. 'As a matter of pure historical fact, Matthew, I had not noticed any particularly quixotic quirks embedded in your dour taciturn nature, nor indeed any quirks whatever that might have remotely made you into a recognisable human being.'

Mulligan scowled beneath his stationary smile. 'You were always the soul of honesty, Sheridan—a very bad trait in a good journalist, by the way.' He returned his beady-eyed gaze to Sonny. 'I have always told my subordinates, maam, to cultivate a healthy streak of ruthlessness. It adds colour, a touch of glamour even, to an existence that otherwise can become dull and common-place.'

'It was the poor horse that had my fullest sympathy.'

'Oh that!' said Mulligan with a casual wave of his hand. 'That was just another example of my quixotic ways, a little case of high jinks shall we say, on the public highway, arising from my sardonic sense of humour. I always did possess a sardonic humour—'

'Sardonic to the point of being black-blooded,' interpolated Luke, tilting back in the chair, hooking his heels on the middle rung of the table. 'Like black pudding, which is merely the congealed blood of slain bulls and butchered bullocks.'

Babysoft suddenly made a choking sound of distaste. 'I could never stomach that stuff—it always makes me want to throw me effing guts up just looking at it.'

Mulligan was resolved to be grimly amiable. 'You see, ladies,' he said joining his hands together and leaning his chin on them, 'in my position a sense of humour is not merely a help, it is a positive asset, because you see in my job, requiring as it does the inner luminosity of a Mahatma Gandhi coupled with the serpent-smooth diplomacy of a U Thant or whoever happens to hold that high august office at any given time in history—'

'The poor horse looked bandjaxed,' Ranter broke brusquely in for the first time. 'It looked sort of demoralised, fit only for Keefe's the Knackers yard.'

'I agree,' said Sonny. 'No beast should be asked to carry such a burden—'

'Such a mountain of disrespect, you might say,' put in Ranter.

Luke sighed. 'Our friend Rambler is quietly eating his oats at this point of time.'

'No ruptured spleen, no dislocated fetlock?' anxiously enquired Sonny.

'He's quietly eating his oats,' repeated Luke quirking an eyebrow in Mulligan's direction. 'In marked contrast to some over-optimistic, over-weight souls in our midst—who shall be nameless, as befits them—who are rather desperately trying to sow theirs.'

'The sowing of oats is a curious thing,' said Ranter with the air of a philosopher preaching to the unconverted. 'It's good in a way, and bad in another. Well—not bad exactly, only not so good. It differs from man to man, I suppose. I mean to say, it never cost Moses a night's sleep one way or another, he was that busy going about writing down the ten commandments on them bleeding big chunks of stone, but look at St Augustine—'

'A lovely man,' said Babysoft impulsively. 'A bit deep for the likes of meself, but a lovely man from all accounts.'

'A lovely man he may have been,' said Ranter crooking a cautious finger. 'I'm not gainsaying that one way or another, but look at what happened to him when he stopped sowing his oats.'

'He became a saint, didn't he?' said Babysoft, and reiterated as if seeking assurance, 'He did become a saint, didn't he?'

Ranter waved a hand. 'That's neither here nor there. The point is, after he stopped sowing his oats he went around telling everyone to forget about women and the joys of the flesh—things that keep a man sane—and ended up being a right bleeding pain in the neck, raving about all the glories waiting for us in heaven if only we'd give up sowing our oats, and all the terrible mortifying things that would happen to us down beyant in hell if we didn't. I'm telling you,' said Ranter with a melancholy squint into his glass, 'there never was such a thing as a democratic saint in the whole bleeding history of the church.'

'A parable for our times,' said Luke, sententious seer dreamily fondling the lobe of his ear. 'Sow ye your wild oats while ye may, before religious men take your balls away.'

Babysoft too had reached the end of her glass and was fretful. 'Jasus, the way you go on about sowing wild oats and the like, anybody would think you were farmers. You'd think grownup men would have something better to do than yap on and on about effing oats.'

Ranter sighed. 'It isn't the agricultural variety we're talking about—'

'I know what kind of oats you're talking about,' replied Babysoft. 'Do you think I'm bleeding thick or what? Oats is oats one way or another, and it makes little difference in the end what you do with them.'

'There comes a point in life,' said Sonny deliberately as she toyed with a ring on Otto's finger, 'when the ritual sowing of one's oats becomes a pathetic thing of the past, though sad to say the onset of age does not necessarily bring decorum, let alone wisdom. However, one should at least try to temper censure with charity, shouldn't one?'

Mulligan's ruddy features darkened to a choleric degree but his trapped smile remained fixed and showing like the desiccated wing of an impaled butterfly as he emptied his glass and banged on the table. 'Landlord fill our flowing bowls!'

'Thanks be to Jasus,' muttered Ranter. 'I thought he had lost his memory or something.'

Mulligan chortled expansive and bland. 'I feel in a festive mood tonight, stumbling by the pure magic of chance, you might say, upon these two delectable torches of wit and beauty—' he bowed to the two women—'when nothing in my zodiac had prepared me for such a happy event. Landlord!' he shouted, a shower of spittle accompanying his imperious command as he thumped the table again. 'Landlord, over here post-haste! We mustn't let the juicy paps of friendship dry up and wither!' He closed his eyes and let the word play about on his tongue like a grape to be crushed. 'Paps. Now there's a fruity peach of a word.'

'I don't like the looks of that bloated oul' bastard,' Babysoft asided to Ranter next to her on the long narrow wooden settle. 'Sitting there like some oul' redundant rajah on a white charger.'

'Humour him, for Jasus' sake,' urged Ranter as he swallowed down the frothy remains of his pint. 'Humour the oul' sod as long as he's buying.'

'I'm not that stuck for a gargle,' retorted Babysoft with unquenchable pride. 'I saw the day when I wouldn't take as much as a pinch of snuff from the likes of that oul' shit!'

'Lookit, we all saw better days,' reasoned Ranter. 'You don't have to throw yourself at his feet.'

'I'd bite the effing toes off him if I did!'

'As long as he keeps digging into his skyrocket you should try and restrain your natural inclination to throw up in his face,' chided Ranter. 'I know it's a bit over and above the call of duty.'

'You wouldn't want to have any blood in your veins.'

Ranter spat into his palm. 'You can have blood in your veins any day of the week, bejasus—I'm ready for something stronger right now.'

Ultan had stepped out from behind the bar and stood now at their table, white towel draped across arm, picking up some of the empty glasses. 'Would you be wanting the same again, sir?'

Mulligan leered out of moist whiskey-inflamed eyes. ' "Would you be wanting the same again, sir?" ' he mimicked grotesquely. 'What side of the Liffey did you get that accent from, boy?'

'Your order, sir.'

'You're not the landlord, are you? I called for the landlord, not for a puny run-down yellow-arsed little shit like you. Who the hell are you, anyway, and why aren't you out in the yard milking the cows?'

'I am Ultan McSweeney, sir, the proprietor's son. Would you like me to take your order now, sir?'

'The proprietor's son!' Mulligan echoed leaning back in his chair. 'How do you like that, ladies and gentlemen, boys and girls, lads and lassies—this undernourished country scallion is the proprietor's son, no less!' Mulligan stuck his face closer. 'You can tell he's from the arsehole of Connemara—he hasn't wiped the stirabout off his mouth yet!'

Babysoft's gay summer-blue eyes darkened ominously. 'That's no way to talk to a nice young lad, and him the height of good manners and breeding.'

Otto's large genial countenance glowed with paternal amity as he put a protecting hand on Ultan's shoulder. 'Hansel is the name I give him, all fresh and pink he is.'

'Leave the young man be, Matthew,' cautioned Luke in a quiet tone, 'if you don't relish the possibly unsavoury consequences of such infantile behaviour.'

'I am sure Ultan is quite adept at coping with bumptious over-bearing boors,' commented Sonny, 'and honourable enough to resist the urge to bash them resoundingly over their oafish pates with the nearest bar-stool, though I doubt very much if I could resist such a thrilling temptation.'

Mulligan turned on them unctuous and urbane at once. 'My friends, my friends, a little lighthearted bantering helps to establish instant rapport between the social classes, between upper and lower in all walks of life—' he reached out and gripped Ultan's other arm—'He knows I am but indulging in a little light raillery —don't you, boy, eh?'

Ultan stared back impassive. 'Would you like to give me your order now, sir?'

Mulligan's grip tightened. 'What did you say your name was, boy? I am afraid I didn't hear aright.'

'You heard it right enough, sir.'

'I did, eh? Well now, maybe I did or maybe I didn't,' said Mulligan domineeringly, leaning forward in the chair his face up close to the youth's, 'but would you mind repeating it again?'

Otto grunted and stirred uneasily. 'The very son he is like to me.'

Ultan gave him a quick grateful smile. 'It's all right, Count Otto. Sure I don't begrudge telling anyone my name.'

'And what is your damned name, boy?'

'It's Ultan, sir, Ultan McSweeney.'

Mulligan sniggered and dug his fingers in deeper. 'And what class or manner of name is that to be labouring under, eh, boy? Would you say now,' he went on with a broad wink around at the others, 'would you say that that name comes from the north or south side of the Liffey?'

'I would hardly know, sir. It just happens to be my name.'

'Name?' roared Mulligan with absurd falsetto mirth. 'Name, is it? In my business you come across all kinds of mad ridiculous outlandish names but never until now have I heard a more diabolical travesty of a name than your own, boy! You know what,' Mulligan said as he wiped his eyes wet with maniac glee, 'you know what it is, boy—that isn't a name at all, but a bloody affliction. That's what it is,' he repeated slapping his knee hilariously, 'a bloody affliction!'

Ultan aware of Sonny's grave sombre eyes like stars glimmering on the edge of his vision stood quietly and stared back into the leering glistening face of Mulligan looming a few rank-smelling inches away, and he had about him the poised alert immobility of a young forest animal warily watching something it did not understand and instinctively distrusted.

'Tell me now and tell me true,' said Mulligan, 'what is your real name, Oh boy of the stirabout mouth and hobnailed boots?'

Luke began lazily to pick his teeth with a matchstick. 'Speaking of afflictions, Matthew,' he said easily. 'I would imagine you would regard it as a severe affliction if our jolly host yonder should come over and connect with sharp incisive uppercut to your grossly slack chin as you are gasping from the solid one-two he has just delivered to that flabby solar plexus of yours, not to mention the thorough-going kick in the crotch that immediately preceded it. But by all means suit yourself.'

Mulligan grinned a limp bile-greenish grin. 'We understand each other, don't we, boy? We stand as equals, don't we, eyeball to eyeball? Ultan Aroon here or whatever his damned fairytale name is isn't the type to be ground under by a little manly horse-play, are you, boy? Why, I believe,' said Mulligan squeezing hard, 'I do believe I can feel the stirring of manly muscles under that ladylike skin!'

Otto grunted deeper in his throat. 'Do not our Hansel molest.'

Mulligan opened his eyes ingenuously. 'Hurt, is it? Me hurt? Sure I wouldn't hurt a spider—would I, Luke? Tell our stout teutonic comrade here that a veritable spider I would not hurt.'

'Too late, Matthew,' sighed Luke, 'too late for false gentility, but not, I fear, for tears of retribution. Your harmless little bout of badinage, I am afraid, is not going to be much appreciated.'

'What, might I ask, is going on here?' enquired Octavius as he ambled up amiably puzzled.

'Nothing, Father, nothing at all.'

'I was not aware of directing my question to yourself, Ultan. As I recollect, I put it to the gentleman at present holding your arm in a grip that I would not describe as friendly.'

Mulligan looked up mistily. 'Ah, there you are, landlord.'

Octavius coughed and cleared his throat. 'Before we enter into any discussion of whatsoever nature, might I be so bold as to politely ask you to remove your hand from off my son's entire person, before I proceed to break every contaminated bone in your body?'

Mulligan blinked blandly. 'What's that? As I was explaining to your boy here, landlord—'

'How is your state of hearing?'

Mulligan hiccupped. 'My state of hearing, landlord? My hearing, I am glad to report, is quite excellent.'

'And I daresay you wish at all costs to keep it that way?'

'Certainly,' Mulligan said with idiot smile, 'most certainly.'

'Then let me most earnestly assure you,' continued Octavius snapping his braces in a jovial friendly way, 'that in exactly five seconds from now, whether you prefer Greenwich Time or Eastern Standard Time or Ballygogatherwhileyemay Time, it's not only hard of hearing you'll be, but very short of sight, smell, taste and touch and any other sense you may possess, after I'm through knocking the living daylights out of you if you haven't taken that dastardly and offensive limb of yours away from my son's person. In exactly five seconds' time.' Octavius began to count in a slow rather dreamy voice as he gazed up into the tobacco haze swirling to the rough oak beams.

'Now look here, landlord, if you think I'm to be intimidated—'

All talk in the close heat-filled front parlour ceased and pints stayed suspended in hardknuckled fists as cheerful clients looked on with expectant goodnatured curiosity, the silence so live and intense the garrulous logs could be heard hissing and spitting in the firegrate and from the far domestic reaches of the kitchen crackled the caterwauling bleat of bagpipes from the superannuated wireless set.

Octavius rocked easily on his stockinged feet. 'Four—'

Mulligan with an inaudible curse withdrew his hand scowling and picked up his empty glass as there came a long-drawn-out disappointed sigh from the crowd and talk lifted again.

Mulligan tried to squeeze minute drops of succour from his glass to rekindle his bullying dominance. 'I must protest, landlord, most strenuously at your attitude, highly insulting as it is in front of my friends.'

Luke smiled and flicked the matchstick into the fire. 'Matthew's friends do either one of two things. They either die young from despair or grow old and insane. Either way it's a happy release.'

'I, sir,' spluttered Mulligan trying to stand up amid a barrage of hiccups, 'I am a paying customer, and I deplore and deprecate your insolent behaviour—*Mr* Landlord.'

'Sit down before you trip over yourself,' advised Octavius pushing him none too gently back down. 'Hold your peace, like a good man, for I have to admit patience was never me strong card, and mine is wearing as thin as a newborn babby's spit right now.'

Mulligan looked up with badly mauled indignation. 'You can threaten all you like, but you can't gag *me*.'

'For Jasus' sake, can't you shut bloody well up, man, and not be provoking me wrath?'

Mulligan banged the table like a tearful schoolboy being reprimanded before the entire classroom. 'I will *not* be bullied and intimidated by any demagogue of a glorified hen-run keeper! You are but a common garden or vegetable innkeeper.'

Octavius laid a heavy hand on the other man's shoulder. 'And that's another thing—stop calling me "innkeeper" in that sneering tone of voice, as if I was some kind of greenhorn pageboy or court jester. If you haven't the courtesy to call me by my proper name,' said Octavius diligently dusting Mulligan's shoulder, 'which my poor Mother, Lord be good to her, gave me and paid for, don't bother your fat bourgeois arse to call me at all. Do we understand one another now, me fine upholder of freedom and democracy?'

'The—the insolence of office!' faltered Mulligan.

'And now we'll consider the matter closed—'

'I should think so, too!'

'—As soon as you have apologised to me son here—'

'Apologise!'

'—*And* bought a round of drinks for your pains.'

Mulligan's eyes rolled in futile rage. 'I'll be damned if I will be spoken to in this manner!'

'Just to show there's no bad blood between us,' added Octavius with disarming simplicity.

Luke put his hands behind his head and yawned. 'Sounds eminently reasonable to me. After all, Matthew, you're getting off from the short sharp uppercut and that pulverising punch to the solar plexus. Take it while the offer still stands, dear old mentor of mine.'

Mulligan glared balefully at Luke. 'Iscariot!'

Octavius clasped his hands together benignly. 'Well—which is it to be, Walter Cronkite, sir?'

Mulligan's waning belligerence flared momentarily. 'If you think or imagine I'm going to go down on my knees to you—'

'Ah, no,' said Octavius after a moment's rumination, 'I wouldn't in all conscience ask you to do that.'

'Too bloody true you wouldn't!'

'Ah no, sure I was never a despot,' said Octavius. 'Just apologise to Ultan now, like a reasonable man, and then we'll take your order.' He paused. 'As an act of contrition, you might say.'

Talk once more stopped in mid-sentence as faces turned and ears were cocked as Mulligan mortified wriggled and squirmed like a hooked worm. 'Taking advantage of my temporary state of inebriation,' he muttered ponderously dabbing at his perspiring face and neck with a large rather unhygienic handkerchief. 'A low vile act of animal cunning.'

'Your apology, Mr National Press,' Octavius droned, 'and if it's not forthcoming in ten seconds flat it's your obituary we'll be reading in tomorrow's first edition.'

'Are you threatening me?' demanded Mulligan attempting to gain once more at least the dignity of the perpendicular.

'Of course I'm threatening you, you dribbling oul' bugger!' replied Octavius pushing him down again. 'And I never hand out idle threats. I'm being generous now by giving you ten seconds this time, and I might point out that four of them have already elapsed.'

Mulligan very nearly blubbered. 'I've never been so insulted, so damnably humiliated—'

'Five,' counted Octavius. 'Six.'

Mulligan shot a furtive appealing look at Luke. 'Damn it, Sheridan—don't just sit there!'

'I'm not,' answered Luke. 'I'm counting too. With keen anticipation, let me add.'

'Seven,' intoned Octavius. 'Eight.'

With a last bileful glare of bellicosity Mulligan fumbled in his breast pocket and threw his wallet on the table. 'Order what you damn well like!'

'Hold on there a minute now,' Octavius stopping Ultan as he

started to resume picking up the empty glasses. 'There's still the little matter of an apology to be dispensed with first.'

'To be sure there is, Octavius,' nodded Luke. 'We must at all times endeavour to get our priorities right as you pointed out to me recently in another context.'

Mulligan's breathing was ragged as he looked around. 'Now look, all of you, I've gone as far as I'll go—you'll not demean me any further!'

Octavius shot out his hand and gripped Mulligan by the lapel of his short overcoat. 'I've had more than me bellyful of you, bejasus, coming in here and throwing your weight around like James Cagney on an off day.'

Mulligan's eyes bulged alarmingly. 'Let me go at once.'

Octavius shook his quarry as he might a captive jackrabbit. 'Acting the big newspaper tycoon, bejasus, Randolph Hearst and Beaverbrook rolled into one!' Octavius looked up, his eyes hot and bright with anger. 'All the oul' bastard was short of saying was calling out "My man!" each time he ordered a gargle!'

'You're—you're choking me!'

Octavius went on shaking. 'I'll effing well guzzle you, you ignorant oul' bastard! I must've been mad, bejasus, to let the likes of you get up on me poor oul' horse, for any decent self respecting nag would keel over with shame and mortification rather than let you put a leg across him!'

Mulligan's arms waved wanly in the air like a broken-down windmill as he was lifted bodily an inch or two off the ground, his face remarkably like an over-ripe pulpy tomato waiting ignominiously to be squashed.

'Are you going to apologise to me son for attempting to belittle him,' asked Octavius, losing sight in his roused anger of the fact that no articulate reply was likely to be forthcoming, 'or do I have to bate it out of you?'

Luke leaned forward in his seat with the look of an interested spectator. 'Er—if I might make a humble suggestion, Octavius?'

Octavius looked across still mightily at loggerheads with every-one within radius. 'What is it?'

'Nothing in the least inflammatory, Octavius, I do assure you,' said Luke with a conciliatory wave of his hand. 'I merely wish to point out that it would facilitate a speedy reply from our friend Matthew if you were to relax your grip somewhat around the general region of his larynx—purely as a temporary measure, if it is your intention to throttle him to extinction, something which is entirely your own affair.'

Octavius seemed a bit baffled and bemused. 'Oh aye,' he grunted abruptly letting go of his prey who fell gasping across the table. 'I suppose it would be a bit rash to guzzle him into the next world and him not having made reparation for the wrongs he committed in this one.'

Luke bowed. 'So good of you, Octavius, to place such a charitable interpretation upon it.'

Mulligan was moaning and making strange gurgling noises as he fingered his throat, eyes swimming and tongue lolling out the corner of his mouth.

Ranter leaned crossarmed on the táble and peered closer. 'He doesn't look too rosy to me, bejasus.'

'The poor oul' bugger,' said Babysoft touched by the spectacle. 'You didn't have to go and nearly strangulate him all the same, Mister,' she added reprovingly to Octavius. 'We all get our deserts in the end, true enough, but murdering someone without benefit of priest or clergy is going too far altogether.'

Octavius looked contritely down at the hapless form heaving spasmodically in the chair. 'Jasus, I meant no harm. I got carried away, sort of. I don't know me own strength when me goat is got going.' He turned to his son. 'Get a drop of brandy, Ultan, and see if we can fan some life into him itself.'

'Righto, Father.'

Ranter looked still closer. 'I think he just had a bit of a turn meself.'

'So he would have, right enough,' said Babysoft nodding, 'and him nearly having the life throttled out of him.'

Ultan soon returned.

'Here we are now, Sundown,' urged Octavius, gently drawing back Mulligan's limp head and placing the neck of the bottle to his mouth. 'A drop of this and you'll be as right as rain.'

At the first few fiery drops Mulligan moaned and spluttered and looked around with fearful eyes. 'Jesus Christ, what happened to me?'

Octavius patted his shoulder. 'You're gameball now, oul' son.'

'Did I have a blackout or something?' asked Mulligan grabbing

Octavius by the hand tightly. 'Don't lie to me, man—I can take it. Did I have a blackout?'

Octavius scratched his head ruefully. 'Er—I suppose you could say that, oul' flower, I suppose you could well say that. Have another slug out of this—it's me own special bottle.'

Mulligan took a grateful swallow and blinked rapidly. 'I'm forever fearful of passing out in the depths of drink in the middle of nowhere with not a soul or sinner nearby to whisper a prayer or two in my ear.'

Babysoft sniffed loudly and brushed her eyes with the back of her hand. 'Jasus help him just the same. I wouldn't wish that on me worst enemy.'

'He looks remarkably himself again to me,' said Sonny surveying Mulligan unprepared to join in the general melting. 'One might almost add to the point of painful vulgarity.'

'Has that wan got no heart in her a'tall?' hissed Babysoft. 'All them foreigners is the same, not an ounce of human charity in them.'

Mulligan looked around with chastened eyes. 'I've never divulged this to anyone before, but the very same thing happened to my Father—' he made the sign of the cross—'years ago.'

'You mean he suffered from blackouts too?' asked Babysoft. Mulligan nodded. 'Just one. The final one.'

'Not in the middle of O'Connell Street?' asked Ranter.

'It was in front of a train, actually,' said Mulligan.

'That was a bleeding stupid thing to do. I don't suppose the train happened to be stationary at the time?'

'It was the Dublin to Cork express,' informed Mulligan with a mournful shake of his head. 'Travelling at full throttle,' he looked quickly at Octavius, 'I mean speed.'

'Was there anything left of him afterwards?' enquired Babysoft.

'There wouldn't be, would there?' growled Ranter. 'Except a gansyload of fond memories.'

Mulligan spoke softly, absently, fingers stroking his throat. 'We found his watch a mile or so up the track. It was made of stainless steel.'

'Whereas your oul' fella wasn't,' said Ranter.

Octavius drew up a chair and sat down. 'Jasus, that's a melancholy tale altogether, no blotting it out.' He filled glasses for all. 'Let's all have a gargle in the name of God, before we start choosing what kind of habit we'd like to be laid out in.'

Mulligan put his hand on that of Octavius with heavy emphasis. 'But first let me say how deeply I regret having caused that little fracas just now—'

Octavius waved airily. 'Think nothing of it, man. Sure if you were to count up me own little indiscretions I'd be hung, drawn and quartered.' He held up his glass. 'Let's drink to the memory of your poor dead Father—'

'Who was so inconsiderate,' interjected Luke, 'as to fall under the wheels of the Dublin to Cork express, and him not knowing what day of the week it was.'

'Now in my opinion,' said Babysoft, 'when a man falls under a train, the day of the week or the month of the year, for that matter, is neither here or there, and the poor man lying mangled under the wheels of fate, you might say.'

'That is all too true,' said Luke. 'I am duly chastised for being unforgivably facetious. It just struck me,' he went on, 'as unbearably risible that all this time friend Matthew was harbouring such a dark tragedy. It is a bit like someone pausing in the middle of "Don't Dilly Dally On the Way" and plunging recklessly into the *De Profundis*.'

'Let me apologise to the gallant youth,' insisted Mulligan downing another glass of brandy. 'In all conscience I must, if only to salve my own insufferable pangs of remorse.'

'Well, if you feel that strong about it. Ultan!'

Ultan stepped forward at a brisk military pace.

'Shake hands with the gentleman, Ultan son, and show him you bear no ill-will or malice despite his great ignorance.'

Mulligan clasped the youth's hand in both his own. 'My dear boy,' he quavered, 'do you forgive me?'

'Sure there's nothing to forgive, sir.'

'That wasn't the question the gentleman put to you, Ultan,' reprimanded Octavius. 'The point is, whether there's anything to forgive or not, are you prepared to forgive him?'

'If you put it like that, Father—'

'I'm not putting it like anything, Ultan son,' corrected Octavius. 'It is the gentleman here who is putting the question to you. I am merely clarifying matters a little, so that you are sure in your mind when you give him your answer.'

'Then I do forgive him—' Ultan stopped hastily and turned to

Mulligan. 'I accept your apology, sir, and am glad to shake your hand.'

Mulligan gazed raptly into Ultan's face, not letting go his grasp. 'Jesus Christ, boy, but you're a splendid young man.' He turned to the others with glistening eyes: 'Isn't it a grand and wonderful thing to be responsible for bringing such a noble upstanding young man into this bleak and weary world?' He turned back to Ultan: 'In you, my dear boy, in you I behold the hope and promise of mankind, and more, much more than that.' He squeezed Ultan's hand tighter: 'The son I might have had, had my life taken other, more purposeful directions—'

'Matthew, Matthew, do please desist,' said Luke, 'or else we are all undone with the sheer unrelieved pathos of it all.'

Mulligan let go of Ultan's hand and dived for the voluminous handkerchief, clapping it to mouth and nose. 'You, Sheridan, are a cold unfeeling brute.'

Luke looked pained. 'Et tu, Brute?'

'Leave the poor man alone, Lukey love,' said Babysoft moist and sweet with renewed brandy. 'Maybe he's not as black as he paints himself, and anyway he's had a bit of a shock, thinking he had passed out under a train.'

'That was his Oul' Fella, you eejit,' said Ranter.

Mulligan threw up his hands in appeal. 'It's true! The world only sees me as a tireless dynamo of energy, a scion of industry and productivity, a hard ruthless merchant driven by ambition, whipped by the will to succeed—'

'You're beginning to sound quite attractive, Mr Mulligan,' said Sonny.

'It's true!' repeated Mulligan near to tearful hysteria. 'I'm seen only as a heartless tyrant seated implacably behind a desk, driving myself beyond the bounds of human strength, with no time to indulge the ordinary human foibles and failings—'

Luke held up a protesting hand. 'Oh, I wouldn't go that far, Matthew; the last time I saw our Miss Springett she looked every bit a foible and falling rapidly to your endearing if slightly over-the-hill charms.'

'Kindly leave Miss Springett out of this!' Mulligan growled.

'Coyness I find distinctly incongruous in you, Matthew,' pursued Luke, leaning forward across the table in an attitude of confidence; 'By the way, I have never been able to unravel a certain mystery about Miss Springett—what the "M" in her name stands for.'

'I told you, Sheridan,' Mulligan responded with surprising fervour, 'I don't wish to discuss Miss Springett with a low dirty-minded lout like you. Her memory is dear to me—*dear*!'

'Oh come on, Matthew,' rebuked Luke. 'You talk as if she, too, had thrown herself under the Dublin to Cork express. I am merely filled with mild curiosity about her Christian name—surely even in your black, black book that does not constitute either criminality or perversion? It is one of the smaller but no less intriguing enigmas of life, not knowing what the "M" in Miss Springett's name could possibly signify, and I thought that you, knowing and revering the lady as you do—'

Mulligan brightened and blew his nose, unable to resist flattery. 'You mean you don't know?' he cackled. 'Hah-hah, Sheridan, that's one thing that has eluded your cunning devious methods of worming things out of people, eh?'

'I humbly admit defeat, Matthew,' admitted Luke readily. 'And as always when something sorely puzzles and outwits me, it is to you I turn for enlightenment and the benefit of your superior perspicacity.'

Mulligan drank and glowed. 'Sure what else in all the world would it stand for, man, if not for Mercedes?'

'Mercedes?' echoed Luke.

'I always thought that was a car the fellas in Fitzwilliam Square drive around in,' said Babysoft.

'Mercedes,' repeated Luke.

A look of positive horror had come over Mulligan's face. 'Jesus Christ, whatever possessed me to tell you that?'

Luke grinned and slapped his forehead with open palm. 'Mercedes. Of course! What else could it be indeed, Matthew! Let's see,' he said picking up his glass with a pensive air. 'Matthew and Mercedes . . . or is it the more cosy and familiar Matt and Merc? Yes, it definitely has an alternative ring about it. As I'm sure Miss Mercedes Springett would love to be able to say about that certain finger on her left hand . . .'

Mulligan looked crestfallen. 'Whatever possessed me?' he wailed. 'I'll never forgive myself for betraying her trust, for violating her confidence.'

'As long as that is all you have violated, Matthew.'

'What evil impulse possessed me to divulge something known only to one person outside her dead parents, and that person myself?' cried Mulligan liberally drowning his remorse.

'Nil desperandum, Matthew. Thy perilous secret is sacrosanct within this manly bosom.'

Mulligan pressed his handkerchief convulsively to his mouth again. 'I will never again be able to look that dear sainted woman in the face, knowing I have wantonly betrayed the one harmless little secret she had kept hidden all these long-suffering stoical years from the cruel mocking eyes of the world.'

Sonny made a small polite noise. 'I don't quite grasp the significance of these exchanges. Am I to understand there is a Dark Lady unseen in our midst, who is romantically attached to our bluff and blustery Mr Mulligan?'

Luke turned to explain. ' "The Lay of the Last Minstrel", you might say in poetic parlance. Or on the other hand you might, in more prosaic and less gracious terms, say "The Minstrel's Last Lay" . . .'

Mulligan banged down his glass. 'I won't sit here and suffer Miss Springett's name to be sullied by that foul and damnable tongue of yours, Sheridan!'

Babysoft looked anxious. 'Don't get him narky again,' she urged. 'He might decide to have a real effing blackout this time and not bother to come out of it.'

'Suicidal, if you ask me,' rejoined Ranter.

Babysoft considered awhile. 'I suppose he's the type,' she agreed. 'Sure he's starting to foam at the mouth already, bejasus.'

Octavius refilled glasses all around. 'Take it aisy, oul' cock,' he told Mulligan patting his arm. 'Get stuck into that now and you won't call the Queen your aunt . . .'

'Aunts is born, not made, is what I always say,' Babysoft stated. She held out her glass as the bottle went around. 'You've a real kind face on you, Mister.'

'And me Missus is in the back kitchen boiling onions,' Octavius told her with a wide beatific smile. 'I'm a bugger for boiled onions.'

'And I'm a hoor for greasy water,' rejoined Babysoft gaily.

'Don't let's start talking about our professions,' muttered Ranter as his glass was filled. 'Life is hard enough as it is.'

'Sure I never took me work home with me once—that's one thing they can't say about me.'

'You wouldn't have to, would you,' reasoned Ranter, 'and you up to your eyeballs in soft quilts and Napoleon brandy. Sure Cleopatra was only in the farthing place compared to you, and she was the greatest hoor in recorded history.'

'Jasus, Ranter, you must've swept poor Gertie off her feet talking like that.'

'She came from Goatstown, let me remind you.'

'And you mean to say there's no hoors in Goatstown? Jasus, what a dismal place to live in!'

Mulligan gave a loud belch and a fart all at once. 'An honourable man was my Father—'

'But so are we all,' Luke intoned, holding his glass up to the flames, 'all honourable men.'

'Night editor he was for over twenty years on the now defunct *Dublin Evening Mail,* and never as much as looked at another woman—'

'Was he a nancy boy?' asked Ranter, 'or something more drastic, like bad eyesight?'

'He loved but one woman to the end, and that woman was my angelic beloved Mother,' Mulligan declared. 'To the end of the line he lavished her with singular devotion—'

'To the end of the railway line anyway,' amended Ranter.

'An honourable man. Used to stand for hours on O'Connell Bridge.'

'Why,' asked Babysoft, 'was he a beggar or something?'

Mulligan lowered his glass and looked sternly at her. 'Madam, we are all beggars.'

'God's curse on you anyway!' fumed Babysoft. 'I'm no beggar, whatever your oul' fella might've been! I earn me living hard, catering to decrepit oul' bastards like you, hardly able to mount the bleeding stairs, never mind anything else.'

Luke held up a peace-keeping hand. 'Forsooth, dear lady, forsooth. Our friend Matthew was merely speaking in a figurative fashion.'

'Used to stand there on O'Connell Bridge,' Mulligan murmured into his glass. 'Last thing at night, first thing in the morning, drunk or sober. Watching the passing parade, observing the foolish populace, the gaudy rags and tatters of Vanity Fair, communing with nature, looking down into the black mysterious waters of the Liffey . . .'

'Otto, show some restraint, do,' commanded Sonny as her companion proceeded to gnaw at her earlobe like an over-affectionate puppy. 'You have been good for so long, don't spoil it now.'

'Very much I have the want in me, mein Gretchen,' slobbered Otto nuzzling the soft side of her neck. 'I am now in our little villa in Baden-Baden under dem net of den stars—'

Ranter had returned to the talkative flames half speaking with moist musing misted eyes:

> 'It was there Maggie dear
> with our hearts full of cheer
> we strolled 'neath the moon's gentle beam . . .'

Babysoft in a melting mood slid her hand along the edge of the bench and laid it upon Ranter's. 'I always loved that oul' song, Ranter,' she said softly touching his shoulder with her cheek. 'Such lovely words. Words with real meaning. They touch me here,' she said putting a hand on her left breast, 'right here. Feel if you don't believe me.'

'Is it seducing me you are?' said Ranter shrugging her off.

Babysoft picking up her glass. 'I'm off duty.'

'I thought hoors was like priests or doctors,' Ranter said, 'always on call, twenty-four hours a day.'

'We have to have our rest times too in or out of bed.'

Ranter drank and turned again to the fire elbows resting on knees:

> 'Beneath it the stream gently ripples
> above it the birds seem to trill—'

'Jasus, Ranter, you're full of song as well as wit,' marvelled Babysoft with a touch of sarcasm. 'You must've had broken blades for breakfast. Anyway, you might as well go on with your song as anything else.'

'Always brings back me coortin' days, that song does,' Ranter reminisced wiping his mouth. 'The days when meself and Gertie used to go for walks along the canal and linger awhile on the locks.'

'Sounds terribly romantic,' sighed Babysoft toying with his hard knobbly fingers.

'It was, till I fell in and woke up.'

'Into the canal?'

Ranter snorted. 'Into bleeding marriage, woman.'

Mulligan snapped jerkily out of a brief snooze. 'The call of nature is insistent,' he said getting ponderously to his feet. 'Luke, old comrade, will you kindly lead the way?'

'Why, Matthew,' said Luke unwilling to relinquish the satiny feel of Sonny's foot now imprisoned between his knees, 'you cannot fail to find it—can he, Octavius?'

'What's that?'

'Our editorial friend here wishes to avail himself of your excellent plumbing facilities.'

'Eh? Oh, the jacks you mean.' Octavius nodded towards the back of the room. 'Just bear due north by the sign of the Ram as you leave the bar and you can't miss it. Failing which,' he continued rocking back in the chair, 'just keep sniffing.'

'As a matter of fact, Luke,' said Mulligan with a weak apologetic grin, 'I'm none too steady on my old pins and would appreciate the assistance of your strong sturdy young arm.'

'In that case, Matthew,' sighed Luke getting to his feet, 'and couched as it is in such affecting language . . . lean on me, my venerable hackneyed friend.'

'Do hurry back, Luke,' said Sonny with a meaningful smile. 'You are such a comfort to us all.'

'I'll go that far with you, lads,' said Ranter rising.

Mulligan stumbled up against Luke clutching his arm. 'Isn't there any privacy left in the world?' he hissed into his ear. 'I wanted a quiet word with you.'

'A man of your vast and varied experience, Matthew,' said Luke as they wove their way through the crowd, 'should know that next to the confessional, there is not a more private place on earth than in the hallowed precincts of a lavatory in an Irish public house.'

'You must be joking!' puffed Mulligan.

'I jest not,' assured Luke. 'Everyone is so busy desperately seeking relief you could divulge the highest and most explosive of State secrets and nobody would raise an eyebrow, or anything else, for that matter. And afterwards they're so vastly relieved and happily spent they wouldn't be bothered to eavesdrop anyway.'

They passed through the tight-packed narrow garrulous spaces of the bar, out the door into a gloomy passageway redolent of onions and boot polish into the narrow pen-like cubicle lit by a single electric bulb bobbing in its socket from the wind whistling in through a small open window high up, the pungent acrid smell of piss instantly assailing the nostrils, rising from a thin gulley running along the bottom of the rough white-distempered wall stained and scarred with naïve obscenities and crude chalk hearts and arrows pledging erotic troths and pre-womb fantasies, the permeating stench of urine starting tears in unwary eyes and a vague unnamable sense of burning at the backend of throats.

Mulligan looked about him with grandiose distaste as he un-zipped and straddled over the gulley. 'I deem it an insult to a man's prick,' he said, 'being asked to piss in a kip like this.'

'I don't exactly remember being asked,' said Ranter, fiddling with conventional buttons.

'Expected, then,' amended Mulligan.

'In my humble opinion,' pursued Ranter perusing the low sloping corrugaged iron roof, 'our good friend Octavius couldn't give two fucks whether you piss or not.'

'But surely you find this sorry excuse for a latrine highly objectionable, even by the sub-standards one expects to meet in outer Dublin?' asked Mulligan with the knowledgeable air of someone who is being blindingly reasonable.

'I didn't expect the Taj Mahal,' said Ranter, 'and if you don't expect the Taj Mahal you're never disappointed.'

Mulligan laughed. 'Oh come now, friend, surely that is a fatalist's attitude! I have waged a campaign in my paper for years,' he confided, 'to obtain more hygienic facilities in public-house urinals, especially as I say in the primitive belt existing in outer Dublin, as Luke here will testify.'

Luke standing in the line nodded. 'True, Matthew, true. Many's the leading article you have embellished with scatological pearls of wisdom and peerless prose in defence and support of a more salubrious slash, displaying therein a high civic awareness and sensitivity. In fact,' Luke elaborated, 'it might truly and with high moral justification be said of you, Matthew, that you were the embodiment of that well-known Dublin character, a piss artist, par excellence.'

'You will have your little joke, Sheridan,' chuckled Mulligan complacently. 'A man can only do his best.' He squeezed up his pudgy eyes in pleasure—'Jesus Christ, I needed *that*!'

'If, unlike bold Robert Emmet, the darling of Ireland, your epitaph comes to be written one day,' continued Luke contemplating a spider drowning just below his foot in the swirling waters of the gulley, 'I might well take it upon myself to do you funereal honours—

> Here does gentle Matthew lie
> of the whiskey-nose and bloodshot eye
> whose reward is in the next world if not in this
> for trying to win us all a more hygienic piss.'

'Ah,' exclaimed Mulligan with fast-closed eyes knotting himself up in a minor convulsion, 'squeeze the last drops out of the bugger!' He seemed to go limp and stepped back hunching forward as he zipped up his fork. 'That was sweet.'

'As far as I'm concerned,' said Ranter as he too concluded, 'a piss is a piss, whether it's in outer Dublin or outer Mongolia, and there's no mollycoddling that fact.'

'Ah yes,' said Mulligan fishing out the handkerchief and mopping his face, 'I would agree that pissing, per se, is a very simple straightforward process, but the question then arises not when or how you piss, but *where*. I mean to say,' he went on putting the hankie back into his side pocket, 'a man is taking his life in his hands when he comes into a place like this—' he stopped to consider the marvel of his own wit and grinned—'That's not bad, eh? Not bad for an old journalistic warhorse like myself, eh? Taking his life in his hands. Get it?' he nudged Luke slyly in the ribs—'get it, eh?

'Indeed I do, Matthew,' answered Luke, 'indeed I do. Send this urgent dispatch, Ranter, to the nearest Reuters office: "Matthew Mulligan is alive and well and cracking superannuated lavatorial jokes in a public latrine in Howth!"'

Mulligan darkened angrily but retained his nervous anaemic smile as he smoothed back the sparse sandy strands of his hair. 'Might I have a private word in your ear, Luke?'

Luke finished and inclined his head forward. 'By all means.'

'Er—umm—I mean, in private.'

Ranter adjusted his cap at a more flamboyant angle. 'I'll see you in the bar.' He paused at the door. 'We'll have one more round, and then we'll head for the holy city—fair enough?'

'Fair enough. I must admit I pine for urban airs once more.'

'I don't think your man likes me,' said Mulligan after Ranter had left.

'Your perspicacity sometimes takes my breath away, Matthew.'

'Yes, well, I have other things on my mind besides the opinion of a sordid little taximan—'

Luke stared at him. 'Careful, Matthew, or I might break my hitherto fervent vows of non-violence and pacifism and finish what Octavius so lamentably left unfinished.'

'Acting tough, Sheridan? Bit late in the day for that, isn't it?'

'On the contrary, Matthew. The very sight of your mottled ugly countenance fills me with an exhilarating urge to render it mercifully unrecognisable in one fell swoop—' he picked up a toilet plunger that stood in a corner—'possibly with the appropriate aid of this, which appeals strongly to my sense of poetic justice.'

Mulligan's weak smile resurfaced. 'Come off it, Sheridan, I didn't come out here to indulge in fisticuffs with you—'

'Then state what you did come out for, Matthew, for I am rapidly wearying of your company so rudely enforced upon us all.'

'I am here to give you your job back, Luke.'

'Most magnanimous of you, Matthew, and you must also surely know by now exactly where you can stuff the selfsame job. I am going back to rejoin my friends—'

Mulligan put his hand on the other's arm. 'I want you back, Luke.'

Luke smiled. 'This sudden sense of being wanted is heady stuff indeed, and an hour since I would doubtless have fallen on my unworthy knees to you in abject gratification, but now I can truly stand back and declare with hand fast held on heart: stick thy job up thy obese back passage, Oh Matthew of the foul body odours and gargantuan farts.'

'Look, Sheridan, look,' Mulligan persisted pulling out the ever-serviceable handkerchief again; 'I'll double your wages, make you a fucking sub-editor if that pleases your vanity—'

'You pile the platter high with Satanic wiles, Matthew.'

'Then it's okay, you accept?'

'Then it is not okay and I do not accept.'

'But Jesus, Sheridan, be reasonable. I can't go any further.'

'The furthest I want you to go, Matthew,' said Luke removing Mulligan's hand from his arm with studied distaste, 'is back to that rathole of an office in the Quays, there to indulge your grey little fantasies of industry and journalistic expansion as you conjure up erotic visions of poor virginal Miss Springett and spend numberless hours of self-torture wondering what colour knickers she is wearing on any particular day.'

'Be sensible, Sheridan.'

'I assure you, at this moment in time, I am filled to the utmost and outermost limits of my being with supreme sensibility.'

Mulligan fell to a cagey sneering. 'You won't fill your belly with either bread or porter while we wait with bated breath for you to fling that masterpiece of horrific genius and art upon the world.'

Luke pondered. 'I agree with you, Matthew.'

'Hah!' croaked Mulligan. 'What did I tell you?'

'I agree with you, I shall probably be ravaged and torn apart for the first ten years with pangs of sheer physical hunger as I struggle to complete my momentous opus. But ah, the mere prospect of never having to encounter that vile visage of yours after a night of honest dissolution is enough to make me want to rush headlong upon an upturned sword and count myself among the blessed!'

Mulligan's eyes had grown smaller and he fought for breath. 'And women—what will you do for women, eh, with not a juice in your pocket or the prospect of one—eh? You'll not be able to pick up the cheapest wine-sodden pox-ridden oul' prostitute in the whole fucking city of Dublin as you sweat your balls out over your secondhand portable Remington! What will our brave genius do then, eh, our Dublin Dostoevsky, sitting there in his bandbox of a bedsitter, shivering with cold and going off his rocker for the want of a fuck!' Mulligan clutched at the wall to steady himself as he gasped for breath. 'What'll you do then, eh, Fiodor?'

'In that event, Matthew, I hope I shall have the strength not to call upon you for the benefit of your own vast experience in such matters of furtive self-induced carnality as you mentally ravish poor Mercedes over a lukewarm mug of morning coffee and an empty flask of Bushmills.'

Mulligan grew purple. 'You—you bastard!'

Luke put out his hand as the older man tottered. 'My dear Matthew, once again you appear to be on the threshold of eternity. Let me help you to a seat.'

Mulligan let himself be led to the solitary toilet seat enclosed at the end of the cubicle behind a green timber door and sat heavily down, shirtfront and collar askew, the perspiration coursing in rivulets down his face. 'You'll—you'll have my death on your conscience yet, Sheridan.'

'An awesome burden, Matthew, were I afflicted with so worrisome an appendage as a conscience. Where's that colossal pocket hankie of yours, Matthew?'

'In here.'

Luke found the handkerchief and proceeded to wipe the other's glistening face as he sat wobbling on the toilet-pot.

'You can't leave me now, Sheridan.'

'Relax, Matthew. Verily, I am with you till the end of your days.'

'You'll come back to the paper?'

'I didn't say that, Matthew.'

'But you will, won't you?'

'Would you have me be unfaithful to my own high purpose just to placate your own ludicrous paternalistic whim?'

'You know fucking well I would, Sheridan.'

'But why?'

'I'm an old man in an impossible position.'

'Marry Mercedes.'

'Fuck off.'

'It would be by far the best and most unselfish thing that you have ever done in your life.'

'Let Sidney Carton rest content in his quicklime hole, for fuck sake, man. He was hung because of a hooring woman!'

'I always assumed he was guillotined.'

'That's what I'd be if I married Miss Springett. She'd have me dead and buried within a month.'

'How so?'

'A pent-up frustrated middle-aged woman like that—it'd be suicide, like stepping into a cage with a starving tigress.'

'She's such a genteel creature.'

'Genteel my bollocks. You don't see the way she looks at me sometimes when she thinks I'm not watching.'

'Fantasising again, Matthew,' reproved Luke as he continued his ministrations to Mulligan's sweating features. 'Your fantasies will be the death of you sooner than anything else.'

'You think I'm making it all up, don't you? Well, I don't imagine the way her nostrils twitch and the quick convulsive way she grips her pencil when I come and stand over her when I'm dictating. And what's more,' affirmed Mulligan gradually getting his normal breathing back, 'she looks at you the very same way when you come into the office.'

'The very same way, Matthew?'

'As if you hadn't got any trousers on, or as if your fly was wide open and you were airing it, bejasus.'

Luke looked thoughtful. 'Hmm. I must put your theories to the test sometime. Now that I think about it, she has a very good back, has our Mercedes, and her legs aren't bad either.'

'You think so, eh?' asked Mulligan eagerly.

'Indubitably. Always accepting,' said Luke as he stepped back to survey his patient, 'always accepting that she is in a remarkable state of preservation for a woman of her age, that is.'

Mulligan looked displeased. 'You make her sound as if she was fucking mummified or stuffed by a taxidermist or something.'

'Better stuffed by a taxidermist than by you, Matthew. Well now, you seem to be back to your old pugnacious repulsive self. You look like a giant king toad sitting on his throne.'

Mulligan struggled hastily to his feet. 'Then you'll return to the fold and let bygones be bygones, eh Luke old son?'

'I didn't say that either, Matthew.'

'But you will, you hoor's melt, won't you?'

'I am always reluctant to let bygones be bygones,' said Luke stuffing the handkerchief back into the other man's pocket. 'Because of course they never are bygones, are they? For instance, when I look at you, Matthew,' he continued measuring up his companion, 'I know to my chagrin and despair that you will never be a bygone.'

Mulligan instantly retrieved the hankie and dabbed at his eyes. 'Jesus Christ, Sheridan, that's the nicest thing that's ever been said about me.'

Luke shook his head. 'You are one of life's incorrigibles, Matthew. One minute you are dying of apoplexy, the next you are laying on the hot butter of humility so thick and fast it sizzles and renders honest indignation impossible.'

Mulligan gave a diffident grin. 'I always was a very complex character, not as one-dimensional as I let on. That's why I've held this job for so long. I like you, Sheridan.'

'You're killing me, Matthew.'

'No—straight up. I mean it. Together, you and me, we could really shake up this fucking paper and make it go with a bang.'

'I've always thought it could do with some gelignite attached to its somewhat pallid tabs.'

'You have integrity, Sheridan, integrity, and despite my—umm, er—my seniority of years, you can't deny that I have a certain flair—a certain penchant, shall we say, for the bold flamboyant gesture—'

'Talking of bold flamboyant gestures—you nearly killed that poor horse tonight. A good thing for us all that Ranter, our sordid little taximan, had sound brakes and keen reflexes.'

Mulligan pulled the lapels of his coat straighter. 'I take back whatever derogatory thing I said about your man—what's his name again?—oh yeah—Panther—'

'Ranter, Matthew, Ranter the unrepeatable.'

'That's it—Ranter. Most humbly I take back whatever I may have said about him, and remind me to buy him a double Paddy when we get back to the bar.'

Luke shut his eyes. 'He is quite liable to blind you with it.'

'Then it's okay, sub-editor Sheridan? Like the black sheep of old you'll return to the fold?'

'You realise of course that I am selling my birthright?'

'Sure isn't that what birthrights are for? From now on you'll be confined exclusively to features and leave all the other shit to the galley slaves downstairs.'

'But what becomes of my fierce determination to be a novelist as I sit at my dreary desk writing about the latest epidemic of swine-fever in County Limerick and gloomily contemplate Miss Springett's untouchable anus?'

'You don't want to waste your time, surely to God, writing fucking novels?'

'Well,' said Luke as they stepped out into the passageway, 'not necessarily novels of that precise description, or in which an inordinate amount of that fine immemorial activity takes place, but I should like to write something relatively meritorious before they trundle me off to join the Glasnevin silent majority.'

'Why?'

'Why what?'

'Why do you want to write a novel in the first place? It's hardly a suitable thing for a bright energetic young blackguard like yourself to be doing, and all them females around just begging to be screwed as soon as you unbuckle your belt.'

'Oh,' said Luke blithely, 'I just thought my energies ought to become a bit more creative rather than procreative, if only for a change—which they say can be as good as a rest.'

They were feeling their way along the dark dank unlit corridor when Mulligan stopped and put out his hand. 'By the same token,' he said in a low guarded voice, 'how did you get on with the two virgins out there?'

'Extremely amicably, I'm happy to say. Charming ladies both.'

'How do you think I'd be fixed?'

'Fixed, Matthew?'

'I don't have to spell it out for you, do I?'

'I don't know, Matthew. Depends what you want to spell out —there's always the hazard of misspelling.'

Mulligan's breath was fetid as he inclined his head closer. 'What I want to know is—which one of them should I try first?'

'You do seem to have this very persistent death-wish.'

'I'm serious,' croaked Mulligan fingers tightening. 'I've been going mad with the horn ever since I saw them, but I don't want to barge into your stable, if you know what I mean.'

'You're learning to be very courteous in your autumn years, Matthew, but if you wouldn't consider it impertinent for one of my own tender years to offer you a word of advice—don't.'

'What do you mean?'

'I mean,' said Luke patiently, 'don't try it.'

'I get it now,' sneered Mulligan. 'You've booked the two of them for yourself. Now that's what I call the essence of cupidity —trying to screw two birds with the one flute at the same time!'

'Alas,' sighed Luke, 'even I would not be capable of performing such a highly intricate gymnastic feat. Let's get back.'

'Wait,' said Mulligan with once more a detaining hand. 'I wouldn't go as far as that German bit—she looks as cold as icing on a cake anyway—but the other one now—she's a scrubber if ever I saw one! I don't think I could go far wrong there, eh?'

'O Matthew, thou rude and frantic beast,' declaimed Luke, observing with a stirring of unwanted pity the bloated covetous countenance hovering hopefully, glimmering in the gloom of the hallway. 'The slightest of false moves in that direction and you risk irreparable injury to life and limb. Especially that limb which you so ardently desire to exercise.'

Mulligan laughed. 'Come on now, Sheridan—you make her out to be some kind of padlocked Prioress with a black belt in judo. Jesus, man, I only want her for less than ten minutes—after that she can retire into the Poor Clares and spend the rest of her life praying for the redemption of my immortal soul.'

'Haven't you, even in that dim primitive brain of yours, any lingering conception of the dignity of womanhood?' asked Luke with measured pedantry. 'Any redeeming comprehension of a woman's place in society?'

Mulligan's uncertain comradely grin faded and he grew impatient. 'Holy fuck, man! You'd think we were talking about the Jewels of the Madonna or something! The likes of that cheap-arsed little pro are going for ten-a-penny in town—'

'Then I suggest,' said Luke with extreme reasonableness, 'that you gather together every available penny in your possession and beat a hasty retreat back to the idyllic and most economic delights of town.'

Mulligan snorted. 'Where did you pick her up anyway—in some notorious knocking-shop along the Quays? What is she, for fuck's sake?' he asked growing increasingly indignant: 'A broken-down run-of-the-mill clap-pedlar that has sent more poor bastards to the Lock Hospital in her time than I've had wet dreams!'

Luke sighed. 'Is it your intention, then, to stand out here in this dark malodorous place as you crack the whip and send your frenetic little fantasies jumping through the lurid circus hoops of your imagination all over again? If so, I'll gladly leave you to it and resume the healthier debauchery of getting pissed.'

Mulligan again grabbed his wrist with nervous insistence. 'Look, Luke old friend, look,' he pulled crumpled wads of notes out of his pockets and shook them in his fists, 'I've got bread! And there's more where that came from. More than that painted little prick-teaser in there would earn in a month of Sundays.'

'You need more than a gargantuan gulp of brandy this time,

Matthew—you require a complete body transplant from head to toe, and even then I fear you would not be worthy to kiss the hem of Miss Brogan's mini-skirt.'

'For the love and honour of God, man,' gasped Mulligan feverishly, 'can't you see I'm desperate and distracted out of my mind for the want of a good ride!'

'In that case, Matthew,' said Luke hitching up the waistband of his jeans, 'I can only further suggest that you hire out the services of our equine friend, Rambler, once more in order that you may derive that particular equestrian pleasure, for I greatly fear that the only thing you'll be mounting this night, Matthew, is the gallows.'

Mulligan rammed the notes back into his pockets quivering with wounded pride. 'You think so, eh—you think I can't get it anymore, eh, you think I can't rise to the occasion anymore? I'll show you, bejasus, I'll show you.'

'I do honestly wish you wouldn't, Matthew—I just don't relish the prospect of scooping you up off the bar room floor bit by bit.'

'I'll show you!' fumed Mulligan. 'The day hasn't come yet when I need the likes of *you* to give me a leg up on a common hoor, and if it ever does I'll borrow a rifle from the Master of the Kildare Hounds who's married to a first cousin of mine and blow my fucking brains out, so help me!'

'A consummation devoutly to be wished.'

'Fuck you anyway, Sheridan!'

Mulligan in highest dudgeon shoved past in the direction of the bar and sighing for the sad quirks and fixations of the man Luke turned to follow but found himself facing a door he had not seen before. It was ajar and emitting a pale congenial light, and Luke was compelled to pause and listen to a thin weedy quaver of a woman's voice singing in a keening lament over the sound of clinking glass:

'O to think of it, O to dream of it fills my heart with tears.
O the days of the Kerry dances
O the ring of the piper's tune
O for one of those hours of gladness
Gone, alas, like our youth too soon . . .'

Caught by the wistful somehow girlish strain of the voice Luke toed the door further apart and peeped into what he then saw was the bottling stores, stacked to the ceiling with bulging crates of beer, with an old-fashioned stove in the centre stuffed with red burning coke at which a cat and a large collie dog lay curled together in perfect equanimity and the voice of the unseen singer rose again on a quaver:

'Lads and lassies, take your places,
up the middle and down again
and the merryhearted singing
flowing out of the happy glen
O to think of it, O to dream of it fills my heart with tears.
O the days of the Kerry dances
O the ring of the piper's tune
O for one of those hours of gladness
Gone, alas, like our youth too soon . . .'

The collie twitched its long fleecy ears and with languid wagging tail looked up as Ethel-May came into view dragging a large crate of beer over the uneven stone floor. Stooping with accustomed ease and large-boned agility gripping it at the edges and heaved it upon a row of similar merchandise stacked neatly out against the wall, lifting a thin angular wrist to brush back frail wisps of her greyish-red hair from her forehead, sitting down tiredly on a wooden box and gazing into the glow of the stove hands loose in her lap.

'Ah dear, oh dear,' she muttered with a sigh, nodding wearily several times. 'Never did I think I would end my days like this, a drudge of a creature, God help me, feeding babies and bottling stout from the time I get up till the hour I lie down, long lonely miles away from my own kith and kin, with a drunken wretch of a man to lie beside me in the dark night and him too far gone with the booze to show me a morsel of affection.' Ethel-May sighed again deeply and raised her smock to her eyes—

'Was there ever a sweeter colleen in the dance than Eileen Orr
or a prouder lad than Tadghi as he sweetly took the floor?
Lads and lassies to your places
up the middle and down again
and the merryhearted laughter flowing out of the happy glen.
O to think of it, O to dream of it fills my heart with tears—'

Ethel-May rose and stood at the stove where the dog lazily stretched and shook itself free of the clinging curling cat and pressed itself against her bony flanks as she absently stroked its head.

'Ah yes, indeed,' she murmured, her silhouette long and gaunt in the fiery radiance of the stove. 'O to dream of it indeed . . . the dancing at the crossroads of a summer evening, the lads passing around the jug and the girls at twittering and laughing waiting to see who'd ask them up . . . them ruffians from Listowel and Ballybunion swaggering into our village like they were the cream of God's creation . . .'

Her voice dropped and she began to half-speak half-sing the words to herself as she fondled the ears of the dog:

'Time goes on, and the happy years are fled
and one by one the friends I loved are dead.
Silent now is that wild and lonely glen
where the old glad songs will echo ne'er again.
Always dreaming of days gone by
in my heart I hear—'

The cat, aroused at last, meowed softly and sprang lithely upon the back of the collie, creeping along its neck until it too reached and was dreamily stroked by Ethel-May's fingers as that tall lost ruminative woman stood framed against the glowing stove, lowered head a little to one side as she spoke the words in a remote recitative undertone:

'Loving voices of old companions
stealing out of the past once more
and the sound of the dear old music
warm and sweet as in days of yore . . .'

'Ah still,' she sighed picking the insistent cat up in her arms and shushing it against her; 'we loved each other once, before that cursed bottle came between us . . . a wild man you looked then, Octavius McSweeney, with your hair as red as a roaring bog on fire, and knowing little or nothing about the life of the birds and small animals and flowers that my people taught us and instilled into us from the cradle up, but I loved your gay rough ways and the strangeness of your speech . . . and now see what I've come to, God help me, haggard and broken before my time, trapped as sure as a rabbit in a snare, and the mountains of Kerry as far away from me now as the mountains on the moon itself . . .

O to think of it, O to dream of it fills my heart with tears . . .'

She stood a while longer bathed in the hot glow shimmering out from the stove, and then with a tired puzzled shake of her head she moved away and returned towards the darkened rear of the stores as the two animals yawned and settled back again into a furry companionable huddle in the drowsy heat.

Shaking himself as if from a sleep Luke stirred and moved back down the dim hallway and into the din and smoke and bustle of the front parlour where waited Ranter who without preamble handed him a glass.

'Do justice to that and we'll be off,' he said, 'before mayhem is let loose upon the land.'

'In what particular shape or form?'

Ranter pulled his cap further down over his eyes and nodded towards their table. 'Need you ask? Your fat friend over there, slobbering all over Babysoft like she was a bitch in heat and him a big horny bulldog with a dose of the rabies.'

'A rash and importunate creature is our Matthew,' said Luke putting the glass to his lips. 'Dense and intractable and dismally slow to learn.'

'Fair play to the bloke for trying,' conceded Ranter, 'and him in the state he's in, but all I can see him getting for his pains is a knee in the bollocks and his face in ribbons.'

Luke finished off his drink. 'Loth as I am to depart this haven of gentle souls, I would be loth still to have this particular Vesuvius erupt and blow up in our faces, so I reluctantly fall in with your suggestion, to head for the relatively calmer waters of Madame Lala's establishment.'

'What about your man there—Darby O'Gill? You're not dragging him along with us, are you?'

'A rather awkward problem arises, Ranter. I've more or less become reconciled with the ogre and agreed to take my old job back on very advantageous terms.'

'Did he make you president or something?'

'I doubt if such a position exists in the corporate body of our whimsical little shitrag,' said Luke. 'But I restart at a decided advantage to my sweet and industrious self, all the same, and to suddenly up and discard him now might send· my promising career plummeting to subterranean depths once more. I mean to say,' explained Luke, 'I don't want to spend the best and most formative years of my life as a budding enfant terrible of the literary world staggering round Ireland in glassy-eyed pursuit of would-be murderesses and assassins, notwithstanding the considerable fringe benefits of such an enterprise.'

'So what are we going to do with Rupert the Fox over there,' pressed Ranter disconsolately, 'put him in the boot?'

'Now that,' said Luke snapping his fingers, 'is not as far-fetched as it sounds.'

'Forget it,' said Ranter, 'me boot's not big enough.'

'Perhaps our good friend Octavius might know of a way out of this little conundrum.'

'What's your trouble, oul' cock?' asked Octavius coming up behind them. 'I heard my name being mentioned—not in vain, I hope?'

'I hope not, Octavius.'

'What are you having while you tell me?'

'Really, Octavius, in this unhappy age of rampant indifference and coldhearted commercialism, you are the soul of decency and fraternity and we'll have the same again, please.'

'It's your man again, isn't it?' said Octavius as he set up their drinks at the counter. 'The blue-eyed lover from Burgh Quay.'

'Do you dabble in clairvoyancy in between pulling pints and multiplying the earth, Octavius?'

'A blind man could see what the caper is,' demurred Octavius. 'You don't know what to do with Walter Cronkite over there—that's it, isn't it, lads?'

'That in a nutshell is it, Octavius.'

'A nice clean plunge over Howth Head wouldn't do him a ha'porth of harm,' opined Ranter arms folded on bar.

'And what if he can't swim?' enquired Octavius with an admirable show of solicitude.

'I'm praying to Jasus he can't.'

'We can't drown the poor oul' sod,' reasoned Octavius, 'and him not knowing why we're doing it.'

'I don't know about that,' said Ranter. 'When you see a dog trying to get up a bitch, what do you do? You fuck a bucket of cold water over it, that's what you do! That soon restores it to its doggy senses, bejasus.'

Luke coughed deferentially. 'Unfortunately, gentlemen, he once more occupies the position of being my employer, so in the circumstances I would appreciate it if your combined conspiratorial talents were to come up with a slightly less drastic solution.'

'What about that oul' horse of yours?'

'You mean Rambler?'

'He could always fall off its back, couldn't he, and break his bleeding neck?'

'Now I couldn't countenance that.'

'Why not, for Jasus' sake? Nobody would know—'

'You're forgetting Rambler,' chided Octavius. 'Rambler wouldn't have it on his conscience. He was brought up very strict, with the fear of divine retribution in his heart.'

'The effing Christian Brothers must've been at him so.'

'He is a very moral and upright horse.'

'And I suppose he's a daily communicant as well?'

'No,' said Octavius solemnly, 'no then, he's not. But there's a Sacred Heart oil lamp hanging in his stall which he sometimes regards with touching adoration.'

'Maybe he'll be canonised yet and be the first horse to be made a saint,' said Ranter and then added on reflection, 'though that wouldn't be all that surprising when you think about it, for the horse has always been the only real Patron Saint of Ireland.'

'Excuse me, gentlemen,' Luke politely intervened, 'but aren't we straying a little? What about our friend Mulligan?'

'Who?' blinked Octavius, checked in his stride.

'Our friend Matthew, of whom we were supposed to be devising ways and means of smoothest disposal, remember?'

'Oh aye, so we were. Well now,' said Octavius picking up his glass and studying it carefully, 'I think there's a simple solution to that little problem.'

'You think so, Octavius?'

'I think so, yes. And you could say that Rambler is indirectly responsible for that solution.'

'God bless Rambler, a wonder horse indeed.'

'What have you in mind?' asked Ranter puzzled.

Octavius scratched his belly. 'When Rambler isn't feeling too rosy, when he's feeling fidgety and fettlesome and can't settle down in his stall at night, there's a little something I always give him.'

'A little something, Octavius?'

'You might say a little sleeping draught, a few drops of something I got from Francie Sullivan, our local vet, that I slip into the bucket of stout Rambler always has at night.'

'With what results, Octavius?'

'Out he goes like a light, with not as much as a whinny out of him till morning. Powerful stuff. Francie Sullivan swears by it.'

'But has it been known to work as well on homo sapiens?' enquired Luke with an intrigued air.

'I thought we were talking about Mulligan?'

Luke nodded abashed. 'I stand corrected, sir.'

'More important,' said Ranter, 'will it do the job?'

'Well,' said Octavius, 'I usually give Rambler four teaspoonfuls, and it does the job fine, so if I give your man, say, two teaspoonfuls—'

'But will that be enough?' Ranter wanted to know.

'I guarantee he'll have the sleep of a lifetime.'

Ranter rubbed his chin. 'I suppose if it's good enough for the horse it's good enough for him, right enough.'

'Francie Sullivan is the best bloody vet in Ireland, sure,' swore Octavius. 'I'd put him before our local GP any time, bejasus.'

'And you're reasonably certain it won't result in culpable homicide, Octavius?'

'It won't do him a bit of harm, and might on the other hand do him the world of good.'

'Well,' admitted Luke, 'he *has* been complaining of chronic insomnia of late.'

'There you are, then!' said Octavius, folding his arms and beaming. 'It's a favour we'll be doing him into the bargain, the lecherous oul' demon.'

'It does add a certain quality of mercy, that is true.'

'I've heard of doping horses,' said Ranter with gleeful anticipation, 'but doping night editors seems a more rewarding thing altogether.'

'As long as the end result is not a permanent state of rigor mortis,' said Luke afflicted with a minute twinge of doubt.

'The only place that horny oul' bastard will get rigor mortis,' scoffed Ranter, 'is under his Kingston shirt.'

'Go over to the table now, lads,' advised Octavius, 'and I'll follow with a round of drinks after a suitable interval, with the special little nightcap for your man.'

'Octavius,' spoke Luke thumping his breast, 'I salute you, Oh peerless Pict.'

Babysoft looked wrathfully up as the two returned to the table, her eyes dark and warring. 'I thought you'd fallen down the pot or something!'

'A thousand pardons, ladies,' said Luke. 'I was, you might say, unavoidably detained by matters of much import.'

'Why—did you have the runs?'

'Nothing quite as simple as that.'

'Would you ever get this shagging oul' effer off me,' breathed Babysoft tensely, 'before I give him something to remember me by for the rest of his days?'

Mulligan gurgled on the bench beside her, one arm around her shoulders as he fumbled with the buttons down the front of her blouse, a thick sluggish sliver of saliva seeping out the corner of his mouth.

'Lots of bread, darling,' he was muttering, eyes tightened up in comic exhortation, 'lots an' lots of bread for a good li'le girl like you . . . Jesus,' he belched, 'such tits . . .'

'I have been debating during your prolonged and ungentlemanly absence,' said Sonny, 'whether or not I ought to let Otto loose upon him.'

'He should the Softbaby not molest like that!' murmured Otto in a tone like the ominous roll of distant thunder. 'I could in one swipe—hah!—distemper him.'

'Dismember him, Otto dear.'

Otto nodded his massive head. 'Ja, ja—dismember him—hah!' Here he made a swift cutting movement with the side of his palm against his other hand, 'Like der slice chopped from der loaf.'

'Peace in our time, dear friends,' counselled Luke. 'We have a little scheme under way which I can assure you will considerably dampen our obstreperous friend's ardour in no uncertain fashion.'

'Will it necessitate violence, this scheme of yours?' asked Sonny with keen interest.

'Personally, I think the example of Gandhi will be best suited to our little enterprise.'

'You intrigue me so much, Luke, I think I have forgiven you for your momentary descent from my good books.'

'Never saw such tits,' Mulligan slobbered, fingers ineffectually trying to pry a blouse button loose. 'Never in my life saw such tits.'

Babysoft shoving him off, 'If you don't stop pawing me I swear to Jasus I'll castrate you.'

'Patience, Hortensia, patience,' urged Luke looking around towards the bar. 'Help is near at hand—'

'What are you complaining about anyway?' demanded Ranter unsympathetic. 'Sure it's all in the day's work to you.'

'I told you before, Ranter O'Rourke,' panted Babysoft vehemently, 'nobody likes to be pressurised into work when they're not in the humour. What about you?' she challenged. 'Would you get up in the middle of the night to drive a drunk down to the Markets at five in the morning for a gargle?'

'A fair question, Ranter,' said Luke. 'Can you answer it?'

'It's not the same thing,' Ranter said. 'It's altogether different.'

'Look,' said Luke. 'The lady claims she is off duty, and is therefore under no contractual obligation to work. Now it follows that were you in bed with your estimable spouse in the middle of the night you, too, would be considered to be off duty.'

'You don't know Gertie,' rejoined Ranter woefully.

Mulligan tried to haul himself up straight as once more his fingers essayed an erratic journey to Babysoft's blouse. 'Did you ev—ever see such tits as these, Sheridan?' He hiccupped loudly. 'Betcha never saw such fine tits as these.'

'You effing oul' shit!' hissed Babysoft, tensing her hard capable knee ready for action. 'Is there no gentleman present?'

Ranter jumped to his feet his cap all awry. 'I'm going to do him!' he shouted struggling to get out of his overcoat. 'Me blood can only take so much—I'm going to do that fucking oul' bastard proper! Get out of me way now, till I send him through the wall.'

'Me life on you, Ranter!' cheered Babysoft her eyes alight. 'There's one left in Ireland anyway!'

Luke was on his feet with a restraining hand on Ranter. 'Don't spoil our little plot, exercise forbearance, do.'

'Forbearance me bollocks!' roared Ranter as he strove to rid himself of the cumbersome overcoat, his face flushed to a bright fighting-cock red. 'Me blood is curdling with the antics of that fat fornicating oul' hoormonger! I'm not a violent man, but bejasus I'll be dug out of him!'

'God save Ireland!' yelled Babysoft swept by a wave of irrelevant patriotism. 'Up the rebels!'

'Now lads, now lads,' said Octavius coming up with a tray of drinks and placing it on the table. 'I'm surprised at you,' he reproved, turning to Ranter whom Luke was gallantly holding in check helped considerably by the troublesome overcoat. 'You looked like a man of peace to me, a man of vision I could rely on when things got rough.'

'Me blood got the better of me,' said Ranter allowing himself to be led sheepishly back to his chair. 'Sure it's more than human nature could stand, the way he insulted me lady friend here, even if she's a hoor itself.'

'Me sowl man Ranter,' beamed Babysoft reaching over and squeezing his hand. 'I'll never forget the way you were willing to lay down your life for me,' she vowed, 'without even being asked.'

'You are to be congratulated, Mr O'Rourke, on your chivalrous if impetuous behaviour,' said Sonny. 'It shows an uprightness of spirit sadly lacking in my own generation,' she added with a sidelong accusatory glance at Luke.

'It seems I march unmourned to the gibbet,' sighed Luke. 'Ah well—the way of the arbiter is a thorny way. So it was in the beginning, is now and ever shall be.'

'Let's all sit down and have one for the road,' suggested Octavius, handing out the glasses with meticulous precision and winking at Luke as he nudged Ranter in the ribs. 'Sure as the saying is, a bird never did fly on one wing.'

'You don't mean you're giving that oul' shit another one,' cried Babysoft as a rather large glass was put before Mulligan, 'and him trying to ravish the life out of me for the last hour!'

'Your generosity, Octavius, is excessive,' said Sonny, 'but also excessively immoderate and most unwise as far as Mr Mulligan is concerned.'

Mulligan lifted his drowned satyr's face from off the table. 'Wha's that? I need no phoney German countess to tell me when I've had enough—or should that be cuntess?' He twisted round and squinted at Luke. 'Eh, Sheridan, you sly hoor's melt—should that be cuntess—hah?'

'Drink up, oul' soldier,' said Octavius taking hold of Mulligan's fingers and twining them round the glass. 'Drink up and show us what a generous forgiving heart you have.'

Mulligan leered ghoulishly around him. 'I don't know about my heart, but I'll show you what a generous something else I have—'

'Drink up, for Jasus' sake,' Octavius muttered, guiding the glass upwards to Mulligan's moist mouth. 'Drink up and take your troubles to the Lord.'

'Oh for a draught of Lethe,' murmured Luke.

Mulligan opened his mouth. 'This is ver—very kind of you, Mr Landlord, ver' kind 'deed.'

'Sure me friends assure me I'm the soul of decency,' twinkled Octavius, putting a hand behind Mulligan's head and tipping the contents of the glass down his gaping throat. 'There now, me oul' segotcha—that'll bring you sweet dreams and hump the begrudgers.'

Mulligan fell back all asplutter. 'Wha'—wha's tha' in th' name o'—o God?'

'Swing low, sweet chariot,' hummed Luke.

'What *is* going on?' asked Sonny. 'I must say, Octavius, it all seems rather obscene, you practically pouring the drink down the man's throat like that.'

'The means will admirably suit the ends, I assure you,' Luke said.

'If you think,' gurgled Mulligan falling back on the bench, 'if you think or eve—even imagine . . .'

'Jasus, what's wrong with him?' gasped Babysoft as Mulligan gently slid under the table. 'A randy oul' bastard, I grant you, but all the same I'd wish nobody any real harm.'

'Der man he go to sleep, ja, in the eye of a twinkling, nein?' said Otto putting out a cautious hand and shaking the comatose form.

'He rests in the arms of the Lord,' said Octavius, 'for twenty-four hours at least.'

Babysoft looked down. 'Jasus you don't mean to say he's dead, do you?'

'Dead to the world, ma'am,' said Octavius rubbing his hands heartily together. 'Dead to the world for now.'

'The euphemism for that, I think,' said Sonny, 'is one Mickey Finn.'

Ranter stooped and looked under the table. 'Holy Jasus,' he said as he came up. 'He's out as cold as a dead mackerel. What in the name of Jasus are we going to do with him now?'

'Do with him, you say?' echoed Octavius leaning back in his chair to peer down at the already snoring figure laid out under the table. 'Do with him? Sure isn't he as happy as a pig in shit as he is?'

'Octavius,' said Luke reaching for his hand. 'Octavius, you are assured of a place in heaven.'

'Sure I knew that years ago.'

'We'll be together in Paradise some day, Octavius.'

'I've been in worse places in me time, I'm telling you.'

'But what about your man?' persisted Babysoft, unable to resist looking under the table again. 'Will he be all right?'

'Him, maam?' replied Octavius as he raised his glass to his mouth with an inclining salute of his head to all present. 'Him, is it? Ah, sure, maam, you can let him rest content for the night in the Arms of May!'

IX

'I'll walk beside you thro' the world tonight
beneath the starry skies ablaze with light
and in your heart love's tender word I'll hide
I'll walk beside you thro' the eventide—'

The treacly strains of Mongoose quavered from the cramped
raised dais at the end of the room, sounding once more as though
he had never left off and in the smoky shadowy background
Freddie, hushed and pale over the piano, weaved a tenuous train
of limp accompaniment above the chatter and din rising from the
crowded floor.

'Doesn't that oul' bastard ever give his tonsils a rest, bejasus?'
growled Ranter as they found a free table and sat down.

'Ah sure, he's harmless,' Babysoft put in loyally and then
reflected, 'but I hope he doesn't come looking for anything off
me tonight, still and all. I'm not in the mood for him and me
worried sick about poor Rosie.'

They sat uncertain and restless, looking at each other under
the garish lights as the ravaged painted face of Madame Lala
came wobbling unsteadily into view, her hands fluttering up and
down in nervous greeting, a large ostentatious brooch at her neck
gleaming like the baleful eye of a serpent as she came up.

'Ah, Luke son, I miss you all these weeks, so long away from
us. Where have you been hiding yourself, eh, boy?' she cackled
as she nudged him slyly in the ribs. 'Where have you been
skulking?'

'We've been out in Howth today, Lala,' he told her, 'catching
the sea air.'

'Howth, you say?' repeated Lala as she ran her dark heavily made-up little eyes over the newcomers. 'Howth, you say, eh? Did you catch any nice fish?' she asked and broke into a thin squeak of pleasure at her own humour. 'Ha ha ha—did you catch any fish!'

'You might say I returned with a fair catch, Lala.'

'And you don't have the good manners to introduce me to your friends—Luke, oh Luke, that is bad!'

'Let me rectify that glaring omission at once. May I present the Count and Countess Fustenhalter, all the way from Baden-Baden via Howth? This is our true spiritual Mother, Madame Lala, patroness of the arts and comely custodian of all our mortal desires.'

'You are such a clown, Luke son,' giggled Lala and then turned to the visitors with a regal inclination of her head. 'You are very welcome indeed to my little establishment, Count and Countess.'

Otto sprang to his feet with a precise click of heels, bowing deeply over Lala's hand as he raised it to his lips. 'Our own the pleasure all is, Madame Lolo—'

'It's Lala, Uncle Otto,' corrected Babysoft. 'Madame Lala.'

'What do names matter?' cooed Lala a little breathless at such lavish attention. 'What a beautiful gentleman!'

'He is,' said Ranter with acrimonious grin, 'as long as he doesn't get you in a headlock or a cross-buttock stranglehold.'

'I should be so lucky!' trilled Lala. 'Such a perfect gentleman is hard to meet these days when courtesy is a dead art.'

Sonny smiled and looked around. 'What a charming place! Do you stay open quite late, Madame Lala?'

'Till the cows come home,' this from Babysoft.

'We stay open for special customers only, countess,' explained Lala and then turned on Babysoft a dark malevolent glare. 'And where have _you_ been all day, _Miss_ Brogan? Out catching the sea air too?'

Babysoft lowered her head. 'I meant to get back sooner.'

Lala snorted and folded her massive braceleted arms. 'You mean you meant, but you didn't, did you?'

'I'm sorry, Madame Lala—I never felt the time going—'

'All my other poor girls are working overtime tonight—a half-day in the country, you see, early closing in the shops—everywhere's swarming with farmers up for the day—and you have to go missing, absent without leave!' Lala's several chins wobbled with indignation. 'Out you were catching the sea air, no less, while we fretted and worried that something had happened to you!'

Luke stood up. 'I'm afraid I am entirely to blame for Miss Brogan's little holiday, Lala. It was I who cunningly waylaid and enticed her out to Howth in the first place—completely against her will, let me add.'

'She was kicking and scratching all the way out, bejasus,' Ranter sarcastically related. 'We nearly had to tie her up with the belt off me trousers.'

'Shut bleeding well up, Ranter O'Rourke!' Babysoft lifted her head to Lala, stung into retaliation. 'And anyhow I'm no slave. I've a mind of me own that God gave me.'

'What are you complaining about anyway, Madame Goldilocks?' Ranter challenged Lala. 'Isn't she after bringing you back two new customers, and them descended from the effing Kaiser and all? I think you ought to give her a rise in pay for that, instead of standing there and berating her in front of everyone!'

'I, Otto, am with der dear Softbaby all der day it was long—no harm did she get at.'

'Come to, Otto darling.'

'What so, mein Gretchen?' asked Otto in confusion.

'No harm, did the lady come to, dear. Do watch your syntax.'

'Ja, ja,' said Otto with a vigorous nod at Lala. 'No harm did der lady come to.'

'No thanks to you, mate,' Ranter amended. 'You were chasing her all over the kip all day, bejasus, like a jackrabbit after a doe.'

'I am what-do-you-say a jackrabbit?' wondered Otto becoming still more befuddled. 'How so, der good Ranter, hah?'

'Forget it, Otto, for Jasus' sake.'

'So, dear Lala,' said Luke, 'will you accept my apologies and gather us all back into thy bounteous grace once more?'

Lala suddenly gave a quick gargoyle grin and patted Babysoft fondly on the head. 'Sure I let my tongue run away with me, Luke son. I know your intentions were well meant, though you're a deplorable scoundrel and arch seducer of hapless females. Call the boy and tell him what you want—it's on the house.'

'You are much too good, Lala—I really must protest.'

'You refuse my hospitality?' asked Lala, wounded.

'He accepts,' said Ranter, 'on behalf of all his friends.'

'And tell me, Lala,' said Luke as he sat down again, 'where and how is the fair Miss Hand?'

'Rosie, is it?'

'The same. Where might she be found at this hour?'

'Upstairs,' replied Lala, adding, 'She isn't feeling so well tonight, poor Rosie. An upset stomach. Must be something she ate.'

'That's one way of putting it, I suppose,' said Ranter.

Luke raised his hand and the floorboy came over swaying expertly between tables, tray balanced on fingertips, young pimply face flushed and harried, smelling of tobacco and peppermint.

'A bottle of the choicest Martell, Pinocchio.'

'Certainly, Mr Sheridan,' the boy grinned showing yellow stunted teeth.

'On the house, Reginald,' ordered Lala.

'There's a name to give a creature,' said Ranter as the boy scurried away. 'Reginald, bejasus! His Oul' Fella must have come over with the Normans.'

'Did she have her baby yet, Madame Lala?' Babysoft asked, abruptly sitting up straighter in her chair.

'Did who have her baby, girl?' Lala queried puzzled. 'Who or what are you talking about, child?'

'Rosie, of course.'

'Our Rosie? What would she be doing with a baby?'

'What would any girl be doing with a baby, and it put there by mistake?' wailed Babysoft, ensconced once more under the maternal wing and yielding easily to tears. 'I was forever telling her she should take precautions, but she was too effing religious, and now look where it's landed her!'

'Keep a civil tongue in your head, child, when there's company present—what sort of a house do you think I run?'

'A very profitable one, I'd say,' Ranter speculated as he scanned the surrounding tables. 'The carnal appetites of this city is ferocious, no blotting it out!'

Sonny looked ceilingwards. 'I just adore those gorgeous old oak beams don't you, Otto dear?'

'Ja, ja,' said Otto sitting happily erect, hands on knees, looking about him with twinkling eyes. 'All der place is very well looking.'

The acne-faced boy returned and set the bottle on the table.

'Let us all now have a little sustenance,' said Luke pouring, 'back in the fold of creature comfort with our good Mother Lala to fuss and watch over us in her own inimicable way. Cheers, everyone!'

'Cheers!'

'All hail!'

'Achtung!'

'Welcome home, Luke my son,' said Lala as she raised her glass and then turned worried eyes on Babysoft still sullen and downcast in her chair. 'I only wish I knew what our daughter here is talking about a baby.'

'Don't be minding her,' said Ranter settling back at ease, full glass in hand. 'It's the sea air has her brain all arsed up. The only baby that Rosie wan is going to have is a baby Power.'

'You don't care, do you?' accused Babysoft picking up her glass and drinking vengefully. 'None of yous bleeding well care whether poor Rosie lives or dies! She could be wriggling and turning about now in the height of labour, moaning and going green in the gills with the birth pains, and all you can do is sit on your arses pouring drink down your gullets!'

'Said she as she reached for another,' remarked Ranter.

Otto squared his shoulders manfully and cleared his throat.

> 'In der fair Dublin city
> where die Fräuleins they are pretty
> mine eyes they do set on die Molly Malone—'

'Not now, Otto dear,' said Sonny, patting his hand.

'I've checked you already about that tongue of yours, Babysoft,' Lala rebuked. 'Such a tongue is not becoming in a young lady, especially with gentlemen present.'

'I'm worried about Rosie, that's all,' sniffed Babysoft, wiping her eyes with her fingers. 'Sure she'd be the same about me if I was in the same condition.'

'You keep talking about babies and birth pains and positions!' Lala snapped with flashing eyes. 'Is it soft in the head you are?'

'Ask *him*,' retorted Babysoft pointing an accusing finger at Luke. 'Sitting there like Little Boy Blue as if all he ever did in his life was box the fox!'

'Luke?' asked Lala in surprise. 'What has Luke got to do with any birth pains, in the holy name of God?'

'He knows he didn't get it for stirring his tea!' said Babysoft with absurd vehemence. 'Putting a girl in that condition and she only doing what she was paid for.'

Luke reached for the bottle. 'My dear Lala, to unravel the intricate workings of Miss Brogan's mind would demand more intellectual stamina than even I have at my beck and call. She has been making these veiled innuendoes all day.'

'Speak bleeding English, can't you!' This from Babysoft.

'Apparently,' continued Luke filling his glass, 'it would seem my manhood has been put fully to the test, the acid test you might say, and has not been found wanting.'

Lala blinked. 'You both talk in riddles, all riddles. I don't understand a word.'

'It happened that night—' Babysoft began.

'And it *wasn't* in Monterey,' put in Ranter.

'Will you ever bleeding well shut up, Ranter O'Rourke!'

'Your tongue, Babysoft, your tongue!'

'I'm sorry, Madame Lala, but that man would provoke a Trappist monk into swearing, making smart remarks like that when a person is doing his best to explain.'

'Explain what, child?'

'About that night.'

'What about that night?' Lala enquired, her jowls beginning to quiver again. 'I was in attendance myself personally all the last time Luke was here,' said Lala, 'and I saw nothing untoward happen.'

'You wouldn't, would you,' Babysoft declared, 'seeing that what happened took place upstairs. In Rosie's room,' she added darkly as if imparting some unnamable secret on a wild wave of daring.

'Now tell the nice ladies and gentlemen,' said Ranter bringing his chair forward more, 'what Mr Sheridan was doing in Rosie's room at such an ungodly hour. Maybe they were saying the rosary together,' he persisted with a serious shake of his head. 'Did that never occur to you?'

Lala appealed to Luke with outspread hands. 'Luke my son, tell a poor old woman what they are talking about or I go truly mad!'

'I must go down to the sea again,' murmured Luke abstractedly, 'and with as much dispatch as possible.'

'More riddles, Luke!' wailed Lala, the bracelets on her arms jingling as she shook them in agitation. 'Just tell me, were you with Rosie in her quarters that night, and if so, for how long?'

'Lala, dear lady, you *know* I was with Rosie that night.'

'Till when, Luke son?'

'Till the bells of Christ Church were tolling out the first dawn-light,' answered Luke. 'And if you ask me what exactly we were doing, I shall finally abandon all faith in mankind and enter a nunnery.'

'Oh, Luke, Luke,' chided Lala gently tapping him lightly on the arm. 'I am the mistress of my own house, am I not? I provide a service, do I not?'

'You do, dear Lala, indeed you do,' said Luke, and continued: 'In the nuttiest of nutshells, dear Lala, rumour has it that I am well on the way to paternity via our friend Rosie. That, if one were so abysmally gullible to believe it, is the source and cause of her mild indisposition tonight, the secret of her little stomach upset.'

Lala stared. 'I still don't understand.'

'What our friend Hortensia here is trying to convey,' said Luke, is that Miss Hand is with child—'

'What you might call in the rude vernacular,' said Ranter, 'up the pole.'

'Not to put too fine or fussy an edge on it—yes,' continued Luke. 'And I am alleged to be responsible for her exalted position.'

'Not to say son and holy ghost all combined,' said Ranter. 'Sure I always told him he'd end up in Quare Street if he didn't end his wild and woolly ways with the lilies.'

'The lilies, Mr O'Rourke?' gently quizzed Sonny.

'Mots, maam. Women. Ladies. Like yourself, maam.'

Lala was still looking at Luke fixedly. 'Are you implying,' she said slowly and paused to take a long sip of her drink before framing the query once more, 'are you implying, Luke son, that you have got one of my daughters into trouble? Baby trouble?'

'That,' nodded Luke with a melancholy sigh, 'would seem to be the general consensus of opinion.

'Invoke the Fifth Amendment you thick,' Ranter cautioned. 'You know, in case anything might incinerate you.'

Lala's mountainous bosom heaved. 'And it is Rosie?'

'So it would seem.'

'Rosie,' echoed Lala mournfully. 'One of the best daughters a woman could hope for. I can't believe it.'

'She was like a sister to me,' affirmed Babysoft, tearful again. 'More than a sister, for we were always together. We shared everything together through thick and thin, good times and bad, laughing and crying—'

The strident valiant strains of Mongoose seemed just then to reach a higher pitch of maudlin prophecy:

> 'And if ever I'm left in this world all alone
> I shall wait for my call patiently
> but if Heaven be kind I shall wait there to find
> those two eyes of blue still Smilin' Thru'
> at ah-ah-aat me!'

'Oh Jasus, poor Rosie,' wailed Babysoft as the tears spilled down her cheeks. 'Smilin' Thru'—that's her, always Smilin' Thru!'

'Best of all my daughters!' cried Lala, small pudgy eyes sunken with maternal grieving. 'Always ready she was with a tear or a smile to comfort or console! My poor lost little lamb—'

Sonny flashed a malicious smile across the table. 'How does it feel to be on the brink of proud fatherhood, Luke?'

'Indescribably alien,' he replied getting to his feet. 'Alien to the best and finest instincts of my nature.'

'Where are you scarpering to now, me noble stud?' asked Ranter.

'I think it's time I went on a little reconnaissance tour,' said Luke straightening his shoulders. 'Just to see how the love of my life is bearing up to the sudden shock of notoriety.'

Lala looked up as he passed and touched his hand. 'You are leaving us, Luke son?'

Babysoft flung up her head. 'Snaking out the back door, that's what he's doing—running away from his responsibilities, like all bleeding men!'

'I am on my way to see Rosie and confront the grotesque truth for myself.'

'You know the room, Luke son?'

'Certainly,' he answered.

With a dull pounding of blood in his temples blurring all other sound he mounted the dim contorted stairway, unsteadily grasping the ornate banisters, ascending into the hushed, darkened upper reaches of the house, once more going down twisting corridors in gloom past doors half unseen behind slumbrous brocaded curtains, his fingers taut touching embossed walls, a low throb of memory stirring in him leading him unerringly, coming at length to the door he sought. He brushed aside the heavy veil and turned the handle.

'Rosie . . . are you awake, Rosie?'

Something stirred beneath the quilt and presently a hand crept over the edge pushing back the covers.

'Who is it?'

'It's me, Rosie. Me.'

She struggled up and sat back against the pillows, eyes dark and heavy with broken slumber. 'What do *you* want?'

Her voice had a drugged petulant sound. 'Aren't you pleased to see me?' he asked sitting down on the side of the bed. 'Home is the sailor, home from the sea.'

'What have you come back for?'

Her hair heavy and lustrous coiled upon her shoulders and the sharp oddly cruel streak of scalp down the middle of her head gave her a sullen defenceless naked look. 'Ah, Rosie,' he said reaching over and taking hold of her hand, 'have you no small word of greeting for your weary traveller?'

'Get stuffed, I'm tired.'

She looked at him all unsure as she snatched back her hand and snuggled back down, pulling the eiderdown up to her chin.

'That, in a way, is what brings me back.'

'What does?'

'Are you very tired?'

'Tired enough.'

'But not unwell.'

'Who says I'm unwell? Well I'm not. And anyway, what is it to you if I am or not?'

'That is precisely what I want to find out—the state of your health and its exact relationship to me.'

'I don't know what you're talking about, for Christ's sake.'

'Give me your hand, dearest.'

'Piss off. You have this thing about hands, haven't you?'

'Have I, dearest?'

'This kinky thing about hands. I never saw a bloke for holding hands like you.'

'But, dearest—'

'And stop calling me dearest, for God's sake! You look stupid when you say it, it makes you sound like Omar Sharif with chronic constipation.'

'But I came back to you, Rosie.'

'I never asked you to.'

'I thought you'd be glad to see me.'

'Well,' she said drawing deeper under the bedclothes, 'I'm neither glad nor sorry. I just want to have a good kip, that's all, and I can't do that, can I, if you're going to sit there spouting bullshit all night?'

'What do you want me to do, Rosie?'

'Get me a drink, that's what you can do. Under the bed.'

Luke got down on hands and knees and felt along the carpet, finding a bottle and heaving himself back again.

'Where's the glasses, my dear?'

'Jasus, I told you to cut out that crap!'

'Sorry. It's just my deplorable middle-class pretensions.'

'There's tumblers on the cabinet there.'

He found two tumblers and poured.

'What do you want with yours, Rosie?'

'Bleeding more.'

'Ask a stupid question.' He handed hers over. 'Here's to the present moment. The future doesn't bear thinking about.'

She took some and spluttered a little and resolutely took some more. 'I hear that Babysoft wan was missing all day. I suppose she was off flying her kite with yourself.'

'I did have the pleasure of her company, yes, though any kite-flying was strictly limited.'

'Where did you get yourself off to anyway? Paris, Rome or New York?'

'It was Howth, as a matter of fact. I went out there in the line of duty. On a case, you might say—'

'A case of Hennessy or Power's.'

'Rosie, you are unkind. I went there to check out the story of some poor lady who tried to murder her husband.'

'More effing power to her!' she said sitting up straighter upon the pillows. 'I hope she succeeded.'

'She didn't. The gentleman in question is downstairs at this moment quaffing brandy and crucifying everyone with his mangled version of "Molly Malone". The dog it was who died.'

'What dog?'

'Never mind, Rosie. There's something I must know.'

'What's that?'

'Are you perchance pregnant?'

'I've never been pregnant in me life.'

'Can I have that in writing?'

'WHAT?'

'A jest, Rosie, a jest. I feel quite lighthearted.'

'It's all that gargling you've been doing all day.'

'I think it's more a feeling of merciful release. You're quite sure, Rosie?'

'Sure that I'm not in the club?' she said with a certain patently unconvincing swagger as she drank. 'Do you take me for a eejit or what? Do you think I'd let meself be caught like that and me one of the best pros in the business? Give me a drink.'

Luke refilled his glass. 'I'm sorry in a way—a convoluted paradoxical self-sacrificial way, true, but sorry just the same.'

'Sorry for what?'

'I don't quite know, Rosie. I suppose sorry that all that you had was a sort of phantom pregnancy.'

'Jasus, I thought only cats and dogs had things like that!'

'Women too, it seems.'

'What would it matter to you anyway, whether I was that way or not?'

'I think you'd agree it would matter quite a bit, if it transpired that I was the father.'

'You the father? You fancy yourself, don't you? Do you think you're the first bloke I've gone to bed with?'

'Assuredly not, but from what I could gather that night you're still not the hardened veteran and campaigner that you like to make yourself out to be.'

'Look,' she said a little wearily, 'mine is a job, just like yours. You know how to do your job and I know how to go about mine. That's all there is to it.'

'But I believe you are rather lax about taking what are discreetly called precautions—'

'Precautions! I suppose you heard that from that bleeding Babysoft.'

'She merely happened to mention it in passing.'

'You'd want to take whatever she says not just with a pinch but with a whole effing pillar of salt! Going around saying things about me behind me back, and me not there to defend meself.'

'You do her a grave injustice, Rosie,' he said. 'She is a true friend, kind and openhearted and generous with her sympathies—'

'Is that all she's generous with, I wonder? I suppose now you'll be telling me it was only Ireland's Eye you were admiring all day.'

'You wouldn't be jealous, Rosie, would you?'

'Me, jealous of her? You must be joking! The day I'm jealous of her it'll be time to purchase a plot in Glasnevin.'

'Then why this display of indignation that is not in the least righteous?'

'Look, would you just piss off and let me go back to sleep. I didn't ask you to barge in here and put years on me with all them big words out of you.'

'Fair enough,' he said rising and setting his glass on the cabinet. 'I shall leave you to your beauty sleep and not darken the door of this hotbed of lust ever in my young life again.'

'If I see you in twelve months' time it'll be too soon!'

He turned at the door raising an apostolic hand. 'Angels guard thee, sweet love, till morn.'

He was already stepping out into the dark corridor when she called after him in a muffled voice—

'Wait.'

He turned slowly back into the room hand on doorknob. 'You called, madam?'

'I didn't mean that about Babysoft.'

'But you meant what you said about me, eh?'

'I don't know what I meant. You have me all mixed up.'

'Let me try to unmix you, then.'

'You're mad—stone mad. Do you know that?'

'It has been more or less hinted once or twice, though I could not bring myself to believe I could attain to such a joyous condition.'

He came and sat on the bedside again.

'Have you missed me even once?' she asked, her fingers toying idly with the fringes of the eiderdown.

'Yea, though the night was loud with song I was sick and weary of an old passion,' he declaimed hand on heart, picking up her hand and kissing it finger by finger.

'Don't be telling me lies, you!' she warned angrily as she pulled her hand back.

'I thought you wanted me to lie to you.'

She was silent a moment and then sighed. 'Yeah—I suppose I did, but you're a bastard to remind me of it. You're certainly no gentleman.'

'My pretentions don't reach that far. You'll have to take me as I am, Rosie.'

'I don't want to take you at all! I don't want to have any truck with you whatsoever.'

'Look straight in my eyes when you say that, Rosie.'

'You're very bleeding sure of yourself, aren't you? Coming in unasked and disturbing me sleep and expecting me to dance attendance on you at a snap of your little finger.'

'I haven't snapped my fingers once since I came in here, Rosie. Do be fair, my precious.'

'Jasus, would you ever stop rabbiting out of you!' she said exasperated. 'You're giving me a headache.'

'Rosie,' he yawned, 'I am overcome with an overwhelming desire to sleep until Judgement Day.'

She paused a moment. 'Lay your head down so.'

'You are kind beyond the telling of it, Rosie.'

'Shut up and lie down.'

'The animal comfort of two bodies touching in peace, Rosie, is the greatest incentive I know for remaining alive.'

She moved over to make room for him and they lay quietly side by side, fingers lightly intertwined, the rise of voices from downstairs and the remoter swell of night sounds from the city comfortably dim and muffled, her hair just touching his cheek the warm nearness of her a pleasant undemanding pleasure lazily lapping his mind. 'I won't marry you,' she said into the gently throbbing silence.

'Of course you won't, Rosie,' he murmured contentedly.

'Wouldn't marry you, not if you were the last man on earth.'

'Very sensible, Rosie. Very wise.'

'I mean,' she went on, 'you don't exactly work for a living, do you?' She leaned up on an elbow and looked down at him. 'Well —do you?'

'Do I what, Rosie?'

'Work for a living?'

'I write, or should I say I try to write.'

'That's what I mean,' she retorted justified. 'You don't exactly work.'

'If you say so, Rosie,' he mumbled, turning onto his side away from her. 'If you say so.'

'I mean,' she continued developing the theme as she toyed with the silky edges of the quilt, 'how would we live?'

'In the depths of direst penury, my dear.'

'I told you to cut out that crap.'

'Sorry.'

'And anyway,' she elaborated, leaning back and placing her arms behind her head, 'you wouldn't want to marry the likes of me, would you? Well—would you?' she repeated annoyed and sticking her big toe into his flanks.

'Would I what, Rosie?'

'Want to marry the likes of me?'

'Rosie, there's not the likes of you anywhere in the whole besodden township of Dublin.'

'But you still wouldn't want to marry me, would you?'

'Don't think so, Rosie.'

'There—you see!' she cried sullenly her chin sinking deeper into the fluffy neck of her nightrobe. 'You think I'm beneath you, don't you?'

'The blood races madly at the mere thought, Rosie.'

'What thought?'

'The thought of you beneath me.'

'You make a laugh out of everything I say!'

'Rosie, I consider you the quintessence of native charm.'

'But you wouldn't marry me?'

'Don't think so, Rosie.'

'Maybe you're right,' she said after thinking for some moments. 'Maybe it would spoil everything.'

'Your perspectives are right up my alley, Rosie.'

'I mean, look at your woman Tessa—'

'Tessa? Who's Tessa? Oh—*Tessa* . . .' he swallowed sleepily.

'Yeah—the wan you were supposed to be heartbroken over, remember. The girl that walked out on you, or so you told me. I don't believe she ever bleeding well existed. I think you made her up.' She nudged him in the ribs. 'Do you hear me? I think Tessa was all in your mind!'

'Maybe you're right at that, Rosie. I certainly wouldn't dream of contradicting you at this hour of the night.'

'But you seemed so heartbroken that evening.'

'I *was* heartbroken, Rosie. I make it a rule to be utterly heartbroken at least once a week. It staves off excess emotional fat.'

There was another pause. 'You and Babysoft,' she murmured, 'you didn't have it off with her today, did you?'

'Satan tempted and consistently refused to get behind me,' he told her, 'but I've come through this long day with my manly honour intact and inviolate, and all parts and appurtenances more or less in their rightful preordained places.'

'What does that mean?'

'It means I have been faithful to thee, Cynara, in my fashion.'

'Not that I give a fiddler's curse, mind you.'

'Of course not, Rosie.'

'I was just—well, just curious, that's all.'

He gave a prolonged yawn and curled up shell-wise. 'I am boneweary unto death, Rosie.'

'Are you staying the night, then?'

'With your permission.'

'Do you always go to sleep in your trousers?'

'It has been known, but if it offends you—'

'Couldn't care less one way or another,' she said quickly and then added, 'but the bleeding buttons are sticking into me!'

'My apologies.'

With tired half-instinctive movements he wriggled wearily out of his jeans and footed them out under the quilt onto the floor.

'I don't remember whether you snore or not,' she said.

'And I have no points of reference.'

She reached over and switched off the bedside lamp. 'It feels funny,' she whispered snuggling close and sliding an arm around him as she nuzzled her cheek in the bony hollow of his shoulders, 'sleeping with a bloke the whole night through . . .'

He did not answer, already curled into an abbreviated question-

mark and after a few minutes she sighed, 'Jasus, you snore enough
to wake the dead!'

'Will you look at the goings-on of your man!' giggled Babysoft
nudging Ranter's foot under the table. 'If ever I saw a fella going
mad for his oats!'

Otto in a corner alcove was tugging at Sonny's arm.

'Do behave, Otto dear.'

'Nein, nein, mein Gretchen,' he slobbered making erratic
essays with his mouth at her neck and earlobe. 'Much the want I
have for you, und in der room in Baden-Baden you lie waiting
on der balcony in your fine kemist—'

'Chemise, dear, chemise.'

'Oh ja, und die burning spears from der moon slice into your
hair—'

'Shine through it, Otto.'

'Ja, und dann I come under you, Gretchen—'

'Behind me, Otto.'

'Und jump up into your arms—'

'Step up, Otto dear.'

'Und bump-bump-bump I feel der heart go in me und the skin
on you was soft as lambbelly in der Spring und your paps felt
nutmeg all over der place—'

'Otto, your syntax is going wild.'

Ranter eyed them across smoking wastes of cluttered tables.
'Your woman is dropping her mask now, bejasus,' he said, 'and
she'll drop a hell of a lot more before the night is out.'

'Sure ladies are born anyway,' said Babysoft, 'not made. I saw
through that wan from the start. A respectable class of hoor, if you
ask me, all airs and graces to start off with, but as soon as the oul'
gargle's down her she's not superstitious who touches her garter.'

Madame Lala waddled up, arms folded over her bosom, a
smug complacent satisfied smile on her rouged mascaraed face.
'Such a nice couple, the foreign lady and gentleman,' she said
with slurry sugared tongue nodding over at the discreetly wrestling
pair in the alcove. 'So refined. So mad as they for each other.'
Lala sighed with nostalgia. 'Ah, so nice a thing to see in this day
and age. I recall the time when my poor Freddie . . .'

One black-dyed tear formed, glistened and trickled down Lala's
pitted cheek, leaving a thin smudged trail in its wake.

'They're not a couple, you know,' informed Babysoft piqued at such misplaced sentiment. 'Not a married couple anyway.'

Lala looked disapproving. 'What do you say, child?'

Babysoft shrugged. 'There's a bit of a mystery about them. Isn't that so, Ranter?'

Ranter coughed. 'Ah now, sure isn't there a bit of a mystery about all of us?'

'Ah yeah, I know,' said Babysoft doggedly, 'but there's a limit to mysteries, isn't there. I mean, when a man goes and poisons his wife—'

'It was the other way round,' said Ranter patiently.

'And then he goes chasing after another woman like a dog that's been held in quarantine for six months getting the scent of a bitch.'

Lala's pencil-thin brows drew together. 'Babysoft, you are not being very nice tonight. What is this about some man poisoning his poor wife? And chasing dogs. Why do you talk this way, hah?'

'Put it all down to the sea air,' advised Ranter. 'Sure most city people go bleeding mad when they get a whiff of the sea.'

'Don't be minding me, Madame Lala,' faltered Babysoft. 'It's true what Ranter says—sure I could never pass Dollymount in a bus without me stomach turning, and when me stomach turns I get all sorts of quare ideas in me head.'

Lala's chins quivered as she shook her head. 'No more you go near the seaside, girl—no more, you hear? You come back with your head full of birth pains and babies and strange men poisoning their wives—no more the seaside for you, hear?'

'I'm finished with Howth forever, Madame Lala,' murmured Babysoft contritely. 'Sure I'm lost the minute I step outside Dublin.'

Lala clucked satisfied and returned her fond gaze to the couple in the corner. 'Such a nice lady and gentleman.'

Folded arms jingling pleasantly with bracelets she smiled and nodded her way among tables to the dim alcove and stood blinking and nodding at the disparate twosome, her entire body exuding gross congenial pleasure.

'The gentleman is enjoying himself, yes?'

'The gentleman is enjoying himself hugely, thank you,' answered Sonny as she caught Otto's hand and held it in check.

'It really is a delightful place you have here, Madame Lala. So old-worldish.'

Lala glowed. 'It is just a humble meeting-place where friends congregate,' she demurred. 'Once it was famous throughout Europe, many's the royal head reclined upon our pillows, but now it is old and creaking in its bones, like myself.'

Otto stumbled to a half standing position, making a gallant effort to salute and click his heels. 'Once in Baden-Baden there was a place like here, und mein Onkel Fritz took me when a boy was I, to die Fräuleins like here, und below beneath der beds we play der games—'

'Do be seated, Otto dear,' said Sonny pulling at his coattails. 'He is such an excitable type.'

With staunch jocular resolve Otto teetered forward and tickled Lala's massive jowls as though she were some kind of grossly overgrown kitten, winking at her.

'Ah, meine pretty Madame Loojo!'

'Oh sir, oh *sir*!' squealed Lala screwing up her eyes in delight. 'Such a cheerful gentleman!'

'Otto dear,' reprimanded Sonny, with a more determined tug pulling him back down beside her. 'Really, my dear, you must restrain your natural high spirits—' Sonny turned to Lala smiling sweetly—'Rather unusual in one of Germanic extraction, don't you think?'

'Believe it or not, countess,' said Lala in a hushed voice leaning over the table, 'but I always thought the Kaiser was a great man.'

'The—er—the Kaiser?' said Sonny politely. 'How interesting.'

'Another thing I tell you, countess,' said Lala casting precautionary glances around her. 'My Freddie, you know, that is him onstage now,' Lala made a quick furtive movement with her head, 'our resident pianist my dear Freddie—well, he has German blood in his veins.'

'Indeed?'

'Nobody knows,' said Lala nodding vigorously, 'but it is true! On his Papa's side, you understand. His real name—' here Lala paused and looked about her again—'his *real* name is Friedrich Mannhauser—but not a word to a soul, I beg you, countess, not a word to a soul!'

'I do assure you, Madame Lala.'

Lala gripped Sonny's free hand between her own and held on

to it so tightly that the younger woman winced. 'Your word, countess, your word!'

'My dear Madame Lala, you have it a thousand times over!'

Lala smile happily and released the imprisoned hand. 'I know I can trust you, countess.'

'Thank you so much, Madame Lala.'

'Not that I am ashamed of my Freddie's blood, you understand.'

'Certainly not, Madame Lala.'

'It is just tnat he is rath⎯ ⎯ensitive on the subject. He feels,' went on Lala with a sigh, 'he feels he has let you all down.'

Sonny coughed slightly. 'Let us all down?'

Lala mournfully nodded. 'His race. His ancestry. His heritage. He feels he has squandered his native genius away. And do you blame him,' said Lala turning to look towards the makeshift stage, tears suddenly welling in her eyes, 'sitting up there night after night playing the Tennessee Waltz to people who do not listen?'

'I am sure,' consoled Sonny, 'your Freddie is not alone in feeling he has failed to realise his full potential. I am equally sure he plays the Tennessee Waltz superbly well.'

'A sad day it was for poor Freddie when he married me,' said Lala for once moody and brooding. 'I stunted his growth.'

'Oh, I am sure that is not so.'

'I stunted his growth,' insisted Lala stubbornly fat fingers joined. 'As a pianist. As an artiste. As a second Paderewski, perhaps—who knows?'

Without warning or preamble Otto lifted his head.

'Meine Lili of der lamplight
Mein' own Lili Marlene—'

'Quiet, Otto dear.'

He lurched towards her. 'Very much the want I have for you, mein Gretchen,' then slipped and sank below the table, his head ending up in Sonny's lap.

'He trained as a concert pianist, my Freddie. Herr Goggleheim, his tutor—German, you understand—he said my Freddie had beautiful hands.'

'And I am sure Herr Goggleheim was right, Madame Lala.'

Lala stared into the smoke and blurred middle distance. ' "And each one kills the thing he loves . . ." Which German writer was it who said that, countess?'

'If I remember correctly, dear lady, it was your compatriot Mr Wilde.'

Lala heaved with disappointment. 'I could have sworn it was a German writer. But it is true, is it not, countess?'

'It is very true, Madame Lala.'

'I killed my poor dear Freddie,' said Lala absently fingering one of her bracelets. 'I started to kill him the day I married him, and killed him completely when his hands got crushed.'

Sonny picked up the bottle on the table and poured for two. 'Is it a very sad story, Madame Lala?'

Over at the other table Babysoft again nudged Ranter's leg. 'Your woman is trying to catch your eye.'

Ranter pulled the cap down further and settled back in the chair. 'So I see.'

'I wonder what she wants?'

'A man can't be too careful in a dump like this. I'm afraid if I go near her she'll ravish me or something.'

'Maybe she only wants a bit of fatherly advice, Ranter.'

'She wants a bit of something, all right. Sure they all fall for the peak of me cap.'

'It's dead kinky, right enough,' said Babysoft reaching across and tweaking it. 'Was that what drew Gertie to you?'

'That, and the power of me intellect.'

'That's what I like about you, Ranter—you're so effing modest. I suppose the next thing we know you'll be writing a book or play or something—'

'You won't catch me at that game, bejasus. There's enough bleeding chancers at it as it is, and anyway I wouldn't like to be doing our friend Sheridan upstairs out of a job.'

'Is he really writing a book, Ranter, or is he just dreaming out loud?'

Ranter made a derisive noise. 'He's writing a book ever since I knew him, and that's not today or yesterday. He couldn't write in a fit, if you ask me.'

Babysoft looked pensive. 'On the other hand, Ranter, maybe that's the only way he could write.'

'Bejasus, you have something there, right enough. Ah sure, Dublin is crawling with fellas writing books,' affirmed Ranter rubbing his chin. 'Walk into any pub in this town and the words would blind and bother you, except that they never get put on paper. A shower of bleeding latchycoats, the same writing fellas. Hoors for porter they are.'

'Well, in that case,' said Babysoft gazing ceilingwards, 'Luke came to the right place.'

'Aye,' agreed Ranter following her gaze meditatively, 'it's not thinking about writing effing books he is now, and him in the middle of the Elysian fields.'

Lala meanwhile had caught the rather anxious looks that Sonny was sending past her. 'May I make so bold, countess, ' she said with elaborate formality, 'as to ask what it is you might be wanting?'

'I was trying to attract the attention of our friend Mr O'Rourke at that table over there.'

Lala frowned. 'A nice man when you catch him in the right mood, but he has such a tongue in his head.'

'One easily accepts such minor idiosyncrasies in those who are basically goodnatured and kind.' Sonny waved. 'I do wish he'd look this way.'

'You are not thinking of leaving us, countess?'

'I was about to see if I could prevail upon Mr O'Rourke to drive us home,' answered Sonny. 'I am reluctant to leave, but as you see, my poor dear Otto is sleeping like a babe just now, and we do have quite a way to go.'

Lala put down her glass and rose with as much majesty as she could command. 'My dear countess, I will not hear of it! I would not be found guilty of such a glaring act of inhospitality as to expect you and the count to travel so late at night.'

'It is most kind of you, Madame Lala—'

'I had taken it for granted that it was understood yourself and the good count were to be my houseguests tonight.'

'Again, Madame Lala, it is most terribly kind of you.'

'Kind—kind?' echoed Lala, drawing herself up to her full foreshortened height, revelling in the role of hostess. 'It is not in the least kind! It is an honour, a privilege to have such a distinguished and loving couple under my roof.'

'We could not possibly accept—'

'You would thus inflict such a wound on me, countess?' queried Lala her voice tremulous. 'Such a deep hurt?'

'Such, I assure you, would be furthest from my mind.'

'I should take it as a personal affront if you decline my hospitality, and as a great personal pleasure if you do stay.'

Sonny spread her hands in a helpless gesture. 'Put like that, Madame Lala, it would be monstrously churlish of me to refuse.'

The older woman's wrinkled map of a face shone. 'Splendid! I have just the room for you, in my own private wing of the house.' Lala paused unsure her fingers moving uneasily. 'If you would not object to one small thing, countess, which I feel I should mention.'

'And what is that, Madame Lala?'

'We—Freddie and I, you understand—call it the bridal suite, the very room in which we spent our first night on this earth as husband and wife. You would not object, countess?'

'Object? My dear Madame Lala, I in my turn feel honoured by such a charming thought.'

Lala paused still further. 'I might mention also there is a baby grand in the room too.'

'A baby grand? Delightful! Otto sometimes has this sudden nocturnal urge to mutilate the Moonlight Sonata.'

Lala clapped her hands joyously together, strangely radiant under the naked lights. 'Oh, such a night this is,' she exclaimed. 'Such a happy night!'

Hours later Ranter woke up abruptly, his cap almost toppling and looked blearyeyed round. 'What did you say?'

'I never opened me mouth, Ranter, except to drink.'

He looked over at Babysoft splayed on the broad lap of a semicomatose Mongoose.

'Where was I?'

'You just dozed off.'

'Was I away for long?'

'An hour or two, that's all.'

'What time is it at all, in the name of God?'

'Jasus only knows. All hours. Everyone's gone home or adjourned upstairs to their boodwar.'

' I never felt meself dropping off, true as Christ.'

'They say that's a bad sign, Ranter, when you drop off in the middle of a gargle without any warning. I hope Gertie has you well covered itself.'

Mongoose opened his eyes and halfheartedly his hand started to roam over Babysoft's revealed haunches.

'You effing oul' eejit!' she said, giving the offending hand a tired slap. 'It's not in the humour for you I am at this hour of the morning.'

'Lovely girl you are,' Mongoose mumbled. 'Lovely fine young girl you are, fresh as flowers newly plucked.'

'You talk beautiful in your sleep, Mongoose.'

Ranter looked round at the empty tables. 'Where's the German Clockwinder and his mot?'

'Madame offered them a room for the night. On the house.'

'Did they take it?'

'They had no choice, for your man Otto was bleeding footless, not knowing whether he was in Dublin or Düsseldorf.'

Mongoose sleepily stole his hand up her thigh. 'Lovely young girl . . .'

'Would you ever say your prayers, Mongoose, and stop trying to rouse me to a boiling pitch of passion!' She yawned. 'You've as much life in you as a well-sucked lollipop.'

Ranter rubbed his mouth. 'And your man Luke, the wandering minstrel—has he not come down from on high yet?'

'Not a sign or trace of him.'

Ranter pushed back his cap and looked wonderingly up at the rafters. 'Bejasus, he must be hard at it, hammering another job on your woman the blushing Rose of Ringsend. Is there any danger of a gargle round here, do you think?'

'Wouldn't a bowl of oxtail soup be more in order, Ranter?'

'I'll get all the oxtail I want when I get home, not to mention lamb's tail and cow's tail as well as the bleeding cat-o'-nine-tails,' countered Ranter. 'I always wake up with a terrible drought on me after a bo-peep.'

'You're bound to find a bottle somewhere. Madame is the essence of trustfulness.'

Ranter yawned. 'I could get to like this place.'

'Yeah—it grows on you, like a wart.'

'I think you're a great girl, Dolores,' mouthed Mongoose, hand veering erratically towards her left breast. 'You put me in mind of me poor dead daughter that's lying beyant now in Bodenstown.'

'Bejasus then, you must've had quare times and high jinks with your poor dead daughter,' retorted Babysoft slapping his hand down in wavering midflight. 'And I'm not Dolores—she left hours ago with that pork butcher from Clanbraisal Street.'

'Sure I knew who you were all the time, Veronica—'

'Veronica? Who the bleeding hell is Veronica? There's nobody working here called Veronica, thank Jasus.'

Mongoose spread his almost deserted gums in an imbecilic grin. 'I'm just teasing you, love—sure aren't you my favourite here?' Mongoose looked suddenly morose. 'But all the same, I wish you were called Maud.'

'Is that your poor dead daughter lying out in Bodenstown?'

Mongoose shook his head. 'No, it was her mother. There was this song I always used to sing to her before me voice went—' Mongoose lifted his head and with fluttering eyelids began to serenade the bleak echoing walls and rafters:

'Come into the garden, Maud,
For the black bat night has flown;
Come into the garden, Maud,
I am here at the gate alone;
I am here at the gate alone;
I am here—' Mongoose rose a few inches in his chair—
'I am here
at the gate—'

He suddenly choked and spluttered with rolling startled eyes as Babysoft elbowed him sharply in the abdomen, causing a spray of saliva to shoot out of his mouth.

'Would you ever be quiet for the love of Jasus, before you have the law in on top of us!' she hissed as she wiped her face. 'You have me effing drownded!'

'You—you took the wind out of me,' wheezed Mongoose sprawling back in the seat. 'You have a wallop like Jack Dempsey in his heyday.'

'Ah, no wonder!' snapped Babysoft getting to her feet. 'You'd put effing years on anybody, warbling out of you like a canary with diarrhoea and at all hours in the morning!'

Ranter came ambling back with a bottle under his arm, gait unsteady as if he were gingerly walking a gangplank. 'I would say the cultural relations and diplomatic exchanges will be fierce tonight, with the two blond Germans under the roof,' he said as he sat down and poured.

'That's a quare set-up all the same, isn't it?' mused Babysoft holding out her glass. 'You wouldn't know what to make of it. I mean, are they related by blood or fancy or what?'

'Hansel and Gretel. Little Red Riding Hood and the big bad wolf. Except I think it's her who'll be doing all the gobbling up.' He squinted over at Mongoose. 'Does Twinkletoes there want a drop of this?'

'Leave him be,' she advised. 'He is after dropping off again. If you as much as say "boo!" to him he bursts into song, bejasus. The lark in the clear air is only trotting after him.'

Ranter drank slowly looking at her. 'Did you ever think of leaving, Babysoft?'

'Leaving here, you mean? Certainly I thought about it,' she replied her eyes remote and brooding. 'I have brothers and sisters over in England, scattered all over the kip. I could always scarper over there to one of them if I wanted to. We get on well, when we're not scratching the eyes out of one another.'

'Why don't you go then, if that's the case?'

She shrugged. 'I just never got round to it, I suppose.'

'What keeps you here, for Jasus' sake, in this dump?' asked Ranter. 'What sort of future is there in it for you, catering to the likes of that dilapidated oul' pisspot over there, for instance?' he said nodding towards the snoring obese bundle of Mongoose slumped in the chair. 'What future is that for a young girl like yourself?'

'Leave poor oul' Mongoose alone,' she said tiredly. 'He's harmless. It wouldn't be a bad world if they were all like Mongoose.'

'That's neither here nor there. I meant this place,' went on Ranter with a swing of his hand. 'It's nothing but a dive. It's like waiting at a deserted railway station for a train to come in, knowing in your own heart and soul that it's never coming in because no bleeding trains are running at that station anymore.'

Babysoft looked at her glass. 'Maybe you're right, Ranter, about the trains, but I happen to like the station very much, to say nothing of the station-master. Or should I say station-madam. It's the only trade I know, Ranter, the only thing I'm good at. How long have you been at the taxi game?'

'All me effing life.'

'And could you pack it all in tomorrow, just like that—' she snapped her fingers—'and take up something else?'

'I'm not saying I could—'

'Well, there you are,' she said filling her glass and then his. 'I've been at this game since I left the nuns—before it, as a matter of fact, and I wouldn't know the first thing about turning me hand to anything else.'

'Look,' said Ranter, holding up his hand, 'I'm not saying you should give it up, only do it somewhere else where there's more of a future, more of an opening you might say.'

'Yeah—you might say that, Ranter, all right.'

'You know what I mean,' he persisted annoyed. 'I mean, there's hoorhouses over in England, for Jasus' sake—lashings of them. You might say they were bleeding well invented over there, when all's said and done. In fact,' he continued adamantly, 'you couldn't go wrong over there, for everyone agrees that England is just one big hoorhouse from tip to bottom, and if you as much as look crooked at a bloke you're away. You wouldn't have to stir out of bed at all—they're queuing up, bejasus, like a shuttle-service—'

'Or a shuttlecock-service. If I ever do go over there, Ranter, I'll make you me agent.'

'I'm only trying to advise you.'

She patted his hand. 'Sure I know you are, Ranter, but I'd be like a lost soul any place else. All me friends are here. This is me heart and home, in a manner of speaking. Sure Madame Lala has been like a mother to me, and she'd never forgive me if I left her and skidaddled across to pagan England.'

'I'd be the last in the world to deprive anyone of a job,' Ranter said. 'But there's no harm in trying to better yourself, is there? If you do something well, you might as well get the best wages for it, the best rates going. You're not a bad-looking mot, all things considered—'

'Don't strain yourself with the compliments, Ranter.'

'You're no raving beauty or anything, but still your face wouldn't crack a mirror, and it's a pity to see you wasting your talents in this hole.'

'You're bringing the hot burning tears to me eyes, Ranter,' she said, slinking out a leg bared to the hip. 'Can I interest you a'tall in staying the night, Big Jim?'

'I've been toying with that idea on and off all day, to tell you the truth.'

'Is that all you've been toying with, Ranter?' she asked idly undoing some blouse buttons.

'But the fact is,' he went on finishing his drink, 'Gertie looks after all *my* medicinal purposes.'

'Ah well,' she sighed drawing back her leg, 'you can't win them all, and anyway it might spoil our beautiful friendship.'

Ranter refilled their glasses. 'I'll be ate, bet and thrun up again as it is when I get home.'

'Are you happily married, Ranter?'

He looked at her puzzled. 'Am I happily married?'

'I was always meaning to ask you.'

'Sure I'm as happy as a pig in shit.'

'That's a pity.'

'Don't tell me you fancy me that much?'

She winked at him. 'Don't you know I do, pet? Don't you know you're the love of me life and if I can't have you I'll throw meself off the Halfpenny Bridge?'

'Yes,' he said drinking. 'I can tell by the way your ears twitch every time I come near you.'

'You're a funny bloke, Ranter.'

'I'm a bleeding pantomime when you get to know me.'

'I could fancy you a lot.'

'I'm kind to animals too.'

'I could do with a real man once in a while,' she sighed, buttoning up her blouse. 'Somebody that wouldn't nod off the minute their head touches the pillow, like dream-lover over there.'

'Sure maybe you were meant for God, a bride of Christ.'

'Ask me arse, Ranter.'

'All this talk about men and women,' he said lifting his leg and scratching at his shin. 'There's too much made out of it. Sure it wouldn't cost me a thought to go back and start living on me own again, on me tod.'

'I thought you said you and Gertie got on all right together?'

'Oh aye, we do, we do,' he said eyes puckered up as he enjoyed the scratching. 'But it's not much of a crack for her or for me. I'm out till all hours with the Joe Baksi, and in bed half the day, so what we see of each other is harmless.'

'You still managed to squeeze five little God-forbids in between going and coming,' she reminded him.

Ranter gave a twist of his head. 'Oh that. There's too much made about *that* too, if you ask me. Sure the animals do it too, don't forget, and make less of an effing song and dance about it.' He resumed drinking. 'It's all in the oul' mind, I'm greatly afraid —half the time anyway.'

'It's the other half that does the damage.'

'Bejasus you have something there.'

Babysoft looked up at the ceiling. 'I wonder if that's what Luke is thinking this very minute.'

He followed her eyes upwards. 'I hope Rasputin beyant will be able to talk himself out of this little caper!'

'Sure he's more to be pitied than envied,' sighed Babysoft. 'Like the rest of us.'

'I won't argue with that,' rejoined Ranter. 'No—I won't argue with that at all.'

Into the pause the asthmatic chimes of the time-eaten grandfather clock from the darkened cloistered hallway beyond struck the long witching hour of three in the morning lending sonorous credence to what Ranter had just said, and somewhere in the torn and tossed sky the moon had the grace to dip out of sight behind a feathery flotilla of cloud, turning a kind blind eye on the antics below.